MUSIC MACABRE

MUSIC MACABRE

Sarah Rayne

This first world edition published 2019
in Great Britain and the USA by
SEVERN HOUSE PUBLISHERS LTD of
Eardley House, 4 Uxbridge Street, London W8 7SY.
Trade paperback edition first published
in Great Britain and the USA 2020 by
SEVERN HOUSE PUBLISHERS LTD.

British Library Cataloguing in Publication Data
A CIP catalogue record for this title is available from the British Library.

ISBN-13: 978-0-7278-8896-9 (cased)
ISBN-13: 978-1-78029-643-2 (trade paper)
ISBN-13: 978-1-4483-0342-7 (e-book)

All Severn House titles are printed on acid-free paper.

Severn House Publishers support the Forest Stewardship Council™ [FSC™],
the leading international forest certification organisation. All our titles that
are printed on FSC certified paper carry the FSC logo.

Typeset by Palimpsest Book Production Ltd.,
Falkirk, Stirlingshire, Scotland.
Printed and bound in Great Britain by
TJ International, Padstow, Cornwall.

ONE

P hineas Fox had not expected to find evidence of murder linking a famous and esteemed nineteenth-century composer at the end of his life to a notorious music hall dancer at the start of hers. But incredibly, he was looking at it.

He had not been searching for murders. He had been enjoying his new commission, which was the gathering of background material for a light-hearted biography about the life and loves of virtuoso composer-pianist, Franz Liszt. Phin had been treading a cautious path between speculation, rumour-mongering, and the Victorian version of fake news – Liszt's life and his character were intriguing and complex. To call him a philanderer was probably an exaggeration, but he had certainly been gallant, and the search had already taken Phin from the dizzy heights of grand duchesses' boudoirs to the lush beds of dancers and music hall performers.

But until today, his research had not turned up anything particularly startling. The morning had been spent in scouring the shelves of a favourite antiquarian bookshop just off St Martin's Lane, and in the foxed pages of one tome he had found a reference to a music hall performer for whom Liszt, in his later years, had apparently conceived a great admiration. Phin scooped up the battered volume eagerly, added a few others that might yield some useful information some-time, and carried them all back to his flat. On the tube he remembered the overflowing state of his bookshelves, and supposed that he would have to have more shelves built in his small study. But books could perfectly well be stacked on windowsills and floors, and at the moment Franz Liszt and his ladies were more interesting than trying to get esti-mates out of carpenters – always supposing Phin could track down a reliable carpenter in the first place, which probably he could not.

Inside his flat, he turned on the desk light against the dull afternoon, and began to read. The music hall performer who had caught Liszt's eye had been known as Scaramel; there were two slightly faded reproductions of photographs. One was a conventional pose, suggesting she had been curvaceous in the way the late Victorians and Edwardians had admired. The other, however, showed her dancing with considerable abandon – and very little clothing – on the top of a concert grand. It was lively and vivid, and Scaramel's costume was mostly black with touches of defiant scarlet.

Phin smiled, liking the lively sauciness of the figure, wished there were more details that might identify the venue or indicate the date, and turned the page.

It seemed that during the 1880s and 1890s, Scaramel had been a favourite turn at somewhere called Linklighters Supper Rooms. As well as dancing on concert grands, she was also credited with dancing on tables – in one case there was said to have been a naked performance for the Prince of Wales. The book's author did not know if Lillie Langtry or Alice Keppel had been present on that evening, but was inclined to think not. Phin was inclined to agree.

But it seemed that among the tally of Scaramel's admirers had been the ageing Franz Liszt. This might be gossip, but it could be true. Everything about the lady was in accordance with what was known of Liszt's reputation and preferences; what was not in accordance with anything at all, and what sounded a definitely discordant note, was a paragraph at the end of the chapter.

> Scaramel enjoyed considerable and affectionate notoriety during her career,' wrote the author. 'However, there is a somewhat discreditable rumour that she was tangled up in a crime – and that the crime was the most heinous one of them all. Murder.

Murder. The word seemed to leap off the page, and present itself in blood-dripping letters, like a strapline for a hammy horror film. Phin stared at it, re-read the previous paragraph in case he had missed something, saw he had not, and read on.

In (somewhat slender) support of the rumour of a murder, reproduced on page 24 is a sketch thought to be from Scaramel's era, and probably the mid-1890s. Sadly, the artist did not sign the sketch, so his – or her – identity is not known. Much of the legend's information appears to be third-, if not fourth-hand – sketchily remembered fragments of casual conversations in taverns, and gossip supplied by descendants of music hall artists or backstage workers. Nor is it known what eventually became of Scaramel, who appears to have faded from the public gaze at the very end of the 1800s.

Phin checked the book's publication date. It was 1946, which meant that even if any of the sources could be traced, the sources themselves would probably be long since dead. He turned to page 24 for the sketch.

It was not in the least what he had been expecting, and it smacked against his senses like a blow. It looked like a pen-and-ink sketch, lightly touched with colour here and there. There was a cobbled square with narrow buildings on three sides, and an alley leading off. In one corner was a tall street gaslight that cast softly coloured, diamond-shaped shadows. Harlequin shadows, thought Phin.

But it was the two figures in the sketch that drew his eye, although it was impossible to decide which one dominated the picture. One stood beneath the streetlight; it was wrapped in a dark cloak, the face in deep shadow, the stance imbued with menace. The other figure was in the forefront and it almost looked as if it was begging the artist for help. Its hands were clapped over its ears, and it was plainly flinching from the figure beneath the gaslight. Phin thought he had never seen an air of such terror portrayed in a sketch. It was so disturbing and so eerie that he felt as if something cold and menacing had stepped up to peer over his shoulder. He made an involuntary movement to look behind him, then was annoyed with himself.

There was a scribble of initials in one corner, but Phin could not make them out. Beneath the sketch, though, were the words, 'Sketch by unknown artist. Titled, *Liszten for the Killer.*'

Liszten for the killer.

Phin stared at these four words for a long time.

Liszten for the Killer. *Liszten.* It's a misprint, he thought. Or somebody misread what the artist wrote. Or the artist was foreign and got the word wrong.

He looked at the sketch more closely. A tiny, pale oblong had been drawn against the brick wall behind the gaslight – was it a street sign? Phin hunted out a magnifying glass, and focused it on the page. It was a street sign. He tilted the desk lamp to get a stronger light, and moved the glass again. Was it Headley Street? No, it was not street, it was court. And it was not Headley, but Harlequin. Harlequin Court. Of course it was. Why else would the artist have painted in those chequered shadows? Phin frowned and turned back to the main text.

> Although the legend of this murder can not be verified, several of the interviewed sources maintained that there is a song from the era referring to it. One source has suggested that the song's lyrics were written by a Welsh writer. Sadly, that writer's name is not known, and nothing of the song itself seems to have survived.

Phin sat back. There could not be any connection between any of these facts. The sketch with its curious title could not have anything to do with Franz Liszt. And yet Liszt had apparently admired Scaramel. Scaramel, thought Phin. It's a version of Scaramouche, of course, and Scaramouche was one of the prancing figures in Columbine and Harlequin. He looked again at the just-readable lettering on the street sign.

The sketch had probably come from the artist's imagination. Or it might have been an illustration – for a Bram Stoker-type bloodfest novel maybe, or a *Grand Guignol* theatre programme. *Maria Marten in the Red Barn,* or *Sweeney Todd, the Demon Barber of Fleet Street.* And the title could still be a printing error.

And yet . . . Scaramel and Harlequin Court, and a sketch that might conceivably have Liszt's name in it . . .

It was at this point that enthusiastic knocking sounded on the door. Phin swore, and abandoned Liszt and Scaramel to answer the door, already knowing who it was. Nobody knocked on a door with quite the same exuberant optimism as Toby Tallis.

'I haven't shrivelled a promising bit of research, have I?' said Toby, bouncing cheerfully into the flat. 'Because if so, I'll vanish like a pantomime villain through a trapdoor – well, not literally a trapdoor, not in your flat, because that would mean materializing in Miss Pringle's flat downstairs, and the dear old love would have half a dozen heart attacks on the spot.'

His straw-coloured hair had flopped over his forehead, and he was wearing the ingenuous smile that Phin knew from experience heralded a request for Phin to get involved in some plan destined to end in chaos.

'I won't stay long,' he said, removing Phin's pile of books from the deep window seat. 'You're starting to get crowded out by books, aren't you? I tell you what you need – you need someone to knock up a couple of extra shelves.'

'It's a question of finding someone who'll do such a small job—'

'Oh, I know someone who's just started a DIY company,' said Toby, sitting down on the space he had cleared for himself. 'Joinery and plumbing. Why don't I have a word—'

'No, thank you,' said Phin, who had vivid memories of past domestic disasters into which Toby's enthusiastic helpfulness had precipitated him.

'Well, anyway, I saw your light so I knew you were in, and I thought you'd want to talk about that letter and the email,' said Toby. 'You have had the letter and the email, have you?'

'Now you mention it, there was a letter this morning,' said Phin, recalling picking it up from the mat, and putting it on his desk. 'I haven't looked at my inbox today, though. It's distracting when you hear an email come in.'

'It's a good thing I opened my post, then,' said Toby, 'because we've had the half-yearly statement on that book we collaborated on, and sales are very good indeed. *Bawdy Ballads Down the Ages* – you do remember it, I suppose? We did most of it when you came with me to visit my godfather. Or are you trying to pretend you had nothing to do with it, in case people think you've abandoned the intellectual stuff and fallen amongst bad company?'

'Of course I remember the book, and I'm not trying to forget it at all,' said Phin, indignantly. 'You inveigled me into doing it, but I enjoyed it,' he said, opening the errant letter which he had now found. In fact, working with Toby on the book charting bawdy ballads over the centuries had been extremely enjoyable. It had gone into what to Phin, accustomed to the leisurely pace of academic publishing, had seemed very fast production, and Toby had organized a lively launch party. This had mostly been attended by his fellow medical students and the rugby club to which he belonged – several rugby clubs had turned up, in fact. Phin had only meant to stay at the party as long as politeness required, but Toby's cousin, Arabella, had accompanied him, and it had turned out to be an unexpectedly agreeable evening. It was remarkable how events that Phin normally avoided became entertaining if shared with Arabella.

Toby had been right about the sales of the book. Even allowing for the fifty-fifty division they had agreed, and the percentage due to Phin's agent, the statement indicated that it had already earned about five times as much as Phin's last book, which had dealt with exiled German and Jewish musicians in the run-up to World War II.

'Those figures are very good indeed,' he said, pleased. 'What's in the email?'

'It's from the editor we worked with for it, and she suggests that they'd be very interested if we felt like embarking on a follow-up.'

'But,' said Phin, opening the email, 'there are only so many bawdy ballads to be found, and we've already plumbed a fair few depths, so—'

'Ministers and angels of grace defend me. We wouldn't do bawdy ballads again. We'd make it different but similar. I've got it all worked out,' said Toby, beaming. 'Street ballads. Raucous news-sheets describing the latest hanging or the newest scandal in Bohemia – no, sorry, that's Conan Doyle, isn't it? But things like those halfpenny news-sheets about royal births and deaths and murders and wars and scandals in high places. And Victorian song sheets – that'd be very much in your field of work, wouldn't it? It'd be light-hearted and occasionally saucy, but informative. And very sellable.'

'Street literature,' said Phin, thoughtfully. 'I believe I can see that working. We could include material from cartoonists and lampoonists . . .'

'So we could.'

'There'd be no copyright to worry about . . .'

'Nor there would.'

'And plenty of primary sources to plunder,' said Phin, catching Toby's enthusiasm. 'Newspapers were heavily taxed in the nineteenth century, and the broadsheets and ballads were all the ordinary people could afford, so there were torrents of them. We ought to be able to track down a fair few and pick the juiciest ones. They were sometimes called catchpennies, I think.'

'I thought you'd know all about them,' said Toby, happily. 'And before we agree to anything, we can check the terrain to see what we can turn up. If you can tear yourself away from your current scholarly commission for a couple of hours, we could have a bite to eat later and make a start – oh, unless you're likely to be entangled with my cousin, Arabella, tonight? If you are, don't tell me the details, because I've always felt I ought to be a bit protective towards Arabella – ask what people's intentions are and all that kind of thing. But I'd rather not do that with you.'

Phin said that his intentions towards Arabella were currently a wish that she was not decamping to Paris for the best part of a month to work for a perfume company who wanted to gain a foothold in the English market and required some inventive and imaginative PR proposals from somebody who spoke reasonable French.

'That's fair enough. I'll miss her as well,' said Toby. 'What about tonight, though? We could start with Soho. And then maybe Limehouse – or Whitechapel. I don't mean all on the same evening.'

Phin had the sensation of being swept along to an inevitable fate by a wave of such cheerful enthusiasm he suspected he might not be able to resist it. Arabella had the same effect on him, although with Arabella the fate was generally an extremely pleasurable one. He was aware, again, of a pang of regret that she was going away. A month was hardly a lifetime, but it was still thirty days. Not that he would be crossing the days off on a calendar, of course.

As far as tonight went, he had thought, vaguely, that he would break off work at some point, and put together a meal from whatever was in the fridge. But Toby's idea was alluring, and the possibility of more royalties on a par with *Bawdy Ballads* was tempting. He might even be able to afford some new, properly built bookshelves. And it might clear his head of the clutter accumulating from Scaramel and Liszt.

He said, 'I'd like to do the book, but I don't know if I can concentrate on the current commission and romp through the street life of the nineteenth century at the same time. What about you? Could you balance it with studying anatomy and physiology and all the rest of it?'

'I'm a mature student,' said Toby, with dignity. 'I'm allowed to lapse a bit; in fact it's virtually expected of me. And I should think Victorian street life will give you a nice change from all that scholarly research.'

'It isn't as scholarly as all that, it's background for a biography on Franz Liszt,' said Phin. 'And there's no need for you to look politely interested. Liszt was a very lively gentlemen indeed. He worked his way through a series of courtesans and minor royalty, and ladies used to throw their undergarments onto the stage when he played. They even called it "Lisztomania".'

'Eat your heart out Mick Jagger,' observed Toby. 'How about we have a meal this evening, and see if there are any leads? If I could find a phone book I could look up likely areas and restaurants – no, wait an online directory'd be better. Can I take over your computer?'

As he seated himself at Phin's desk, Phin looked back at the sketch, and without realizing he had been going to say it, he said, 'Toby, see if there's anywhere in London called Harlequin Court.'

'All right. Where exactly might it be?'

'I don't know. It might not exist.'

'It does, though,' said Toby, after a few moments. 'Here it is. Harlequin Court. It's in the St Martin's Lane area, and it's only just about marked. It looks as if it's one of those little alleyways that you walk past without noticing.'

'Theatreland,' said Phin, getting up to look over Toby's shoulder. 'Of course it would be. Does it have anywhere nearby to eat?'

'Can't see anything – hold on, I'll zoom up the screen . . . It looks as if there's a pub on one corner – oh, and a hamburger place, but that's all, except – no, hold on, here's a restaurant. It's called Linklighters, and . . . What have I said?'

'Linklighters,' said Phin, staring at him. 'Then it's still there.'

'What's still there?'

'I'll explain in a minute. But does Linklighters have a website? Or is there one of those "Places to Eat" websites where it's listed or reviewed? Would you have a look while you're at the desk?'

Toby tapped a few keys, frowned at the screen, then said, 'Yes, here we are. "Linklighters Restaurant, restored earlier this year, has good food – all Victorian style – and the décor is a pleasant nod to its former life as a supper room and night cellar." What on earth's a night cellar? It sounds like cesspits being drained under cover of darkness. And what in God's name is a linklighter?'

'Night cellars were small – or smallish – music halls,' said Phin. 'Sometimes called supper rooms. There were dozens of them in the nineteenth century – often in pubs. Mostly under pubs. As for linklighters . . . I'll have to check, but I think they were boys who'd light people through those thick old London fogs.'

'Pea-soupers.'

'Exactly. They'd have sticks with rags wound around them, dipped in tar and set alight. I only know it because I came across it somewhere recently,' he said, a bit apologetically. He handed Toby the book with the section on Scaramel. 'Read this.'

'Scaramel,' said Toby, scanning the page. 'Scaramel?'

'Yes. Not her real name, of course.'

'You surprise me.'

'All I know so far is that she was a music hall performer,' said Phin. 'But Liszt refers to her in a letter he wrote to his daughter, Cosima, shortly before his death. He said – hold on, where are my notes – yes, here it is. Liszt said that Scaramel reminded him strongly of the notorious cabaret dancer Lola Montez. Liszt had quite a fling with La Montez in his youth,' said Phin. 'He wrote that he recalled Lola dancing naked on a table when he unveiled the Beethoven Memorial in Bonn.'

'Not something you'd forget,' agreed Toby.

'No, and Liszt's supposed to have said, "Scaramel puts me strongly in mind of Lola. She has the same spirit and the same leaning towards the outrageous, and I have conceived a great admiration for her." And then he adds, a bit wistfully, that, "sadly, such admiration as I have for ladies these days is a matter of the mind only."'

'Peculiar thing to write to a daughter, I'd have thought,' said Toby.

'I haven't checked that letter's provenance yet,' said Phin. 'But the thing is that I think Scaramel might have been a murderess.'

'Oh, God. Phin, *don't* tell me we're murder-hunting again . . .'

'No, of course we're not. I think the murder's almost certainly a myth,' said Phin, very firmly. 'Victorian urban legend. Even a publicity stunt. What did you think of the sketch?' he said, as Toby put the book down thoughtfully.

'*Liszten for the Killer?* Good title, isn't it?' He regarded Phin. 'It's got to you, hasn't it?' he said, suddenly. 'That sketch.'

'Yes, and I don't know why.'

'You're probably recognizing it from late-night horror films,' said Toby. 'Or that Munch painting – *The Scream.*' He got up. 'But let's try Linklighters, shall we? Three birds with one stone. Your Liszt commission, our street ballads, and a music hall murder . . . Oh, now that sounds like a good title for a crime novel, doesn't it? Anyway, at least we'll be getting a decent meal, if that website can be trusted. I'll phone and get us a table. Seven thirty?'

'All right.'

'They do steak and ale suet pudding,' said Toby, looking back at the screen. 'Oh, and beef and oyster pie.'

TWO

Phin would not have been surprised if Harlequin Court and even Linklighters had turned out to be non-existent.

But in a narrow space between two buildings, set into the old brickwork, was the street sign exactly as it had appeared on the sketch. *Harlequin Court.* The glow of streetlights from Charing Cross Road was dimmer here, and the traffic sounds were muffled. If the ground had been cobblestoned, Phin might even have wondered whether he had stepped into a time warp, or been fed magic mushrooms on the sly, because, either by accident or by collective intent, Harlequin Court was very nearly Dickensian. The square itself had an old gas streetlamp, which Phin thought was in the exact place where the old sketch had shown it. That was where that menacing figure had stood. The other corner was where that terrified figure had been . . .

If he stood here for long enough would he see those figures printed on the air, like cut-outs pasted on to cellophane? For pity's sake, said his mind, it was a sketch! It probably wasn't drawn from reality, and even if it was, it was a long time ago . . .

But he liked Harlequin Court. The three or four shops all had bow windows with small panes of glass. One sold books, antiquarian from the look of it; another displayed antique jewellery, and a third appeared to be a small printing company.

'This is one of those tucked-away little squares you sometimes stumble upon in London,' he said, looking round. 'Well, in any old city, I suppose.'

'Never mind tucked-away squares,' said Toby, 'there's our destination.' He indicated a sign over a door in the far corner. The lettering was crimson on a gilt background, and said: *Linklighters Restaurant. Good food. Open from 6.00 p.m. to midnight.*

'It looks as if it's a semi-basement.'

'Yes, but it would be if it was one of the old cellar music

halls. It's directly under the bookshop by the look of it,' said Phin.

'The bookshop's called Thumbprints, and it says it was established in 1825. Nice. And possibly useful for our street ballads.'

Immediately inside the restaurant's door were steep narrow steps leading down. They were carpeted in crimson, and the stair wall was lined with framed theatre posters and playbills. The restaurant was larger than either of them had expected.

'Very Edwardian,' said Toby appreciatively. 'Fleur-de-lys walls, and a general air of the Naughty Nineties.'

'It's quite busy,' said Phin, looking around. 'Pre-theatre people, I expect.'

'Good thing I booked a table.'

Their table was in an alcove, and above it were more of the framed playbills and posters.

'They had colourful names in those days, didn't they?' said Toby, reading them, appreciatively. 'Dainty Dora Dashington with Dances to Delight You. A couple of comic acts, a juggler . . . Oh, and a lady billed as Belinda Baskerville, the Gentlemen's Choice. You'd have to ask yourself if Conan Doyle ever saw her perform, wouldn't you?'

'There's one here of Scaramel appearing in Collins' Music Hall,' said Phin. 'In 1887. That would have been a really upmarket booking in those days. This one's not so grand, I don't think – Whitechapel Road. The Effingham.'

'That sounds like the first line of a limerick. 'Twas at the good pub, Effingham, Where everyone was—'

'*Don't* start reciting,' said Phin hastily, having had some experience of Toby's facility with impromptu limericks. 'Or at least not so loudly. And this looks like our waiter coming over.'

'Snazzy outfit he's got on, isn't it?' said Toby, approvingly. 'Brocade waistcoat and velvet bow tie. Could I get away with wearing that, do you think?'

'It'd go down a storm at the rugby club,' said Phin, gravely.

'It'd cheer up the ladies on the maternity ward, though. Is this the menu? Thank you,' said Toby, to the waiter. 'I don't know about you, Phin,' he said, 'but I'm going to have beef and oyster pie. And let's have a bottle of red, as well. In fact, let's make it a couple of bottles. Good for the heart. And neither of us has got to drive.'

'We'll ask the waiter to decant us into a hansom cab,' said Phin, gravely.

London, 1880s/1890s

Daisy would never forget the first time she travelled in a hansom cab. It had been the night it had all started. Later, she came to think of that night as a signpost – but a signpost that was all bloodied and smeary, pointing to the dreadful road she was about to step on to.

Living in Rogues Well Yard, you did not have much to do with carriages and cabs, well, you did not have anything to do with them at all; and on the very rare occasion that a hansom rattled its way down Canal Alley, people peered through their windows to watch, and children ran out to follow it, and try to cling on to the back of the carriage to get a ride for a few yards.

People in Rogues Well Yard walked everywhere, or, if they had to travel a long way and there was enough money, they took a tram. For very long journeys, they went on a train, although when Daisy first went to work for Madame, she did not know anyone who had actually travelled on a train.

Since being with Madame, she had got a bit more used to hansom cabs and such things, although it had been a bit bewildering at first. There was so much to learn. Cleaning and polishing furniture, and washing china so fragile you could almost see through it. Ironing beautiful fabrics – silk and velvet and lace-edged underthings. There was food she had never heard of, and there was the laying of a table. In Rogues Well Yard, you did not lay tables – not many people had tables, anyway.

Then there were the performances at Linklighters Supper Rooms, and at some of the big theatres, as well. Daisy went with Madame, to help her dress and make sure she had everything she needed. Famous people came to watch her – they all knew her as Scaramel. Daisy would not have dreamed of calling Madame that, but when she saw the posters and the programmes with the name in big bright letters she wanted to run all over London and shout to people that this was the lady she worked for.

Scaramel, performing her newest, most daring dance . . . said the posters. Or, *Scaramel, as you've never seen her before . . .* Daisy was proud that she could read it all; there had been a lady in Rogues Well Yard who had been a teacher, and she had taught Daisy, and later her young brother, Joe, how to read and write.

Madame lived in the whole top floor of a big house in Maida Vale and they had their own front door. Daisy had never known anyone who had their own front door. In Rogues Well Yard you were lucky if you only shared a landing with two other families. But here there was a green-painted door with a brass door knocker.

It was a lovely house, and Madame was a lovely lady to work for, although you had to be a bit cautious first thing of a morning, because you never knew who you might meet coming out of her bedroom. And you had to shut your ears late at night, too, on account of the giggles and shrieks, and the bed often creaking as if it might be about to break.

And then, after a few months of living there, came the night Daisy would never forget.

She had gone to visit Ma, which she did every week. Ma had had the most wretched of lives, married to that drunken layabout who would not know an offer of honest work if it came and bit him on the bum, and who beat up Ma regular as the Thames tide. He was not averse to a bit of how's-your-father with other females, either, and when the randy mood was on him he was not particular if he happened to shove his hand up his own daughters' skirts, and pull their hands down between his legs. He was a nasty old lecher, but Daisy and her two sisters had not grown up in Rogues Well Yard and played in Canal Alley without learning a trick or two. So the second time he tried it, Daisy kicked him hard between his legs, and Lissy and Vi ran for the bucket of cold water from the yard, and poured it straight on to his todger. It had been January so there were lumps of ice in the water. And as for the squeal that Pa gave . . . Well, you'd have thought someone had chopped his todger off altogether, and a good thing if they had.

Lissy and Vi had left home soon after that – they'd never really taken to the bit of teaching the old schoolmistress had given Daisy and Joe. Not for them, they had said, and scoffed when Daisy tried to talk like the schoolmistress, and said, Blimey, hark at our Daise, and, Who does she think she is, Lady Muck?

It was all good-natured, though. Lissy and Vi got factory work in Wapping, with decent regular wages, and left home. 'Can't stand Pa no longer,' Lissy said, apologetically. The two of them shared a room near the factory, and after a time they both got hitched to decent blokes, who respected them. Daisy had been pleased about that, although Vi had told Daisy much later that her wedding night had been a nightmare: 'And a good many nights afterwards, too,' she had said. 'On account of what *he* done to us when we were kids. *You* know what I mean, Daise.'

'Yes. Oh, yes.'

'Had to grit my teeth that first night I was married,' said Vi. 'Found I was clutching the bedrail, too, till it was over. Same for Lissy. Don't think Lissy ever really got over it. I did, though. Not sure what happened, but – well, somehow it got to be all right for me.' She winked. 'Matter of fact, it got to be pretty good.'

'I'm glad,' said Daisy, fervently.

'You an' me both,' said Vi, grinning.

Vi was all right, and although Lissy was not really all right, and probably never would be, she seemed to be coping.

But Joe was different. He was so much younger than Daisy and her two sisters, and somehow he was never quite able to cope with the world and the kicks life could give you. Daisy would always look out for Joe. Even when she got the work at Linklighters, which meant going right across London each day, she went home every night, never mind how late it was. Lissy and Vi said it was mad, Daisy ought to find a place nearby, a room somewhere, and not traipse across London on trams at such hours. You never knew who might be about. But Daisy could look after herself, and she did not trust Pa. He might

set about Ma again. He might even start on Joe, if the mood
and the drink took him that way. Anyway, she liked tram
journeys. They were lively and friendly. You could get sixty
people in one carriage, and all it took were two horses to pull
it along the lines, and it was only a penny a mile.

Linklighters was like nowhere Daisy had ever seen. It was
all lights and dazzlingly dressed people and unfamiliar scents.
Everyone rushed round and shouted, and there was music and
dancing and men hammering bits of wood that turned as if by
magic into trees or castles or ships. As for the clothes the
women wore . . .! Daisy told Lissy and Vi and Ma that you
wouldn't believe the half of it unless you saw it for yourself.

After a bit, though, she got used to it, and although the
work wasn't much at first, just washing-up and a bit of cleaning,
she hadn't minded. But then had come the real piece of luck
– Madame had taken a fancy to her, and said how about going
to live with her as maid and to be her dresser.

Daisy had hesitated because of leaving Ma and Joe with
Pa, but she could visit them every week, and Lissy and Vi
were nearby. Between them they would make sure Pa didn't
get up to his viciousness. And living with Madame meant
Daisy could often take a bit of money out to Ma. Sometimes
Madame gave her clothes to take, too, saying they were things
she no longer needed. They were not clothes Ma would ever
dream of wearing, of course – walk along Canal Alley in
scarlet satin or a black and pink feather boa, and you'd be a
laughing stock, or you'd be the butt of a dozen rude suggestions from the men coming out of the Cock & Sparrow. But
the clothes could be sold to Peg the Rags for a few pence so
it all helped.

The time went along. Daisy got used to being in Maida
Vale, and she began to think life was not so bad.

It was even better when Pa went, falling into the canal,
pissed as usual. Nobody mourned him and nobody missed
him, least of all Ma. Soon afterwards, Ma got into the way of
helping Peg the Rags; they'd pick over the clothes folk brought
in, and Peg would give Ma a coin or two for the work.
Sometimes they had a nip of gin while they did the picking
over, and why not? Ma had a bad enough life, and Daisy was

glad to think of her having this companionship. Next time she visited Rogues Well Yard, she took along a peck of gin for the pair.

Then came the night in October when she was a bit later than usual setting out to visit Ma, and the tram got stuck in fog. Daisy hated fog. It had been a night like this when Pa fell into the canal. She peered through the tram's misted window, trying to see where they were. Ma and Joe were expecting her – Joe often came to wait for the trams so the two of them could walk back to the yard together. So Daisy was not going to turn back and disappoint him.

Then somebody in the street called in to the driver that everything ahead was at a standstill, and it would be just as quick – and probably a sight quicker – to get out and walk, especially if anyone was bound for Whitechapel, because it was not far off at all.

Grumbling good-naturedly, most of the tram travellers got down, telling each other that they were nearly home anyway, and they could all go along together. But somehow, once out of the tram, they all melted away, and there was only the fog swirling into Daisy's face. It all began to feel a bit scary, even though she could recognize some of the buildings. The street-lights were being lit, though – they made fuzzy discs of colour overhead. She went cautiously along. Here was the rearing outline of The Thrawl now, with its barred windows and the massive iron gates, just about visible. The Thrawl was a land-mark, but people living here hated it. They told how poor demented souls were locked in there – for their entire lives, some of them – and how, on dark nights, you could hear them screaming to be let out. Bad children were told that if they did not behave, they would be taken off to The Thrawl – which was a terrible thing to say to a child. Like saying the bogeyman will come to get you.

Daisy always scuttled past the grim walls very quickly, not looking up at it. Still, at least this meant Rogues Well Yard was not very far, and she would get to Ma's all right, although she might not be able to get back. She was not sure what time it was, but it must be quite late. But she could stay the night with Ma if she had to. Madame would understand.

Some people called these fogs London Particulars, and told how you could never be sure what might be lurking inside a London Particular. Things sounded different in the fog, as well. Daisy's footsteps echoed a bit oddly, so that she kept thinking someone was following her – creeping along behind her. Twice she turned sharply round, but each time there were only the other travellers, walking as quickly as the fog would allow, some of them holding on to the railings as a guide. Or had someone darted into that alleyway just then, as if not wanting to be seen? Daisy went on, walking as quickly as she could, trying not to clop her shoes on the pavement so that no one would hear her or know where she was.

But here was Canal Alley, and on her left was the turning into the little lane that went down to the canal itself. She was almost within sight of Rogues Well Yard when a small figure came hurtling through the fog, and almost knocked her over. Hands clutched at her, and a voice she knew and loved better than any voice in the whole world, cried out her name.

'Joe?' It was not quite a question, because Daisy knew it was Joe; how could she not know the beloved skin and hair scent, or the feel of his small, thin hands grasping her. He had come to meet the tram as he so often did, waiting patiently for the glimmer of the lights and the clop of the horses' hoofs, anticipating seeing her with his own self-contained delight.

But he was not delighted now; he was terrified, and it was more than just the fog that was terrifying him. He was shaking so badly Daisy thought he might break apart. In a voice from which most of the breath seemed to have been squeezed, he said, 'I saw . . . Daisy, I saw the man—'

'What man? Joe, what's frightened you?'

There was a half-strangled gulp, as if Joe might be about to be sick, then he said, 'Knives, Daisy. There were knives. He had them in a bag. And he had a saw. Like a butcher . . . He sawed into her . . . The blood went everywhere . . . Bits of bone—'

'Oh God,' said Daisy, her arms tightening around the small, frail figure, but her heart lurching with terror. 'But Joe, you're safe. I'm here now. No one'll hurt you.'

But Joe was still shaking and clinging to Daisy's hand. Tears streamed down his face, and then he said, 'But he saw me. He looked up, and he saw me watching him.'

It was as if something that had been hiding inside the fog crept nearer, and Daisy, still holding on to Joe, looked about her. Rogues Well Yard was some way off – it was beyond the swirling fog, and there was no one about who might hear if they cried out. And they were only one slightly undersized girl and a small boy who was scared half out of his wits.

Keeping hold of Joe's hand, she began to walk towards the sound of crowds – the horses' hoofs and the rumble of wheels from hansom cabs and carriages. But the fog was so thick that at every corner Daisy thought they had taken a wrong turn. And there were footsteps behind them now. As they turned a corner, almost blundering into a row of railings jutting blackly out of the mist, the footsteps quickened, coming closer. It would only be someone a bit lost like themselves; at any moment a cheerful voice would probably call out that it was a shocking night, you couldn't see your hand in front of your face, and did the lady happen to know exactly where this was?

The owner of the footsteps behind them did not do that, though. The steps were much nearer, and Daisy could hear the sound of someone breathing quite fast and quite loud. She tried to think that anyone, and especially someone elderly or bronchitically inclined, would huff and puff from breathing in the fog. But anyone elderly or bronchitic would not walk as fast as this.

She paused, desperately trying to see where they were. A movement came from behind, and Daisy spun round. The mist parted and a figure stood there. Joe's cry of fear tore into Daisy's brain, and his hand clutched hers so tightly she gasped with the pain. In a terrified whisper, he said, 'It's him. It's the man I saw.'

For a dreadful, never-to-be-forgotten second, Daisy's eyes and the man's eyes locked and held. Something that might almost have been a smile lifted his lips, and then he came towards them.

Daisy was not conscious of having moved, but somehow she and Joe were running blindly away, into the fog, not caring where they went or if they ran into the paths of carriages and

horses. The world whirled and spun around them, but as long
as they kept hold of one another, it would be all right . . .

After several panic-filled moments it began to seem as if it
might be. They had come to streets with people and brighter
streetlights. The fog was a bit wispier now, and hansom cabs
were rattling along. Safe. But for how long? Because if one
of you has seen a murder being committed, and if both of you
have seen the murderer clearly enough to identify him, you need
to get as far away as you can, and you need to hide as
completely as possible. They mightn't be able to get as far
as Maida Vale in this fog, but they could probably get to
Linklighters. The thought of Linklighters and its lights and
bustling people, and of the friendly square with the shops, was
so reassuring that Daisy did something she had never done in
her whole life before. She stepped into the road and waved
down a hansom cab. Incredibly it pulled up, and she told the
driver to take them to Linklighters. Clambering inside, half
pulling Joe with her, she realized she had no idea what the
cab driver would charge. She only had a few pence in her bag,
but Madame would be at Linklighters, and Madame would
pay whatever it cost. Daisy would tell her to take it from her
wages. Then she would send a message to Ma by one of the pot
boys or one of the linklighters who lit people through the
streets – nothing to frighten Ma or worry her, just explaining
that Joe would stay with her for a time, and that she would
tell Ma all about it tomorrow or the next day.

What could not be so easily dealt with was the future.
Because the murderer had seen Joe and Joe had seen the
murderer. That meant Joe could identify him. And Daisy had
seen him as well. That meant Daisy could also identify him.

Daisy already knew, without anyone needing to tell her, that
this was the man about whom all of London was talking. A
man who had killed several times already. It did not matter
that the killings had all been women – most of them prostitutes.
A murderer who ripped open his victims and dragged out their
bowels and their kidneys and their guts would not hesitate to
do the same to a young boy and his sister who had seen his
face and who could send him to the gallows.

THREE

M adame's generosity on that night and on all the nights
that followed was something Daisy would never forget.
It was Madame who said Joe could not possibly return
to Rogues Well Yard, and who found lodgings for him two
streets away from Harlequin Court with one of the barmen at
Linklighters. The barman's daughter had recently left home
to marry, and his wife was a motherly soul who was very
pleased to let the daughter's room.

As for earning his keep, said Madame, to be sure Joe was
a bit young to be coping with that, but there were plenty of
his age who had to do so. There was no reason why he could
not help at Linklighters, afternoons and early evenings,
washing up glasses and running errands and suchlike. The
money wouldn't be much, but it should be just about enough.

Somebody suggested Joe might go out with other boys to
help light folk through the fogs, as well. It was a tradition of
Linklighters, what with the name and everything, and he would
earn a bit extra – there were always tips from people who
were grateful to be lighted along their way home.

'Joe won't go out in the fog, not ever,' said Daisy, so firmly
that it was not mentioned again.

Surprisingly, Joe liked Linklighters. He liked the life and
the colour and the music, and being with people all the time.
He usually walked home with the barman after they locked
Linklighters up, but Madame made sure that neither Joe nor
Daisy ever went home alone. Daisy repeatedly told herself
that the mad killer could not possibly know where they were
or anything about them.

And presently Joe found little nooks and crannies in
Linklighters – tucked-away corners that people scarcely knew
existed – where he could disappear. It made him feel safe,

Daisy explained to Madame, not admitting that she too sometimes darted into one of those places if anyone resembling the
killer came in.

In the quiet spells at Linklighters, Joe did what he used to
do in Rogues Well Yard. He drew little sketches of all the
people who came and went and the various performers. He
would curl into a corner on the side of the stage, with a folded-
up piece of old velvet curtain as a cushion, out of sight of the
audience, but able to watch the artistes who danced and sang
and performed acrobatics across the stage. He was wide-eyed
with wonder, and Daisy sometimes thought it was as if he was
peering through a half-open door into a magical world he had
never known existed.

When Madame saw some sketches which Joe had done on
a bit of wrapping paper, she bought him a sketchbook and
pencils. A real artist's sketchbook it was; Joe stroked the satiny
paper almost reverently, and would not let it out of his sight.
After that he drew everything he saw. Sometimes the people
who came to watch the shows called Joe over to their tables
so he could do sketches of their wives or sweethearts. Joe
drew them all – not like posh painted pictures you saw hanging
on rich folks' walls, but lovely, lively sketches. The people he
drew were very pleased and gave him a few coins or bought
him a pie and mash supper.

The Linklighters owners were very pleased as well,
because this was something different, and it would mark
them out from all the other supper rooms and halls. They
encouraged Joe and gave him a bit of extra money so he
could buy more sketchpads and pencils. He bought a set of
coloured pencils from Thumbprints in the Court, and began
to add colour to the sketches. This brought them even more
vividly to life.

There did not seem to be any way of repaying Madame for
all this, except to work as hard for her as Daisy could. And
there was plenty of work to be done, not only making sure
Madame's beautiful costumes were clean and pressed and at
the theatre or the club for each performance, but also in her
home. Madame enjoyed inviting people to the rooms at Maida
Vale – it was usually for lunch, because most of her friends

were at theatres or music halls in the evenings, as Madame was herself.

Ladies were often asked to what posh people called afternoon tea. This was not the kind of tea Daisy's family had in Rogues Well Yard, where tea was eaten when the men were home from their work, and where the meal might be onion soup, or stewed ox cheek, if you were lucky enough to have a stove. Even Pa used to say there was nothing so grand as a plate of ox cheek of a cold night. Or it might be a kipper or jellied eels, which were cheap enough from a street stall. Daisy and her sisters used to fetch them. Vi always insisted on buying whelks, because she liked the boy who helped at the whelk stall.

Afternoon tea at Maida Vale consisted of delicate little sandwiches with the crusts cut off and fillings of watercress, or cucumber sliced so thinly you could almost see through the slices. There had to be cakes, generally from Fortnum & Mason's, which was a palace all by itself, and which Daisy had at first been terrified to enter, handing in Madame's written order to a lady who looked at Daisy as if she might be something to scrape off her boot. Daisy glared, and when the woman turned away, put out her tongue.

Food at the afternoon teas had to be served on the best china, and the ladies would sip tea, and tear to shreds the reputations of people who were not there. Madame never tore anyone's reputation to shreds; she was kind and tolerant and she saw the best in almost everyone. The only exception was a lady called Belinda Baskerville, who performed what were called *poses plastiques*, which in plain terms meant she stood absolutely still on the stage wearing draperies so flimsy she might as well have been stark naked, and trying to look like the statues in the British Museum. Madame said Belinda Baskerville was a greedy, blood-sucking harpy, and was not to be trusted from here to that door.

'And we once fell out over a gentleman, Daisy. Someone the creature wanted for herself.'

'But you got him?' Daisy dared to say, and Madame gave her sauciest wink.

'Of course I did, and Baskerville's never forgiven me for

it. A very nice man, in fact. He went on to do very well for himself. But there was once a New Year's Eve party – wild gambling all night, and Baskerville was there, throwing out her lures. It didn't do her any good. Still, it was a splendid party,' said Madame. 'I remember, I danced on the card tables later on,' she said, reminiscently.

There had not, however, been any enmity or reputation-clawing with the lady who had come to the house that autumn. Also, she had been so different from Madame's usual visitors that the visit had lodged in Daisy's mind.

'No names,' Madame had said before the visitor arrived. 'She prefers not to attract any attention – she's only in London for a short time, anyway. So just call her Madame – like you do with me – and bring her into the drawing room. Then serve tea and bugger off back to the kitchen.'

Madame could be quite refined when she had to, but occasionally a touch of earthiness slipped through, and there were times when her language was what the schoolmistress had called 'street urchin'.

Daisy said, forthrightly (they were on those kind of terms by now), 'I hope you won't use language to this visitor if she's that important,' and Madame had laughed and said of course not, what did Daisy think she was, and now please sod off and don't forget lemon slices with the smoked salmon sandwiches.

The lady was foreign, which was not unusual – Madame knew all kinds of people. She was not especially pretty, but Daisy thought the word for her was elegant. She wore black, which either meant she was in mourning for somebody or that she simply liked wearing black. Ladies often did; they thought it flattered their figures.

Daisy did not listen at the door, of course, but going in and out with plates and hot water meant she could not help hearing a bit of the conversation.

'I have brought you a small souvenir in memory of an old gentleman who admired you,' the visitor said.

There was a silence, then Madame said, 'You mean your father.'

'Yes.'

'I don't need anything to remind me of him,' Madame said,

quickly. 'I remember him very well indeed. It was an honour to meet him – it was after a performance I gave. He came to my dressing room afterwards. We had a glass of wine together – if I'm honest, we had more than one glass. And there were a few other nights when we had supper together.' Daisy heard the reminiscent smile in Madame's voice. 'Even at the age he was then, your father was remarkable – there was such energy and such intelligence. Also,' she said, and now there was unmistakable affection in her voice, 'also there was a decided smile in his eyes.'

'He never lost that,' said the visitor. She sounded pleased. 'He told me that you brought back to him the memory of a lady he had known in his youth – a dancer. Rather a wild lady, but she—'

'Became the mistress of Ludwig of Bavaria?' said Madame. 'Yes.'

'I thought that was who you meant. We're talking of Lola Montez, aren't we?'

'We are. My father admired her – if I am to be honest, I think he did more than just admire her. Ah, we are women of the world, the two of us – we do not need to pretend. But yes, there was a brief liaison between Lola and my father. When he saw you dance, all those years later, he told me that he saw much of Lola's spirit and mischievous rebelliousness in you. It revived some pleasant memories for him. That is why I have brought you these small souvenirs.'

'Then,' said Madame, 'I am greatly complimented and very grateful.' Madame always found the right words, no matter how unexpected the situation.

There was the rustle of papers; Daisy was carrying out the tray by then and she did not like to turn round to look, but as she went out, she heard the visitor say, 'He composed these pieces around the same time as he composed the *Mephisto Waltzes* – those are filled with devils dancing and all manner of abandonment, and they were brilliant, of course. Well received by everyone. These pieces I have brought to you were written on the crest of that success, but my father said afterwards that they were not as good. They were too dark, he said, and he refused to allow them to be performed. I never heard them, but as you know, he was a maestro. His wishes were honoured when it came to these pieces and they were never performed in public. But when the scores came to me, I remembered you. I think he might have liked you to have some small memory of him. Perhaps one day they can be brought into the light. Perhaps one day they might even be worth large money.'

'Even if they were, I would never sell them,' said Madame, very seriously. 'I shall keep them in his memory, on that you have my word. Another cup of tea, now?'

'Thank you, yes. And perhaps just one more of your delicious cakes.'

As Daisy washed the cups and plates – doing so carefully, because Madame, for all her generosity and kindness, was a bit of a tartar if her expensive china got broken – she thought about what the visitor had said.

'When the scores came to me, I remembered you.' Scores meant sheets of music with all the music notes on them – Daisy knew that. There had been a few times when she had had to fetch Pa out of the Cock & Sparrow, and Bowler Bill was nearly always there, playing the battered old piano for all he was worth, music scores propped up on the stand. People often got up to sing and everyone would join in. Rhun the Rhymer sometimes sang his own versions of the songs, most of which nobody could understand, on account of Rhun generally lapsing into Welsh after the fifth drink.

But all kinds of songs there'd be, and Bill liked to boast that he could play anything that was put in front of him. So Daisy knew what a music score was.

It sounded as if the father of the unknown foreign lady had been famous. Daisy put the scores neatly inside an envelope in Madame's desk drawer.

Every night she told herself that the man she and Joe had seen could not possibly know where they were, or anything about them.

'You're safe,' she said to Joe, not once but many times. 'He won't find us. He'll be too frightened, because he knows we saw him that night. He knows we can tell what we saw. He won't dare to kill again.'

But he did.

It was Madame who showed Daisy the news-sheet from one of the street sellers.

Across the top, in thick black letters, were the words, *LATEST GHASTLY MURDER IN EAST END . . . DREADFUL MUTILATION OF VICTIM . . . LEATHER APRON STILL AT LARGE . . .*

Leather Apron was one of the names given to the killer, and at the sight of it Daisy shivered.

The news-sheet said that Leather Apron had taken a new victim, and told how the victim had been a street woman – that meant a prostitute, of course. Whitechapel – the entire East End – teemed with prostitutes. The whole of London teemed with prostitutes, but the killer seemed to be focusing on those living in the East End. As far as Daisy knew, nobody had been able to explain this.

The news-sheet wanted to know what the police were doing to catch the man.

'It has been suggested that the police know the killer's identity, but dare not move against him,' said the news-sheet. '*Why*? Is he someone in the government? Is he a member of the police force? We say, no matter who this butcher is, the people of London – and very especially the people living in Whitechapel – must feel safe.'

There was a description of how viciously the victim's throat had been cut – 'So violently the neck had almost been severed all the way through' – and how several internal organs had been cut out and taken away. The news-sheet did not speculate as to if this had been done before or after death.

Daisy stared at the black print, her mind tumbling. So it was not over. It never would be, of course, because neither she nor Joe would ever be able to forget what they had seen that night. The man's features and the glaring madness in his eyes were stamped on their minds. The dreadful thing was that her own features and Joe's must be stamped on his in turn.

After a few moments she was able to hand the news-sheet back to Madame, and to say how terrible this was.

Madame did not appear to see how violently Daisy's hands were shaking. She said, very thoughtfully, 'They talk about protecting people, but they don't suggest how it can be done.'

'The police ought to be able to think of something,' said Daisy. 'Or people in the government. Clever men like that ought to think of a way for folk to warn one another.'

Madame said slowly, 'Warn . . . *Warn* . . .' She frowned, then said, 'Such as sending out a signal if they think he's prowling around?'

'Yes.'

'You'd feel safer from him with something like that, wouldn't you?' said Madame. 'Joe, too. I won't let Joe see this, you know.'

'I know you won't. But how could you warn people about the killer?' said Daisy. 'How could there be a signal that would do that? Unless – could people be given police whistles? So as to blow them as a warning?'

'I don't think that would work,' said Madame. 'Even if they'd spend the money, it's not . . . not specific enough. You often hear a police whistle, and you ignore it, because most of the time you know it's a drunken brawl, or some wretched starving urchin's stolen an apple or a loaf of bread from a street stall. People wouldn't take any notice of a police whistle.' She paused, clearly still thinking, then said, 'Daisy, do you think a warning could take the form of a piece of music?'

'You can't play music in the middle of Whitechapel at midnight,' began Daisy.

'No, but you could sing it. Or even whistle it. A tune – only a few bars, but something unusual that people would recognize. Something that a lone female would recognize as an alarm – as a warning. Run for your life – get to a place where there's people – because there's someone prowling these streets tonight who might be dangerous. Someone who might be *him*.' She began to walk up and down the room. 'But what kind of music could it be? *What?*'

Daisy waited.

'It'd have to be something nobody had heard before,'

Madame said at last. 'Something really different. Not anything popular that's sung on a stage at the moment, or that all the errand boys whistle. Something nobody's ever heard.' She suddenly spun round to face Daisy, her eyes bright. 'How about an unknown piece of music composed by a real composer? A maestro?'

'What . . .?'

'A piece of music that's never been played in public, because its composer thought it was too dark, too macabre, for its time.' Madame's eyes were brilliant, and she was already across the room, and opening the drawer of the little desk. She took out the envelope enclosing the music given to her by the foreign visitor.

'This is what we'll use, Daisy,' she said, holding it up, her eyes glowing with fervour. 'One of these pieces of music composed by a man dead these two years. He was a wonderful composer, and this is his work. It will be—'

'Good?'

'Oh, it'll be better than just good. He was a genius. And we'll write words to his music, then we'll make people in Whitechapel learn it. To use it as a warning.'

'How can we do any of that?' This would be no more than Madame off on one of her wild fantasies, and none of it would work.

'Well, first, we need someone who could play the music,' said Madame.

'One of your piano players?' Madame's acts were generally accompanied by a small group of musicians attached to whichever hall she was performing in, but she had two or three gentlemen who often accompanied her on the piano as well, and who she sometimes rehearsed with.

'Well, yes, we could use them, but whether they'd want to risk being involved . . . We really need someone who would understand – who would want to be part of it.'

Daisy thought: someone who would understand . . .

She said, eagerly, 'I know who we can use. His name's Bowler Bill. He plays at the Cock & Sparrow most nights. Sometimes the Ten Bells, too.'

'If that isn't Whitechapel, nowhere is,' said Madame.

'I bet he'd do it like a shot. He'd understand – he knows the people there, and he'd do anything that would help. And,' said Daisy, 'he reckons he can play any piece of music put in front of him.'

'Then,' said Madame, 'Bowler Bill it is.'

Daisy had not been to Rogues Well Yard since that night she and Joe had seen the killer, but Lissy and Vi made sure Ma was all right. Twice Lissy and Vi had brought Ma out to Maida Vale, where they'd had a cup of tea in the kitchen, and then gone along to Joe's lodgings, so Ma could see for herself that he was safe.

But now Daisy was going back to Rogues Well Yard and into the Cock & Sparrow in order to introduce Madame to Bowler Bill. But Rogues Well Yard was part of *his* hunting ground, and for all she knew he could still be looking for her. Would he recognize her? Stupid, said her mind. Of course he would.

Madame guessed most of this, of course, and said she could perfectly well go on her own, but Daisy was not having that. In any case, they would be taking a hansom cab, and afterwards Bowler Bill or one of the other men would very likely walk along with them as far as the Commercial Road, where they could get another hansom back.

Their cab had to go past The Thrawl, because it was a wider road. Daisy shivered as they approached it, but they rattled smartly past, and then they were pulling up outside the Cock & Sparrow. Once inside, she felt better, because there was warmth and noise and a sense of familiar ground. There were a few people she recognized – several of them called out cheerfully.

Bowler Bill was in his usual place at the battered piano, the hat that was his legend firmly jammed on his head. A tankard of ale stood on the piano's top, and Bill was playing away, even though it was still early. But that meant the place was fairly quiet, which was what Daisy and Madame wanted.

Bill was charmed to meet the famous Scaramel, standing up and even going so far as to take off his hat, which he did not do for many people. He shook Madame's hand, and said he knew all about her; in fact he had seen her perform at the Canterbury in Lambeth last year, and at the Effingham, too.

'You did "My Grandfather's Clock",' he said, and Madame nodded delightedly.

'So I did. They liked it, didn't they?'

'Two encores,' agreed Bill.

'It was a good night,' agreed Madame. 'Now then, Bill, to business.' She sat down next to him on the piano stool, and Bill listened as she explained what they had in mind. He nodded a few times, frowned, then said, Blimey, that was an idea and a half, and he'd bash out tunes until kingdom come if it'd act as a warning and stop that madman butchering any more victims.

'Good. This is the music we've got,' said Madame, spreading out the four music scores.

'Classy stuff,' said Bill, studying them. 'These weren't written by a hack musician.'

'No, they weren't, but never mind classy, can you play them?'

'It ain't my sort of music,' said Bill, 'but I've never seen a piece of music yet that I can't play. Give us that top one and we'll have a go.'

He propped the first piece on the piano stand and played it straight off, only hesitating a couple of times, and that very briefly. Daisy thought that – even played on Bill's jangly old piano – the music was beautiful. The notes floated into the smoky bar.

'Real class,' he said, again. 'Thought it would be. Drawing-room stuff.'

'Yes, but we don't want drawing room,' said Madame. 'We want something that'll yell to people to run for safety.'

The second piece was different, and Daisy looked hopefully at Madame.

'Better,' said Madame. 'Bit like footsteps, but—'

'But more like marching footsteps,' said Bill. 'And you don't want marching, like an army's coming down the street. This ain't a band of soldiers we're dealing with. Let's try number three.'

This time the music did not float and it did not march. It

seemed almost to prowl its way into the room, and Daisy felt as if an icy finger had traced its way down her spine. This was music that made you think of hunched-shoulder figures tiptoeing through shadows, pausing in narrow alleyways. It made you think of hands clutching glinting knives, and faces twisted up with madness . . . Of one face in particular – the face that had glared through the swirling fog that night, and the face Joe had seen bent over the killer's grisly work. Daisy would never lose that memory. Joe would not lose it, either.

'That's the one,' said Madame, when Bill stopped playing.

'It'd frighten the life out of you to hear that of a night,' he said. 'By God, you'd know you were being sent a message about danger, wouldn't you? Send old Leather Apron to the rightabout, as well, I shouldn't wonder. Daisy, no need to look like that, he ain't here tonight.'

'Course he ain't. But we'll have a drop of porter to cheer us along.' Madame waved to the barman.

'And now what?' said Bill, after the porter had been brought.

'The music's exactly right,' said Madame, slowly. 'But I reckon it's a bit too long.'

'I reckon so, as well. You only want something the women can sing to warn everyone. Like a verse of a song. No more than three or four minutes, say?'

'Can we shorten it?'

'Course we can. Easy as kiss your hand.' He pointed to the music. 'We could skip from that bar there down to here. Only needs a chord or two adding here to make a transition. I can do it while you wait, if you like.' He felt in his pockets and produced a stub of pencil.

'What about words?' asked Madame.

'Ah, now, there's the thing. I'm not good on words. There's Rhun the Rhymer, though. He'll be in soon – well, if he can tear himself away from his current lady, he will.' He sent Daisy a wink. 'But he'll probably be able to come up with something. If he can't, it'd be the first time in his life. He'd be glad to be part of it, too.' He looked back at the music. 'We could get Old Shaky in on this, too,' he said. 'He'll be along soon, looking for his supper ale and a pie to go with it.'

'And his banjo,' said Daisy, smiling.

'Yes, give him a pie and a glass of something and he'd play for the devil himself, Old Shaky would.'

Daisy said, eagerly, 'It'd make it a bit more of an evening, as well. Kind of thing folk'd come along to hear.' She glanced at Madame. 'And we want as many people to know about it as possible, don't we?' she said.

'Yes, we do. Can we wait for them now – Rhun the Rhymer and the banjo man?'

'Course you can.'

'In that case we'll all have another drop of porter,' said Madame. 'And a couple of those meat pies, as well.'

FOUR

'Isn't it lucky that you found this place,' said Arabella Tallis, delightedly facing Phin over a table in Linklighters, three nights after Phin and Toby's visit. 'I bet you'll find masses of leads here that you can follow up.'

'I'm hoping so,' said Phin, and thought, not for the first time, that one of Arabella's many attractive traits was her enthusiasm for almost everything.

'But I'm sorry I got my heel stuck in the grid outside just now,' she said. 'Although I expect it was my own fault for wearing boots with four-inch heels. You wouldn't have thought it would take three people to prise a stiletto heel free, would you? Aren't people helpful?'

'Will you be able to get it put back on to the boot?' asked Phin, as Arabella contemplated with pleasure the plate of food which had just been placed before her. 'And what's that you've ordered?'

'Fricasseed chicken. It was either that or something called pork griskin, which I thought sounded like the name of Snow White's eighth dwarf. What did you have – oh, you had beef and oyster pie, didn't you? It looks good. I think the heel can be stuck back on my shoe. I rescued the actual heel, after all, and the leather's only torn the very smallest bit. Although at

one point I thought the entire boot might fall all the way
through the grille, and end up in one of London's lost rivers.
D'you know, Phin, I'll swear I could actually hear water
somewhere below that grid, glugging and sloshing.'

'Not impossible. London's got quite a few forgotten underground rivers.'

'Isn't the Fleet one of them? I'll bet if my boot had fallen
all the way through that grating it'd have been the Fleet where
it ended up,' said Arabella. 'You wouldn't believe how many
people have prophesied I'm destined for a debtors' gaol,
although I think they've usually meant the Fleet prison rather
than the Fleet river.'

Phin was never sure how far to believe Arabella's flippant
claims of impending bankruptcy and her extravagant stories
of bailiffs about to camp out on the doorstep. It was strange
how you could become extremely intimate with someone on
practically every level, but still find the subject of money
awkward. Set against the possible bankruptcy was the fact that
Arabella was always wanting to share the bill for a meal or
the theatre and usually appeared to have sufficient money to
do so. Phin nearly always managed to override her, but she
tended then to cook him a lavish meal a few days later, or
suddenly announce that she had been given two tickets for a
concert or a film which she thought they could enjoy together.

'It was worth a broken stiletto to come here, though,' she
said. 'And I love Harlequin Court – that marvellous old streetlight. It'd have been gas originally, wouldn't it? When I get
back from France I'd like to spend an entire day, if not longer,
wandering around the shops in the square. Will you wander
with me?'

'To the ends of the earth and back again.'

'Ah, one of the last real romantics. But if we're going as
far as that I'd better remember not to wear four-inch stilettoes.'
Arabella surveyed the restaurant. 'Whoever did the renovations
here made a good job of it,' she said. 'It's just enough to make
you feel that you're dipping a toe into the Naughty Nineties.
I wouldn't be surprised to see Edward VII walk past our table
– smacking ladies on the bottom as he goes, the old goat. Or
should we make it the ghost of Henry Irving? How close are

we to the Lyceum? I'd like to think of Sir Henry popping in
here on matinee days for something to eat. Did music halls
serve food, do you know?'

'Jellied eels. Whelks. Oh, and pickled oysters?'

'Honestly?'

'It's a known fact that Irving wolfed down whole barrels
of pickled oysters between *Richard III* in the afternoon and
Othello in the evening,' said Phin, solemnly. 'Although I don't
think he was greatly given to smacking bottoms. Arabella, I
do wish you weren't going away for a month. Apart from
everything else, I'll miss all the inconsequential talk.'

He reached for her hand, and she took it at once. 'I'll miss
it, too,' she said. 'I've never met anyone else I can be incon-
sequent with. I don't exactly wish I wasn't going to Paris,
because it's a good commission and it'll be interesting work,
and I know it's only three and a bit weeks, but . . .' She
made what was almost an impatient gesture, and, as if determined not to accidentally talk herself into anything emotional,
said, 'Anyway, while I'm away, I'm having the bathroom
refitted. You remember I knocked over that container of
sulphuric acid while the plumber was trying to unbung the
washbasin last week? It practically ate the carpet there and
then, and corroded all the taps and pipes.'

Phin remembered this event vividly; in fact the thought of
Arabella and an unstable bottle of sulphuric acid in the same
room had haunted his dreams for several nights afterwards.
But he only said, 'Did the insurance company pay up?'

'Practically the whole amount. So while I'm away, Toby's
arranging for all the refitting of the whole bathroom.'

'Oh, God.'

'No, it'll be fine. They're going to start the day after
tomorrow, by which time I'll be in Paris. Toby knows someone
who's started a DIY and plumbing company.'

'I know he does,' said Phin. 'He wants me to have some
new bookshelves built.'

'What a good idea. I'm always tripping over piles of books
in your flat – I usually trip as far as your bedroom, don't I,
although to be fair I don't actually mind. In fact I'll miss it
rather a lot,' said Arabella.

'The tripping over?'

'The bedroom.' She looked at him from the corners of her eyes.

'I'll miss it, as well,' said Phin.

'Really, Phin?'

'Oh, God, yes.'

She smiled, then said, 'I might manage to dash back for one of the weekends. Or you might dash over. You won't be perpetually immersed in Franz Liszt and the music halls, will you?'

'I'll come up for air if you're around,' promised Phin. 'I do want to trace some of the acts in these posters and playbills, though.'

'Let me find my glasses so I can have a better look at them.' Arabella rummaged in her bag, and found the spectacles, which turned her from slightly dishevelled imp to untidily earnest academic. 'Oh, yes, I can see them now. I love the names. Belinda Baskerville, the Gentlemen's Delight. Dainty Dora Dashington . . . Oh, and is that one in that corner Scaramel?' She leaned across the table to read it. 'Yes, it is. It's something about a "Triumphant return to London after her Parisian successes including her appearance at the Moulin Rouge".' She sat back, thoughtfully. 'Interesting that she was in Paris.'

'And that she performed at the Moulin Rouge,' said Phin.

'She was up there with the best of them, wasn't she? I wonder if I could find any traces of her while I'm over there,' said Arabella, thoughtfully.

'It'd be a bit of a long shot, although . . .'

'What is it?' said Arabella, as he broke off.

'I've just noticed a framed song-sheet in that corner,' he said. 'Over there on the left – d'you see it? Toby and I looked at several of the playbills and things, but we didn't see that.'

'Is it relevant to your street ballads?' asked Arabella, turning to look. 'Or is it just that any unexplained piece of music is the siren's lure for you?'

'Whatever it is, I think I'll be lured,' said Phin, getting up.

'I'll come with you. I'd better take these boots off altogether first, though. I don't mind limping out to a taxi, all dot-and-carry-one,' said Arabella, 'but I'm blowed if I'll limp across a restaurant for people to think I'm sloshed.'

'They'll think you're a leftover from the hippie era,' said Phin, as Arabella discarded the boots under the table and padded barefoot across the floor.

'I'd rather be thought of as a leftover hippie than a wino. Is this the song-sheet? It looks as if it's been torn, or as if it simply crumbled at the edges from age. Pity it's lost the title.'

'It's very faded, as well – the actual music's hardly visible.' Phin peered as closely as he could at the framed song-sheet.

'I shouldn't think anyone could make out more than a couple of notes here or there,' he said, regretfully.

'The lyrics are readable, though.'

The lyrics were faded and damp-spotted in places, but, as Arabella said, they were readable.

Listen for the killer for he's here, just out of sight.
Listen for the footsteps 'cos it's very late at night.
I can hear his tread and he's prowling through the dark.
I can hear him breathing and I fear that I'm his mark.

Now I hear the midnight prowl,
Now I see the saw and knife.
Next will come the victim's howl.
So save yourself from him, and *run* . . .
. . . run hard to save your life.

Phin and Arabella looked at one another.

'That's possibly the eeriest thing I've ever heard,' said Arabella, at last. 'It's almost a warning, isn't it? Could it be the murder song the book mentioned? Late 1800s, wasn't it?'

'That's a huge assumption to make,' said Phin, still staring at the framed song. Even though the music notation had faded beyond legibility, he could almost conjure up its cadences. Prowling, menacing. Footsteps-in-the-fog music – music for killers hiding behind the bedroom door, or peering down from the attic . . .

And there, again, was that line. *Listen for the killer.*

'But we could make a small assumption, couldn't we?' Arabella was saying, hopefully. 'After all, this was Scaramel's place, and the rumour was that she was tangled up in a murder, and that somebody wrote a song about it.'

'A Welsh lyricist,' said Phin, frowning. 'But this mightn't be anything to do with that. It might be one of those spoof horror things – a comedy turn. There were plenty of them. There's that one about the Tower of London, and Anne Boleyn.'

'*With Her Head Tucked Underneath Her Arm, She Walks the Bloody Tower*,' nodded Arabella.

'Yes, and there's a really ghoulish one called "Eggs and Marrowbone". But this might even be a saucy one, like Marie Lloyd's stuff.'

'What about the music publisher's name?' said Arabella, indicating the tiny print at the edge of the song-sheet. 'Does that tell you anything?'

'Not really. It's Francis & Day,' said Phin. 'They were one of the leading music publishers from the 1870s on – actually they were very active in promoting music copyright. But this could be an old score published purely as a curio. Still . . .' He glanced round the restaurant, then reached into his pocket for his phone.

'What are you doing?' demanded Arabella. 'Oh, God, you're not going to photograph it, are you? Phin, the camera will flash and people will see—'

'I'm going to read the words aloud with the memo record on,' said Phin. 'I don't think it'll attract attention, and even if it does I'm not doing anything wrong. But in case I press the wrong button on the phone, or we get interrupted, can you possibly scribble down the words as well? You'll do it quicker than I can.'

'All right.' Arabella scooted back to their table, seized a table napkin and foraged in her bag for a pen.

Phin repeated the song's words into his phone, and as he reached the final line and put the phone away, Arabella said, 'I've got it. Let's finish our dinner, shall we, before it goes cold.'

Back at their table, she speared a piece of chicken with her fork, then said, 'Are you going to talk to anyone while we're here? About looking at any old archives? An owner or a manager or someone?'

'Would you mind? I wouldn't take long, but if I could
arrange to have access to any old documents or records they
might have stashed away . . .' He looked back at the framed
song-sheet.

'Of course I wouldn't mind,' said Arabella. 'I'd have been
surprised if you hadn't wanted to do so. Are you going to say
anything about that *Liszten for the Killer* sketch? Phin, is it
coincidence, that line? "Listen for the Killer"?'

'I don't think I will,' said Phin. 'I can be quite open about
the book on Liszt's life, though. And I can say I've found
some evidence of a friendship between Liszt and Scaramel. I
could even produce Cosima's letter as proof.'

'Cosima? Oh, his daughter.'

'Yes. Francesca Gaetana Cosima Liszt. But she was only
ever known as Cosima. She married Richard Wagner,' said
Phin.

'*The* Richard Wagner? *The Flying Dutchman* and *The Ring*
Wagner?'

'Yes.'

'You can't say she didn't keep things in the family, that
Scaramel,' observed Arabella. 'But it all sounds nicely scholarly, and it ought to add to your credibility.' She looked round
the restaurant. 'There's a lady at the desk over there. Black
frock, and one of those faces that looks as if it belongs in a
painting of Spanish olive groves. Or if you don't want to
approach her, we could go undercover,' she said, hopefully.
'Steal furtively down into the nether regions of the building
while nobody's looking. Although I don't think I can be very
furtive in one heelless boot.'

'You aren't really dressed for furtive stealing around, anyway,'
said Phin. 'You should be in a balaclava and camouflage jacket.
That's not to say I don't like the patchwork-patterned velvet
jacket.'

'The skirt doesn't go with it, does it?'

'Well . . .'

'I thought it mightn't, but I can't get at the full-length mirror
in my flat on account of the bathroom disaster – the bath's
still upended in the hall. Good thing I can get at the shower.
Shall I come with you to talk to the olive-grove lady, or will

I cramp your style if you're going to exert your understated charm?'

'I didn't know I had any . . .'

'It's the eyes,' said Arabella, regarding him. 'Silver with black rims. I'll bet Svengali had eyes like that. If he'd been real, I mean. I'll stay here, shall I, and order some pudding. There's a champagne soufflé which sounds nicely decadent. Oh, or something called Love's Cartridges. It says it's a kind of ice-cream pudding with cherry and violet glacé embellishments. It sounds quite suggestive. I bet it'd stop you being understated later on.'

'What time did you say your flight is tomorrow?'

'Not until midday,' said Arabella, demurely.

'That's what I thought. Order two helpings,' said Phin, getting up from the table. 'We can test the effects when we get back to your flat.'

The lady whom Arabella had pointed out was called Loretta Farrant.

'I'm the owner,' she said, shaking Phin's hand. 'Well, I'm part-owner if we're going to be accurate, along with my husband. But he's not here tonight.' This was said almost as an afterthought, as if the husband was not especially important. Closer to, the Spanish look was less noticeable; Loretta Farrant's eyes were smaller and shrewder than they had looked from a distance, and her lips were rather thin. Even so, she was a striking-looking lady. Phin thought she was probably in her middle thirties.

He explained about his commission for the research on the Franz Liszt book, and about the tenuous link he had found between Liszt and Scaramel.

'She was a music hall performer,' he said. 'And I've turned up fairly reliable information suggesting that Liszt admired her in his old age – and that she used to perform here when it was one of the old supper clubs.'

'I don't know about Liszt, but this certainly used to be a supper club – well, you can see that from the décor, I expect,' said Loretta Farrant. 'And there was indeed a performer here called Scaramel. I – that is, we – took over the place last year, and the legend was that Scaramel was the main attraction. The 1880s and 1890s – fascinating era, isn't it? But this place was in a shocking state of dereliction, and the renovations took months – as well as a good deal of money. But I was determined to recreate as much of the original music hall as possible.' Something flickered in her eyes, then was gone.

'You've made a brilliant job of it,' said Phin, pleased he could say this with complete honesty.

'Thank you. It mattered to me to get it right.'

'What I really want to ask,' said Phin, 'is whether there were any old records around? Or any old accounts or invoices that came to light during the renovations? I'm after anything that might turn up more information about Scaramel. Land deeds or anything like that when you took it on? Anything attached to the lease, maybe?'

And about whether Scaramel really committed a murder, and about that curious song hanging on the wall over there, he thought.

'I had a new lease written when I took the place on,' said Loretta, thoughtfully. 'There weren't any deeds with it, though, and I don't think there was anything about previous occupants, either. Leasing isn't like buying a property outright, is it, where you'd have lists of previous owners. Epitome of title, isn't it called?'

'Something like that.'

'There are a couple of boxes of stuff still in the cellar, though. I threw some of the contents out – the really mildewed stuff, but I kept as much as I could, because – well, you never know, do you? And I think there were old papers relating to some of the properties in Harlequin Court itself. I'm sure the bookshop – Thumbprints – was mentioned a couple of times. It's been there for well over a century. There were a good many old playbills and posters – we used the best of them for décor.'

'Where did they come from?'

'I forget exactly. I think a lot of them were already here – stored in the cellars.'

'Would you be prepared to let me look through the boxes?' said Phin, eagerly. 'I wouldn't take anything away, of course

– but if I could make notes or take photos or copies? And I'd be sure to give the restaurant – and you and your husband, of course – acknowledgements in the eventual book.'

'Would you really?' Clearly, this snared her interest. She's scenting a bit of publicity, thought Phin. And why not?

He said, 'Yes, certainly, I would. The book's commissioned and contracted, and it's being written by a couple of very eminent musicologists. One's attached to King's College, Cambridge.'

'I'm sure we can arrange for you to look at the old documents,' said Loretta, apparently impressed. 'They're all in what used to be known as the deep cellar. I turned it into an office – it was the only bit of space we could utilize for that. But I'm not really supposed to let people – members of the public, I mean – down there, because of Health & Safety regulations. The thing is . . .' She broke off, glancing round the restaurant, and said in a much lower voice: 'The thing is that there's an old sluice gate behind one wall. It's all sealed off, of course, but there was an underground river beyond the gates. Not a pleasant thought, to have that behind your wall, is it?'

'I shouldn't think so at all.'

'Still, whatever it was, it's long since dried out – it's what they call a ghost river. The channel's still there, though, and you can see the course of the river on some of the really old maps. It ran south down St Martin's Lane, and out into the Thames near the Embankment.'

'Well, I promise not to investigate behind any walls,' said Phin. 'And I'd only need an hour or so, to see if there's likely to be anything that might provide a definite lead to Scaramel.' He spread his hands ruefully. 'I don't even know her real name,' he said. 'I don't suppose you do, do you?'

'No. Sorry. But the legend is that she was the typical East End girl who achieved a degree of fame and caught the eye of one or two prominent gentlemen of the day. Well, when I say *eye* . . .' A shrug of amused tolerance. It was not quite a knowing wink, but Phin had the impression that she was drawing him into a vaguely sexual intimacy.

He said, politely, that he thought Scaramel had had several lovers, and Loretta, clearly sensing his lack of response, changed tack.

'I shouldn't think that we'd be contravening too many bylaws if you went down there, Mr Fox,' she said. 'I'd have to be with you, of course . . . What about coming in tomorrow? We're open between twelve and two, but it's a very easy service for us – just a cold buffet, salad and sandwiches.' Her eyes went to Arabella, who was in enthusiastic discussion with the waiter over the menu. 'Will your companion be coming with you, Mr Fox?'

'No. As a matter of fact she's going to France tomorrow. She'll be there for the best part of a month.'

'I see,' said Loretta. 'Well, then, you could come in just after the lunch service. I could stay on to let you in. There'd be just the two of us.'

There was again the impression that she drew nearer to him, and Phin said carefully that it would be easier if he came a little earlier. 'Perhaps around half-past one, just before you close?' When there are people still around, he thought.

'Yes, that would be all right. I'll have the boxes ready for you.'

'I have to say,' said Arabella much later, 'that those Love's Cartridges seem to have been remarkably effective, don't they? Not,' she said, a smile in her voice, 'that you've ever needed any help.'

Phin turned to look at her. Her hair, which had earlier been pinned into Arabella's version of a chignon, was untidily spread over the pillow. The velvet jacket had been thrown over a chair in a corner of her bedroom, and the heelless boot kicked under the bed with its fellow.

'It's remarkable how quiet and . . . almost self-effacing you are most of the time,' she said, studying him. 'Even a bit reserved. But underneath that polite academic demeanour . . . Well,' she said, with a pleased chuckle, 'when it comes to the crunch – do I mean crunch? – you aren't reserved or quiet or self-effacing at all. I always suspected you weren't, all the way back to those days when I used to see you from the window of Toby's flat. You'd come and go with an armful of books and a kind of abstracted look, as if you were thinking about some obscure scholarly point or trying to work out some frightfully arcane piece of research. And I used to think – he'd be really interesting to know; I bet there are hidden depths there. I was right, as well.'

Phin said, 'I used to hear Toby's stories about you and think you were a frivolous scatterbrain, and that you'd be absolutely maddening to actually meet.'

'Am I? Maddening and scatterbrained?'

'Beautifully so.'

'It's all very good, isn't it?' said Arabella, then propped herself up on one elbow and looked down at him. 'Isn't it?' she said, with a sudden note of doubt.

'Oh, yes,' said Phin, reaching for her again. 'It's all *very* good indeed.'

It was almost two a.m. when Phin finally got home. He managed to pick up a taxi outside Arabella's flat. He liked being driven through London at this hour. The streets were never really deserted, and London was never entirely quiet, because London, like all cities, never really slept.

He let himself into the big old house and went softly across the dim hall, moving as quietly as he could because of Miss Pringle who lived in the garden flat, and who was a lady of a rather timid disposition. The smallest scrape of noise after ten p.m. usually sent her anxiously peering through a chink in the door to see who was abroad at such a dissolute hour. Toby always invited her to his parties – he invited the entire house, in fact, which he said saved complaints about noise. The parties terrified Miss Pringle, but she generally presented herself for a polite half-hour, before retiring to the security of her flat to watch DVDs of *Midsomer Murders*, *Inspector Morse* and, more recently, *Endeavour*, all of which had her unswerving devotion. Arabella sometimes took her out to lunch at the trattoria on the corner, and the other residents of the house occasionally invited her to supper, but that seemed to be about the extent of Miss Pringle's socializing.

Phin tiptoed past her door, wincing when a floorboard squeaked, but reaching his own flat without mishap. He was physically tired, but mentally wide awake – which was partly due to Arabella, of course. He smiled, then remembered she would be away for three weeks. Still, there was the intriguing 'Liszten for the Killer' sketch to be investigated. And the curious song tonight.

And it would be interesting to see Harlequin Court by daylight tomorrow and look through the old papers that Loretta Farrant had promised to look out. He considered Loretta. She had said she and her husband owned the restaurant jointly, although she had seemed somewhat dismissive of him. He wondered vaguely what kind of man such a forceful lady would have married. It would either have to be somebody very strong-minded who could stand up to the lady's assertive manner, or it would have to be a complete wimp who would happily fill a role of subservience and think everything she did was marvellous.

FIVE

Roland Farrant had not met up with Loretta until they ate breakfast together. Sometimes he waited up for her after her evening session in the restaurant, but she had not got in until almost half-past one last night, so he had gone to bed by himself.

It was not unusual for her to get home so late. People sometimes stayed on after their meal in the restaurant, lingering over a final cup of coffee or a liqueur. You could not point crossly to the time, Loretta said, although you had to be careful about not serving drinks and food after hours. You never knew when the licensing authorities might be setting sneaky traps to catch you out. She knew all about these things, because she had worked in hotels and restaurants for years. When they first met, Roland had loved listening to her tales about the hotel guests and their quirks and foibles.

But Mother had not cared for Loretta. 'False,' she had said, the first time Roland took her back to Dulwich. 'All that gushing and bringing me flowers and saying how marvellous the food was at lunch. I saw through all that right away. I can always tell if someone's not genuine. She's not good enough for you, Roland.'

Mother had not thought any of the girls Roland had tentatively taken out good enough, and it had usually been easier not to argue. If they were not dubbed as forward little madams, then they were colourless brown mice with no personalities. There had not, in fact, been many of them, and Roland had not been especially keen on any of them anyway.

He was very keen indeed on Loretta, though, and certainly nobody could have described her as colourless. Spanish, he had thought when they met. Like something out of a painting – olive skin and dark brown eyes and high, slanting cheekbones. She liked to wear rich dark reds and vivid sapphire blues, and she had unusual jewellery – not precious stones, but modern designer jewellery. Necklaces of chunky gold or jade. Earrings of jet or amber.

Quite soon after meeting her, he began to hope that she might feel the same about him. She came to the house several times, and she was very good with Mother, very patient and interested, wanting to help with little household tasks like putting up some new curtains, and offering to help with pasting some old photographs into albums. She liked old photos, she said; she had several of her grandparents – even her great-grandparents. Links to the past mattered, and she would be really interested to see any photos of Roland's family.

'Pushy,' said Mother, later. 'Prying into things. It's my opinion it's not family photos she's interested in – it's money. She wants to find out how much money we've got.'

'She hasn't got any family left of her own,' said Roland, who was delighted that Loretta was taking so much trouble, and gratified to think he must be the reason.

The real gratification came a month later. They had had dinner in a small restaurant that Loretta had suggested, and afterwards she invited him back to her flat for a drink. It was not so very late, she said; he would not be expected home quite yet, would he? Roland, who had casually told Mother that he would be having a few drinks with his office colleagues, said at once that it was entirely up to him when he got home. They took a taxi to the flat and they held hands in the back, and it was probably, but not necessarily, an accident that Loretta's hand brushed between Roland's thighs, and then lay there for a few moments, the fingers curling around him . . .

Her flat was quite small, but it was very comfortable. The softly cushioned sofa was very comfortable indeed, and presently, Roland ventured on more explicit embraces than he had attempted with Loretta before. They were actually more explicit than he had attempted with anyone, because on the few occasions he had been in this situation in the past, Mother's disapproving visage always came into his mind, and Mother's steely remarks about girls who went to bed with men before marriage sounded in his brain. He knew it was impossibly old-fashioned and very nearly Victorian prudishness, but it was what always happened. It always had an embarrassingly shrivelling effect, and it meant he had never really managed to get as far as anyone's bedroom.

But that night with Loretta was different. She was exciting and assertive and they did not even bother to reach her bedroom; it all started happening there on the sofa almost before Roland realized it, with buttons torn off in passionate haste and zips frantically undone and no thought about condoms, which Roland did not have anyway.

There was a frenzied bouncing of the sofa springs, and the sensation of being out of control of his own body and of being rushed towards a conclusion. And then the conclusion took him over, and it was marvellous and shattering. Roland did not think Loretta would know it was his first time ever, and he privately vowed never to admit it to her.

Afterwards, Loretta padded into the kitchen to make cups of tea for them; she put on Roland's discarded shirt which was so intimate – so very nearly loving an action – that Roland thought she could surely not refuse a proposal of marriage.

He made the proposal nervously while they drank the tea. If it was not exactly inept, it was certainly nowhere near the glossy romantic proposals you saw on films and TV, and heard about in the press. He more than half expected her to refuse, though.

But Loretta did not refuse. She accepted it with an enthusiasm that astonished and delighted him so much, that he

discovered he was capable of making love to her all over
again.

After this second excursion, she said, a bit hazily, that she
supposed his mother would not object.

'Because I had the impression she didn't care for me very
much.'

Roland tightened his hold on her. 'She'll get to know you,'
he said. 'And in any case, I won't let her stop me from marrying
you.'

'No? You promise?'

'Nothing will stop me from marrying you, Loretta.'

In the end, he had not needed to fall out with Mother about
marrying Loretta, because Mother died several days after that
memorable night on Loretta's sofa.

Roland told himself it was very sad, and that it would
leave a massive hole in his life. He had to repeat this several
times, and even then he did not really believe it. He told people
what a happy evening they had had on that last night, and that
this memory was a great consolation.

Loretta had been to supper for the evening – in fact she had
provided supper, arriving in a taxi with a casserole which she
had made, and which only needed to be heated up and served
with a salad. The casserole had been very good indeed, because
Loretta was a very good cook. Roland had opened a bottle of
wine, and had suggested that for once Mother had a glass.

'It's very soft and light. Very relaxing.'

'Well, perhaps I'll have half a glass just this once. It might
help me to sleep. I'm a martyr to insomnia,' Mother told
Loretta.

'How miserable for you.'

Mother was not a martyr to insomnia at all, but she liked to
promote the image of herself lying wakeful throughout the night.
She had the wine and went up to bed. She liked her bedroom
– she was private up there, she said; she had her books, her TV,
even her own shower room next door, put in by a previous
owner who had a big family and a live-in au pair.

Once, when Roland had asked if the extra flight of stairs
might be getting a bit of a haul, she had said sharply that she

might have a touch of arthritis and a twinge or two of angina, but she was not so decrepit that she could not manage a few stairs once a day.

'Two flights of stairs,' Roland said.

'I can manage perfectly well.'

But on the morning after Loretta came to dinner, Mother had not managed well at all. Coming downstairs for the day, she had fallen all the way down both flights of stairs, stumbling over a rucked piece of stair carpet outside her door. She had broken several bones, of course, but, most crucially of all, the fall had broken her neck.

Everyone had been kind, and at the inquest the coroner said Roland must not feel guilty. Wynne Farrant's death had been tragic and unfortunate, but carpets did come away from their moorings and people did trip over them and tumble to their deaths. He directed that the jury bring in a verdict of Accidental Death, and said that no blame whatsoever could be attached to Mr Farrant, who clearly had been a devoted and attentive son.

Loretta had been marvellous. Roland had been grateful to her in the days that followed. She had helped with all the bewildering practicalities – the post mortem and the inquest and all the paperwork. She said it was a wife's job to do things like this, and she was practically his wife. And Roland should remember that she had had to do it all herself a few years earlier for her own mother, and a few years before that for her grandmother, as well. It meant she was familiar with all the procedures, she said, and she was not letting Roland go through it on his own.

There was a good deal to sort out. Mother had been highly insured – there were two policies that Roland had not known existed. There were bonds and investments, as well, from Roland's father who had died many years ago. Overall, there was far more money than he had realized. Everything came to him.

Loretta accompanied him to the meetings with solicitors and bank staff and financial advisers. She was surprisingly knowledgeable, and Roland was immensely proud of her. And when life had settled down into some kind of normality again, it was marvellous to tell people at the office the exciting news that he was engaged. There were surprised celebrations; Loretta was invited to a drinks party with the office staff so they could meet her and congratulate her. There was wine and modest snacks, which two of the girls had brought in. The following week Roland went to the hotel which Loretta managed and which was part of a chain, to be introduced to her friends and colleagues there. There was another celebration, this time with champagne and snacks that were slightly more upmarket. He felt he was moving into a whole new life.

Loretta did not mention the house, not directly, but Roland did not think she liked it very much. It was a rambling old place, of course, not to everyone's taste. When Loretta said, quite casually, that she supposed there were a great many memories in it, Roland agreed, but he did not say that a good many of the memories were unhappy. When Loretta next remarked that properties in Dulwich were fetching some very good prices, he contacted an estate agent, and was staggered to find that Loretta had been right, because the agent thought a very high figure could be achieved. Why not try offering it, he said. Roland agreed, and was even more staggered when two people wanted to buy it at what was practically the full asking price.

After this, there was no reason to delay their wedding, and they were married shortly after probate was granted. There was a brief honeymoon in Scotland.

Linklighters was mentioned three weeks later.

'It's something I've always dreamed of,' Loretta said. Her eyes were shining. Roland had never seen her look like that, not even in bed when she told him he was the most marvellous lover in the world.

'My own restaurant,' she said. 'Our own restaurant.'

'Yes, but . . .' The enormity of what she was suggesting rose up like a gibbering monster. Roland took a deep breath and said, 'Where is this place, exactly? And how did you hear about it?'

'Oh, it was one of those chance remarks,' said Loretta, vaguely. 'I forget exactly – or it might have been someone staying at the hotel. Yes, I believe that was it. And the thing is, Roland, that I've already been to see it – I didn't tell you,

because I wanted to see what it was like first. It might have
been a complete ruin.'

'Isn't it?'

'No,' she said, softly. 'Oh, no, it isn't a complete ruin at
all. It doesn't look anything very much at the moment, but it
could be made really terrific.'

'You still haven't said where—'

'It's quite near Charing Cross Road. You have to walk along
a little alleyway – only a few steps – and then you're in a
kind of small courtyard. It's close to St Martin's Lane, so we
could do early meals for theatre-goers, and late suppers for
when they come out. All it needs is the right kind of advertising. It was a Victorian music hall in the late 1800s – you
can still see traces of that, even under all the dirt and rubble.
It was called The Linklighters Supper Rooms. Beautifully
Victorian, isn't it?'

'What were linklighters?'

'Usually young boys who would light people through those
thick old London fogs with lanterns.'

'You're very knowledgeable.'

'I read it up,' said Loretta, offhandedly. 'Anyway, my idea
is that we'd recreate the original music hall ambience as far
as possible. The food could be things like steak and oyster
pies and even jellied eels. Game pie and champagne jelly. I
know one or two chefs who have a real feel for that kind of
food – I think I could tempt them to come in.' She glanced
at him. 'I know this is all a bit out of the blue, and I never
thought it could be possible,' she said, and for the first time
since Roland had met her, she sounded shy and even a bit
nervous. His heart melted, because she had never allowed him
to see a vulnerable side before. He thought – she's had no one
and nothing for most of her life.

'I could get estimates and talk to builders and architects,'
Loretta was saying. 'And find out about planning regulations
and things. None of it will commit us to anything, of course.'

'But I don't know the first thing about running a business,'
said Roland, worriedly. 'I wouldn't know where to start.'

'Rubbish. You're an accountant. You're dealing with people's
business affairs all day. Of course you'd know.'

It was nice that Loretta thought him so capable and knowledgeable, so Roland did not remind her that he did not really
deal with people's business affairs – that he had somehow
gravitated to the audit and tax section of the company, which
the partners seemed to think was more suited to his abilities.

But when Loretta showed him the estimated cost for trans-
ferring the lease, what he said was that they could not possibly
afford to lease and run a restaurant in central London.

'We could, you know,' said Loretta. 'It's the tail-end of a
lease that's being offered. There're only four years of it to run
– which means we could get it fairly reasonably. We can do a
lot in four years, and by the end of that time, if we've made
a go of things, we might be able to afford to renew.'

'But there are other costs,' said Roland, trying not to be swept
along by her enthusiasm. 'Ground rent and a service charge.
And business rates – they'll be colossal.' He felt on safer ground
with this; he knew all about business rates.

'Well, let's look at the statement for those bonds – I
remember noticing how well they'd done. It should be in this
file here.'

She had organized the paperwork into folders, each one
neatly marked. She was a marvel when it came to this kind
of thing. And she was right in saying that the bonds had been
extremely profitable.

'We could cash them in,' said Loretta, studying the statement. 'And with the money from the house I think we'd have
enough for a proper renovation and refurbishment job.'

Staring at the statements and then looking at Loretta's
columns of figures, Roland could almost hear Mother's indrawn
breath of disapproval at the idea of risking what looked like
three-quarters of his entire legacy. But it was his legacy. It
was his money, and that meant he could do what he wanted
with it. The thought was a heady one.

Even so, he said, 'But weren't we going to buy a house?
This wouldn't leave enough for that. Where would we live?'

'We'd go on living in this flat for the time being,' said
Loretta, clearly surprised. 'It wouldn't be for ever.'

They had lived in Loretta's flat since Wynne's death,
although Roland was spending most weekends at Dulwich,

sorting out her possessions. The sale was going through, and he had assumed that they would use the proceeds to buy a smaller house in the same area.

He had, in fact, grown up in that part of London, and he had been articled at the nearby accountants' office where he still worked. Mother had known someone at the firm and she had arranged it all, saying that accountancy was such a safe profession and Roland had always been so good with maths.

'It will be just the thing for you, Roland,' she had said, and had set up an interview for him there and then.

Roland had gone to the firm straight from school. They had their own training programme, and he had gained diplomas and qualifications as he went along. It all meant he was used to travelling to and from home each day; the office was only two tube stops away, and he had generally gone home to have lunch with Mother.

But it was a long, tiring journey between Loretta's flat and the office, and Roland had looked forward to moving back to Dulwich. He had even earmarked a couple of houses they could view. Still, he supposed he owed it to Loretta to at least take a look at this derelict-sounding restaurant. Not that anything would come of it.

SIX

Loretta borrowed the keys that weekend, and took Roland to see Linklighters on Sunday afternoon.

On the way there, she said, 'You'll be able to look beyond its present condition, won't you – but of course you will; you have such a gift for seeing beyond the obvious to what's real. Like you did with me.' She smiled and slanted her eyes at him, pressing against him for a brief moment. Roland was grateful that for once his body did not betray him. The truth was that he was too worried about Linklighters to be giving way to unruly desires on Leicester Square tube escalator.

'I know the alley looks a bit narrow and tucked away,' said Loretta, when they reached Harlequin Court, 'but the court itself is charming and beautifully quaint.'

Roland did not think Harlequin Court was charming or quaint. He thought it was distinctly seedy. The shops that fronted the square had small-paned windows and there was the impression that their interiors would be cramped and dim. There was a conventional modern light at the entrance to the square, but within the square was only an old street gaslight that should have been rooted out decades ago. It would be dangerously easy to bump into it on a dark night. Was this really a place people would seek out in order to have a meal?

Loretta said, 'You can see how it must have looked, can't you? And over here –' she led him across the square – 'over here,' she said, on a note of pride, 'is Linklighters Supper Rooms.'

Roland stared in dismay at the door next to the bookshop which Loretta was unlocking. Most of the paint had peeled off it and there were faded fragments of old posters which probably went back decades, and might have advertised all kinds of questionable events. The door itself had a furtive air, as if it did not want to draw attention to itself or what lay behind it.

'We'd have a new door, of course,' said Loretta, pushing it open to reveal a flight of dark stairs. 'Be careful how you go down, because there's no electricity.'

'None at all?'

'There is electrical wiring, of course, but it's turned off at the moment. Anyway, I think it was put in a long time ago, so it'll have to be redone.'

She's talking as if it's already been agreed, thought Roland, even more worried, but he said, 'Let's get inside. It's starting to rain.'

'Yes, all right. The stairs are a bit rickety, but we can have them ripped out and a new staircase put in. Don't grab that railing, it's coming away from the wall.'

The rain spattered against the old door as they went down, and a smeary light came in through a narrow, very grimy

window halfway down. Through this window and seen through
the curtain of rain, Harlequin Court looked somehow older.
The ground seemed to be uneven, almost as if it might be
cobbled, and the streetlight took on a vaguely sinister appearance. Roland was grateful when Loretta took a couple of
torches from her bag and handed him one.

'This was the music hall itself,' she said as they reached
the foot of the stairs. 'It's much larger than you'd think from
upstairs.'

'Yes.'

'In its heyday it'd have been jam-packed with people –
probably sitting in rows or on ledges or at round wooden
tables. And there'd have been raucous music and loud singing,
because the audience would have joined in with most of the
songs,' said Loretta. 'Can't you just imagine them – waving
tankards of drink, and the men shouting lewd comments at
the scantily dressed females on the stage?'

She looked at him, her eyes bright, clearly wanting him to
share the images, and Roland said, 'It doesn't sound very
different from today's pop festivals and club scenes.'

'No. Nothing new under the sun.'

There were no windows at this level, of course, but in the
light from the torches it was easy to see that the place really
was derelict. Roland was just thinking it was remarkable that
it had not been broken into and used as a squat, and even
wondering about rats, when the torch's beam showed up a
couple of tattered blankets and several greasy foil trays that
had once contained curries and takeaways. Nearby were a
number of empty beer bottles, along with several discarded
condoms.

'I suppose it's better than strewing them all over the square
outside,' said Loretta, seeing Roland look at these. 'Still, food,
drink and sex. And a roof over your head. Covers all the basic
needs, doesn't it?'

Roland moved the torch around. Cobwebs hung down in
thick swathes and clung to the walls. The walls themselves
had huge leprous patches and large sections of plaster had
fallen away. There were gaping holes in the floor, and the
whole place stank to high heaven.

But Loretta was saying, 'Isn't it all brilliant? Can't you see the potential? So much space, and—'

'What's that stuff spilling out of the walls? Like wire wool.'

'Where? Oh, that. It's a sort of wall stuffing. Apparently parts are the old wattle-and-daub construction – that's kind of wooden strips made into a frame, then stuffed with clay and earth and crushed stone. It'll be easy to rebuild those sections though. Try to look beyond the dereliction. There's masses of room for – well, about a dozen small tables I should think, and three or four six-seaters. And it won't be hard to recreate what the place used to be. That wall over there, for instance – you can still see bits of the old flock wallpaper. Fleur-de-lys. It's grey now, but it would probably have been crimson originally – velvety and gorgeous. We'll look for the nearest match.'

'But some of the walls look as if they're almost falling in.'

'No, the builder says everywhere just needs properly replastering, and once that's dried out and papered and painted, it'll be fine. OK, maybe an odd ceiling joist here and there. And we can have the kitchens through this door here – you'll have to prop it back, though.' She shone the torch around. 'Stoves against that wall, and hobs alongside. Plenty of space to put in cupboards, and a preparation area at the centre. Freezers and fridges in that recess. This would have been the backstage area, of course.'

'Where was the stage?' said Roland, looking back at the main room.

'Long rotted away, but it would have been at that far end – can you see where I mean? Can't you? Well, never mind.' She walked back across the floor, her footsteps echoing in the emptiness. 'This other side is where the performers would have got ready. I don't think there were dressing rooms as such, but there were a couple of rooms where they'd have changed and kept their props and things . . . Look out, there's a hole in the floor . . . I said look out—'

There was the sound of wood splintering and Roland let out a yelp. 'My ankle's bleeding,' he said, bending over his foot. 'And these are my new shoes. The leather's all scratched.'

'It'll polish out, and your ankle's only grazed.' She turned away, clearly more interested in their surroundings. 'Those recesses under the stairs open out and go quite far back,' she said, pointing. 'They'd convert beautifully into cloakrooms. The plumbing's fairly ancient, but the basic pipework's there and my plumber says he can lay new pipes.'

My plumber. Again, there was the impression that she had already lined up a team of workmen who would leap into action when she gave the word.

'What's beyond that door by the stairs?'

'There're steps beyond it going down to a deeper level. It couldn't be part of the restaurant, but spruced up it'd make a bit of an office. Or a storage place.'

Roland walked across to the door and opened it, then flinched.

'God, what's that smell?'

'Well, there's an old sluice gate down there. Only a small one, though, and it can easily be walled off.'

'Why is there a sluice gate?' asked Roland, suspiciously.

'Because there's an old ditch down there. It's long since dried out, though. Ghost river, they call it. The gate seals it off.'

'Not if the stench is anything to go by, it doesn't.'

'If you must know,' said Loretta, sounding a bit annoyed, 'that ditch is the reason that the lease is being offered at an absolute knock-down figure.'

'Dear God.'

'The gate would have to stay and be reasonably workable, but the builders say they can put up a false wall – with one of those panels like you have across water tanks in airing cupboards, so the gate can be reached. Only larger, of course. And if we put a fire door at the bottom of these stone steps, the Health and Safety people will be perfectly happy,' said Loretta, confidently. 'I've checked that. I know it sounds a bit grim, but come down there with me now, and I'll show you what can be done.'

She took his hand, and led the way, shining the torch as she went. The stench increased as they went down the steps, and there was a faint dull echo of water dripping somewhere. Once at the foot, Loretta moved the torch across the stone walls, pointing out a section of wall on the far side.

'The sluice gate's through that narrow bit of opening,' she said. 'There's a kind of inner cellar. If you go right up to that part of the wall, you can see straight in – you can see the gate itself.'

'No, thanks. It looks as if somebody once tried to knock part of that wall away, though,' said Roland.

'I know. The stones are all jagged and broken up. But the builders can make that good, and they'll plaster over everything.'

Roland shivered and turned up his coat collar. 'Can we go back upstairs now? And out into the fresh air, because if I stay down here any longer with this stench I'm likely to be sick.'

As he went back up the steps he was thinking that this place was little more than a massive derelict cellar over an ancient ditch. Renovating it to match Loretta's vision would eat up a very large portion of Mother's money.

But, even as he was thinking this, another thought was pushing upwards. Risky as this would be, mightn't it be rather exciting? Loretta certainly thought it would, so perhaps Roland ought to try thinking of it in the same way. His life had not held much excitement so far, and he had always known that the people at his office had regarded him, albeit tolerantly, as a bit dull. But he had made them blink a bit by presenting them with Loretta, and he had enjoyed that. What would their reactions be if he casually announced he was opening a smart, trendy restaurant in the middle of London? And if that restaurant were to be a success . . .? After all, the money was his money.

Standing in the semi-shelter of Linklighters' door, Loretta unfurling an umbrella for the walk back to the tube, and rain washing bits of unsavoury debris into the gutters, the words danced temptingly across Roland's mind. *The money was his money.* And it was his decision as to how it was spent.

He looked back at Harlequin Court, and at the battered door leading down to Linklighters. Could it be done? Mother would have sneered and told Roland he was being a fool even to consider this. With the realization of how furious Mother would have been, something seemed to seize Roland's mind and wrench it completely around, causing him to see the project from an entirely different angle. He was seeing how Harlequin Court could be tidied up, swept clean, and how Linklighters could be turned into a smart and comfortable restaurant, filled with people wanting a meal before an evening at the theatre, or a late supper afterwards. There would be lights glowing and nicely printed menus and thick carpets.

That was the moment when he knew he was going to do what Loretta wanted.

Loretta plunged into the Linklighters project enthusiastically. Roland must be company secretary, she said. He would be marvellous; he would know how to deal with the legal side and the finances. Roland did not know anything about the legalities of starting a business, but one of the partners at his office knew, and guided him through it. It was not necessary to tell Loretta about that.

The solicitor, preparing the assignment of the lease, frowned over some of its requirements, and said it was to be hoped no major repairs were ever needed, because it would be a night-mare to decide who owned which bits. He dared say the entire court was very charming and picturesque, but parts of the foundations joined up, and it was impossible to say which bit belonged to which owner. It was to be hoped that Mr and Mrs Farrant did not find they were liable for the replacing of some ancient underground sewer pipe or a crumbling wall that might be propping up something overhead. As for the old ditch . . . He shook his head and said that ditch by itself was a lawyer's nightmare.

Loretta did not find any of it a nightmare. She glowed with excitement and energy, and she met builders and plumbers and interior designers. She came to bed every night wanting to talk about her plans, and wanting to make love fiercely and with an abandonment – and a frequency – that Roland had not really bargained for. Embarrassingly, there were one or two occasions when he was unable to get himself into a satis-factory state of arousal. Perhaps there were more than one or two. Nobody was keeping a tally, for goodness' sake.

SEVEN

London, 1880s/1890s

P eople in Rogues Well Yard and Canal Alley and the streets around were mildly interested to hear that there was to be a bit of a concert at the Cock & Sparrow on Saturday. Probably it would only turn out to be Bowler Bill and some silly girl he'd taken a fancy to, but who had a voice like a corncrake. Still, Old Shaky would most likely be there, plunking his banjo, and Rhun the Rhymer would be in his usual corner, wearing the long black overcoat that trailed the ground, his hair tumbling over the collar. Might be a bit of a sing-song. Might be a lively night, in fact.

The Cock & Sparrow had put a poster on a wall about it. People who could read told people who could not what it said. Drinks would be half-price and there was to be a famous music hall performer. No, it was not Marie Lloyd, of course it was not, silly bugger, you wouldn't expect Miss Lloyd to prance around the Cock & Sparrow, would you? But it was somebody quite well known. Hackney Empire, and Wilton's and the Cambridge, and everything. Might as well go along to watch, specially with drinks half-price.

Wives warned their husbands not to get soused, half-price drinks or no, and not to start fights, neither. Most of these gentlemen retorted with spirit that if you could not get sozzled after a week's graft in the factory or down at the docks, or dragging a brewer's dray, you might as well curl up your toes and die. Fisticuffs might well develop, you could never tell. Then the Cock & Sparrow announced that anyone starting a fight or getting involved in one would be flung outside into the street and sluiced down with the overflow from the privies.

It was thought most people would behave reasonably well, though, what with wanting to see this music hall female.

* * *

She was called Scaramel, and people said they had heard of her, even if they had not, because you wanted folk to think you knew what went on in the world.

The big upstairs room of the Cock & Sparrow had been opened up, which was not something that happened very often, and although there was no charge to go in, you had to write your name in a book at the door. If you couldn't write – and no shame if you couldn't! – somebody was there to write it down for you, and you could add your cross.

Seats and tables were set out, and a small stage had been rigged up at one end. Scaramel, when she came out on to it, was certainly a looker, never mind who had or hadn't heard of her. Some of the younger men cheered and whistled, and the older ones said, by God, you didn't often see females the like of that, and would you look at that display of ankles. Older ladies sniffed that it was shameless, while the younger ones wondered, enviously, where Scaramel got her stockings, because they were thin as cobwebs, but very likely cost a week's wages for the likes of most folk.

Scaramel clearly enjoyed the cheers. She dropped a very saucy curtsey, Bowler Bill began playing and Old Shaky perched himself on the edge of the stage, and joined in.

The first song was the Lily Morris one, 'Why am I Always the Bridesmaid?', very cheekily sung, with a good many bum-juttings and winks to the audience, which everybody cheered. Then they had 'Hot Codlings', with everyone shouting the last lines, and Rhun the Rhymer coming up with one or two versions of his own. After this was 'The Putney Bus', and then George Leybourne's famous 'Champagne Charlie'.

When she finished this last one, Scaramel came to the edge of the stage, and put her hands on her hips and looked round. A sudden hush fell on the room, because anyone with half an eye – anyone who wasn't half soused by then – could sense that something serious was going to be said.

Scaramel said, 'Good bit of a fun, a sing-song, ain't it? But you haven't been having so much fun round here lately, have you? Well, I know you haven't. The whole of London – the whole of England – knows that.'

There was a faint murmur of slightly puzzled agreement,

then Scaramel said, 'Police ain't been much help to you, either, have they?' She appeared to wait, and there were one or two shouts of agreement, and calls about bloody useless peelers, sat on their arses in posh offices. A female voice from the back of the room said the peelers weren't nothing but mutton-shunters anyway.

'Move a gel on for trying to make a penny or two, that's all they do.'

'Tell you it's the law,' added another. 'Bleeding law. Move you on, and drive you into the arms of *him*, more like.'

'You don't like naming him, do you?' said Scaramel, looking at the two women who had spoken.

'Give him a name? I wouldn't give him the steam off my piss.'

'I understand that,' she said, seriously. 'Give him a name, and he's suddenly more real. Don't matter what he's called or what he isn't called, though. Because, people like us – and I'm not from so very different a background as yours – we've learned to look after ourselves, haven't we? To look after our own. But how do you look after yourselves with that mad butcher creeping around? You got to go about your ordinary lives, that's for sure, and do your work – and never mind what kind of work it might be. But the police are never there when you want them—'

''cept for mutton-shunting,' said the disgruntled voice from the corner.

'And as for sounding an alarm, well, you can't carry trumpets or bells with you all the time,' said Scaramel. 'Anyway, they cost money to buy. It'd be easy enough for me to hand out whistles to you all, but I don't think it'd work. Whistles get lost, they get pinched, they get forgotten. And even then, would anyone take much notice of a whistle being blown, never mind how loud it was? Folk'd think it was a street fight, or somebody pilfering something. And if *he* was prowling up on you . . .'

She paused, and people shivered again.

'. . . You'd likely not be able to get the whistle to your lips,' said Scaramel. 'Difficult, isn't it? You saw we got you to give your names at the door here earlier on – that's so's we'd know that everyone who's here is all right.' She looked round the room, and in a lower voice, said, 'To be sure there's no one here who shouldn't be.'

Several of the females looked nervously about them.

'Now, here's my idea. How'd it be if you – the ladies mostly, but nothing to say the men can't join in – were to be taught a bit of a tune that'd sound an alarm. Only a few notes, nothing difficult. But something easy to recognize, and something that could be sung or even whistled if you see or hear . . .'

A pause, then, 'If you see or hear anyone you don't like the look of,' she said. 'Because a song – something you'd all know – would send out a warning. People hearing it would know to run for cover, and also to run to get help. Either to the nearest peeler – if you can find one – or a bunch of your own folks.'

This was unexpected. Nobody had thought of this, but people were nodding. Hadn't they all of them said the police ought to do something to give them a bit of protection from this mad killer? And had the police done anything? Had they buggery? Somebody from the back called out that the truth was that the police didn't give a tuppenny fart if a gaggle of prostitutes got murdered, and there was a murmur of agreement.

From the back of the room, somebody said, 'But what about *him*? Hear it a couple of times, then *he'd* get to recognize it, too, wouldn't he?'

'I hope he would,' said Scaramel, at once. 'Because if he did, he'd know he'd been spotted and he'd know a call for help had been sent out. He'd fear that half of Whitechapel would come running. He'd be off like greased lightning.' She suddenly walked to the front of the little dais, and in a soft voice that still managed to reach every part of the room, she said, 'Jack? You in here with us, are you? You here, listening and watching? I wouldn't put it past you.' She paused, looking round the room. 'But if you are here tonight, Jack, you'll know that we're setting a trap for you.'

This time the shudder that went through everyone was much more pronounced. People turned to look over their shoulders, and somebody got up to peer through the door.

'He ain't here,' said a man.

'Ain't he? How d'you know?'

'Wouldn't have the balls.'

'That's where you're wrong, that's just what he would have!'
This was Rhun the Rhymer, draped over his table in the corner.

'Wouldn't have any at all if I could get my hands on him,'
said somebody else, and this broke the tension slightly.

'Never mind what he's got or what he mightn't have in the
future,' said Scaramel. 'What about this song?'

'I reckon it'd work,' said the man, who had refused to
believe the Ripper was in the room. 'I say we hear it.'

'Ask me, it's a bloody good idea,' called someone else, and
a ragged cheer went up.

'An' we don't care if he is here, the evil sewer rat. You sing
this tune for us, darlin'. We'll learn it.'

Scaramel stepped back from the dais edge, and nodded to
Bowler Bill who seemed to know all about it, and then to Old
Shaky who also seemed to be part of it. There was an imme-
diate hush. The music began, and Scaramel started to sing.

'Listen for the killer for he's here, just out of sight.
Listen for the footsteps 'cos it's very late at night.
I can hear his tread and he's prowling through the dark.
I can hear him breathing and I fear that I'm his mark.'

She paused, as if wanting a reaction to this, but a number of
people – almost all of them women – were nodding, because
they knew how it felt to think someone was creeping along
after you, and they all knew what a 'mark' was. You didn't
live in the East End all your life and not know that. They
waited to see what came next.

'You don't need much more than those four lines,' said
Scaramel. 'But there's another verse if you want it.'

She looked round the room, and for a moment no one spoke.
The truth was that most of them wanted to hear the music
again, and they wanted to hear the second verse, too. The
strange, dark music was like no music they had ever heard; it
was music that made you think of tiptoeing footsteps coming
at you along an alley or down a passageway. Even creeping
under your own window towards your own door, which was
a very bad thought. They wanted to seize this idea and hold
on to it as a safety line.

But there was a tiny part of them that wanted to push the whole thing away and forget about it, and believe that *he* would not walk through the night streets again.

The moment hung in the balance. From her corner, Daisy saw Madame looking round the room, and for a terrible moment she thought Madame had made a mistake. But then somebody called out that they'd hear the rest – they'd have the thing in full or not at all.

Bowler Bill and Old Shaky started the music again. By now they were all thinking that it wouldn't matter if it was sung or hummed or whistled – or even tapped out on the spoons, for heaven's sake! – you'd only have to hear the first few notes of this and you'd know at once that *he* was around.

As for the words of the second verse – they were chilling, in fact they were downright bloody terrifying.

> 'Now I hear the midnight prowl,
> Now I see the saw and knife.
> Next will come the victim's howl.
> So save yourself from him, and *run* . . .
> . . . run hard to save your life.'

The music stopped and Scaramel looked round the room.

'Dark music, isn't it?' she said. 'What they call macabre. The man who wrote it thought it was a bit too dark for his own audiences, and it only came into my hands after his death. As for the words – well, they're dark too, aren't they?' She sent a grin towards Rhun the Rhymer, and people exchanged glances, because they might have known Rhun would have had a hand in the words, what with him being Welsh and given to spouting poetry at the sniff of a gin bottle, never mind a lady being involved

'You needn't even use any of the words, not if you don't want to,' said Scaramel. 'I know words aren't always easy to memorize – and I'm speaking as one who went completely blank on the stage at Collins' one night, and had to make up an entire verse! Died the death that night, I did! Thought I'd never go back on a stage after that!'

This went down well. They'd already been feeling friendly

towards her, but at this they felt even closer. She really was
one of their own kind, and you couldn't help liking somebody
who admitted to what she had called dying the death, and at
Collins', as well, posh hall that it was, not that any of them
had ever been there, but they all knew about it.

'But if you can't remember the words, you can remember
the tune,' she said, and in fact people were already trying it
out, humming and la-la-ing. Bill and Shaky played it over
once again, and then again. It was surprisingly easy to get
your head round, nor it wasn't something you'd mistake.

'Sing your own words to it if you want,' said Scaramel.
'Never mind if they're a bit saucy, neither. Whistle it if you'd
rather. Well? What do you think?'

What they all thought was that this was a very good idea
indeed; it was setting up a simple alarm network they could
all use. It wasn't foolproof against *him*, nor would anything
be, but it'd mean looking after their own a bit, yes, and
sticking out their tongues at the police as well.

'But listen to me,' said Scaramel, 'there's to be no cheating.
You're never – *never* – to sing it unless you believe he's around.
There's to be no scaring of people with it. You've got to agree
to that. You've got to promise.'

'Agreed!' shouted the room. 'Promised!'

'I'm taking it to a couple of other pubs,' she said, and,
picking up a comment from one of the tables, said, 'Yes, I
know about the Ten Bells. That's on *his* patch, isn't it, and
it's all been arranged. Next Friday night. Come along again
if you want. Bring people with you. You'll all have to sign in
like tonight, but that's only as a bit of a safeguard. And I'll
go to anywhere else you want to suggest. Any other pubs in
the area.'

'Horn of Plenty,' called out somebody.

'The Princess Alice,' said another. 'And anywhere in the
Commercial Road.'

'Good,' said Scaramel. 'I'll go to both those places if they'll
have me.'

A wit at the back of the room called out that he reckoned
anyone would have her, and he'd be first in the queue.

'I'll book you in for special treatment,' she said at once,

quick as you like, and they all cheered, pleased that she could give as good as she got.

'No charge at any of the pubs for this,' she said. 'Tell everyone that. And tell them that, like tonight, I'll be putting a few sovereigns behind the bar, so folk can have cheap drinks for the evening. In fact, now I've said that, we'll have another round on me.' She nodded to the barman, who leapt forward.

Daisy was so fiercely proud of Madame during the days that followed the Cock & Sparrow night that she wanted to run all over London telling everyone about her and what she was doing.

They were calling it the 'Listen' music by now, and Lissy and Vi came along to the next evening, which was at the Princess Alice pub on the corner of Wentworth Street. Lissy was wearing a new bonnet – very smart it was. Daisy was pleased Lissy had taken the trouble, but of course Lissy had always been one for nice outfits.

They had brought their husbands with them. Madame had met Vi and Lissy when they came out to Maida Vale, but she hadn't met their husbands, so Daisy had to do introductions. Madame, of course, was as nice and as friendly to them all as you could have wished.

'She don't make out she's something she ain't,' Lissy said afterwards. 'I noticed that the first time.' Vi said they were all glad to think that their Daise had such a good place and that Madame was looking out for Joe as well.

Shortly after the night at the Princess Alice, Madame told Daisy that someone had let the police know what they were doing.

'About "Listen" and the pub nights, I mean.'

'Do the police mind?' asked Daisy.

'I don't give a farthing fart if they do. Not costing them anything, and we're not breaking any laws. Matter of fact, I think they thought it was worth trying,' she said. 'And it'd be grand if it ended in them catching him, wouldn't it?'

'As long as he don't catch us first,' said Daisy. She hesitated, then said, 'He'll know about it by now, won't he?'

'I should think so. But I can't see he can do anything about it.'

'He might try to stop us – I mean you and me – from teaching more people the song.' Daisy did not voice her worst fear, which was that through all of this *he* would find where she and Joe lived and come after them.

But Madame understood at once. She said, 'Daisy, he doesn't know where you live nor where Joe lives. He can't. I'm watching out. You're both perfectly safe.'

Perfectly safe. As the days went along and nothing happened, Daisy began to believe that Madame was right. And then came the night at the Ten Bells.

EIGHT

1880s/1890s,

A great many people came to the Ten Bells.

'Word's got round,' said Rhun the Rhymer, pleased.

'So it should, all the posters stuck up in pubs and everywhere,' said Bowler Bill.

'They've spelled it wrong,' said Rhun, 'silly devils. We said to call it "Listen for the Killer". But they've put a *z* in *listen*, which oughtn't to be there.'

'That's what Madame told them to put,' said Daisy, who had taken Madame's costume along to the pub ahead of the evening, and had stopped to share a meat pie with Bill and Rhun. '"Liszten for the Killer", that's what she wants it calling. Something about it being a nod to the bloke who wrote the music years ago.'

Bill observed that most folk wouldn't know the difference between an extra *z* and the entire alphabet on a poster, anyway.

Bill would be playing the music for the Ten Bells night, and Old Shaky was coming as well, pleased to be included. Rhun the Rhymer was going, too. Madame had said Rhun felt a personal interest in the song on account of writing the words for it. Daisy thought Rhun felt a personal interest in Madame as well, but she did not say so.

The evening started well. Daisy found a seat just inside the door of the big upstairs room. She could see everyone coming in. Ma had come along with her friend, Peg the Rags. Peg was decked out in what looked like the best pickings from her rag shop. They waved to Daisy, and found themselves seats on one side of the room. Daisy thought she would get a couple of glasses of gin sent over as soon as she could. But the room was already crowded, and there were so many people that the two men in charge were having quite a struggle to get all the names. There was some jostling and pushing for tables nearest the stage, and Daisy was glad to have this small corner table to herself. It was all very good-natured, though, because people wanted to hear the song that was meant as an alarm signal if Leather Apron was creeping around. Also, there were half-price drinks.

But as the room filled up and the gas jets flared and popped, Daisy felt a trickle of fear. She remembered how Madame had come to the edge of the dais that first night, and said, very softly, 'Jack? Are you here?'

It was stupid to wonder whether he might be here tonight, but she looked nervously round the room. The point of getting names at the door was to know who was here, but people could give false names. And *he* was clever; he would know how to blend in. He might be disguised – wearing a false beard, for instance. Or he might have a hat pulled over his brow like the dockers over in that corner. Or a grimed face from having just come off a shift at one of the factories. There were quite a few of those. And she would recognize him, even through a disguise. Or would she?

With so many people turning up, the performance began later than planned. The first two songs went well; in fact they went so well that people were soon cheering and raising their glasses. A couple of the women got up to do a bit of a dance between the tables, causing the men to whistle and shout rude comments, and dig one another in the ribs and say would you just look at that Rosie Grady showing her drawers for all to see, saucy creature.

The room was becoming very warm. It was thick with cigarette smoke, and there was the stink of clothes that didn't often get washed, and also of bodies that didn't often get washed, either. Daisy tried to remember that if the only tap you had was down in the yard and you shared it with six other families, you were lucky to get even a bit of a sluice down in the morning. Before she went to work for Madame, Daisy had never noticed things like that. Living with Madame meant you did notice, though.

But this was disloyal. Daisy had lived among these people – or people very like them – and when she had, she had probably smelled just as bad.

Madame was starting to tell them about the 'Listen' song, and it was then that Daisy sensed a movement to one side of her table, by the door. She looked round, thinking someone had come up to speak to her, then realized the movement had been the opening of the door. But it was not opening in an ordinary way; it was being slowly and quietly pushed, an inch at a time. Daisy's heart began to race. Most likely it would be somebody's nippers, who had crept giggling up the stairs to see the famous music hall singer. She twisted all the way round in her chair to look.

The door was still only open a very little way, but it was possible to see the shadowy landing beyond. It was possible to see the figure who stood there.

Daisy's nervousness shot all the way up into outright terror. It was not inquisitive children who stood there; it was the man she and Joe had seen that night – the man that Joe had seen looking up from his grisly work. He was exactly as she remembered. The face was the face that had stared at the two of them through the swirling fog. He was looking straight at Daisy now. He was *recognizing* her. Panic twisted at her stomach so viciously that she gasped and half bent over. When she looked again, there was no one there, only a bit of curtain moving at the window, because somebody had opened a narrow window to let in air. There was no dark figure with deep dark eyes. Had there ever been? Had it just been Daisy's own stupidity, turning a fluttering curtain into the outline of a menacing figure?

She dared to get up and walk the few steps to the door. Everyone's attention was on the stage, and she reached the door without anyone looking round. There was no one there; there was only the landing, a bit dusty, and the flapping curtain, and the stairs going down to the main bar. It sounded a bit rowdy down there, but it was a comforting sound, because it meant plenty of people were around. Daisy drew in a slightly shaky breath of relief, closed the door softly, and went back to her corner seat.

'Now then,' Madame was saying, 'this is the music, and we don't want any whistling or jeering for the next five minutes – nor any dancing around tables. Just listen.'

Listen for the killer . . . Liszten . . .

She nodded to Bowler Bill and Shaky, and the music began.

The music and the strange words had always had an effect on people; Daisy had noticed that at the Cock & Sparrow and the Princess Alice. But tonight was somehow different. Tonight it was as if something had crept into the room, and as if that something was listening and whispering a warning. *I'm here, my dears . . . I'm among you . . . And I'm watching you . . .* Daisy, her heart pounding with fear, looked back at the door. It was still firmly shut, but he might be on the other side of it. Listening. Watching.

After Madame had finished singing, people called out with questions, and then several of them came up to talk to Madame, wanting to know about the music and its composer. Madame said what she always said when people asked this: that the composer was dead, but that he had been very gifted and his music had been given to her.

Around ten o'clock, just as they were getting ready to leave, a huge tray of meat pies and newly fried sausages was brought in, and Madame said quietly to Daisy that they could not go yet, not after somebody had gone to all that trouble. So they stayed and ate a pie apiece, and Daisy was able to have a word with Ma and Peg the Rags.

Then Madame got into what looked like a very close conversation with Rhun the Rhymer. Daisy tried to think they would be talking about the song – perhaps they were going to alter the words or even write another verse. But they seemed to be enjoying themselves, although as the big clock over the bar ticked its way towards eleven, she started to feel uneasy. What if *he* was still out there? Or waiting down in the street? They had always been very careful not to return home too late – the later you left it, the more difficult it was to find a cab, especially in Whitechapel, where there were never many cabs anyway. And the longer you were likely to be walking through the dark streets with no one around, the more you were in danger.

It was almost a quarter past eleven when Madame eventually came over to Daisy, and Daisy saw that of course she and Rhun had not been discussing 'Listen', because Madame was wearing the expression she normally wore when she was about to embark on a new assignation. There were probably going to be a few nights when Daisy would have to be careful to keep to her own room in the Maida Vale apartment. It might be a bit embarrassing to encounter Rhun coming out of Madame's bedroom – not that you could imagine Rhun being embarrassed about anything. But at least he wasn't likely to go boasting about how he'd slept with the famous Scaramel. He liked to be thought of as a gentleman.

It was after half-past eleven when Daisy and Madame eventually reached the Commercial Road. They walked along, looking out for a hansom. Daisy was becoming used to waving them down. 'To the manner born,' Vi had said proudly when they all came out of the Princess Alice the other night, and Daisy hailed a cab for them. But Daisy knew she didn't do it to the manner born, because she had not been born to it, and she still felt guilty about bowling along London streets in a horse-drawn contraption. Sometimes the cabs smelt disgusting when you got in, and you had to look where you sat and where you trod, because people were sometimes sick, or worse, over the seats.

It was starting to rain, and Madame was wearing her extravagant velvet cloak – velvet in the East End, for pity's sake! But at least the cloak had a hood which she could pull up over her head against the rain. Daisy was going to have a hard job getting it all dry and back into shape tomorrow. A drop of rain never hurt anyone, though, even if it did send up a bit of a mist. She turned down the brim of her bonnet to stop the rain going down her neck.

Generally hansoms rattled along this bit of road quite often, but because it was so late, and because of the rain, there were none at the moment. Madame said they would keep walking and one would come along. They were going in the right direction for Maida Vale anyway, although it was to be hoped they did not have to walk all the way.

One or two groups of people walked past them, and some called out a cheerful 'goodnight'. But then they turned off on to a narrower section, and suddenly there were no cheerful late-night drinkers going home, or friendly pubs. The houses were set back behind railings; they were narrow, mean-looking buildings, with not a single light showing at any of the windows. There were narrow alleyways at intervals, a bit like the ones at Rogues Well Yard.

The rain was getting worse; it dripped off the railings, and came slooshing down from overhanging rooftops and street-lights to run along the gutters and glug down to the sewers and the old underground rivers. It was remarkable how loud that sound was. There was almost a rhythm to it as well – or was it just that 'Listen' was still beating in Daisy's mind?

'Listen for the killer for he's here, just out of sight . . .'

She clutched her cloak more firmly around her shoulders, and was aware that Madame was starting to walk faster, as if the rhythmic rain spatters were making her nervous as well, and as if she wanted to get away from them. Her heels rang out sharply on the cobbles – she was wearing a pair of glacé slippers, which were just about the most impractical shoes you could imagine for a night like this.

They were coming up to where the road divided itself into three, and Daisy was about to say they should make for the left-hand one, when Madame suddenly grabbed Daisy's arm, and said, 'There's someone following us.'

Daisy's heart seemed to come right up into her throat, but she tried to think that the footsteps would be just someone walking along the same street, walking at the same pace . . . She risked looking over her shoulder, and a blurry shape dodged into the shelter of one of the buildings. It moved too fast to see any real details, but the impression of a dark-clad man had already printed itself on Daisy's vision. Terror

flooded over her. It was him. He really had been there at the
Ten Bells – he had looked into the room and he had seen her;
he had recognized her. And he had stolen down the stairs and
waited for them to come out.

Madame said, very softly, 'Keep walking as fast as you can,
Daisy.'

'It's him, isn't it?'

'It's more likely to be a drunk going home. I can't hear the
footsteps now, anyway.'

They were walking alongside shops and small warehouses
– all of them deserted at this hour, of course, and although
there were a couple of streetlights, the flares were blurred from
the rain.

As they turned a corner, the footsteps came again, and
Daisy glanced back. He was there. He was not bothering to
step out of sight, now. She started to say that someone would
appear at any minute, or a cab would come rumbling along,
when Madame slipped on the wet cobbles, turning her ankle
because of the ridiculous shoes. She half fell, and Daisy
grabbed her, but Madame had already tumbled headlong, the
velvet slopping in the puddles, her face twisted with the pain
of her foot.

The footsteps quickened, and he was there, within yards of
them. He stood very still, looking at them, his head tilted to
one side. Daisy tried frantically to drag Madame to her feet,
and then tried to find enough breath to scream for help. Or
would screaming mean he would leap on them that much
faster? She looked wildly about her for help. Nothing. No one
within earshot.

There was a sudden movement within the dark coat and
something glinted for a second in the street lamp. A knife?

Now I see the saw and knife.

Next will come the victim's howl.

So save yourself from him, and run . . .

The words came at them softly and mockingly, and Daisy
was just drawing breath to scream anyway, when out of the
dark rainy shadows came the sound of clopping hoofs and
the rattle of wheels. The faint glimmer of a hansom cab's light
appeared, and now Daisy did yell out. She ran towards the

cab, waving her arms for all she was worth, because it must not be allowed to drive past, and she did not care if the horse reared up in fright, and she did not care if the Queen herself was riding inside.

Blessedly – oh thank you, Lord! – the hansom pulled to a halt, the horse snorting, its breath cloudy in the rain. Daisy managed to haul Madame to her feet and towards the cab.

'Bit of trouble, luv?' It was the familiar gravelly hansom-driver voice, bronchial from constant exposure to rain and fog, immensely reassuring in its normality.

Daisy gasped out an explanation about a twisted ankle.

'And we thought someone was following us—'

'Odd folk about at the moment,' said the driver, poking his head out of the woollen scarf wound around his neck. 'You're all right now, though. Get in by yourselves, can you? Can't let go of the horse in this. Where we going?'

Daisy said, without thinking, 'Maida Vale.'

'Where? Sorry, bit hard of hearing. Damp in me chubes.'

'Maida Vale,' said Daisy, leaning nearer to him.

'Shoulda guessed it'd be that or 'ampstead.' He sent a leery grin towards Madame's velvet cloak. 'Right you are, darlin'. Maida Vale it is.'

They clambered thankfully into it, Madame half laughing with relief, half sobbing with the pain of her twisted ankle.

The driver clicked to the horse, and the cab jolted forward, its rumbling wheels echoing loudly in the empty streets.

Back in the house, once Daisy had locked the doors and closed the curtains and lit the gas, she felt better. She soaked a couple of handkerchiefs in cold water and bound up Madame's ankle. Madame would most likely make the most of it tomorrow, lying gracefully on a couch, languidly receiving any visitors who might call. She would not keep up the languid air for long, though, because it was not in her nature.

Daisy took Madame a cup of hot milk, laced with brandy, then thought she had better try to brush the mud from the velvet cloak before it dried in. She was just doing so, when there was the sudden rat-a-tat of the doorknocker. It echoed loudly and shockingly on the landing beyond the flat, and

Daisy almost jumped out of her skin. It was after midnight, for pity's sake – who knocked on people's doors at midnight?

But then came Madame's voice calling out that it was all right, Daisy, nothing to worry about, only a friend who had promised to come along after tonight's show for a late drink.

It was Rhun the Rhymer. Of course it was. He had walked here, he explained – yes, all the way. Well, yes, it was raining, but rain was beautiful, and he had had his thoughts of a lovely lady waiting for him at the end of the storm. It had spurred him on through the tempest.

This was all entirely in accordance with what Daisy knew of Rhun. She hung his coat in the scullery to dry out, told him to take off his boots, because they did not want mud and rain trodden into the carpets, and poured him whisky from the decanter. But when she offered him a towel to mop his wet face and hands, he waved it aside and said he would allow his lady to dry his face with her unbound hair.

Whatever he was allowed or hoping to be allowed to do, it was clear that Daisy's presence was no longer wanted, and at least Rhun had taken off his muddy boots.

But the next day, and through the days – and the nights – that followed, Daisy no longer felt that the big old house overlooking the park was safe. At first she thought the feeling would get better – that the horror would fade – but it did not. As the days went by, the fear clawed more and more deeply into her mind. She began to wonder, as well, whether Madame's idea of the song, which had seemed so good and which people had welcomed so enthusiastically, was actually going to be of any use. Would it help Daisy herself if the Ripper really was lying in wait for her?

At least Joe seemed all right. He was still drawing everything he saw, and he had become part of Linklighters' traditions. People sometimes even called him 'Links', which Daisy encouraged, because it seemed to her that it was a different identity behind which Joe could hide.

There were nights, though, when she lay awake, listening to the street sounds from below, and hearing the chimes from the church on the other side of the park. Hearing footsteps go along the road, or a hansom cab rumble along. She was used to the sounds of all the steps by now. There were some quite grand houses in this road, and you often saw and heard gentlemen and ladies in evening clothes coming and going, late at night.

But a night came when there was a different set of footsteps. They were solitary and slow. The old church chimed midnight, and Daisy began to feel uneasy. The footsteps stopped – did that mean someone had stopped outside the house? Perhaps she would take a quick look, to reassure herself that there was no one down there in the street.

She wrapped a shawl around her shoulders, went into the big room at the front, and knelt on the window seat to draw back the curtain slightly. Because this was a posh area, the lamplighters always lighted all the lamps outside at dusk. There was a lamp immediately outside this house; its light fell on the railings and the thick bushes fringing the park. Daisy leaned forward as far as she could to see better, and something cold closed around her heart.

He was there. He was leaning against the railings, his cloak wrapped around him, and he was looking up at the windows of this flat. Daisy gasped, and felt the room tilt in a sick blur. It could not be him. It would be a drunk or someone looking to see if any of the houses were worth breaking into. It might even be one of the gentlemen who admired Madame and who lingered at stage doors in the hope of speaking to her. She knew it was none of those things, though. She knew she would never fail to recognize him. There was the remembered tilt of his head, the line of his jaw was clear in the lamplight, and all of it exactly as it had been that night near Rogues Well Yard and then again after the performance at the Ten Bells. In her mind, Daisy felt Joe's terrified hand clutching her that night in the fog, and as the memory unrolled a little more, she saw again the door of that upstairs room being pushed stealthily open. He had stared straight at her, and he had known who she was, just as she had known who he was. *The one who saw me that night*: that was what he had been thinking.

And he knew she was here.

She recoiled into the room, and huddled, terrified and shivering in a corner. She did not know, afterwards, how long she had crouched there, but eventually she managed to return to the window, and peer out.

He was walking away, almost jauntily. As he drew level with the park gates, he stopped and looked back; Daisy thought he looked up at the window again. Then he went on again. This time Daisy managed to make her way back to her bed.

It could not have been *him* down there in the street tonight, it simply could not. How could he know where she lived? But even as the question formed, memory showed her with Madame, both of them half running along the dark street after they left the Ten Bells, knowing they were being followed. Madame had tripped, but then the cab had come along and they had clambered thankfully into it.

And Daisy had called out the address to the cabbie – in fact she had had to repeat it, a bit louder, because the man had not heard it the first time. Could *he* have heard that? Had he been near enough? She had only said Maida Vale, but *he* could have found another cab very quickly and followed them all the way to this house.

However it had come about, Jack the Ripper knew where she lived.

NINE

B ecause renovating Linklighters occupied all of Loretta's time, the packing up at Dulwich was left to Roland. He did not mind this in the least. The house sale was going through, and the place had to be cleared. Most of the furniture would be stored for when they had a bigger place of their own; clothes and shoes could be taken to a charity shop, and he had a garden bonfire of all the old papers that had accumulated over the years.

'Have you been burning all your guilty secrets?' asked Loretta, who had borrowed a colleague's car so that they could make the trip to the charity shop with the clothes and books and some boxes of CDs.

'Every last one,' said Roland, smiling as they loaded up the car, and thinking how happy life had become.

But two days later, the happiness vanished.

He had gone back to the house for one final check, wanting to make sure that nothing had been left behind, and that everywhere was locked up. He paused at the foot of the second stair leading to Mother's old room; he had only been up there once since her death, to help remove the furniture. Still, he had better make sure everything was all right.

And, of course, once he opened the door, the room was simply an empty room, the walls faintly marked with the outlines of where pictures and photographs had hung, or where furniture had stood. But Roland hesitated, because although there were no ghosts, the room did hold one particular memory – and it was a very bad memory indeed.

It was the memory of how he had sat on the button-back chair on that last night, and had told Mother that he and Loretta were going to get married. A spring wedding, they thought, he said. That would allow plenty of time to get everything arranged. They intended to find a flat – a small house if they could manage it – here in Dulwich. That would mean he could still come to have lunch here most days, and he might even be able to call in after the office on some evenings, as well. Loretta was frequently on duty at the hotel until late, so it would all fit in. They could arrange for someone to come in each day – Loretta had even suggested a live-in housekeeper/carer, if they could find exactly the right person. She knew of a couple of small companies that specialized in finding such people.

He had expected Mother to be pleased for him, ready to welcome Loretta as a daughter-in-law, interested in what might be ahead. He thought, later, that he should have known better. What had happened was that she had looked at him for a long time, without speaking. Her eyes were like hard little pebbles, and her lips had puckered into the drawstring line that Roland had always found so ugly.

Then she said, 'So that little bitch will find a housekeeper for me, will she? The impudence of the creature! She's after the money, Roland, that's all she's after.'

'She isn't,' said Roland, stung.

'No? I didn't want to tell you this, but twice now I've caught her snooping around. Prying into private family papers – bank statements and suchlike. As for all that rubbish about helping with old photographs – that was a ruse to get at details about my money.'

'You're wrong.'

'No, I'm not.' She leaned forward, jabbing the air with a bony finger. 'After I caught her the second time, I made discreet enquiries with the hotel chain she works for. They didn't disclose any actual information – I suppose data protection or whatever it's called prevented them. But they hinted very strongly that your precious Loretta has attempted to – to form relationships with gentlemen guests known to be comfortably off. I knew what that meant, of course.'

'I don't believe you.'

'There were complaints,' said Mother, as if he had not spoken. 'That's why she was moved around – transferred to different hotels. Three separate occasions that happened.'

'Those were promotions,' said Roland, at once.

'Don't be naïve,' said Wynne, scornfully. 'We don't know anything about her – where does she come from? Who were her family?'

'I don't know. I don't care. Nobody cares about that kind of thing any longer.'

'There's a wrongness about her. She's as false as she can be, and she's certainly out for your money – I know she is. Well, she won't get it. I won't see you ruin your life and end up broke, because that's what'll happen. If you marry her I'll . . .' She paused, her brows drawn down in a frown, and then a look of such triumph came over her face that Roland flinched. 'I'll make a new will leaving everything away from you,' she said. 'It can all go to charity – all the bonds and the investments your father left. This house. I'll cancel the insurance policies on my own life, as well. And I'll tell her what I'm doing, make no mistake about that, Roland. Then you'll see what happens. The minute she knows there's no money ahead, she'll be off faster than greased lightning.'

She sat back, breathing slightly fast, one hand pressed to

her left breast, as if forcing a pain back. Roland reached automatically for the GTN spray and handed it to her.

After she had used it, he said, in as reasonable a voice as he could manage, 'You've got it all wrong, you know. Why don't you try to get to know her a bit better?'

'I'm not wrong and I don't want to get to know her. I'll phone the solicitor tomorrow morning and get it all in hand. And now go away. I don't know you any more. You're not the son I thought you were.'

Roland had looked at her, then had gone, without a word.

One of the really terrible things was that after she died, he had felt no sadness, no remorse whatsoever. His mother had been mean and selfish and controlling and joyless. His main emotion at her death had been relief, and an astonishing sense of finally being free.

Closing the door on the empty bedroom, preparing to leave the house for the last time, Roland had the feeling that he was finally closing off the memory of that last conversation. He would lock the main door, and take the keys along to the estate agent's office, as arranged. The past would be sealed off.

He paused on the small landing immediately outside the door, and stamped the carpet more securely into place. The purchasers were taking all the stair carpets with the house, and Roland did not want them telling one another that it was no wonder that poor Mrs Farrant had tripped down the stairs with that carpet all rucked and uneven. As he bent down to smooth the corners out, a small object lying under the carpet's edge caught the afternoon sunlight coming through the narrow window.

It was an earring. A smooth oval of jet, with a disc of amber set into the centre. It was distinctive and Roland recognized it at once. The last time he had seen it was the night before Mother had died – the night Loretta came to supper. She had worn these earrings then – Roland remembered how he had commented on them, saying the amber made her eyes almost golden. She had laughed and said they were brand new – bought that very day, so she was pleased he had noticed them.

But Loretta had not come up here that night; she had deliberately stayed downstairs after Mother came up to bed, knowing

Roland was going to break the news about their marriage, giving him space to do it. And she had only come to the house once since then, when she had brought the borrowed car to collect the things for the charity shop. She had not even come into the house that time; she had parked in the drive, and they had carried everything out and put it in the boot.

Then how had the earring got up here? Because they had been new – that evening had been the first time she had worn them. A pulse of apprehension began to tap against his mind, because it was beginning to seem as if Loretta could only have lost this earring on that night. She might have come up the stairs without Roland knowing, wanting to know how the marriage news was being received. If she had heard what Mother had said about her – about how she was supposed to have seduced, or tried to seduce, well-off hotel guests, she would have been furious and hurt. If she had heard Mother say she would make sure the money did not reach Loretta, she would have been even more furious. Was it possible that she had crept back up there while Roland was outside trying to flag down a taxi? That she had deliberately arranged the carpet so that it could be tripped over?

Sick horror washed over him, because he suddenly had a very clear image of Loretta creeping up the stairs, and kneeling down outside Mother's room. Her face would have been twisted and sly – it would not have been the face of his Loretta, the lively, sexy, *loving* companion of these last weeks and months.

The sick feeling increased, and he took several deep breaths, then had to run back into the bedroom, and across to the little bathroom, where he hung over the sink, retching helplessly.

Presently he managed to wash his face, and he made a shaky way downstairs. He sat for a while on the wide window ledge overlooking the garden. The earring was still in his pocket; after a moment he put it in the little zip compartment of his wallet.

Loretta had not mentioned losing the earring. Possibly she had thought she had lost it in the taxi. And the following day had come Mother's death, and all the flurry about the inquest, and then sorting out the money and the will and everything else. A missing earring would not have been worth mentioning.

Was any of this likely? Could Loretta really have heard

Roland's mother threatening to disinherit him, like some ridiculous Victorian parent in a melodrama? Had she set a trap by ridging the carpet, trusting to luck that Roland's mother would trip over it and fall down the stairs?

Had Mother been right, and Loretta had been after his money?

That was a terrible thought, but a far worse thought was that Roland might have married a murderess.

Linklighters had been open for about four months and Roland had managed to push the suspicions of Loretta to the deepest level of his mind. They did not quite vanish, but he thought he had them in check.

But if his mind coped with what he had found, his body did not. It began to let him down in the most embarrassing of ways.

'I believe there are pills you can take for this,' Loretta said one night, after even her most diligent endeavours had still ended in flaccid failure. 'I'd come with you to see a doctor.'

'I'm just tired,' said Roland, who was certainly not going to discuss such a thing with a doctor, and who knew quite well that the reason for his inability to make love was because he had found out that his wife might have killed his mother.

After a while he got into the habit of pretending to be deeply asleep when Loretta got into bed. They did not discuss it again. In any case, she was too busy at Linklighters, which Roland would admit seemed to be doing well. A small regular clientele was building up, and people were booking large tables for late supper parties after a theatre visit. Two flattering reviews had appeared in a couple of well-regarded food magazines.

It's going to be all right, he thought. It really is going to succeed. And I'll be able to stop thinking about what Loretta might have done that night. It will all be fine.

And then Phineas Fox came to the restaurant, and nothing was fine at all.

'He came in for dinner,' said Loretta, over breakfast, as she poured muesli into a dish. 'As a matter of fact I think it was his second visit. I'm sure he was there a week or so ago.'

'Is he so memorable?' said Roland.

'Not at first, but then you find afterwards that you're remembering him – and for longer than you'd expect. He's quite ordinary looking really, although he has remarkable eyes. Very clear grey, with black rims.' Roland had the impression that Loretta was remembering Mr Fox's eyes with pleasure. What had Mother said, about her trying to form relationships with men she believed were well off? Was this Phineas Fox well off?

Loretta said, 'Anyway, he wants permission to delve into the restaurant's history. It's on account of a book being written about Liszt – I mean the composer. Franz Liszt.'

'I have heard of Liszt,' said Roland, a touch tartly, because he was not much liking the sound of this Phineas Fox, nor did he like Loretta so patronizingly assuming he had not heard of Liszt.

'Of course you have,' she said, comfortingly. 'But Phineas Fox has been asked to research his life for a book, and he thinks he's found a link between him and Scaramel. The Scaramel who was a regular performer at Linklighters, you remember? We've got a couple of old playbills.'

'I remember perfectly well.'

'This Phineas Fox wants to follow up this link.'

'That's a bit unlikely, isn't it?' said Roland. 'Classical composer and music hall artiste.'

'Oh, I don't know. It'd be the prince-and-showgirl thing, I expect. Think about Charles II and his actresses. And Edward VII and his.'

Roland did not want to be fed details about promiscuous monarchs over his breakfast. He said, 'What kind of link does Phineas Fox think he's found?'

'I don't know yet,' said Loretta. 'He might tell me more this afternoon. He's coming to the restaurant. There's no need for you to be there, though. It would mean you taking a long lunch hour and getting across London, and I can easily cope.' She paused, then said, 'I got the impression that he thinks if there was a link between Liszt and Scaramel, there might have been some kind of scandal at the heart of it.'

'What kind of scandal?'

'He didn't say. But he's asked if there are any old

documents – records – relating to the past. I told him about those boxes of stuff I found during the renovations. He was very interested, so I've looked them out, and put them in the downstairs office for him to see.'

'You mean the old cellar.'

'I wish you'd stop calling it a cellar. It's an office.'

'Whatever it is, we aren't supposed to let the public go down there,' said Roland.

'It doesn't matter for one person just for an hour or so, and not if one of us is there.'

'Those boxes have only got old accounts from the supper room days, and a few tattered programmes,' said Roland. He frowned, then said, 'Might a scandal about Scaramel really be unearthed? Because if so – well, we wouldn't want to be associated with it, would we? I mean, we wouldn't want Linklighters mentioned?'

'Of course we would!' said Loretta at once. 'And the juicier the scandal, the better it'd be for the restaurant.' She leaned forward. 'Think about it. If Scaramel was tangled up with Franz Liszt – if they had one of those raunchy nineteenth-century affairs and something illegal or even criminal happened, it'd make a terrific story. We'd be booked out for months. There'd be all kinds of publicity. Reviews for the book itself and articles about the whole thing, and Linklighters would be part of it. Can't you imagine the quotes? "Composer of 'Hungarian Rhapsody' and 'Liebestraum number 3', and bawdy music hall dancer from London restaurant".'

'I didn't know you knew so much about classical music.'

'Everyone knows those pieces,' said Loretta, carelessly. 'And anyway, "Liebestraum number 3" is very well known. It was even vamped up for an Elvis Presley song years ago. He sang it in a film. I thought everyone knew *that*.'

'I didn't.'

'All right then, how about this for a headline, "Liszt's lover and the stage where he first saw her"?'

'The stage rotted away years ago.'

'God, you're so pedantic.'

'I think you're getting carried away,' said Roland. 'How do we know this book's actually going to be published anyway?

It's probably some wild idea that won't get anywhere. It most likely won't ever reach a bookshop.'

'It will,' said Loretta. 'It's not just something that Phineas Fox is doing on the off-chance. He's got a publisher and an agent and there are a couple of university lecturers involved – one's from Cambridge as a matter of fact – so it's all quite scholarly. Mr Fox is quite scholarly as well, although I have the impression that he might be capable of being rather unscholarly at times.' Again there was that speculative, pleasurable note in her voice. 'Anyway, people like hearing shocking things about famous people from the past. All those books and TV programmes about whether all the Romanovs really died, and how Edward VII's supposed to have shut a mistress away in a madhouse. Can't you see that this might be the same kind of thing – and that we can turn it to our advantage? We could have a launch party at Linklighters for the book – we'd have Liszt's music piped in, of course, and we can use the old photos and posters of Scaramel. The restaurant will be at the centre of it, and we'll be at the centre of the restaurant. Probably they'd want to interview us. Good thing I bought that Stella McCartney suit.'

She reached for his hand, and Roland hoped she was not about to try to initiate one of her hectic, fast-paced love-making sessions over the breakfast table. He pretended not to have seen the gesture, and said he had better be getting off to the office, because he had a lot to do today.

By the time he reached his office he had managed to quell the slight apprehension. It was not very likely that this Phineas Fox would find anything of much interest about Linklighters. There would not be anything to make him delve deeper, or to result in Roland's private life being pulled into the spotlight.

There was certainly no reason to suppose that any of this might result in anyone suspecting that Loretta might be a murderess.

TEN

As Phin walked towards Harlequin Court, he could almost believe that those long-ago performers from Scaramel's time walked with him, ephemeral and indistinct, like ghost reflections seen in the window of a late-night train.

It was extraordinarily easy to believe he was seeing flickering gas-lit shapes, glimpses of opera-cloaked and top-hatted gentlemen making a leisurely way back from the nearby theatres. Silken-clad ladies, stepping daintily over the cobblestones . . .

Except that those images were entirely wrong, because any fragments of Harlequin Court's past would not be silk- or velvet-clad. This had been the haunt of the ordinary working people – men and women from the factories and the docks and the street markets. They would have dressed up in their cheap finery for their evening out, and they would have been cheerful and lively, singing snatches of the songs of the day as they came down the alleyway. But they would not have worn silk.

He crossed the court and went down the carpeted stairs. As he stepped out into the restaurant he saw that there were only a few people at the tables, and that Loretta Farrant was seated near the door, looking towards the stairs, as if she had been watching for him. She was wearing a black suit with a white silk shirt under it, and large silver and jet earrings.

'It's very nice to see you again,' she said, coming over to him. 'Let's go straight down to the office.' She led the way to a door near the staircase. 'Twelve steps down,' she said, indicating. 'And they're a bit steep, so be careful. I've left a light on, though, and there's a handrail.'

The steps were not carpeted, and their footsteps rang out in the enclosed space. But Loretta – or her interior designer – had made a fair attempt at sprucing up the stair. The walls were smoothly whitewashed, and several framed prints of old street scenes were hung at intervals. They've tried to conceal what this really is, thought Phin, but it's still unmistakably a cellar.

'These are the boxes,' said Loretta, and indicated two large battered cardboard boxes standing on the floor. 'Take as long as you want sorting through them, and feel free to photocopy anything. The copier's in the corner there.'

'I suppose we can't carry them upstairs?' said Phin, not very hopefully.

'Bit difficult. The restaurant's still open.'

'Fair enough.'

'I've asked for a pot of tea to be brought down – or would you prefer coffee?'

'Tea is fine,' said Phin, turning to study the boxes. He could already see that the papers on the top were badly foxed, and probably unreadable, but documents beneath might be in better condition. Fragments of old newspapers, perhaps. Advertisements for cures for ailments . . . Reports of murders, of trials, of executions and disasters. Public proclamations, penny ghost stories, announcements of royal births and deaths and marriages. Playbills relating to Linklighters' own artistes.

'It's a bit small down here, isn't it?' said Loretta. 'I don't work down here very often, of course, but it's useful for storage.'

'You said you had to seal off an old ditch.'

'Yes, the Cock and Pye Ditch – at least that's the name on the old maps. We had to satisfy the insurers and the bank, and we had to create that panel in the wall, in case it was ever necessary to get through to the sluice gate.' She indicated a large panel inset into one wall. 'It unlocks and lifts out. There used to be a culvert somewhere along the channel – I think it came out somewhere near St Martin's Lane. And there's a sluice gate on the other side of that panel.'

'Really?'

'Yes, a massive great thing – it's black with age, and there are iron spikes at the top and chains looping around it. And a monstrous wheel at one side that has to be winched round to lift the gate.'

Phin said, 'Ancient gates are always a bit nightmarish. As if they might be portals into other worlds – and as if the other worlds might be very sinister indeed. You almost expect them to creak open very slowly, and a beckoning hand to come out.'

He was instantly annoyed with himself for saying this – Arabella's influence! he thought – but Loretta said, eagerly, 'Yes, exactly like that. I thought you'd know what I meant, Phineas.'

Phin, who loathed being called Phineas, which he always thought sounded like Trollope's laid-back Irish politician in the Palliser novels, or an annoyingly impractical Victorian traveller, mumbled a vague reply, and knelt down to examine the contents of the boxes. He was slightly disconcerted when Loretta came to kneel next to him. The skirt of the black suit was a bit short and a bit tight for kneeling; it rode up over her knees. She was wearing one of the modern scents that Phin always thought smelled like sweetened mildew. He had a sudden memory of Arabella extravagantly spraying on the absurdly costly perfume that always made him think of ancient Persian rose gardens and warm amber.

But he said, 'Were you able to check the lease of these premises yet? To see if there are any earlier names on it?'

'I did look, but there aren't any names as such. Only that Harlequin Court and a few nearby streets have been owned by a set-up called the Salisbury Estate or the Salisbury Trust since around 1940.'

'Probably ultimately the whole place is owned by the Duke of Westminster,' said Phin. 'Most of Belgravia and Mayfair belongs to him. And if it isn't him, it's the Crown or the Church.'

He reached again for the contents of the nearer box, and Loretta reached out with him. It was probably accidental that as she leaned over, the white silk shirt parted at the neck, allowing a glimpse of a lace-edged bra. Phin was relieved to remember she had mentioned tea, which presumably somebody would soon bring, and which would create an interruption.

'Most of this stuff is from the old music hall years,' said Loretta. 'We used some of the better-preserved playbills for decoration in the restaurant.'

'I saw several of them. Are they all the originals?'

'Most are, although we had to take copies of one or two because they were so fragile . . . Ah, that sounds like our tea.'

She got up to take the tray from the waitress, and set it down on the desk. Phin seized the opportunity to move the larger box to form a makeshift barrier between them.

'Please don't think you need to stay down here with me,' he said, as she handed him a cup. 'I expect you've got masses to do, and I'm more than happy to look through everything on my own. Sometimes it takes ages going back and forth, seeing if you can link up two unrelated discoveries, and recording tiny bits of information. It'd probably be a bit boring for you. I'll let you know if I do find anything of interest, of course. Oh, and I promise not to venture anywhere near the sluice gate panel.' He looked over his shoulder at it again.

'Well, all right,' said Loretta, clearly reluctant. 'I'll be in the restaurant if you want anything. I'll leave the door at the top of these stairs open.'

Phin waited until he had heard her steps go all the way back up to the restaurant, then he began systematically to sort through the boxes' contents.

There were a great many old programmes for performances that had been held in the supper rooms; these dated mainly from the late 1870s to the middle of the 1890s. Phin looked through them all, but most were so faded and tattered they were barely readable. He was hoping to find something about the macabre song that hung in a frame upstairs, but there did not seem to be anything.

He was, though, delighted to turn up several mentions of Scaramel. She appeared to have danced her way through those years in various guises and costumes – most of the descriptions of her routines sounded lively, several sounded suggestive, and a few had clearly been downright outrageous.

Phin thought that whatever else she might have been, and whoever's bedsprings she might have bounced, she had certainly been part of the saucy naughtiness of the Victorian and Edwardian music halls. He particularly liked a report of how she had presided over several gaming tables at a card party one evening. The party was described as having been attended

by, 'A number of very estimable personages, best not named.'
At the end of the night, with the tables littered with cards and
IOUs and empty wine and brandy bottles, Scaramel had apparently performed a lively routine with the remarkable title of,
'If Only They Knew Where I Keep My Little Bit of Luck'.

Phin smiled at this. He hoped that Scaramel had amassed
enough money to make life smooth and enjoyable, and he also
hoped she had not been tangled up in a murder.

He made a number of notes, set aside the programmes that
were clear enough to be copied, and ploughed on. But although
Scaramel's name and image continued to bounce through
the tattered playbills and programmes, nowhere was there the
smallest reference to Franz Liszt.

He was no longer aware of the time passing, or of his
surroundings, although several times he heard sounds from
the restaurant above – doors opening and closing, voices calling
out, the rattle of crockery. He was working through the second,
smaller box now; he had almost reached the bottom, and was
reluctantly acknowledging that this whole thing was starting
to look like a dead end. The trouble was that dead ends had to
be checked, to make sure they were really dead ends.

There were a number of what looked like old news-sheets,
and he lifted them out. Hadn't it been Charles Dickens who
had called such things the rags of last year's handbills? He
began to look through them. There were a few advertisements
for a Christmas event which had been held in the square and
which would have been handed out to passers-by. Phin put
these to one side to make copies in case he and Toby could
make use of them in their proposed book.

It was now almost four o'clock, and the restaurant seemed
to have settled into silence. Probably this was an in-between
time for them. But it was not completely silent down here.
Phin could hear faint rustlings and creaks, which were certainly
not coming from overhead. He glanced uneasily at the sluice-
gate panel, then turned determinedly back to the boxes, blotting
out the impression that the sounds beyond the wall panel were
footsteps that echoed slightly. But there would be some perfectly
ordinary explanation. All kinds of people might have to go
down into the depths of London's sewers and rivers and ditches,

by way of all kinds of peculiar methods. Presumably there were departments whose task it was to ensure that nothing unwholesome could slop its way up to the streets from the depths. But this last thought was so much like the start of a garish horror film that Phin relaxed and grinned, and then thought he must remember to tell Arabella about it. She would promptly come up with several explanations for the sounds, none of which would be remotely possible, and most of which would involve aliens, spectral visitations, and/or megalomaniac scientists. Before Phin met Arabella it would never have occurred to him to think on such lines.

Remembering Arabella's cheerful fantasizing made him feel better, and he returned to the remaining papers. He lifted out one on the top of the pile which was faded, but reasonably legible, and began reading.

> Information is sought regarding the whereabouts of the young artist known as Links, who has not been seen at his lodgings for over a week. Links's work has been exhibited in Thumbprints bookshop, and he is best known for his vivid sketches of the area immediately around Harlequin Court and of the performers and patrons of Linklighters Supper Club. The sketches have been much admired for their liveliness and originality.

Links. Could it be an abbreviation of Linklighters? Could one of those vivid sketches have found its way into a modern book?

Whoever had distributed this news-sheet had included a small head and shoulders sketch, and beneath it were the words, 'A self-sketch of Links'. Phin studied it, interested to see the artist who might have created that eerie sketch – *Liszten for the Killer* . . .

The self-portrait was surprisingly clear, even allowing for the cumbersome nineteenth-century printing processes. Phin, his interest caught, tilted Loretta Farrant's desk light so that it shone directly on the paper. Under the light it was possible to see the features in the sketch much more clearly. The face was thin, with high cheekbones and large dark eyes. There was a tumble of dark hair that would always flop forward, no matter how firmly it was combed back. It was a face that would stay in your mind, and its owner looked heartbreakingly young – no more than nineteen or twenty – and unbearably vulnerable.

The news-sheet did not give any more information about Links, but there was a brief appeal for information.

> Persons having any useful information are asked to kindly communicate details to Mr Thaddeus at Thumbprints in Harlequin Court.

Phin put the paper down, but he went on looking at it. How likely was it that this long-ago artist had drawn that *Liszten for the Killer* sketch? How possible was it that the sketch was connected to the framed song-sheet upstairs? '*Listen for the killer for he's here, just out of sight . . .*'

He remembered that Loretta had said he could use the photocopier, so he switched it on, and made two copies of the news-sheet, being careful not to damage the original. Then he made copies of the pages from the programmes which featured Scaramel.

He put the originals back in their box, and put the copies into his briefcase. Then he went back up to the restaurant, thankful to be leaving the underground room. Loretta Farrant was talking to two people in chefs' outfits, and Phin was grateful that this allowed him to make a brief goodbye, and to say he would phone later.

Shadows were already forming in the corners of Harlequin Court when he went out. Had that long-ago artist seen these very shadows? Had it been the mysterious Links? If so, had Links seen that frightened figure by the old gas lamp in reality, or had it just been his imagination? Those wide-apart eyes might be capable of seeing anything – of looking beyond the commonplace to the dream worlds beyond.

Phin paused by the old streetlight, thinking about the people who would have come here and who would have come to Linklighters. Shopkeepers and clerks and housemaids and navvies and costermongers. The linklighters themselves would have been here, of course, young boys scurrying through the famous pea-souper fogs – the London Particulars that Dickens and other Victorian writers had described and used to chilling effect.

There would have been people from the seamier, darker side of the city, too: pickpockets and cutpurses, all eagerly on the watch for opportunities. Beggars, hopeful of being given a few coins here and there to buy their next meal or a night's lodging, some of them soldiers maimed in the Crimea or the Transvaal. And those ladies who plied the oldest of trades, and who, whether they were kitten-faced teenagers or haggard-eyed harridans, would all have been prepared to stand up against a dank wall in a dark corner for a stranger . . . Was it Boswell who had recorded having sex with a sixpenny whore in one of the alcoves in Westminster Bridge?

What place had Links had in all of that? Where had he belonged? He must have belonged to somebody, because that somebody had arranged for those news-sheets to be distributed in an attempt to find him, and had taken the trouble to include that self-sketch.

And who had been the killer referred to in the song and the sketch?

ELEVEN

Back in his flat, Phin propped up the copied news-sheet on his desk, and sat for a long time looking at the image of Links's face. Then he frowned, pushed it into the folder containing the miscellaneous notes so far gathered and put the folder away in a drawer. Chimerical fragments about long-ago artists could not be allowed to push through into the present. They did not pay bills. Disinterring information for the book on Liszt did.

Phin had already amassed a reasonable amount of back-ground, some of which had resulted from leads provided by the two academics who were collaborating on the actual writing

of the book. He had immense respect for both of them –
Professor Liripine was a professor of musicology at Durham
University, and Dr Purslove was a fellow of King's College,
Cambridge. However, it was becoming extremely difficult to
reconcile the wildly differing views held by these gentlemen
as to how the book should be written. They were, in fact, locked
in polite warfare with each other, and Phin was in the middle
of it.

Dr Purslove was of the cheerfully robust opinion that what
he referred to as Liszt's bed-hopping activities should be the
springboard for the book. This, he maintained, would help sell
it, because readers did love a bit of scandal and sauce mixed
in with their solemn musical studies – Phin would surely agree
with that. Two days later, he had sent him a gossipy snippet
regarding the tempestuous affair between Liszt and the
infamous night-club dancer, Lola Montez. La Montez had
apparently discovered that Liszt had sneaked out of a
Constantinople hotel bedroom in the early morning while she
was still asleep, and had consequently given way to an extravagant fury and smashed up the entire room. Mirrors had been
angrily splintered, and what was delicately referred to by the
hotel staff as 'bedroom china' had been hurled out of windows.
Dr Purslove thought this spicy little episode must certainly be
quoted in the book, and nor must they omit a statement, apparently made by Herr Liszt later, that he had been so exhausted
by the exigencies of his nights with La Montez, he had decided
to flee, since he 'feared her importunities were starting to
damage his sanity, his constitution, and his virility.'

The image of the fiery Lola throwing chamber pots around
and of Liszt furtively tiptoeing out of the bedroom like a
character in a French farce was a lively one, and Phin had
noted it all down.

But the following day, Professor Liripine had written, reiter-
ating his view that they should focus on the composer's later,
more contemplative, years, and on his generosity to various
humanitarian and charitable organizations. With this in mind,
the professor thought that Phin might direct his main research
towards Herr Liszt's monastery years, and his religious and
liturgical compositions.

'We want to present a scholarly study of a fine man and a great composer,' wrote the professor. 'With that in mind, I'm enclosing copies of several letters written from within the Madonna del Rosario monastery near Rome. As you know, in later life Liszt was ordained in that monastery, and was even sometimes known as Abbé Liszt. Sadly the dates are vague, but perhaps you can pinpoint them.'

Phin had still not been able to decide how best to reconcile these two opposing points of view, and he was currently wondering whether to explain that there might now be a murder complication in Liszt's background. He slid Professor Liripine's photocopies out of the envelope, and he was about to start reading them when an email pinged in.

It was from Arabella, and Phin put the professor's letters to one side, and opened the email gratefully. He had not really been worried about not hearing from Arabella, but still . . .

'Very dear Phin,' Arabella had written. 'You're probably blamelessly asleep in your bed, so I'm emailing instead of phoning. After a bit of a tussle, and some crawling around in corners and jiggling those universal adaptor plug things, I've finally got the laptop set up and connected to Wi-Fi. The agency here have housed me in one of the company's studio apartments. It's a very comfortable bed-sitting room, with miniature kitchen and bathroom, so I can make meals for myself, but there's also a bistro on the ground floor, which is very useful.

'Didn't we have a truly memorable and brilliant time last night! It stayed with me all the way across the English Channel. Thank you. I'm counting down until the next time.

'I didn't phone earlier because of a small misunderstanding at Charles de Gaulle airport about a piece of my luggage – you wouldn't believe how long it took to get it sorted out. My case had unaccountably got mixed up with somebody else's luggage, so I had to go along to an airport office and identify it. This was fair enough; the trouble was that I discovered I had lost the key to that particular case, (which could happen to anyone).

'But then it seemed that claim was also being laid to the case by a French Monsignor, who had lost an identical piece of luggage. Can you believe the airport staff asked me to list the contents of my suitcase? I had to do so in a crowded airport office, with masses of people milling around listening. I swear the officials beckoned in one or two travellers whose planes were delayed – presumably with the idea of providing a bit of entertainment to help them to while away the wait.

'Anyway, I said, very firmly, that there were clothes and shoes in the case, but they said that was too vague, and pointed out that the French Monsignor had also said clothes and shoes. So please, could I be more specific?

'I said if they couldn't distinguish between the garments of an English lady and those of a French cleric, matters had come to a pretty pass. (He was seventy-five if he was a day, for goodness' sake. Although an absolute lamb.)

'So then I said there was a set of black silk underwear, which I supposed no one would ascribe to a gentleman of the cloth, after which I threw discretion to the winds by telling them I had packed it because I was expecting my lover to join me for a weekend. You'd think the French would understand such a thing, wouldn't you, but they looked scandalized, although to be fair that might have been due to the Monsignor's presence. (He was very politely pretending not to understand – what a gentleman.)

'Then I remembered that there was a hot-water bottle in the suitcase with a knitted pink cover (present from Miss Pringle, the dear love), and I thought that would clinch my ownership, although it threw them for a few moments, because you could see that although they could certainly slot together a lover and black silk lingerie, the inclusion of the hot-water bottle confused them utterly.

'Thankfully, at that point the Monsignor stepped forward and said he must retract (or it might have been rescind or even recant) all claim to the suitcase, because he certainly did not have a hot-water bottle amongst his luggage, although he thought I was very wise to have brought one, because Paris could be *très froid* at nights. (We didn't mention the black silk underwear.)

'I signed one or two forms, and somebody went off to make a new search for the Monsignor's missing case. We all parted very amicably; in fact the Monsignor invited me to take you to have lunch with him if you do manage a weekend. He's a very charming gentleman and he's given me his card and it looks as if he lives in a very respectable part of the city.

'While I'm here I'll see if there are any traces of Scaramel. That poster in Linklighters referred to her being back "Fresh from her triumphs in Paris". I don't suppose there will be anything, but I'll try.

'And I'll look forward to hearing about your explorations into the underground river cellar. Don't fall into that, will you, and don't get tangled up in anything dangerous or seductive while I'm away.

Arabella.'

Phin enjoyed this missive very much, although he thought that the chances of Arabella finding any trace of Scaramel in Paris were slight.

He sent a reply, promising to see about fitting in a weekend, pointed out as diplomatically as possible the necessity for being wary of charming and courteous gentlemen in airports, no matter their apparent religious affinities, and requested Arabella on no account to mislay the black silk underwear before he, Phin, could get to Paris.

After this, he returned to Professor Liripine's letters in a much happier frame of mind, and began to sift carefully through them.

In the main they were, as the professor had said, from Liszt's more decorous years, but they were interesting and they would be useful. Phin worked systematically through them, typing notes on to the computer as he went.

It was getting on for midnight when he turned over the last of the letters, and he was just thinking he might call it a night. All around him the house and its various occupants had fallen into silence, although there had been a series of thuds from Toby Tallis's flat shortly after eleven, followed by some muffled feminine giggling, which suggested Toby had not returned home alone from his night out. Good for Toby.

The last document from Professor Liripine was a photocopy of a newspaper cutting from an old French newspaper. Phin saw with relief that the professor, efficient and thorough as ever, had sent a separate sheet with the translation.

He adjusted the desk lamp so that its light fell more strongly on the page, and began to read.

SPLENDID AND MOVING TRIBUTE TO
MAESTRO
TEN-YEAR ANNIVERSARY OF THE DEATH OF
VIRTUOSO FRANZ LISZT CELEBRATED

Music lovers and faithful admirers of the works of Franz
Liszt gathered at the Hall de la Mélodie on Saturday
evening to celebrate the great man's music ten years after
his death at a concert aptly titled, 'Liszten to the
Symphonies'.

Liszten. The word seemed almost to explode off the page.
Liszten. As in, *Liszten for the Killer*, thought Phin. I won't
leap to any conclusion, though, not yet. That play on Liszt's
name must have been used many times.

Or had it? Could this be the definite link between Scaramel
and Liszt he had been trying to find? There was no date, but
the ten-year anniversary of Liszt's death would have to make
it 1896. He read on.

The concert was a glittering and well-attended occasion;
the hall being packed with people from many walks of life,
although it is understood that the organizer wishes to remain
anonymous. This newspaper does, of course, respect that,
although one source has suggested that it was a lady whom
Herr Liszt had greatly admired in his last years.

[We courteously remind our readers that Herr Liszt
was a gallant gentleman when it came to the company
of ladies.]

The orchestra was applauded enthusiastically, and
encored several times. After the performances a lavish
supper was provided by Maison dans le Parc. M'sieur
Alphonse himself presided over the tables.

A charming note came immediately before supper,
when bouquets and beribboned magnums of champagne
were carried out by two small children and presented to
the conductor, the soloists, and the first violinist.

We understand the children to be twins, and they curt-
seyed and bowed with grave politeness. It was not possible
to obtain their full names, but it is understood that they

are English, and that their first names are Morwenna and
Mervyn.

They were delightfully dressed in the costumes of
Harlequin and Columbine.

Phin read the article a second time and then a third. It's all
there, he thought. The pieces from the mystery. Or is it? Let's
look at it fragment by fragment.

First of all, the anonymous organizer. Scaramel? She had
not sounded like a lady who would have shied away from
publicity, but perhaps she had wanted to be discreet about a
liaison with Liszt. Did the dates fit for an actual liaison, though?
Liszt was born in 1811, and Scaramel's heyday seemed to have
been the late 1880s and early 1890s. So she could have been
born anywhere from 1840 to 1860, which would have meant
an age gap of anything from thirty to fifty years. Phin
conceded that a liaison would not have been impossible, but
remembered that Liszt had written to Cosima that while he
had a great admiration for Scaramel, he had added rather sadly
that nowadays such admirations were a matter of the mind
only. So Phin was inclined to think there had not been any
actual bed bouncing, and that what Liszt had felt for Scaramel
had been an old man's benevolent but sexless passion.

How about the play on Liszt's name? *Liszten* – this time it
was 'Liszten to the Music'. Was that coincidence? Or had
Scaramel known about the *Liszten for the Killer* sketch?

But for the moment it was the twins who were attracting
his attention – the two small children dressed for the glittering
occasion as Harlequin and Columbine. It's the *commedia
dell'arte* motif again, thought Phin. The famous Italian
'comedy of art' from the sixteenth and seventeenth centuries.
Harlequin and Columbine and all those other characters –
Punchinello and Pantalone. And, of course, Scaramouche – the
feminine version of which was Scaramel.

Would anyone other than a flamboyant music hall artiste
known to the world as Scaramel – a lady who performed at
a place situated in Harlequin Court – have dressed those two
children in those particular costumes?

Staring at the names, the images dancing tantalizingly across his mind, Phin was gradually aware of a tugging in his mind. Something he had found earlier, was it? Relevant to the twins? Their costumes? Their names? Their *names*. He reached for the book in which he had found the original mention of Scaramel, and flipped through the pages. Here it was.

'There is a song from the era (i.e. the 1880s and early 1890s), which referred to the murder . . . The composer of the song's music is not known, but one source suggested that the song's lyrics had been written by a Welsh writer.'

Welsh. A Welsh writer. And here were twins, turning up at a concert connected to Liszt and probably to Scaramel as well. And those twins had unmistakably Welsh names – names that were not very common, and that surely would not have been common at all in late nineteenth-century Paris. Phin closed the book thoughtfully. He still could not see how any of these pieces fitted together, but he would certainly have to find out more. He went to bed with an increasing conviction that there was something in Linklighters he had missed.

TWELVE

The morning brought Toby Tallis, who came breezily into Phin's study.

'I've found a promising hunting ground for our book,' he said. 'I don't mean your academic one, I mean the one we're doing on ballads and news-sheets and related spin-offs. It's a pub near Marble Arch – I was there last night as a matter of fact.'

'I heard you come home,' said Phin, then, in case Toby wondered what else might have been audible, he hastily added, 'I mean I heard your door open and close.'

'She's a physiotherapist from the hospital,' said Toby, apparently feeling clarification was required. 'I'm still on rotation – three months in osteology, so I'm meeting quite a few new people. It's a subdiscipline of anatomy, really, and it's not compulsory, but I thought I'd take it in, because you never know, and it's actually rather an interesting area of medicine. Bones and a bit of archaeology and forensic stuff.'

'And an interesting physiotherapist in the mix?'

'She is interesting, as it happens. Very good company. And somebody had recommended this pub – it has a bit of a theme, you know how they do these days – and it makes great play of the fact that it was on the site of the old Tyburn gallows. Well, the general area of the gallows, because nobody seems able to agree on the precise spot.'

Phin observed that Toby certainly took his girlfriends to the best places.

'Don't mock,' said Toby. 'It was a very lively pub and we enjoyed each other's company, and . . .' He paused, and then, with unusual awkwardness, said, 'Well, you know how there are some girls you feel really proud to be with when you walk into a public place . . .? Yes, of course you do, you've walked into enough public places with Arabella these last few months, and she certainly makes people look at her twice.'

'Twice and usually three times,' said Phin, smiling and knowing exactly what Toby meant. To smooth over Toby's moment of near-embarrassment, he said, 'What was the pub like?'

'Very good. We had a very nice meal, too. But the evening wasn't all given over to pleasure, because I was looking out for material for our book.'

'Did you find anything?'

'Odds and ends,' said Toby. 'They don't have framed stuff on the walls like Linklighters – but they've got huge scrapbooks of the pub's history and the history of the area. They've been put together over the years – a bit here and there; people contributing old newspaper cuttings from attics, and ancient photographs and woodcuts. It's an ongoing project. The bar staff let me make a few notes, and they said they'd be happy to photocopy anything I wanted. Did you know people used to buy what they called execution ballads – the printers churned them out by the ton. And when there was a hanging, crowds would gather round the gallows to sing them – very *Les Misérables*, isn't it?'

'I expect it was a day out for most of them,' said Phin.

'Yes. And nowadays terrorists post videos of live executions on Facebook and YouTube,' he said, his cherubic face suddenly serious. 'Human nature doesn't change so very much, does it?'

'You're unusually philosophical this morning. Is that the physiotherapist's influence?'

'Well, it might be. But,' said Toby, 'I do think we could use some of the ballads. I only glanced at a few, but they all looked very solemn.'

'So we'd need to find lighter ones for balance.'

'Yes. You get the impression that whoever wrote or distributed most of them was trying to convey a sense of bells tolling and of people watching in awed and respectful silence. Whereas probably everybody was cheering and shouting rude comments and blowing raspberries.'

'And scoffing pies and jellied eels from street vendors between times,' agreed Phin.

'Anyhow, I did find this, though, which is nicely quirky,' said Toby. 'I think it's about London's underground rivers. Listen . . .

"Never be lured to the ghost river beds,
Only sleep in a bed where you're safe.
In a ghost river bed, you could end up quite dead.
On some terrible night, you'll be Pigged in the Dyke,
Or Kilned in the Lime – what a terrible crime,
You'll be Cocked in the Pie and then left there to die,
You'll be Tied in the Burn or Sluiced by the Earl –
And that is a fate that will make your toes curl.

"You'll be chopped, you'll be strangled, or fed to the mangle,
And most of your guts will be left in a tangle,
Your bones will be spread on the dark cobblestones
And you're too deep below to make heard your moans."

'That,' said Phin, 'is possibly one of the most macabre things I've ever heard.'

'It is grim, isn't it? There's a bit more,' said Toby, with a grin. 'Listen again.

"And there's really no use
To try raising the sluice.
Street grids and street grilles will not help your ills,
For you can't reach the grilles when you're dead.
So the bed of a friend – whether new, whether old
Is safer by far than the grue and the cold
Of the ghost river beds down below . . ."

'It's a play on all the old river names, isn't it?' said Toby.

'Is it?' Phin took the verses from him and re-read them. 'I think you're right,' he said. 'And all bawdiness aside, the Cock and Pye – spelled *pye* – is the old ditch, or a river tributary, that runs under Harlequin Court. Loretta Farrant told me about it. She used the term ghost river, too.'

'And Tied in the Burn's got to be Tyburn, hasn't it?'

'I don't know. Was there an underground river there?'

'Bound to be. London's veined with them,' said Toby. 'Is your computer on? Oh, good.' He sat down at Phin's desk and typed in a search request. 'Yes, here it is. Apparently the Tyburn runs directly beneath Buckingham Palace – and if that isn't good material for our book, I don't know what is. I bet we could get several pages on royalty wading through sewage when there was an overflow. We'll call the chapter, "The Night Edward Vll Caused the Loo to Back Up".'

'Did he? Cause the loo to back up?'

'Hasn't everybody at some time? Anyway, nobody could prove he didn't.'

'What about being Sluiced by the Earl?'

'It sounds like a polite term for getting rat-arsed with the aristos, doesn't it, but . . . No, here it is,' said Toby, still at the computer. 'Earl's Sluice. An old waterway near the Old Kent Road. I expect the other references will check out, too. Fun, isn't it?' he said, getting up from Phin's chair. 'Sort of Victorian crossword clues. Anyway, I thought we might go back to the pub tomorrow night – thee and me, I mean – and see what we can turn up. I can't do tonight, because I'm on a late ward shift.'

'Tomorrow would be fine. Yes, let's,' said Phin, pleased.

After Toby had gone, in deference to Professor Liripine's wishes, Phin set about tracking the details of Franz Liszt's soberer years in the monastery. He drafted a possible timeline for Liszt, including what Liszt had termed his *'vie trifurquée'* – the threefold existence he had pursued in later life, when he had travelled between Rome, Weimar and Budapest, giving master classes in piano playing. This was all fine and could be expanded. The trouble was that he could not escape the feeling that Scaramel and Links were eyeing him reproachfully from the shadows. In the end, immediately after lunch, he put Liszt away and went out. Linklighters would be closed at this hour of the afternoon, but there was Thumbprints to explore.

Thumbprints, when he got there, had a pleasingly old-fashioned air. Phin enjoyed it very much, and he wandered along the bookshelves until he found himself in a small section displaying framed paintings and prints. This was what he had really come to see. There were a number of sketches and prints on display – several more in the shop's windows – and there were also large pocket folders hanging from racks, containing unframed prints and sketches. It was not very likely that any of Links's work had survived, apart from the occasional repro-duction in old books, but Phin wanted to make sure. This seemed as good a place to start a search as anywhere.

There were some nice old sketches in the portfolios – mostly prints, but a few originals, with several of the immediate areas around Harlequin Court. Phin thought Arabella might like one of the originals for her flat – it was her birthday next month. There was a particularly nice one of a pub in Covent Garden called Ben Caunt's Head, which apparently had stood on the site of what was now the The Salisbury. Phin remem-bered Loretta saying something about the freeholders of Harlequin Court being the Salisbury Trust or the Salisbury Estate, and he set this sketch aside and went on looking through the rack.

And then he saw it. It was almost at the end, and it was behind a larger print of St Martin-in-the-Fields.

It was not a sketch of Harlequin Court this time but, even to Phin's untutored eye, it was from the hand that had drawn the menacing figure by the streetlight. It was not signed, but when he looked more closely, there was a scribbled *L* in the bottom right-hand corner. It looked as if it had been hastily done – almost as if, having finished the sketch, it had not mattered to the artist about adding his name, and as if somebody had nudged him to at least initial it. But it's Links, he thought. I'm sure it is.

He laid the sketch carefully out on a small display table, and studied it more closely. It was fairly large; in today's measurements, it was probably about double A4 size – perhaps it was A3. It was longways on – landscape rather than portrait. But it was disturbing in the way that the *Liszten* sketch had been disturbing.

This one showed a long, bleak, windowless room, with sections partly divided by iron bars that almost, but not quite, reached the ceiling. They're rudimentary cages, thought Phin. In one corner were two troughs, presumably containing either food or water. In another corner of the room was a pile of straw. Anonymous debris was littered elsewhere on the ground – tattered fragments of paper and shreds of rags. But it was not the room that tore at Phin's emotions; it was the room's occupants.

They were ragged and wretched, and in the main it was impossible to know if they were men or woman. They were chained, the ends of each chain embedded in the wall. But the chains were long enough to allow them to reach the troughs and the straw with its all-too-obvious purpose. Some of the figures seemed to be staring straight at the artist, but others sat in huddles, looking hopelessly at their hands or staring uncomprehendingly at the ground. A gaol? thought Phin. A workhouse? No, it's more likely to be a madhouse. Links, he thought – and I'm positive this is your work – where on earth did you find your subjects?

He bought the sketch. He did not even look at the price tag on it – he would not have cared if it had cleaned out his current bank balance. He bought the Covent Garden pub sketch as well, leaving it with the manager to be framed for Arabella's birthday.

The manager also turned out to be the owner of the shop. He introduced himself as Gregory, and seemed interested in Phin's purchases. Asked about any books relating to the history of Harlequin Court, he said he would see what he could find. No, it would be no trouble at all; in fact he would enjoy the search. This was an interesting part of London, wasn't it? His family had owned this bookshop for nearly two hundred years, so he always felt very much part of its past.

'Of course, there've been a good many changes since then,' he said. 'But people still like books, you know, no matter the format. Once it was clay tablets or papyrus scrolls.'

'And now it's iPads and android screens,' said Phin, smiling.

'Life changes,' said Gregory, philosophically. 'This is a curious subject for a sketch, isn't it?' He was studying the madhouse drawing. 'I wouldn't mind knowing who the artist was – it's only signed with that single initial.'

'Yes. There's something written in that other corner, though,' said Phin. 'It's just about readable. It simply says, "Thrawl". Does that mean anything to you?'

'Not offhand,' said Gregory. 'Although I think there's a Thrawl Street in the East End, if that's any help.'

'It might be.'

'I'd be interested to hear if you turn anything up,' said Gregory. 'And I can certainly let you know if we find anything that looks as if it's by the same artist.'

'I'd be very grateful if you would,' said Phin, handing Gregory his card.

'The framed one of the Covent Garden pub will be ready midweek – is that all right?'

'Yes, certainly.'

'We're open until six most nights, and every Thursday we have a book discussion group. Six thirty to seven thirty. My great-grandfather – maybe one more "great" – started it, and the tradition's stuck. You'd always be welcome to come to that.'

'Thank you.' Phin thought he might very well look in on one of the Thursday night meetings.

He went back to his flat where he propped up Links's sketch on his desk, and looked at it for a long time. Then he opened the book with the *Liszten for the Killer* sketch, and set it alongside. Both so dark. Both so filled with menace and sadness and fear. At some stage in your life, something dark entered it, he said to Links in his mind. But what was it?

Had 'Thrawl' been a real place? It could only have been an asylum or a workhouse, or possibly a gaol. But if so, what had Links's connection been to it? People did not wander in and out of asylums or workhouses or prisons, and set up an easel or sit unchallenged with a sketchbook. Could Links have been an inmate? Phin's mind flinched from the possibility of Links being insane or a violent criminal. Could he have been visiting someone? Working there, even? Or, again, had the place not actually existed – had it been a dark fantasy from Links's imagination?

He put a pan of pasta on the cooker, stirred in a ready-made cheese sauce, and while it was all simmering searched for the card that Loretta Farrant had given him.

'Is there,' he said, carefully, when she answered, 'any chance that I could be allowed a second look at those old papers in the restaurant?'

Loretta sounded pleased to hear from him. 'Yes, of course,' she said. 'Have you found out anything useful?'

'I'm not sure yet,' said Phin, noncommittally. 'One or two small things have cropped up – probably they won't turn out to be important or relevant, but if I could have half an hour or so to look through those boxes again, I'd be very grateful. I'd be looking for different information, this time, you see.' He did not want to say he would be looking for Links and an old asylum or workhouse.

'Could you manage a Sunday morning? We'd be closed then and I could get the boxes out ready. We could go down to the office, and you could take as long as you wanted.'

'Thank you. This coming Sunday?'

'Why not?'

THIRTEEN

London 1880s/1890s

Daisy hated going home late at night after a Linklighters evening, or after a night when Madame had been performing at one of the bigger theatres.

If Madame was with her she felt safe, but there were nights

when Madame went out to supper after a performance. At the moment it was often Rhun the Rhymer who took her out, but there were other gentlemen, too. Rhun was apt to succumb to bouts of jealousy about it, but he was never violent or sulky, and Daisy was sure it was only ever supper Madame had with the other men. Whatever else you might say about her morals, she had never, to Daisy's knowledge, run two men at the same time.

But there were nights when Daisy had to go back to the Maida Vale house by herself, and those were the nights when she believed that *he* was watching her – that he was hiding, waiting his chance to pounce. If he ever caught her by herself, he would be on her, and his knives and gouges would come out . . . After he had dealt with her, he would seek out Joe and do the same to him. The thought of Joe – frail, trusting, infinitely dear – at the mercy of that mad butcher was more than Daisy could bear. But it could happen. He would know that Daisy and Joe could identify him as the Whitechapel Murderer. Leather Apron. Jack the Ripper.

'But could you really identify him?' demanded Madame, when Daisy said all this. 'Could you recognize his face again?'

'Yes,' said Daisy, very definitely. 'You could as well, couldn't you? You saw him that night after the Ten Bells. You'd recognize him again, wouldn't you?'

'Yes, I would,' said Madame, softly, and her eyes were suddenly fearful. 'Oh God, yes, I would. We could both identify him – Joe, too. And the Ripper knows it. That's why we need to be very, very careful.'

'Should we tell the police? Give a description?'

But despite the fact that Madame was a lady who feared very little, Daisy knew that they both flinched from telling the police what they knew and what they had seen. It would draw too much attention to them. The newspapers would find out – they were always eager for a story about these killings, and they would write about it with little care for the consequences. *'Music hall performer and East End girl know who the Ripper is,'* they would say.

As Madame said, they had already risked enough by taking the 'Listen' song around the East End pubs, not that she regretted that. But it was one thing to try to set up an alarm network, and it was another altogether to tell people you knew what the Whitechapel Murderer looked like.

'Even if the newspapers didn't splash it all over their pages, it would still get out,' she said. 'He's clever and he's cunning and he listens and watches. He was there that night in the Ten Bells, wasn't he?'

'Yes.'

'And in any case, all we could describe is a tall man with dark hair and eyes.'

Madame was nervous, Daisy could see that. She worked out a plan for when Daisy had to go home by herself. Daisy was to take a cab from the rank just outside Harlequin Court as they always did. Madame would make sure she always had enough money to pay for it. And before the cab reached the house, Daisy was to have her latchkey ready in her hand, and after the cab had pulled up and the driver was paid, she had only to hop down and run straight up to the front door. And if it looked as if there might be anyone hanging around outside the house, she was to ask the cabbie to wait until he saw her safely inside. None of the drivers would mind doing that, and on those nights Daisy was to give them a small extra payment. The fare was eight pence from Linklighters to Maida Vale and Madame had told Daisy to give ten pence – cabbies worked long hours in all kinds of dreadful weather, and an extra tuppence would be thankfully received. But on nights when Daisy asked them to watch her go into the house, she was to give a whole shilling.

Once she was inside the house, she always locked all the doors and went round all the rooms. She knew Joe did the same. He still drew everything and everyone around him – recently, he had drawn terrible pictures of a cloaked man stalking his prey by the flickering streetlamps.

'He's putting his fears on paper,' said Madame, seeing some of the sketches.

'I know.' It tore Daisy's heart in pieces to see Joe's terrors set down like this, but she would never destroy his sketches. She did not know if she wanted anyone to ever see them, though.

Madame told Rhun the Rhymer about their encounter with the Whitechapel killer, of course. She tried to make a lively story out of it, but her voice shook several times.

Rhun had listened, his frown getting blacker and blacker. Afterwards, he said he would summon the shades of his ancestors to lend him the strength to rid the world of this monster. Those ancestors had fought the marauding British and the Irish, never mind a goodly few of the Scots and the Picts as well, said Rhun, his eyes glowing with fervour. They had stormed down from the mountains and across the valleys, scattering enemies as they went, and, possessing such ancestors as those, he thought he would be more than equal to this madman who was prowling around Whitechapel.

Daisy did not like to say that Whitechapel was nothing like the mountains and valleys of Wales, or ask how the ghosts of Rhun's warlike ancestors were likely to help if a murderous madman got into a house in Maida Vale. Still, on the nights that Rhun stayed with Madame, it was a comfort to know he was there.

But Daisy was not at all sure that Rhun would hear anyone trying to get in, because he had turned out to be very enthusiastic when it came to the intimacies of the bedroom. It was a bit embarrassing to have to hear someone you had known since you were a child shouting about climaxes that were going to explode your brains in your skull. Daisy did her best to shut out the sounds, but it was often difficult. There was an awkward incident one night when the people in the flat immediately below came storming up to hammer on the door. Madame forbade Daisy to open it, but the people shouted through the letterbox that Scaramel could spend her entire life bouncing around in beds with half the men in London if she wanted to, but they did not want to listen to her doing it, and certainly not at one o'clock in the morning.

Rhun stalked out to the landing, and hurled abuse in what Daisy supposed was the Welsh language, and the downstairs neighbours stumped crossly back to their own flat, saying what could you expect from a shameless hussy who waggled her half-naked body at people from a stage. Still, it now seemed

likely that the indignant neighbours would hear anyone
creeping up the stairs and trying to get in.

And then came the night when Daisy and Joe found themselves alone at Linklighters, with midnight approaching.

It ought not to have happened, but it chanced that Madame
was going out to supper with some of the other performers
straight after the show. Dora Dashington was going, and a pair
of tap-dancing twins – Fancy and Frankie Finnegan, who were
particular friends of Madame's, and whose act Daisy always
greatly enjoyed. There were several gentlemen, too, who would
meet them at the restaurant. At the last moment Belinda
Baskerville had somehow got herself into the party. She had
not been invited, but Madame told Daisy the Baskerville creature usually managed to push in if she thought there might be
a rich gentleman to be picked up during the evening.

Madame left Harlequin Court shortly after eleven, in company
with the Finnegan sisters, swirling a fur-trimmed cloak around
her shoulders, all of them laughing about avoiding the rain and
swishing umbrellas. Daisy stayed to help Joe and the barman
to clear up, but just as they were finishing, one of the linklighter
boys came running in with a message for the barman. His
daughter in Canning Town was about to give birth, said the boy
and the barman's wife wanted him to go out there at once, on
account of the daughter's husband being useless.

The barman's wife was a strong-minded lady with a loud
voice and forbidding bosom, and the barman looked worriedly
at Daisy and Joe. Daisy said at once that of course he must
go – they would all want to hear about the new baby tomorrow
anyway, and she and Joe could perfectly well get themselves
home for one night. The barman frowned, then delved in his
pocket and gave Joe one of the keys that locked the main door
leading out to the square. When they had finished washing-up,
Joe was to lock the door on his way out, was that clear? He
was to return the key later tonight or first thing tomorrow
morning, was that clear as well?

'Yes,' said Daisy and Joe, together.

The barman went anxiously off to Canning Town, and Daisy
said to Joe they would walk to the cab rank together, and get

a cab to Maida Vale. Joe could stay the night; he could sleep in the tiny room off the scullery, which he had done before on a couple of similar occasions.

It always felt a bit strange to see Linklighters empty and silent, although Joe said it was never really completely empty. There were always echoes, he said; if you listened you could hear faint voices and snatches of music. As if all the people who had performed here liked to wander back because they were curious about what went on without them.

Once he had drawn Linklighters, showing how it looked after the audience had all gone, sketching the shadowy stage and the stacked-away bits of scenery, and the odds and ends of rope and stage weights and wicker baskets of costumes. But then, over it all, he had drawn half-figures and fragments of music – music notes or half-written lines from songs. He had used real songs, too – just fragments of them, but they were readable, and it had made the sketch all the more interesting. Joe called the sketch *The Ghost Theatre*, and Mr Thaddeus at Thumbprints had liked it so much he was going to frame it and put it in his window to see if somebody would buy it.

When the two of them walked across the main room between the chairs and tables, a soft echo of their footsteps seemed to walk with them, and when they went past the stage the heavy velvet curtains looped at each side stirred slightly. Joe's ghosts. To dispel them, Daisy said, loudly, that they would run all the way along the alley because of the rain.

As they went up the stairs to the main door, Joe was silent, and Daisy knew they were both trying not to think how frightening it felt to be on their own like this, out of sight and sound of other people. But they only had to cross Harlequin Court and run down the alley, and it would not take more than a few moments.

The streetlamp in the court was burning strongly, showering its flickering light over the cobblestones, and Daisy felt Joe relax a little. He said, 'One day I'll draw Harlequin Court, exactly like it is now. Night-time, but with the light coming from the lamp over there, and with everywhere all clean and shiny from the rain. And proper painted bits, too.'

'I'd like that.' Daisy would save every farthing she could to buy Joe the right paints. She had no idea how much such things cost or where you bought them, but she would ask Thaddeus Thumbprint, who would know.

They shut the main door and Joe locked it, trying the latch to make sure the lock had dropped, then putting the key in his pocket. It was only a few yards across the court to the alley, and then a few more to walk down it and join the late-night crowds.

It was as Joe was turning up his jacket collar against the rain that a feeling of menace crept across Harlequin Court. Fear scraped Daisy's skin, because something was wrong somewhere. But what? The rain was blurring everything, but surely nothing was different? There was the door behind them, firmly locked, with the Linklighters sign over it. That was all right. The jutting windows of the shops were all right, as well. Thumbprints, which joined on to Linklighters, had the window displays that Mr Thaddeus took such trouble over – books and several small, framed paintings. The jeweller's and the printing shop were further along and they looked normal, as well. On the far side of the court was the streetlight with its twisty iron post, and the little cage for the gas jets at the very top . . .

The streetlight. Daisy's heart began to thud, because it was the streetlight that was wrong. Standing immediately beneath it, leaning against the post, was the figure of a man. Nobody stood like that, out in the pouring rain, not moving, watching the buildings. He was wearing a long dark coat with the collar turned up, half hiding the face, but the tilt of the head, the extraordinary impression that he wore not a cloak or a coat of ordinary cloth, but one woven out of evil, were all unmistakable. He was unmistakable.

Daisy's heart seemed to leap up into her throat, and in the same instant she felt terror course through Joe. The figure stepped out of the pool of blurred light and came towards them, not hurrying, because he did not need to hurry. They could not get past him to the alley and run to the safety of the bustling street beyond. They could probably not fight, either, because even though there were two of them against his one, Joe was little more than a child and Daisy was small and light-boned. They would be overcome with case. They were trapped . . .

No, they were not trapped, because behind them – no more

than six paces – was Linklighters. Daisy backed towards it, pulling Joe with her. In an urgent whisper, she said, 'The key – unlock the door!'

But Joe already had the key out of his pocket, although as he fumbled to slot it into the lock, his hands were shaking so badly that Daisy was terrified he would drop it. Please God, let him unlock the door, and please let us get back inside . . .

The key turned, and they tumbled into the familiar warm scents of Linklighters – but it might be too late, because *he* had already crossed the square, and if he reached out both hands . . . There was no time to lock the door behind them – they half fell down the stairs, the faint light from the court filtering in so that they could just about see their way. But even as they reached the foot, they heard him push the upstairs door wider, and step inside. He was here – the man some called Leather Apron, and some called the Whitechapel Murderer, but almost everyone now referred to as Jack the Ripper. He was inside Linklighters. The door was shut and there was no other means of getting out.

They were shut in with him.

FOURTEEN

Through the searing panic, Daisy was aware of Joe pulling her towards a small door at the bottom of the stairs.

'Down here,' he said. 'There's a cellar – good hiding place. Come *on*.'

He dragged the door open and pushed her through.

'Twelve steps,' he said, in a whisper. 'Don't fall.'

The twelve steps were dark and steep and very uneven. It would be easy to slip and plunge all the way down to the bottom, but it would be better to die of a broken neck than at the hands of the madman who was coming after them. There was hardly any light, but Daisy tried to think that if she and Joe could not see, then neither could *he*. But even as the thought came, there was a faint scraping sound from above, and a thin flicker of light sprang up. Daisy realized with horror that he had a tinderbox or a pack of matches and that he had lit one. When she turned involuntarily to look back up, he was standing at the top of the stairs, his head and shoulders silhouetted blackly in the tiny flame.

The match burned out almost at once, and although the darkness closed down like a curtain, that brief flare of light would have been enough for him to see the steps and to see the two of them at the bottom. She gasped, and clung to Joe's hand, because she had no idea where they were, and she had not even known this place existed. Linklighters was a cellar itself – it was several cellars that ran under most of the Harlequin Court shops above, and that somebody, at some time, had knocked into one huge space. But this was a deeper level – an older cellar. However far down it was, it smelled dreadful.

Joe was pulling her across the floor.

'There's a bit of wall that juts out,' he said. 'But you can squeeze behind it, and you can get through to a tunnel – where an old ditch was. But it's a very narrow squeeze, and he'll never get through. Only I need to find the bit of wall with the gap and I can't see . . .'

Daisy kept tight hold of his hand, then realized that with the other hand he was feeling all over the wall's surface.

The scrape of the tinder came again, and even though it was madness in the extreme to look round, Daisy did look. He was there in the cellar with them. His face, lit from below by the small, brief flame, was smiling, but it was a dreadful smile. As the light wavered, he lunged forwards, but in the split-second before the light went out, Joe said, 'Found it!' and pushed her forward. For a wild moment it felt as if he was simply pushing her into the blank wall, then Daisy realized that there were two walls, and that the edges of both of them overlapped but did not join. There was a small space where it was just possible to get through. She managed to cram into the narrow opening, and there was the faint brush of colder air.

From behind came a soft whisper.

'*You shan't escape me, Daisy . . .*'

It hissed eerily around the cellar, and new horror flooded over Daisy because he knew her name. Then suddenly she was through the gap, and Joe was with her, and they were standing in a kind of tunnel with a low, arched roof. There was a faint greenish light from somewhere, and the sound of water dripping. The smell was far worse than it had been in the outer cellar.

Immediately in front of them – so close that if she took two strides forward she could reach out to touch it with her fingertips – was a massive door. It towered over them – easily three if not four times their height, and ten or twelve feet wide. Its surface was scarred and pitted and black with age, and iron spikes jutted up from the top. Black chains, each link as thick as a man's forearm, hung from the spikes, like monstrous snakes. Stretching above and on each side of the door were stone walls, shiny with damp, and set into the wall on the right-hand side was a huge wheel, glistening faintly in the dripping dampness, with an immense rusting lever jutting out.

'It's an old sluice gate,' said Joe. The fear was still in his voice, but he was already reaching for the lever. 'You turn the wheel and that pulls those chains, and they lift the gate.'

Daisy looked back at the wall behind them. *He* was still there – she could hear him. But surely a full-grown man could not get through that narrow gap between the walls.

'I'm still here, my dears . . . And I will reach you . . . Both of you . . . And then shan't I do my work on you, oh, shan't I just . . . Because you can't be allowed to tell what you saw me do . . .'

The words were picked up in the enclosed space; they spun and echoed around Daisy's head, and her heart skittered with fear. But Joe was pulling at the lever with all his might, and there was a shiver of movement, and a dull, deep sound, as if something was being dragged unwillingly from the bowels of the earth. Daisy darted across to help him, seizing the lever, hating the cold sliminess of it, but pulling it with all her strength.

'Joe – what's on the other side?' she gasped, although she did not really care what was on the other side, if it meant they would escape.

'Old ditch.' Joe's voice was as breathless as Daisy's, but he said, 'Mr Thaddeus in the bookshop showed me a map. Only it's all dried out now . . . But when I saw it, I thought that – if ever we had to hide from *him* . . .'

Daisy's arms felt as if they were being wrenched from their sockets, and sweat was pouring down her face, stinging her eyes, but they dared not give up, because they could hear the sounds of their attacker trying to get through the narrow gap between the two bits of the wall.

'It's starting to move,' cried Joe, and with the words there was a faint menacing rumble from within the darkness. Above them the chains began to uncoil, and inch by tortuous inch, the sluice gate began to lift. A narrow rim appeared at the bottom, and a breath of old, sour air gusted into their faces. As the gap widened they could see a wide tunnel beyond.

'It's stopped,' said Daisy, suddenly. 'I think it's stuck.' A fresh wave of terror swept over her, and she looked back at the wall.

'Might be as high as it goes. It's far enough up, though – we can get under it. Come *on.*'

They had to bend almost double, but once beyond the gate they saw that the old ditch was not only wider, it was much deeper than either of them had expected.

Daisy had been expecting a narrow trench, maybe with a trickle of water in it, like you sometimes saw in places like Hackney Marshes, but this was far wider. It had to be at least twelve feet across.

'And it isn't dried out after all,' said Joe, standing on the rim and peering cautiously over. 'There's mud and stuff down there.'

Through the thick shadows, they could see that at the very bottom of the channel was black, brackish water and oozing mud. It might be only a couple of feet deep. You could wade through a couple of feet of muddy water if you had to. But if it turned out to be deeper than that, you could drown in it. It would blind you, you would choke, struggle helplessly . . .

'Joe, we can't get down there. It's far too deep.' Daisy's voice sounded unnaturally loud, and the echoes snatched the words greedily, bouncing them back.

'Don't need to. We can walk along this edge,' said Joe. 'It's
a bit narrow, but if we're careful . . . The map said the ditch
comes out somewhere in St Martin's Lane.'

'Can we close the gate so's *he* can't follow us?'

'Don't know.' Joe turned to look, then said, 'Don't think it
closes from this side. There's no handle – no wheel. We got
to go along the tunnel, Daise.'

Daisy shut out a sudden nightmare image of the two of
them becoming lost down here, and said, 'All right. But it's
nothing more than a bit of stone shelf. Keep tight hold of my
hand, so's we don't fall in.'

As they began cautiously to walk along the narrow rim of
the ditch, the faint light began to fade. But although Daisy
could barely see Joe, she could sense that his earlier confidence
had gone. He said, suddenly, 'It's going to be all right, ain't
it? He can't get to us now, can he?' His voice was so pleading
that Daisy could hardly bear it.

She said, 'We're safe. I'll make you safe, Joe.'

'You'll make me safe,' he said, half to himself, and nodded.
His trusting tone tore at Daisy's heart.

The tunnel was only slightly wider than the ditch itself,
but the stone shelf was wide enough for them to walk if they
went singly. Above them the roof was curved, and every few
feet were brick archways that looked as if they might be
holding up the roof. Daisy and Joe had to bend over so as
not to bang their heads at those points. Every few yards were
square iron grids, which they had to step over. An even worse
stench rose up from beneath the grids, and Daisy prayed not
to be sick.

There was hardly any light now, but several times tiny
pinpoints of red showed near the ground. Rats' eyes, thought
Daisy, in horror. Dozens of them. She felt Joe's hand tighten
around hers, and she said, 'They won't come near us, Joe.
They'll be more frightened of us than we are of them.'

Several times they heard the rats scuttling quite close to
them, and their steps and their frightened breathing echoed
loudly. The world shrank to this dreadful place. Daisy no
longer had any idea of how long they had been creeping
through the darkness, but they had to go on. Somewhere in

St Martin's Lane, Joe had said. That might be anywhere, but
it was where they would get out and reach safety. And *he*
could not get through that narrow bit of wall, but if he did
– if he got into this tunnel – he would be on them before they
had time to do anything. Would he have his knives and his
saws with him? He could take his time with them down here
in this secret place – he could do what he wanted to them.
And then what? Would he leave their bodies down here where
no one would ever find them, or know what had happened to
them? And leave them for the rats . . .? No, he would not do
that. He liked people to know what he had done – he liked
everyone to be shocked and horrified. He would make sure
their bodies were found.

Then Joe said, 'Oh! Light – see it? Up there.'

But Daisy had already seen it, and she thought she had
never seen a more beautiful sight. Light was coming in from
over their heads, and it was not the smeary greenish light of
the tunnel, but the clean good dark blue of a London night
street – light that lay on the old stones in a criss-cross pattern,
because it was coming through a street grid.

And, just under the grid, coming all the way down to where
they stood, was an iron-rung ladder.

They went eagerly forward, and they were within a couple
of feet of the ladder, when the light was blotted out, and there
was the ringing sound of footsteps on iron.

Someone was coming down the iron ladder.

'*I told you that you wouldn't escape me, Daisy . . . I know
all the dark places of this City, you see . . . I know about
Linklighters and the ghost river beneath it . . . And it's easy
to get across a city when you know the short-cuts – when
there're cab drivers glad to earn an extra shilling . . .*'

And then, incredibly, he began to sing, very softly, the
sounds echoing in the enclosed space.

'*Listen for the killer for he's here, just out of sight.*
Listen for the footsteps 'cos it's very late at night . . .'

Cold horror swept over Daisy, and she fumbled for Joe's
hand. 'Run back,' she cried. 'Go *on*. Back to the cellar. As
fast as you can.' He does know the song, she thought, and
again came the eerie awareness of her thought.

'Of course I know it, Daisy. I was there – on those nights when it was sung. I heard it – I learned it . . .'

The singing came again, closer this time.

'Now I hear the midnight prowl,
Now I see the saw and knife.
Next will come the victim's howl.
So save yourself from him, and run . . .
. . . run hard to save your life.'

Fingers like steel traps reached out and closed around Daisy's arm. It was like a hand reaching out of a churning nightmare, pulling her into its black core. She struggled, and she thought she shouted to Joe again to run back to the cellar, but the man's arms were around her by now, and he was pressing into her. And, oh God, there it was, that older nightmare, the nightmare with Pa at the core of it – the feel of that hard thrusting stick of flesh between his thighs. Threatening. Ready to inflict that deep secret hurt that no one must ever know about . . .

Terror tore through Daisy's mind. She had finally managed to deal with Pa all that time ago, but this one was different – no one could deal with this one. Even so, the knowledge that she must protect Joe gave her courage. She kicked out and her foot smacked against flesh and bone. But the blow seemed only to excite him more. A throaty laugh bubbled in his throat and he pulled her against him again, pressing into her. Dreadful. Daisy struggled, and tried to kick him again, but he was holding her too tightly. Then Joe's small hands came out of the dimness, pushing at the man for all he was worth.

It took the killer off guard, and Daisy thought, with vicious triumph, that he had not expected an attack from that quarter. The steel-like hands loosened, and Joe pushed him again, sending him falling back against the iron ladder. There was the sickening crunch of bone against iron, and a grunting cry of pain and anger.

Daisy had no idea if the fall had knocked him out, but she did not think they could risk trying to climb over him on to the ladder. Then he turned his head in a confused way, and in the light from overhead she saw his eyes open, and stare straight at her. There was such blazing hatred in them that she recoiled, and, grabbing Joe's hand, began to half scramble, half run, back along the tunnel. After a few feet, she turned to look back, and saw that the man was pulling himself slowly to his feet. He was holding on to the ladder, and clutching his head. Why couldn't the fall have knocked him out altogether? Or why couldn't she have managed to push him into the yawning channel, to break his legs or his neck?

But there was nothing to do but grope their way back to the sluice gate. As they went, they both heard him start to come after them.

'Faster,' hissed Daisy. 'Go *on*. He's stunned from the fall. We can outrun him.'

They went forward as fast as they dared, but with every step Daisy expected one of them to trip and go down into the dark, evil-smelling trench at their side. And the murderer was coming after them now – they could hear him – but he was moving much more slowly. Because of the darkness? Or because he was still dazed from being half knocked out? It did not matter.

Then Joe said, eagerly, 'There's the gate,' and there it was, just as they had left it, raised by about three feet, so that again they had to bend down and crawl through. As they did so, the footsteps behind them quickened.

'Close the gate! Don't let him get through!' shouted Joe, but Daisy was already at the wheel, and Joe was with her, both of them dragging at it.

But the murderer was almost here. Daisy was about to say they would have to leave it, and get out of the cellar and into Linklighters and escape that way, when the deep clanking sounded, and the gate began slowly to descend. But as it did so, *he* appeared. He gave a cry of fury, and lunged forward, throwing himself flat on the ground, trying to claw through the slowly closing gap. His head was thrown back, and mad eyes glared out.

Daisy and Joe backed away, shaking violently, their arms around one another.

'The gate's still coming down,' said Joe, and he darted back to the wheel and seized it. But even in the dimness

Daisy could see that the mechanism was grinding its own way downwards, as if once cranked into life it must complete its journey.

'Daisy, help me. I can't stop it,' said Joe, in a voice of horror.

Daisy darted to his side, and together they dragged at the wheel. It was no use. The gate was descending – doing so with a dreadful slow relentlessness – and the man beneath it was still clawing at the ground, squirming to get through the narrowing space.

Daisy suddenly shouted, 'Go back! You'll be chopped in two!' And then thought this had to be the maddest thing to say, because this was the man who had almost chopped several women in two – who had been set to do the same to herself and Joe.

He was almost flat to the ground now, and in another moment the edges of the gate would be touching his shoulders. His hands came forward, as if to reach out for help, and Daisy shuddered, and felt Joe pull her back.

There was a screech from the old mechanism – or was it a screech from the lungs of the man beneath the gate? Then he suddenly twisted away, back into the darkness, and the gate clanged all the way down. Screams rang out – dreadful piercing screams that sounded as if they were tearing the screamer's throat into bloodied tatters. And then they cut off, as if a door had been slammed on them.

FIFTEEN

'**D**id we kill him?' gasped Joe, as they squeezed back through the narrow wall opening into the old cellar, and shakily went up the stairs. 'Will he die down there?'

'I don't know. But I don't care.' Daisy knew it was wicked and monstrous and evil to want somebody – anybody – to die, but she did wish it.

Harlequin Court, when they stepped out into it, was quiet

and the streetlamp threw gentle shadows on the old bricks and the ground. It was familiar and it almost felt safe – although Daisy was not sure if anything would ever feel really safe ever again.

But she said, as firmly as she could, 'We'll go along the alley and find a hansom cab.'

'No money for a cab.'

'Don't matter. Madame'll pay when we get to her house.'

'Long as she's there,' said Joe, worriedly. 'She might not be home yet.'

'If she's not there, I'll take money from her box in her bedroom.'

'All right.' He paused, then said uncertainly, 'Have we got to tell her what happened?'

'Yes,' said Daisy, after a moment. 'We've got to tell her. It'll be all right, though. In any case, we're covered in mud and filth and stinking to high heaven.'

Madame was at home. Wearing nothing but a silk robe and flimsy velvet slippers, she ran out to pay the disgruntled hackney driver Daisy and Joe had managed to find, presenting him with a guinea so he could have the cab's interior cleaned after all the weed and silt Daisy and Joe had trailed into it.

Once they were inside the flat and the doors bolted against what was left of the night, Madame said, 'Explanations later – hot water and brandy in warm milk for you both first.'

She boiled kettles and brought towels, and filled basins for them to wash off the dust and the dirt of the tunnels. When Daisy tried to help, Madame wanted to know if Daisy thought Madame was so posh nowadays that she had forgotten how to heat up a drop of milk? As for Joe being too young to drink brandy, if you could not swig down a measure of brandy for shock and cold, the world was a sad place.

The fire in the big sitting room was stirred into life, and they sat in front of it. Madame listened, without interrupting, to the story of what had happened. When Daisy told how she had struggled to pull free of the clutching hands, and how, at one point, she had been held against her attacker, Madame shuddered, and reached out to clasp Daisy's hand briefly.

Daisy said, 'We think he ran along to the grid at the other
end of the tunnel while we were still down there.'

'And climbed down and waited for you?'

'Yes. St Martin's Lane or somewhere nearby, Joe thinks it'd
be, that grid.'

'We can have a look by daylight, but it doesn't tell us
anything even if we find half a dozen grids,' said Madame.

'He said he knew all the . . . the dark places of the City,'
offered Joe. 'And how cabbies were always glad to earn an
extra shilling to get you across London fast.'

'And it's not very far from Harlequin Court to St Martin's
Lane anyway,' said Madame, thoughtfully. 'He could even
have walked there if he was quick.'

'He said he knew about Linklighters and the old ditch,'
added Daisy. 'But please . . .' She leaned forward and grasped
Madame's hand again. 'Please – we don't want no one told
about this. Not the peelers, no one.'

She had no idea what she would say if Madame said that
of course they must tell the peelers, but Madame did not. She
said, slowly, 'I think you're right. I don't think we can tell
anyone about this.'

'See, if they find him – if he's dead – we could be branded
as murderers.'

'They could find out it was us,' put in Joe. 'We're both part
of Linklighters.'

'And never mind it's the Ripper, we'd be hanged.'

'Yes. Yes, I think you could be right,' said Madame,
thoughtfully.

A shiver went through Joe, and Daisy put her arms round
him and hugged him hard.

'Except I ain't letting that happen,' she said.

'Nor am I,' said Madame, at once. She thought for a moment,
then said, 'Will you let me tell Rhun about this? He'll be
entirely trustworthy.'

Daisy and Joe looked at one another, then nodded.

Rhun, listening to the story the following afternoon, talked
to Daisy and Joe very seriously. They were to do their best to
put the entire thing from their minds, he said. They had done
nothing wrong – they had defended themselves, as anyone

was allowed to do. As for wondering whether that warped monster might die down there – well, to Rhun's mind, if he did, it would be doing the world a service.

Daisy said, 'But if he died, wouldn't he be found? The – um – the body, I mean?'

'It might,' said Rhun. 'But I don't think it would be for a very long time. I think men do go down there – officials of some kind – to make sure everything's working as it should. Maintenance,' said Rhun, in the vague voice of one who has no real idea of how such things work.

'There was the ladder from the grid in the street,' said Daisy. 'That'd be for men to get to the tunnel from the street.'

'It would indeed. But believe me, Daisy, bodies will sometimes be found in those tunnels, and it's a fair bet that nobody thinks much about it. Death by accident, it'll be. The bodies they find are usually vagrants – people who've somehow got themselves into such places and become trapped. Very sad, but there it is.'

'And,' said Madame, 'any bodies they do find would simply be brought up and given a pauper's burial?'

'Indeed they would. No, Daisy, I'm not trying to make you feel better, that's what will happen.'

Daisy thought: so if Jack the Ripper died down there, he might end up buried in a pauper's grave, unnamed, and no one will ever know.

It was a few weeks after that night that Madame said, 'Daisy, I've got some unexpected news.'

'Yes?' It would be some ridiculously extravagant and unnecessary purchase, or a wonderful booking at one of the big theatres. Or it might be more serious. Through Daisy's mind darted the knowledge of the secrets she and Madame had shared. Things that only the two of them knew about.

But it was not an extravagant purchase or a booking, and it was not anything to do with any of those dark secrets.

With a light in her eyes that Daisy had never seen before, Madame said, 'Daisy, your good friend Rhun the Rhymer has proved himself to be a very capable lover. Not only capable, but effective.' She saw Daisy's puzzlement, and started to laugh.

'I always thought I was clever enough to avoid it,' she said. 'But it's caught me out at last.' The light was still in her eyes, but in a more serious voice than Daisy had ever heard her use, she said, 'Daisy, I'm going to have a child.'

Rhun was at first disbelieving, then astonished, and finally ecstatic at the prospect of being a father. It had not been intended, he said, but there you were, you got carried away at times. He bought champagne for everyone he knew, and made elaborate marriage proposals every other day – all of which Madame refused.

Then he said, almost humbly, that he would be able to contribute towards the child's upbringing. His poems were doing surprisingly well; there was to be a book including a number of them, and he had recently been elected to a rather prestigious society for writers and poets. As a result of that, he was being asked to give talks and readings and lectures, all of which commanded surprisingly generous fees.

'You certainly will contribute to the upbringing,' Madame said. 'There'll be a decent education, as well. I'm not having a child of mine growing up uneducated.'

Daisy thought Madame never did things by halves, and knew that the appearance of the unexpected, unintended child in their lives would not be done by halves either.

She was right.

'Twins!' said Madame, delightedly, reclining in the big bed, a baby cradled in each arm, a froth of lace and silk pillows propping them all up. 'Isn't that wonderful, Daisy? Boy and girl. A complete family in one go. I wonder if we might have to move to a bigger flat, because . . . Nonsense, of course we can afford it.'

Rhun was overcome with emotion and delight at the birth of the twins. He said they were the most beautiful children ever to enter the world; he would write reams of poetry to them, and he would like them to have names from his family. His mother had been Morwenna, his grandfather Mervyn. Good Welsh names, he said, hopefully.

Madame said, consideringly, 'Morwenna and Mervyn. The

names go well together, don't they? And they're sufficiently unusual to be noticeable, which is important. Yes, let's call them that.'

So Morwenna and Mervyn the twins became.

Rhun wrote what he said was a lyric ballad in praise of the twins, using what he called the ancient method of *cynghanedd*. It had more in common with music than traditional poetry, did the *cynghanedd*, said Rhun, and he insisted on reading several verses to them that same night. Daisy, collecting their glasses and supper plates, was quite unable to understand any of it, and although Madame said it was marvellous and Rhun was a genius, Daisy didn't think Madame had understood any of it, either. It was likely that the birth of the twins had gone to Rhun's head a bit.

Later, he wrote what he said was a final banishing of the darkness. It was what Rhun termed a satirical poem about Jack prowling the old ghost rivers, looking for prey. Daisy did not know the word 'satirical', but when Rhun showed her the poem she understood. The poem told how it was better to stay in your own bed – or the bed of someone you knew – rather than go to the beds of one of the lost rivers – the ghost rivers – and be chopped up and have your guts left in a tangle. It even named some of the rivers, but in a comic way, so you had to read the lines a couple of times to be sure what they meant. Rhun said he would probably not do anything with the verses, but you never knew – one day somebody might find them, and speculate as to what the meaning was, and even whether there had been a mysterious murder that had never been solved.

With all this, and with the lively twins in the flat, Daisy was starting to dare to think the darkness really might have been banished. She was able to think that it might be possible to forget the sight of the sluice gate descending, and those hands clawing frantically out from under it.

SIXTEEN

Roland had been concerned to hear that Phineas Fox had been in touch a second time, and that Loretta had agreed to meet him at Linklighters this coming Sunday morning. He thought about it after Loretta left for the restaurant. She had spent the afternoon cleaning out cupboards and washing shelves – she always had so much energy, it often made Roland feel quite tired. He had offered to help with the cupboard-cleaning and shelf-washing, of course, but she had brushed the offer cheerfully away, saying she was better working on her own. Later, she had gone off to Linklighters, saying that Saturday nights were always busy, so Roland was not to expect her until late.

Roland noticed she had on another new outfit. It looked expensive, but then everything Loretta bought and wore was expensive. Roland had been shocked to discover how much she spent on clothes. When he had asked about this once, in the early days of their marriage, careful to explain that he was not being pinch-penny, but that he was worried as to whether such things could be afforded, what with all the outlay for the restaurant, Loretta said she intended to attract to Linklighters customers who were smart and prosperous, which meant that she had to look smart and prosperous. People responded to that kind of thing, and you could not look smart or prosperous in cheap clothes.

After she had gone, he ate his supper off a tray. He did not mind being on his own for the evening, which tended to happen at least four nights out of seven. Apart from anything else, it meant Loretta was not forever flopping down on his lap while he was watching TV, or writhing against him in the minuscule kitchen while waiting for the potatoes to boil.

He did not mind if he had to make his own supper, either – he had cooked for Mother each evening anyway in the last few years – but he had not often had to do that since their marriage. On Sundays, when the restaurant was closed, Loretta often had what she called a freezer day and made huge casseroles or lasagnes and pasta dishes, which she froze in batches and which had only to be reheated. Sometimes she brought food back from Linklighters as well; dishes that could be brought across London in a taxi, and stowed in their own fridge or freezer. Tonight, Roland had a Linklighters meal of jugged hare, which had not gone very well in the restaurant and was going to be taken off the menu, with a cider syllabub to follow.

As he washed up the plates later, he could not stop thinking about Phineas Fox. Was there really anything in Linklighters' past sufficiently disreputable or spicy to attract publicity to the restaurant and consequently to its owners? Phineas Fox seemed to think there might be, and Loretta was clearly hoping so. She did not care if she and Roland were dragged into the light; in fact she would help with the dragging. Roland repeated to himself that there was nothing wrong – nothing incriminating or damning – that could ever come out. But he still did not want people delving.

It occurred to him that it might be useful to find out a bit more about Phineas Fox, on the old principle of, 'Know your enemy.' Fox was not an actual enemy in that sense, of course, but still . . . After a moment, he fetched Loretta's laptop, which she kept in the flat, because it was a nuisance to lug it back and forwards on the tube, and it was as easy to email attachments of any documents between the two places, or to save information on to a memory stick.

He entered Phineas Fox's name in a search engine, hoping there would not be too many results for such an unusual name. There were not, although there was a website, which Roland had not expected. It was very basic, though, almost like a business card, and it merely described Phineas as a music researcher and historian, gave an agent's name, email and phone number for enquiries, and listed Fox's published works. It looked as if he was moderately well known in his field; he had written several books which seemed to have received considerable praise. Two were biographies – one on the jazz musician, Oscar Peterson, and one on a nineteenth-century

Russian violinist Roland had never heard of. There was also a serious-sounding book on exiled German and Jewish musicians prior to World War II, although – as if to prove he had a lighter side – there was also a frivolous-sounding book called *Bawdy Ballads Down the Ages*, which Fox had written in collaboration with somebody called Toby Tallis.

None of this was of very much help, though. It was not Fox's work Roland wanted to know about, it was the man himself – whether he had any weaknesses, any vulnerable points. How about his background? Had he any family, a wife, children? How old was he? Loretta had said he had remarkable eyes, which she would not have said if he had been a desiccated octogenarian.

But there did not seem to be anything about Fox's private life, and Roland closed the website, and sat for a few moments looking at the home screen. It was suddenly dreadfully tempting to look at Loretta's emails, but he was not going to yield to that temptation. In any case, they would all be business emails, relating to the restaurant. Or might there be anything from Phineas Fox – something he had asked about or told Loretta about that she had not passed on? But it would be like reading someone's private correspondence, and Roland would not do it.

He smiled, though, on seeing that Loretta, efficient and organized as always, had sorted all her photographs into separate, clearly labelled folders. They were labelled with things like 'Wedding', or, 'Engagement party at R's office', and 'Scotland'. That one would be their honeymoon, of course; they had taken lots of photos then.

There was also a folder called Linklighters. During the renovations Loretta had said she was trying to make a pictorial record of the progress of the work; it might be possible to use it as a display sometime. They could call it, 'From music hall to ruin to restaurant' perhaps.

It would be interesting to see those photos. Loretta would not regard them as private, and anyway Linklighters was as much Roland's as it was hers. More, in fact, because it had been his money that had made it all possible. He clicked on the folder, and the images opened up. In the main they seemed to be a series of shots showing the various stages of the building work. Loretta had conscientiously allotted them titles and dates. 'Demolition of original supper room door'. 'Dismantling of stage'. 'Laying new floor'.

Roland studied them, but men wielding power drills or swinging sledgehammers at walls, and giving thumbs-up signs to the camera, were not especially interesting.

The earlier ones were a bit better – there were only three or four, but a couple showed the place when it had been Linklighters Supper Rooms. There was a grainy shot of its façade, and another showing the street door half open, and a poster advertising the acts that were appearing. It was a pity the names on the poster were too faded or too indistinct to make out. Loretta had typed in '1890s?' under these.

Alongside these two shots, however, was one which was slightly different. Again it was of Linklighters in its nineteenth-century heyday, but this looked like a small sketch that had been scanned in. Roland tried zooming it up, but it caused what he thought was called pixelation, sending the edges of the outlines into confusing little squares, so he zoomed it back down. But he had the impression that it had been drawn on the nearest bit of paper – a menu card or the back of a programme, perhaps, while the artist had been waiting for something or someone.

Linklighters was unmistakable, of course, and Thumbprints bookshop had been drawn in next to it. In front of Linklighters was a small group of figures – three females and a man. The man looked slightly self-conscious. They were all quite plainly dressed – there was even a rather shabby look to them. The women had long coats with slightly bedraggled hemlines, and button boots, but one of them had added one of the extrava-gant hats characteristic of the era – fruit-trimmed and with several plumy feathers curling over her face. The hat was tilted to a jaunty angle, and Roland smiled. It was rather endearing that someone who had to wear what was clearly a cheap coat and shabby boots had nevertheless managed to brighten her outfit with the addition of a striking piece of headgear.

Whoever the ladies were, none of them was Scaramel. From

all Roland had heard of Scaramel she would never have been
seen – let alone sketched – in such dowdy apparel.

He zoomed the image up again in order to read the title.

Beneath it, Loretta had typed, 'Family group with the great-
great (one more "great"?) aunts, outside L/L, *c*.1890s'.

Roland sat for a very long time staring at the sketch. So Loretta
had had great – several-times great – aunts, who had been drawn
standing outside Linklighters. They might have been there by
chance; they might simply have been looking round London,
perhaps shopping in Harlequin Court itself, and been captured
by a street artist outside Linklighters. But there might be a
stronger connection. And if there was, that could certainly
explain Loretta's eagerness to get the place and renovate it.

But either way, surely there was no reason for her not to
have mentioned it?

Loretta arrived home about midnight, poured herself a glass
of wine, handed one to Roland, then kicked off her shoes and
flopped down on the sofa.

'It's unusual to find you still up when I get back,' she said.

Without realizing he had been going to say it, Roland asked,
'Who were the great aunts sketched outside Linklighters?'

It was not often he had seen Loretta thrown off balance,
but she was certainly thrown by this. She did not flinch physically, but Roland felt her do so mentally. After a moment she
said, in a voice that was just a little too bright, 'How on earth
did you know about that? Oh, of course – you must have seen
that little sketch on my laptop.'

'I did. I wasn't prying,' said Roland, anxious not to be
suspected of this. 'I was looking for . . . for an invoice for the
next tax return.' He was surprised at himself for having thought
of this, but it sounded credible. 'I saw you'd uploaded some
shots of the restaurant,' he said, 'and I was interested.'

'Fair enough.' She got up to refill her glass.

Roland watched her, then said, 'Why didn't you tell me you
had a . . . a family link to Linklighters? Or was the sketch
just coincidence – did they just happen to be in Harlequin
Court one day?'

'It was a bit more than coincidence, and it was a bit more than them just being there one day.' Loretta sipped her wine. 'One of them worked at Linklighters,' she said. 'I don't know which of them it was, though, and "worked for" doesn't necessarily mean performing on the stage. It could have been anything from scrubbing the floors to painting scenery or acting as pot boy. I'm rather sorry you found the sketch,' she said, 'although I suppose I shouldn't have put it on the laptop. But the original's quite fragile, so I scanned it in to preserve it.'

'Why didn't you tell me about them? They all looked nice,' said Roland. 'I rather liked that one who'd tried to jazz up an old outfit with an extravagant hat. I found that quite endearing.'

'One of them's supposed to have had an eye for nice clothes,' said Loretta. 'I've always thought it was that one. None of them ever had a brass farthing, but apparently one of the girls used to scour second-hand clothes' shops and market stalls for things she could adapt or remake.'

'Who drew the sketch?'

'No idea. It was most likely one of those street artists, though. I found it in my grandmother's things after she died. On the back she'd written, "Family group – great-aunts, outside Linklighters, early 1890s".'

'What about the man?' asked Roland. 'Who was he?'

'I don't know. A brother or a cousin, maybe. Or the husband of one of them.'

'Why didn't you show me the sketch?'

Loretta had been staring into her glass of wine, but now she turned her head to look at him. 'There are some ancestors you can talk about quite openly,' she said, slowly. 'You can share their stories, and it's all very nice, and it reminds you that you belong to a family, even though none of them is around. But you only do that for the nice ancestors – the lively characters, or the ones who made a success of their lives. Because there are others, and their stories are far darker . . .' A frown twisted her face, then she said, 'Roland, be honest, would you have married me if you'd known—'

'Known what?'

'That I had an ancestor who was shut away in an asylum?'

This was the last thing Roland had been expecting, but after a moment he said, 'Yes, of course I would. It must have been a very long time ago, and those things – madness and so on – aren't hereditary anyway.'

'I don't think you would have married me,' said Loretta. With a kind of bitter anger, she said, 'And if your mother had known, she would certainly have used it to get rid of me.'

This was true, of course; Mother would have seized on it with triumph. Roland said, 'It was one of those people in the group? The . . . the one who was put in an asylum?'

'They had very bad childhoods,' said Loretta, almost as if she was repeating something learned by heart a long time ago. 'The stories were handed down – those last years of the eighteenth century aren't so very far back, you know. Only three, or maybe four, generations. I expect the details got skewed over the years – bits might have got added on, or other bits might have been forgotten. But at the heart of it is imprisonment in one of those old Victorian asylums. And they were terrible places, Roland. Cruel. Inhuman. I grew up hearing the stories. One version said there had never been any insanity at all – that it had been faked.'

'Why?'

'How should I know? But people did do that for unwanted relatives. There was another version, though, that said it was entirely justified – that there had been violence and cruelty. Even murder. I've no idea how true any of that is. But when I found the sketch, I went to see the place where it was drawn. It was easy enough – if you look closely at the original, you can see where the artist had drawn in the words, *Harlequin Court*, on the edge of a wall.' She made a brief, impatient gesture with one hand. 'And as soon as I found it – as soon as I saw Linklighters, I wanted it,' she said. 'I wanted it for that ancestor whose name I never knew, but who might not have been mad – who might have been shut away for ever, perfectly sane.'

'One of those four people in the sketch?'

'That's how I thought of it. And the dates are about right, I think. I wanted to . . . to make up for what had happened. To put success where there'd been failure and loss and tragedy. Because tragedy faced that group,' she said. 'It was waiting for them in their future. Linklighters became a kind of symbol of that. I was determined to get it somehow. I'd tried two or three times to link up with men with money, but I'd never managed it. Until I met you. You were the best possibility I'd ever found.'

'Yes, I see.' Roland had to stop himself from asking her if it had only ever been about the money.

'D'you know, all those months it was being renovated, I sometimes thought I saw that little group in the sketch,' she said, softly. 'I'd imagine they were standing in Harlequin Court, watching. Approving of everything I was doing. I'd sometimes talk to them, just quietly, when no one was around. Explain to them what was going on. I'd say, "See how it's all going to come right."' She sent him a sideways look. 'And now you'll think there really was madness and that I've inherited it.'

'No. Which one of the four d'you think was shut away in the asylum?' said Roland, suddenly.

'I don't know.'

But even as she said this, something cold and sad seemed to breathe into the warm room, and the image of the figure on the right-hand side of the sketch came back to Roland. Small, a bit birdlike, but with an air of cheerfulness about the way she faced the camera and about the jaunty angle of the lavishly trimmed bonnet. He found himself wondering what her name had been.

SEVENTEEN

Phin had almost forgotten promising to accompany Toby to the Marble Arch pub that evening, and by the time he had disentangled his mind from Links and found a clean shirt, it was already seven o'clock. It was after eight when they reached the pub, and the evening was already in full swing, with a group of people singing ballads from the pub's collection.

'I think it's a bit of a tradition here, this singing,' explained Toby, as the group embarked on a gleeful rendition of a macabre ballad entitled 'The Maid Freed from the Gallows'.

They collected drinks, ordered two platefuls of the pub's pasta bake, and found a table. The food arrived promptly, and they ate to the accompaniment of another, equally lugubrious ballad involving a hapless lady living in Manchester Street and a lascivious but ill-fated coachman. This was cheered loudly, after which Toby went off in search of the promised scrapbooks. Phin had another drink, and somehow found himself drawn into the conversation of an earnest trio who were discussing criminal lunacy.

'They had no rights, those poor sods who were thrown into the madhouses,' explained one of them to Phin, clearly considering that Phin's presence was sufficient credential to include him in their conversation. 'And the treatment they were given . . . Well, for my money, most of them might have been better hanged, because, believe you me, it'd have been a living death in those places. Years and years they'd be there. Entire lifetime for most of them.'

'And the crime didn't have to be serious, either,' put in the girl sitting next to him. She was wearing fashionably torn jeans, and was typing notes on a tablet in the intervals between drinking cider. 'Pilfer a couple of blankets or an apple from a costermonger, and you could be chucked into a madhouse for years. Bethlem, Colney Hatch, Broadmoor.'

'Still, some of them did come out. There are documented cases of that.'

'It was the luck of the draw,' said the girl. 'And whether you'd got money or knew people on high.'

'Yes, think of Charles Lamb's sister,' said the second man, pushing his glasses back on his nose. 'That's Charles Lamb the poet,' he added to Phin.

'Yes. *Lamb's Tales from Shakespeare*. Friend of Coleridge and Wordsworth,' said Phin, then hoped this did not sound as if he was puffing off his erudition.

But the bespectacled one said, 'Praise the gods for a man of knowledge. Have another drink on the grounds of that.'

'Well, I've already had . . . Oh, thank you.' It was easier

to accept the drink which looked like a double. Phin had no idea if it was whisky or brandy. He tried it and still had no idea.

'Anyway, Charlie Lamb's sister stabbed their mother—'

'And should have gone to the gallows for it,' said the girl, at once. 'Privilege of the rich, that's all that got her off. Disgraceful.'

'No, they judged her insane, and she was put in Islington Asylum,' said the man who appeared to be the group's leader.

'But she was let out – that's the point I'm making.'

'Ah, but there's that tale about how she felt the madness starting up again, and she and poor old Charles walked across the fields to put her back inside. Arms around one another, sobbing as they went. Bloody heartbreaking. Where's my drink?'

Phin said, 'You're all very knowledgeable.'

'Wait till you read the book we're writing.'

'If we ever manage to finish it.'

'If we ever manage to even start it.'

'Have any of you ever heard of an asylum called The Thrawl?' said Phin, suddenly. He had not realized he had been going to ask this. He thought the place in Links's sketch was probably an asylum, but it was also likely that it had never existed outside of Links's imagination. But the man who had bought the drinks, said, 'Thrawl. *Thrawl.* There's a Thrawl Street, isn't there? I think it's on one of those Jack the Ripper walking tours.'

'Oh, Jack the Ripper got everywhere if you can believe the tours,' said the girl. 'Like all the beds Elizabeth I's supposed to have slept in. She was never even near most of them. Still, Jack might have bought his tobacco or his newspaper in Thrawl Street, I suppose. If you can imagine him doing something so mundane as reading a newspaper.'

'I don't see why not. Murderers aren't murdering every hour of the day. They have to do ordinary things like – like grocery shopping or paying the rent. I grant you it's difficult to imagine Jack the Ripper asking for a pound of apples or queueing up at the fish shop for a bit of cod for his supper . . . And *don't* say he only ate kidneys, please don't.'

'He'd want to read the papers,' said the man with glasses,

seriously. 'Specially the local ones – to find out what was being said about him.'

'Hold on, though, wasn't The Thrawl one of those old asylums they called tunnel houses?' said the first man, ignoring this side-road.

'What on earth is a tunnel house?' asked Phin, and the man said, 'Means once in you couldn't get out. One-way street. Those were the really grim institutions in those days. Think Broadmoor set in darkest Transylvania, or Dante's Ninth Circle of Hell.'

'There weren't many tunnel houses though,' said the other man, 'because there was that fashion for people to visit asylums – to do – what did they call it? "View the lunatics".'

'Sunday afternoon outing,' put in the girl, disparagingly. 'Ranked about equal with public hangings.'

'At least they stopped in . . . well, around the middle of the nineteenth century.

'Nobody could ever go inside the tunnel houses,' said the trio's leader to Phin. 'Visitors weren't ever let in.'

Visitors weren't ever let in. The words jabbed into Phin's mind. But alongside this was the fact that The Thrawl had existed and had indeed been a madhouse. But if visitors had not been allowed in, there was only one way that Links could have gone in there. But Links did not need to have been inside – he could simply have known about the place, and the sketch might still have come from his imagination.

Phin said, 'Was the place, this asylum – The Thrawl – actually in Thrawl Street?'

'If it was, it isn't there now,' said the leader. 'I only know about it because I remember seeing it referred to in some archive or other. Tower Hamlets library, I think it was. We're making a detailed study of all the London madhouses, so we've been all over the city. Hell of a task it is, as well. Needs a few drinks to oil the wheels.'

'My round,' said Phin, taking the hint and getting up.

He could not, afterwards, remember how it was that he ended up seated at a battered piano next to the main bar, extemporizing accompaniments to several of the songs that were still being sung. He was quite surprised to find he could still sight-read, although it was as well that most of the drinkers were singing loudly enough to cover up all the wrong notes.

Toby, enthusiastically joining in with this, read out the verse about the sinister ghost river beds, which went down well, and resulted in Phin being urged to try to match up music to it so it could be sung with suitable gusto.

He thought it was as well Arabella was not here to witness this uncharacteristic behaviour, but then he realized that Arabella would have loved it; she would have entered into the spirit of it all with great enthusiasm, and she would probably have found several more songs for everyone to sing. He remembered how she had once said she had never yet heard him play the piano, and that he had promised he would play something romantic to her. At the time, he had had in mind something on the lines of Jerome Kern's 'The Way You Look Tonight', or perhaps, 'Take My Hand, I'm a Stranger in Paradise', to a background of a candlelit restaurant over-looking a rose-filled garden. Songs about a maid consigned to the gallows for mangling an errant lover, belted out at top range in a London pub, did not quite meet the case.

'I didn't know you could do that, old man,' said Toby, as they got out of their taxi considerably later, and tiptoed a bit unsteadily into the house.

'Do what? Don't make such a row, you'll wake everyone up.'

'Vamp on the piano like that.'

'I can't,' said Phin. 'Not very well, at any rate. You must have heard all the wrong notes. And you wouldn't have heard middle C at all, because it wouldn't play.'

'It was still bloody good. I couldn't do it.'

'Yes, but I couldn't whip out an appendix.'

'Nor could I at the moment.' Toby made vague stabbing and slicing gestures at the air, almost overbalancing with the effort. 'See what I mean?' he said. 'Ah well, I'll get along to my bed. It's a solitary one tonight, but at least it isn't a Pig-in-the-Dyke ghost bed where you get mangled and tangled.'

He began to sing,

'O, never be lured to the ghost river beds,

Only sleep in a bed where you're safe.

In a ghost river bed, you could end up quite dead,

On some terrible night—'

'For pity's sake don't make such a row,' said Phin. 'It's nearly midnight.'

'Is it?' said Toby. 'By God, so it is. Midnight, the witching hour, as I live and breathe.' He began to sing again:

'It was on the bridge at midnight,

Throwing snowballs at the moon.

She said, "Sir, I've never had it",

But she spoke too bloody soon.'

'Toby, you'll wake everyone up,' said Phin, torn between helpless laughter and a sudden desire to join in with the next verse. 'People will come storming out and complain. And you'll probably give dear old Miss Pringle nightmares.'

'Heaven forfend. You're perfectly right, of course. G'night.' He sketched a vague farewell gesture, followed it with a reasonable attempt at a courtly bow in the direction of the garden flat, then clumped along the corridor to his door.

Phin, letting himself into his own flat, hoped he was not going to dream about Victorian madhouses where people were locked away from the world for ever, and where visitors were not allowed.

With the idea of dispelling these potentially troubling shades, he checked his emails, hoping for something cheerful, and smiled when he saw Arabella's name. If anybody was guaranteed to dispel darkness and chase away ghosts, it was Arabella. He opened the email and began to read.

> I do hope that you're still tangling enthusiastically with Liszt and Scaramel, because I might have found another intriguing piece for the jigsaw.
>
> You remember I said I'd look for traces of Scaramel here? I thought it was a very long shot indeed – and I think you did, as well, although you were too polite to actually say so, of course.
>
> But I hit on the idea of searching through back numbers

of old French magazines – the gossipy kind – early versions of *Hello!* and those other ones that have reports of all the celebrities and the riotous parties and scandals. Scaramel was a bit of a celebrity in her day, and we know she was in Paris because of that framed playbill at Linklighters. So I thought she could have got into a few gossip columns while she was here.

I mentioned at the agency that I had promised to follow up a few bits of research for you, and they were interested. I didn't give anything away about your project, of course, just general information. Somebody suggested *Le Charivari*, and then somebody else offered to make an introduction to the present incarnation of *La Vie Parisienne*. The original magazine apparently closed in 1970, but a paper of the same name started up in 1984, and the thought was that their offices might have old copies of the original set-up.

I dashed along to the offices the next day and it turned out that they did have old copies from the original set-up! Not all of them, of course – there were expressive mutterings about *Les Boches* and the devastation inflicted during WWII – but there was still quite a lot of archived stuff.

At first I couldn't think where to start, but I remembered you emailing about that memorial concert for Liszt – you thought Scaramel had organized it – so I thought that might provide a starting point, because it meant she must have been in Paris in 1896. So I started with that year, and I found an article about her! It's only a kind of gossip column item about a birthday party, but it gives a slightly different slant on things, and there are one or two names that might be useful. The staff let me photocopy the article, and I said if it formed any part of your final work, you would arrange to give them a suitable credit. (Was that all right?)

I'm sending the photocopy as an attachment, with my translation. I'm also sending a request to all the appropriate gods that they ensure both copies reach you intact . . . Is there a god of the internet, or would somebody like St Christopher, who looks benignly on travellers, be best, or maybe Mercury with winged heels? Anyway, I hope they'll reach you uncorrupted and inviolate.

I'm missing you a huge amount, Phin, dear.

Arabella

Phin smiled at the last sentence, and opened the attachment marked '*Translation*'. Across the top, Arabella had typed, 'From *La Vie Parisenne*, dated August 1896.'

It was a report of a party held a week after the formal 'Liszten to the Symphonies' memorial concert, and it was apparently to celebrate the birthday of someone whom *La Vie Parisienne* called '*le très distingué*' Welsh poet, Rhun Rhydderch. Beneath this, Arabella had put, 'Could this be the mysterious Welshman who wrote the murder song?'

LIVELY EVENING AT MAISON DANS LE PARC

A lavish birthday party was given at Maison dans le Parc by the English nightclub entertainer, Scaramel, to mark the birthday of her close friend, the distinguished Welsh poet, Mr Rhun Rhydderch – known among the English community as 'Rhun the Rhymer'.

The couple have been staying in Paris for the last three months, and are often to be seen in Paris's cafés and nightclubs. Readers will no doubt recall the dazzling performance that Scaramel gave at the Moulin Rouge last month, which brought several encores. [See photograph on page 4].

Here, Arabella had added a note in italics: *Phin – sorry couldn't find photograph – page 4 doesn't seem to have survived.*

Scaramel looked stunning for the occasion, wearing a gown of emerald silk, which our fashion editor tells us is from the house of M'sieur Worth.

The tables were presided over by no less a personage than Monsieur Alphonse himself, and a number of English performers had travelled to Paris for the birthday celebration.

Several of them provided entertainment on the restaurant's small dais after supper.

Two charming sisters, Fancy and Frankie Finnegan, tap-danced, and Miss Dora Dashington (Dances to Delight You), treated the company to a spirited rendition of 'A Little of What You Fancy', with a gentleman wearing a hat playing the piano, accompanied by a personage with an English banjo.

Mr Thaddeus Thumbprint [sic] appeared dressed in the manner of Mr Charles Dickens, and read extracts from *The Pickwick Papers*, which were brought to life by three English actors, enacting the scenes.

It is unfortunate that a small altercation marred the later part of the evening. We understand that an English singer, Miss Belinda Baskerville ('the Gentlemen's Choice'), was preparing to give her own performance, but was prevented from it by Scaramel, on the threefold grounds that her style and the song she proposed to sing would not suit the occasion, that she had not been invited, and that she was seldom able to hit more than one accurate note in ten.

Scaramel stalked majestically to the door of the restaurant, and held it open, tapping one foot impatiently as Miss Baskerville collected her cloak, fan and gloves. M'sier Alphonse himself escorted her across the restaurant – ignoring, with his customary tact and politeness, the stares of the diners – and snapped his fingers to an underling to find transport for the lady.

Our photographer was again on the spot, and captured an image of her flouncing into a hansom cab outside Maison. [See page 9].

Again, Arabella had added a note of apology: *Phin, again no trace of any photo of the flouncing Baskerville!*

Readers will know that Scaramel's hospitality has become famous in Paris, even in the short time she has been here, and may recall how this magazine reported on a dinner hosted last month at Maison, when she entertained the

English author, Mr H. G. Wells, and several other notable names, including M'sieur Anatole France, who fell off his chair and had to be helped out to a cab – an incident our photographer was sadly unable to capture.

'She certainly had style, that Scaramel,' Arabella had written at the foot of the article. 'Might you be able to follow up one or two of these names? I don't mean H. G. Wells, obviously. But there's certainly Rhun the Rhymer Rhydderch, and wasn't Belinda Baskerville on the wall at Linklighters? She sounds a bit of a handful, and clearly she and Scaramel had an ongoing feud.'

Phin remembered seeing a playbill featuring Belinda Baskerville's name at the restaurant, although she had not, until now, occurred to him as a possible line of enquiry. It was interesting to see the Thumbprints name mentioned, as well. But other than Rhun Rhydderch, who probably could not be traced after so long, he could not see that any of this was going to get him much further.

As he was climbing into bed, he found himself wondering why Scaramel had gone to Paris in the first place. Had it simply been to arrange that Liszt memorial concert? Or had there been something else – something in London she had wanted to escape from? Such as the consequences of having committed murder?

But Phin did not want Scaramel to have been a murderess. He wanted her to remain in his mind as the insouciant, defiantly disreputable lady who had frequently shocked London, and who had delighted Parisian society. The lady who had danced for the Prince of Wales and other luminaries of the day, and had cavorted across the stage of the Moulin Rouge and enjoyed public and dramatic quarrels with rivals. He had a vague idea that all this was probably the fantasizing of a hopeless romantic, or that he might be seeing things through rose-coloured – or maybe whiskey-tinted – glasses.

Even so, he did not want to find that Scaramel had scuttled out of England like a hunted creature fleeing the gallows.

EIGHTEEN

1890s

'Leave London?' Daisy looked at Madame with a mixture of disbelief and panic. 'Leave England?'

'Yes, but only for a few months. Probably only three – say five or six at the very most. But we'd be leaving all the . . . the bad memories behind for a while, Daisy. *All* of them.'

All of the bad memories. All of the secrets and the menace . . .

Daisy said, 'But where would we go?'

'France,' said Madame. '*Paris.*' Her eyes started to dance. 'I've had invitations,' she said. 'To appear in nightclubs. Moulin Rouge even – no, I know you've never heard of it, but believe me, Daisy, it's very famous indeed. If I can't cause a few flutters in the audiences there, then I'm no kind of entertainer!'

'But where would we live? And would the twins come?' The enormity of the whole thing was engulfing Daisy.

'Of course the twins would come,' said Madame. 'It will be very good for them. Travel broadens the mind. As for where we live – you remember the lady who brought the music we used for "Liszten"? The music her father wanted me to have?'

'Yes, I remember,' said Daisy, hastily, because even now she could not bear to remember that strange music.

'Well, it's partly because of her that I've decided to accept the other invitations,' said Madame. 'She wants to arrange a memorial concert for her father in Paris – it's ten years this summer since he died. I said I'd take charge of it. It'll be interesting and worthwhile.'

'But you can't speak French,' said Daisy, a bit helplessly.

'Oh, that's a small detail. We'll find people who can interpret. Wait a moment and I'll show you the letter,' said Madame, foraging in the desk. 'It's here somewhere . . . This is it.'

'There is an apartment which I could arrange for you to

have for a few weeks, my dear friend,' said the letter. 'A delightful place, with a small balcony overlooking the river. The rent would be a modest affair. If you come, I will send letters of introduction around for you. As you know, I do not live in Paris, but I grew up there, and I know people.

'Most of my time is spent here in Bayreuth. The Festival, which I direct here – to keep alive the music of my beloved husband, Richard – takes up most of my time. If ever you can travel here, you would be most welcome to stay with me as my guest. That is something I should greatly enjoy. For the rest – I am very happy to make these arrangements in gratitude for the concert you are arranging for my father, and also in appreciation of the good memories you gave to him near the end of his life.

I am yours very affectionately,
Cosima Wagner.'

Daisy had supposed that going to France – going to *Paris* – would be a relatively simple matter of packing their clothes and some of Madame's favourite possessions, and getting on a train. There had to be a boat at some point, too; she knew that, of course, although she did not know how that worked. Madame would know, though.

But it had not occurred to Daisy that the Maida Vale flat would have to be dealt with in any way. In Daisy's world you walked out of your house and left a key with the man who collected the rent (when you could afford to pay it), and went on to wherever you were going.

But Madame said the lease did not allow her to leave the flat empty for longer than one month, and since they would be away for at least three, there would have to be what was called a sublet, which was a word Daisy did not know. She felt she was learning a good deal, although she was not sure if she was entirely understanding all of it.

But Madame said she was buggered if she was going to pay out good money to lawyers, who were the most cheating race of bastards in the world. Daisy thought it was to be hoped Madame did not use such language in front of the twins, because it would not be good for them to grow up thinking they could use words like bugger and bastard, and one or two more that Madame sometimes sprinkled around when she was annoyed or impatient. Still, Daisy and Joe – Lissy and Vi, too, of course – had all grown up in a place where people cursed and swore without thinking about it, and somehow they had all acquired an understanding of which words you could and could not use when you needed to be polite.

Rhun made enthusiastic plans to visit them while they were in Paris. He would not intrude on his beloved's riverside apartment, he said; he would find himself modest rooms on the Left Bank for a week here and there. On the Rive Gauche he would be among kindred spirits – he would become part of Parisian café society. Nowhere else in the world could you dine in a restaurant where presidents and poets, artists and anarchists – and very likely a clutch of courtesans – were gathered together at adjoining tables.

But this flat, said Rhun, looking around the rooms, must be sublet in a businesslike way. Property had to be respected, and they did not want to end up with a set of crooks living in the house, spoiling the nice furnishings, defacing the expensive wallpaper and goodness knew what else, not to mention upsetting the neighbours.

'That's true,' said Madame, thoughtfully. 'You sometimes talk quite good sense, Rhun – no, that doesn't mean I shall marry you, because I don't want to marry anyone.'

'Didn't you ever want to get married?' asked Daisy, curiously, after Rhun had gone.

'Maybe once I did.' An unfamiliar expression crossed Madame's face. 'Yes, maybe once there was someone,' she said, then appeared to give herself a small shake. 'It wasn't to be, though. It wasn't possible.' Her face held the very rare shuttered look, and Daisy knew not to press her.

Then, two days later, Madame said, 'Daisy I know what I'm going to do about this flat.'

'What?'

'I'm going to let Thaddeus Thumbprint take it over.'

This turned out to be a very good plan. Thaddeus Thumbprint was the owner of the bookshop above Linklighters – the shop that had sold some of Joe's sketches. It appeared that he had been looking for somewhere larger to live for a while, on account of his own little house being too small to house his collection of books, and so shockingly damp into the bargain that all of his furnishings were becoming mildewed. Also, his cousin was going to come into partnership at Thumbprints and it would be useful and practical if they could share a house. Or an apartment.

Nobody could pronounce Thaddeus's surname, so everyone called him simply Thaddeus Thumbprint. He did not mind at all. His family were all very proud of the shop, which had been started by his grandfather, who had come to England in the days of old King George – the one people said had been as mad as a March hare.

The two cousins were delighted to have the Maida Vale flat for three months, or a little longer; it would give them time to look round for something more permanent, they said. Daisy was called in to the sitting room to watch Thaddeus Thumbprint sign his name on a legal piece of paper that said he could live in the flat for up to six months. She had to write her own name to say she had seen him do it. Rhun wrote his name as well, to say the same thing.

'Witnesses to the deed, the both of us,' Rhun said to Daisy. 'It's a very solemn and important matter to witness a legal transaction.' He had added his name with so many flourishes that Daisy wondered if anyone would ever be able to read it. She was grateful, though, to the retired schoolmistress in Rogues Well Yard who had taught her to write a neat, clear hand.

Thaddeus Thumbprint was delighted with the flat. It was charming, he said, and everything in such good taste – although perhaps there would be no objection if he just moved the scarlet brocade chaise longue out, and brought in his own? And he might, if Scaramel did not mind, put the black silk bed sheets away in the linen cupboard, and make use of his own which were best Egyptian cotton.

He was a wispy, mild-mannered little man, given to wearing high-wing collars and rimless spectacles which he frequently pushed up on to his forehead, and then thought he had lost them. His cousin was mild-mannered, as well, although not quite so wispy. Thaddeus could undoubtedly be trusted to pay the various charges for the flat, and to do so on time each month. He would look after the flat and he certainly would not hold wild parties or permit raucous behaviour on the premises. The two gentlemen would probably give small supper parties for their friends, at which they would discuss scholarly and learned subjects and chuckle over passages in books that hardly anyone read and could not understand anyway.

The neighbours in the flat below, who had hammered crossly on the door during one of Madame and Rhun's livelier bouts of love-making, came up to be introduced to Thaddeus and his cousin. They were very pleased to be having such well-behaved and congenial neighbours, and although they did not quite say that they hoped Madame would take up permanent residence in Paris, Daisy could see that they were thinking it.

Everything was going very well.

Daisy had not expected to like Paris, but even though it was not home and never would be, she discovered she was able to enjoy it. She loved the buildings and the bustle which was not so very different from London, really. There were marvellous shops and cafés, and after a while Daisy even began to understand a little of what people were saying. She started to recognize a few words here and there, and presently she found enough courage to go into a shop and buy things, mostly by pointing, but managing to make herself understood. People did not seem to mind that she could not speak French; they smiled and shrugged and said, quite kindly, *Ah, les Anglais*, which Madame said meant, Oh, the English. She and Madame went to the famous fashion houses, and Madame bought the most beautiful gowns and lengths of silk and velvet for making up that Daisy had ever seen. There was lace-trimmed underwear, fine as cobwebs, and hats so elaborate you would almost be afraid to wear them.

There were nightclubs too, of course, and also some theatres where Madame was invited to perform.

'That's Cosima Wagner's doing,' she said, winking at Daisy.

'I'd better tone down my act, hadn't I? Out of respect for her papa.'

She did tone it down, but not very much and not for very long.

She certainly did not tone it down for her performances at the Moulin Rouge, or for Rhun's birthday party, which they celebrated in a French restaurant with a number of Madame's performer friends travelling to Paris to join in.

She did, though, dress with unusual decorum and behave with an unexpected dignity for the memorial concert. Daisy was extremely relieved at that.

And home did not seem so very far away when there were letters coming to them. Thaddeus Thumbprint wrote quite often – he and his cousin had settled in very well, and he liked to send little reports of the flat, and of how the shop was doing. He and his cousin were going to start a little literary society there on Thursday evenings. They would invite writers and novelists and journalists to give little talks.

'Rhun has already agreed to give a talk,' wrote Thaddeus. 'Cedric and I think our grandfather would have been very pleased to see our prosperity.

'I must let you know that a small patch of damp appeared in the small sitting room overlooking the park. It was beneath a window and seems to have been caused by a leaking gutter immediately outside. The lease states clearly that I am responsible for ensuring the rooms are kept in good order, so I have had the gutter repaired, and have had the room newly wallpapered, with the damp plaster renewed. We chose what we think is a very tasteful silk stripe wallpaper in maroon and biscuit colour. I enclose a small sample, together with a piece of maroon brocade, which has been made up into new curtains for that room. It all matches beautifully.'

Reading this, Madame said that when they got back she would have to have the entire room redone, because she could not possibly live with maroon and biscuit. Still, at least the Thumbprints were taking good care of the place.

There was occasionally a letter for Daisy, too.

'Dear Daise,' wrote Lissy.

'I got Bowler Bill to write this for me – ain't much of a

one for the writing and stuff, as you know. He don't mind writing it, and he'll see about sending it in the post, too.

'He told us all about seeing you for Rhun's birthday and the posh party you had. Wish we could've come to that, but I ain't never been out of London, nor I don't want to. My Albie says wild horses wouldn't drag him across that English Channel! Funny, that, him having that Spanish mother. We called the kids Spanish names, though. Sort of a nod to her.

'I been helping at the Ten Bells of a Saturday night – making the pies mostly. Means a few extra bob every week, and very nice too. We was none of us ever afraid of hard work, was we? I'm bringing my girls up that way – Lita's been helping me with the pies, she's getting to be a real good cook. I told her, there's money to be made from good cooking, gel. Both the girls send their Auntie Daisy lots of love.

'Joe's still at Linklighters, and them two old boys from the bookshop keep an eye on him. I reckon he'll be all right, our Joe. I reckon we'll all be proud of him one day.

'Ma got together with Peg the Rags and they got a little stall in a couple of the street markets now. Me and Vi, we got some smashing bargains there – real good stuff for trimming bonnets, and bits of fur and some nice lengths of lace, too. We found Ma better rooms, as well. 'Bout time she got out of that rat-hole. Bit shabby at first, but we spruced them up a treat – my Albie even painted the walls. He said best not ask where he got the paint. You know Albie! Seth Strumble, that has a market stall alongside Ma and Peg, brought his street-barrow to help with the move. Should have seen us all carting the stuff through the streets! Right old laugh we had.

'We all miss you.

'Fondest love from us all, Lissy.'

Daisy was pleased to hear from Lissy, and she was pleased about Ma's new rooms as well. She asked Madame about sending a bit of money to help with the new place; she had no idea how such a thing might be done, she said, and she did not want to send money in an envelope through the post. But Madame knew what to do, and she arranged everything, and insisted on adding a couple of guineas extra.

'For your ma to buy something special for the new place,' she said.

'Dear Scaramel,' wrote Thaddeus Thumbprint, a few weeks later, 'all is well with our world here. You might be interested to know that my cousin, Cedric, recently met a former fellow-performer of yours, Miss Belinda Baskerville. The encounter took place at Linklighters, where Miss Baskerville had been entertaining a Thursday-night audience. Cedric had been presiding over one of our literary circle meetings earlier, and he met her afterwards. A purely chance meeting it was.

'I recall that you and Miss Baskerville seemed to have some kind of small misunderstanding on the occasion of Rhun's birthday party at Maison dans le Parc. (What a lovely occasion that was – those of us who could travel to it still talk about it. And didn't the dear twins present their bouquets beautifully!)

I do not know the rights of that little altercation between you and Miss Baskerville, of course, but I am sure it will have been something very trivial, for we have both found the lady to be a charming and sympathetic companion. She and Cedric have taken supper together several times now, and last week she came to luncheon here in Maida Vale, on which occasion she brought with her Miss Frankie Finnegan. A very lively occasion, that was! We ate at the oval table which you have in the dining room, and Cedric cooked mushroom omelettes for us, with a *gratin* of potatoes, and a dessert of peaches in brandy. Miss Baskerville was very taken with the rooms, and greatly enjoyed looking round them.'

'Dear God,' said Madame, reading this missive aloud to Daisy. 'Frankie Finnegan's as nice and kindly a soul as you can get and so is her sister, but the Baskerville will corrupt those innocent Thumbprints, and she'll very likely bankrupt Cedric. Purely chance meeting indeed! And snooping around my rooms! I'm not having that! It's time we thought about going home.'

NINETEEN

1890s

G oing home was not, of course, quite as easy as stepping onto a train and then a boat, which was what they had done when they left London a few months earlier. It was, though, considerably easier than Daisy had dared to hope it might be. This was to a great extent because the Thumbprints had written to say that the large ground-floor flat of the house had just become vacant.

'And this is only the merest suggestion,' wrote Thaddeus, 'but we did wonder whether – what with you having that much larger household now – you might want to consider taking it over? Cedric and I would very much like to stay in these upstairs rooms if so.'

'We'll do it,' said Madame, at once. 'That's a very nice set of rooms indeed. They open on to the gardens – there's one of those glass doors, as I recall. Just right for the twins to run in and out. One of the sitting rooms is rather small, I think, but I remember a deep linen cupboard that might be knocked through. It would open up that room very satisfactorily. I daresay it wouldn't be much of a job to knock a couple of walls down. We'll have to paint and repaper everywhere as well, I should think, but we'll go to Fortnum and Mason or one of those Knightsbridge places.'

'Cost a lot of money,' said Daisy.

'Yes, but I haven't cavorted across all those Parisian stages without getting paid. And Cosima was unexpectedly generous over the arranging of that memorial concert, too. We can afford it.'

Daisy had enjoyed Paris, but she was glad to be back in London. She was glad to see Joe and Ma again. Lissy and Vi too, of course. Joe was still in the rooms with the

Linklighters' barman, working at Linklighters most evenings. He still drew everything he saw, though. The Thumbprints were planning to arrange a little exhibition of his work in their shop window. As Lissy had written, they would all be proud of Joe one day.

It was very good indeed to be back – even though workmen began tramping through the Maida Vale flat, knocking down parts of walls so that there was a big airy drawing room. Everywhere was covered with ladders and dustsheets for days; pots of paint and plaster were carried in and out, and the rooms were filled with the sounds of hammering and sawing, and men cheerfully whistling. Madame said it would be worth it in the end, but Daisy said it was a wretched nuisance and she was never done cleaning up.

Still, in the end everyone was satisfied – or, if they were not, they were too polite to say so.

Linklighters put on a special evening – a gala performance, they called it – to welcome Madame back to London, and on to their own stage. Scaramel was delighted. It would be a wonderful evening, she said.

The Thumbprints designed posters and programmes. Joe helped them and Thaddeus Thumbprint insisted on paying him a small fee.

A midnight supper would be served after the performance. Daisy had managed to get Lissy along to help with that, and Lissy brought Lita with her – Lita had some really good ideas about food. Daisy was very pleased indeed that she had been able to put this bit of work their way.

Invitations were sent to all kinds of important people, and Madame said it was a pity the Prince of Wales could not attend. He would certainly have done so in the past, but now that the Queen, game old girl, seemed finally to be failing, Bertie was starting to take his responsibilities more seriously. But he could tell a few ripe old tales, and so could a great many of the ladies he had known. One day, when the twins were a bit older, she would tell them how he had slyly twanged a garter off her leg while she was dancing near the edge of the stage, and had said he would wear it next to his . . .

'Next to his heart?' said Morwenna hopefully as Madame paused. 'That's what princes in stories do for their ladyloves.'

Madame laughed, and said, well, it had not exactly been his heart the Prince had meant, but it had been somewhere private anyway, at which Daisy hustled the twins off to their beds, because you could not have young ears hearing about such behaviour from a man who would one day be the King of England.

Madame occasionally expressed a friendly curiosity that Daisy had never had a young man – there were plenty around Linklighters and here in Maida Vale, she said – but Daisy had never wanted that kind of relationship for herself. Not after all the things she had seen as a child. Not after living with Pa in Rogues Well Yard.

Come over here to me on the bed, my little love . . . Let's put your hand here . . . She could still hear his voice in her dreams sometimes, quiet and sort of treacly. She could still feel his hands, rough-skinned and jagged-nailed, forcing her own hands down between his legs.

'*Feels good, don't it, Daise . . .? And when you get a man of your own, you'll know what it's all about, wontcha . . .?*'

That had been the start. Later there had been other things, far worse. Painful things. Pa forcing himself inside her body – her own voice crying out, begging him to stop. But he had been panting and his breath had been sour in her face; his hands pinned her down on the bed, and he did not care how much he hurt her.

'*Always hurts first time, Daise,*' he had said. '*Won't kill you . . . You squeal like that an' I'll make it hurt worse . . .*'

Afterwards he had said, '*Don't you go crying to your ma 'bout this. She don't care what we do . . . She don't care what I do with any of you . . . Any case, I'll take my belt to you if you tell her . . .*'

The memories had stayed with Daisy all these years. She knew they would never go away, and she knew, as well, that she would never forget how she had struggled with leaving Ma and Joe and going to live with Madame all those years ago. But Lissy and Vi had urged her to do it. They would look out for Joe, and for Ma too, of course, they said. They would not let Pa get up to his evil ways with Joe – not that it was likely. It was the girls Pa liked. They had looked at one another when Vi said that, and although none of them had said anything else, understanding had been there between them.

So in the end Daisy had accepted Madame's offer, although she had asked if she could be sure of visiting her family at least once a week. Madame had agreed immediately. Families were important, she said.

At first it had seemed all right. On the same day each week, Daisy took a tram to Rogues Well Yard – it was a good feeling to have a few coins in her purse to pay the tram driver, and Madame often gave her a few odds and ends of food to take for Ma. Leftovers, she said, even though Daisy knew they were not always leftovers at all. But Ma was pleased to have the food, and always asked Daisy to be sure to thank her kind mistress.

And then had come that day that burned itself into Daisy's mind. When she looked back, she saw the day as a kind of grisly marker jutting up out of the years: like a bloodied milestone that had been set down at the side of a road. Later, there had been other milestones, of course.

It had all seemed entirely ordinary at first. It had been a dark afternoon, with a thin, spiteful rain falling, but there had been part of a leg of ham to take with her, carefully wrapped in waxed paper to keep it fresh. Daisy had hopped down from the tram, and walked quickly along the alley, swinging the food basket and going lightly up the narrow stairway that was shared with several other families. She was looking forward to seeing Ma and Joe and to giving Ma the ham, and she was hoping Pa would be in the Cock & Sparrow, which was likely if he had any money. It was unusual not to see Joe waiting to meet her off the tram tonight, but there could be any number of reasons for that.

She went across the yard with the huddled buildings on each side, up the steps to Ma's rooms, and pushed open the door, calling out that she was here, and that Madame had sent them some ham.

At first she thought no one was at home. Still, if Pa had gone along to the Cock & Sparrow, Ma might have gone with him to get one of their pies for supper. Joe might have gone, too.

Then somehow – she did not know how – she was aware that someone was here after all. She called out again, and there was a kind of scuffling and a half-cry from the inner room, where Ma and Pa had their bed. When Daisy and her sisters were at home they had slept in a corner of this main room; Joe had a pallet in the far corner.

Joe. Daisy had always known she had what was almost an extra sense where Joe was concerned. That sense reared up now, so strong it was almost like a hand pulling her forward. She ran across the room, not noticing that she had let the basket with the ham fall to the floor, and pushed open the inner door, banging it against the wall.

That extra sense had been right. Joe was there – he was lying on the bed, his small face distorted with pain and fear, his face streaked with tears, and the dark hair that felt like silk to the touch, tumbling over his forehead. He was naked, his small limbs spread out, white and thin, and unbearably vulnerable.

Pa was half kneeling over him, his breeches open, his hands clutching Joe's small hands, forcing him to perform the intimacies that once they had forced from Daisy, and from Vi and Lissy as well. Terrible. Ugly and vicious and warped. And only the start of what would happen later on.

Daisy did not pause to think or reason. She flew straight at Pa, not thinking or caring that he was a big, heavily built man, with shoulders and neck like a bull. Her small hands beat at him in blind fury, and she could hear someone shouting words like filth and devil and evil. It was a shock to suddenly realize it was her own voice screaming those words – that she was using gutter expressions that she had always tried not to use. She did not care. It was all true.

Joe had tumbled off the bed, and Daisy saw him reach for a shirt and the ragged breeches he always wore, and scramble shakily into them.

Pa had fallen back against the wall, his face the ugly purple hue it always was when he was angry or drunk.

'Get out of this place,' said Daisy, shaking with such rage she could hardly speak. She aimed a vicious kick at him, feeling a surge of triumph when he yelled in pain. 'Don't come back, and don't never touch Joe again, or I'll take a knife to you,' she shouted.

'Bitch,' he said, spitting out the word. 'Useless bit of rubbish, you are.'

For a terrible moment Daisy thought he was going to grab her and force her on to the bed, but as he clutched ineffectually at his open breeches, she could see that the warped arousal had already wilted.

She laughed. 'You're the useless one. Look at you. Much use as a melting candle, you are. Bugger off, 'fore I take the bread knife to you.'

She had not really believed he would go, but he stumbled across the room, cursing her, his small mean eyes glowering when he looked back over his shoulder.

Daisy watched him go down the stairs and stagger across the yard, then she went back to Joe and knelt down in front of him.

'Joe, you won't have to face this again. I'm going to make it all right. I'm going to make you safe.'

He shivered and wiped the back of his hand across his face.

'Did I ever let you down?' said Daisy. 'Or lie to you?'

He gave a small, scared shake of the head, and looked up at her. It tore at Daisy's heart to see the trust in his face.

'I ain't lying now, and I won't let you down, neither. You won't see that evil creature again, no one will.' She got up. 'Where's Ma – getting pies for supper, is she? You stay where you are, and you'll be safe, I promise you.'

She folded him in a quick hug, and went out.

It was almost completely dark by this time, and the rain had lain a faint mist over the streets. The ground was uneven, but Daisy almost ran, because she wanted to catch up with Pa.

All around her, she could hear the familiar street sounds – cheerful shouts of people, footsteps, wooden wheels rattling across the cobblestones. Then she saw him, making an unsteady way along the street. She quickened her footsteps, but kept close to the buildings, so that the shadows hid her. The hatred was scalding through her, because this monster, this evil creature, could force Joe to bring him to an obscene satisfaction, just as he used to do with Daisy and her sisters. Hands, first. Later, he used their bodies . . . Sluicing them out, Vi had once called it, saying it with such angry bitterness that Daisy had understood Vi was covering up the memories by using the language of the streets and the terms of the prostitutes.

Not for the first time, Daisy wondered whether Ma had ever known what had gone on. Even if she had, she would have been too scared to do anything about it. A bloodied nose, a broken arm or cracked ribs would have been the result – for Ma and probably for Joe, as well. As for throwing Pa out – Ma would not have the courage.

So it was up to Daisy.

Pa would be going to the Cock & Sparrow tonight, of course. He could go across Fossan's Yard, along by the flat, bleak wall of The Thrawl, or he could take the towpath leading off Canal Alley. There was nothing in it for actual distance, but most people avoided Fossan's Yard because of it being overlooked by The Thrawl.

Pa was some way ahead of her, walking unsteadily, which might be because he had already been partly drunk, or because of the kick Daisy had landed. Would he turn left for The Thrawl or right for the canal? *Turn right, turn right . . .*

He did turn right. Daisy's stomach lurched with nervousness, but the memory of Joe's small, scared face – and of those nights when Pa's body had rammed deep into hers, leaving her sick and trembling and sometimes bleeding – was stamped on her mind. She kept her distance, but she kept Pa in sight, dodging back if he looked like turning round, pressing into the shadows of the tall old buildings.

She could see the faint glimmer of the canal now, and she could smell its putrid stench. There were old warehouses along this bit of the path; most of them were abandoned, because the canal made everything so damp that people had given up trying to store anything in them. Windows had fallen out, and rats scuttled to and fro in the derelict buildings.

Occasionally someone who did not have the price of a night's lodging would get into one of them for a bit of shelter, but they were bleak, unfriendly places, and you had to have a strong stomach to go in. But the path itself was a good shortcut to the tavern.

Daisy waited until Pa had reached the part of the path where not even the blind windows of the warehouse overlooked it. Then she ran forward, as fast as her feet would take her, and reached out, pushing him as hard as she could.

It took him completely by surprise, and he gave a cry, falling back, his hands flailing at the air. Then he went over the edge, all the way down into the canal. The muddy water churned and rippled, and Daisy, gasping and shaking, fell back against the warehouse wall.

Ma and the girls said they were shocked, and Ma cried a bit, but Daisy thought they all knew it was relief they were feeling.

'I won't never forget what he did to us,' Lissy told Daisy, much later. 'That first time – I bled so much, I thought I was going to die. Didn't dare tell anyone though.'

'You could have told me,' said Daisy, wanting to comfort Lissy, knowing little comfort was to be had.

'No, I couldn't,' said Lissy. 'Not then. I'll never stop hating him, though.'

'Nor will I.'

No one in Rogues Well Yard and the surrounding streets was particularly shocked to hear about Pa's death. Pissed as usual, said most people, and he'd tumbled into the canal. Good riddance to bad rubbish.

They did not say this very loudly, though, from respect for his wife, poor soul, and they passed round the hat for her in the saloon bar of the Cock & Sparrow and also the Princess Alice and the Ten Bells.

TWENTY

1890s

When the twins were coming up to their seventh birthday, Cedric Thumbprint offered to give them piano lessons. He told Madame he thought they were very musical – particularly Morwenna. He could try them with one or two simple exercises to see if they took to it, he said. It was only an idea, of course.

'He's being very kind,' said Rhun, indulgently.

'It makes a change from him being a silly old fool,' said Madame, not realizing Daisy was in earshot. 'I caught him writing a bank draft for £2,000 to the Baskerville creature last week, did I tell you about that?'

'No!' Rhun was horrified.

'It was the money that came to him from that grandfather who founded the shop. Baskerville told him she wanted it for a sick brother. Doctor's fees and a stay by the sea for his health, she said. Sick brother and stay by the sea my backside,' said Madame angrily. 'I was so furious I tore the draft up and I went straight round to see the Baskerville; she's got the most horrible set of rooms you ever saw – grubby pink satin cushions and simpering dolls lying on couches, and a sort of sleazy feeling, as if none of the beds are ever made. I threw the pieces of the draft in her face and I told her what I thought of her in no uncertain terms. Then I said she could find somebody else to suck blood from.'

'What did she say?'

'She called me a string of names, and threw a scent bottle at me. Fortunately I dodged in time,' said Madame, 'but the bottle smashed against the wall, so Baskerville lost an entire bottle of Otto of Roses, all over the carpet. The place'll stink to high heaven for days. Anyway, Thaddeus is going to make sure she doesn't come to the house again.'

'Poor old Cedric,' said Rhun, rather sadly.

'He'd have been very poor indeed if she'd cashed that £2,000,' said Madame. 'Still, if he can teach the twins how to play the piano, even in a basic way, it would be useful to them later on. I shall insist on paying Cedric a proper fee, of course. And it might take his mind off being lovelorn.'

The lessons went well. Mervyn had declined to learn to play, but he liked to go to the Thumbprints' flat and listen to his sister playing. The twins liked the Thumbprints, who gave them afternoon tea as if they were grown-up, pouring it into perilously fragile china cups which they were terrified of dropping and breaking, and serving warm scones and jam. There were books everywhere, because books were their world.

Daisy liked the Thumbprints, too. Thaddeus often talked to her about the straits to which his grandfather had been put in order to come to England and to London, and begin the bookshop. Cedric told her about Belinda, and how he had been taken in by her.

'I'd thought she was a shy, sensitive soul,' he said, sorrowfully. 'But in fact she was simply after the bit of money our grandfather left to Thaddeus and to me. She didn't have a sick brother who needed sea air – she didn't have a brother at all, in fact. So I'm very grateful indeed to Scaramel for stepping in. But I shall think of it as a lesson learned – part of life's rich tapestry. And as Vanbrugh wrote, "Love, like fortune, turns upon a wheel, and is very much given to rising and falling".'

Daisy had no idea who Vanbrugh might be, but whoever he was, his words seemed to give Cedric some comfort, which was all that mattered.

The twins ransacked the trunks in the flat to find their mother's old song-sheets and music scores, and carried bundles of music up to the Thumbprints' flat, to try them out under Cedric's tutelage. Cedric enjoyed this; he said they were embarking on a musical odyssey, and Rhun went off to write an ode about it.

Most of the squirrelled-away music was lively and a bit saucy, and bounced along. But one afternoon, when rain was darkening the street outside, and the Thumbprints had gone out to collect some food for a little supper party they were giving that evening, Daisy went up to the top landing to put up some lace curtains she had rinsed for the Thumbprints. While she was clambering onto the windowsill, she heard music from their flat that sent such a chill through her entire body; she almost fell off the sill.

It was obviously Morwenna who was playing – she had permission to go into the upstairs flat to practise any time she wanted. But it was also obvious that this was unfamiliar music she was trying to play, because it was hesitant and stumbling, as if she was feeling her way through unknown notes. Daisy stood absolutely still, clutching the folds of curtain, her heart thudding against her ribs. There was no need in the world to suddenly feel this thrumming fear, but she did feel it, because she recognized the music, and she had prayed never to hear it again.

Then Mervyn's voice said, a bit uncertainly, 'I don't think I like that very much, whatever it is.'

'I don't think I do, either. There's words to it, as well, though.'

Don't sing them, Daisy thought, standing on the shadowy landing. Oh, Morwenna, please don't sing them, because it'll bring it all back . . .

But Mervyn must have joined Morwenna on the piano stool, because when Morwenna began playing again, the two small young voices rang out.

'Listen for the killer for he's here, just out of sight.

Listen for the footsteps 'cos it's very late at night.

I can hear his tread and he's prowling through the dark.

I can hear him breathing and I fear that I'm his mark.'

'That's scary,' said Mervyn, after a moment.

'I know. I don't know what it's meant to be, not really, do you? I'll play the rest, though, 'cos if I don't I'll wonder what it was like.'

'All right. But then we'll stop.'

The twins' voices came again.

'Now I hear the midnight prowl,

Now I see the saw and knife.

Next will come the victim's howl.

So save yourself from him, and *run* . . .

. . . run hard to save your life.'

Silence closed down, then Mervyn started to say, 'Don't let's ever play that again . . .' Before he could say any more, Daisy had tapped at the door of the flat, and had stepped inside, calling out.

The door to the room that the Thumbprints used as a study was open, and she saw the twins seated at the piano, staring at the music score propped on the stand.

They had turned at the sound of Daisy's voice, but for both of them the smile had a puzzled look.

Daisy said, 'I heard you playing from outside.'

'Did you? It was this – something I found in one of those old trunks,' said Morwenna, a bit uncertainly. 'It's quite old. I don't know what it is, but we don't like it very much.'

'We're going to burn it,' said Mervyn.

Daisy went over to the piano. 'I think it's something your mother found or was given – oh, years ago, it was. She didn't like it very much, either.' She noticed Morwenna was shivering slightly, but she said, carefully, 'I don't think we'll burn it, though.'

'Why not?'

Daisy thought: because once upon a time, it was written by a very famous composer . . . And once upon another time, it was used to fight back evil and madness . . . And that evil madness might have died in a dark old river tunnel, but it might not . . .

But she only said, 'Well, one day it might mean something to somebody. It might even be worth money. Let's just put it back where you found it.'

They nodded, and the three of them went back down to their own flat. Mervyn pulled out the trunk in which they had found the music, and Morwenna knelt down and placed the music at the bottom of the trunk. Mervyn reached in to pull a bundle of other other papers over it, to cover it.

Then the door to the flat was pushed cheerfully open, and Madame was calling out to know if anyone was at home, and if so whether anybody had thought to put a kettle to boil for a pot of tea, because it was as cold as a nun's embrace outside.

The twins did not mention the music again, and nor did Daisy. None of them told Madame or Rhun about finding it.

TWENTY-ONE

P hin had spread both of Links's sketches out on his desk, and he was examining them minutely. There were times when, if your research hit a brick wall, it could be helpful to go back to your original sources. He did not think he had missed any clues in the sketches, but he was going over them again anyway.

The *Liszten for the Killer* sketch with the macabre figure under the lamp in Harlequin Court did not seem to contain any secrets. Admittedly it was a reproduction and the book it was in was an old one, but the details were quite clear.

He turned to The Thrawl sketch. Now that he knew that such a place had existed and that it had indeed been an asylum – a 'tunnel house' according to the group in the Marble Arch pub – he could recognize the madness in the faces Links had drawn. He looked back at the terrified figure in the Harlequin Court sketch, whose imploring eyes seemed to be beseeching the artist for help. The figures in The Thrawl sketch had the same look, and Phin set about examining the details through the magnifying glass.

He was not really expecting to find anything, but the debris sketched on the floor came more sharply into focus under the glass. The outlines would not yield anything, of course; they were obviously meant to convey the general dereliction of the place, and there were only anonymous, tattered fragments of paper and cloth. But . . .

But some of the debris was not anonymous at all. There were scraps of newspapers. *Newspapers.* And Links, faithful as ever to detail, had drawn in tiny pieces of actual newsprint, so that on a few of the pieces it was possible to make out words. Maddeningly, none of the words made complete sentences, but at the top of two of them was a complete and just-legible heading. It said, *Fossan's Journal.*

Fossan's Journal. It sounded a bit like something from a

Victorian novel – or the kind of name someone might conjure up to lend a Dickensian flavour to a story. It was a place that would have its offices in a dingy backstreet, with the proprietor sitting at a high desk, wearing fingerless gloves, grudgingly counting out the meagre payments to his underlings. On the other hand, it could be the name of a real newspaper or a magazine. A local one, perhaps? But local to where? The East End? Might it even be still in business? Phin swivelled his chair round to the computer, and opened a search engine, typing Fossan and Thrawl as search requests.

The first results were mostly dictionary definitions, explaining that thrawl was an old term for a stone slab in a larder, intended to keep food cool in pre-refrigerator days. But further down the screen was a reference to Thrawl Street, which was indeed in London's East End.

The street's chief claim to fame seemed to be twofold. The first was that by the end of the nineteenth century, it had typi-fied extreme poverty and dereliction. There had been lodging houses of the cheapest, most basic kind, and the street, and its immediate environs, had been the haunt of, 'Thieves, loose women and bad characters of all kinds'. Police had refused to venture there unless in the company of a brother officer. There was a grim photo of the street from around 1900, showing the grey hopelessness of the buildings with a few inhabitants peering suspiciously at the camera.

The other notable fact about Thrawl Street was its connec-tion to Jack the Ripper, who had chosen one or two of his victims there. Again, Phin remembered the Marble Arch trio referring to this. He could not see that the Ripper's appearance on the scene was relevant, however, and he scrolled down to read about the street's history.

> Originally built by Henry Thrall (or Thrale) c.1656, Thrawl Street ran east–west from Brick Lane, as far as George Street, across a former tenter field owned by the Fossan brothers, Thomas and Lewis.

Fossan, thought Phin, staring at the screen. *Fossan.* Had some long-ago magazine or newspaper proprietor wanted to give a nod to the area's past – to the brothers who had originally owned the field on which the houses stood – and named his paper for them? Or had Links simply known the area and its history, and made use of the slender connection for his sketch?

This was worth checking, though, and Phin started with the British Newspaper Archive, whose vast collection he had occasionally scoured when tracking down obscure information. The website provided various links, and if there could be a link to a small site with archives relating to the East End, or a local archives centre . . .

There was a link. There was Tower Hamlets library, which apparently had extensive archives of the area. Again, he remembered the Marble Arch pub trio mentioning this. Was Tower Hamlets close enough to Thrawl Street? Phin checked the map, and thought it was. The library was in Bancroft Road, which was a part of London he had never visited, but there was a phone number, and he dialled it.

Certainly, they were open today, said the helpful voice who answered. They opened every other Saturday, and today was one of those Saturdays. Mr Fox would be asked to kindly complete a registration form for a first visit, and to provide ID, but from there he could have the run of the collection, so to speak. Did he know exactly where . . .? Ah, then Stepney Green was the nearest tube station, or the Number 25 bus went along the Mile End Road. They were just along from Queen Mary University main campus in the Mile End Road, if Mr Fox knew that? Anyway, they would look forward to seeing him.

Phin said, 'Thank you very much. I'll be in later today.'

He liked the Tower Hamlets library. He liked its air of believing it important to preserve the minutiae of the past, and of considering that the past could be relevant to the present. But even as he was finding himself a place at a small desk, he was keeping in mind that he was probably chasing rainbows or will o' the wisps, and also that it was Franz Liszt he was supposed to be researching, not obscure music hall performers and enigmatic artists. Still, Professor Liripine and Dr Purslove were true academics for whom the world moved at a slow and gentlemanly pace. They would not mind – they would probably

not even notice – if Phin took an extra week or so to produce
the information they had commissioned.

The library's archives were extensive. There were records
of the borough and its predecessors going back to the sixteenth
century, and there were deeds showing transfer of properties
and land. There were minutes of meetings held by numerous
organizations and churches and companies.

There was also something called the Cuttings Collection,
which included newspaper and periodical cuttings – articles
and printed ephemera. The description helpfully explained that
a substantial amount of this material dated from the nineteenth
century, but added warningly that searchers should be aware
that the collection ran to more than 400 boxes.

It would take Phin at least a fortnight to work through 400
boxes, and it was not time he could allow himself. But it
seemed that local newspapers from the mid-1850s were on
microfilm and could be viewed, and staff assured him that
printouts could be made and photocopies taken. No, there was
no actual charge, but they tended to suggest that if library
users felt a suitable donation might be made, that was always
gratefully received. Phin resolved to make a donation, whether
he found anything about The Thrawl or not, typed in a search
request for Thrawl and for Fossan, and began patiently to
scroll through the screen.

And incredibly, there it was. A newspaper article that looked
as if it might have been rather raggedly cut from the page,
headed, 'Curious Legend of Burned-Out Asylum'.

> This Journal brings to the attention of its readers, a curious
> legend clinging to the ruins of the old Thrawl Asylum.
>
> It will be recalled that The Thrawl burned down some
> three months ago, [the story was reported with photo-
> graphs in our issue within three days of the tragedy]. It
> is still not known how the fire began, although it is
> suspected that a burning cigarette end may have ignited
> rubbish or old newspapers in the staff's rooms.
>
> The shell of The Thrawl can still be seen, of course;
> the stones are blackened and windows glassless, although
> many of the iron bars remain in place. What was known

as the Paupers' Ward was completely destroyed, and what is left of its walls rear up against the night sky like rotting teeth. It is impossible to see these decaying bricks and stones without being aware of the despair and the bewilderment that still clings to them – also, the rage – all left by the poor mad creatures incarcerated there. In its time, The Thrawl was sometimes referred to as a 'tunnel house', signifying that there was a way inside it, but no way out of it.

[Note: The term *tunnel house* seems to have been either a colloquialism that has since fallen into disuse, or perhaps a local expression, for I have not found it used anywhere else.]

Visitors were never allowed into tunnel houses, except for the occasional medical man, and, of course, undertakers who must needs remove those who died.

However, a strange story is growing up around the ruins. There have been reports that people living nearby sometimes hear strange singing coming from within the blackened ruins or in the streets immediately around. Because of this, many are avoiding the area after nightfall.

'Hear it many a night, I do,' said one Seth Strumble, a street trader, who plies a cheerful trade in several local markets. 'Chill your marrow it would.'

Asked what the song was, Mr Strumble seemed unwilling to elaborate, and even to regret having spoken of it at all. He muttered, evasively, that he could not say what it might be, adding that he was not a great one for music, not unless it might be a bit of a sing-song down the Cock & Sparrow of a Saturday night.

More than that, your reporter could not get Mr Strumble to say. It does seem, though, that the strange singing is generally heard near to the rooms that overlooked Fossan's Yard. [Named, readers will know, for Thomas and Lewis Fossan, the brothers who originally held the ownership of the land on which Thrawl Street stands.]

After the fire, a detailed check of the records and the burned bodies was made, and it was finally admitted that not all the inmates of The Thrawl had been accounted for. Tragically, it seemed that most had perished in the blaze, along with four of the attendants.

However, some half-dozen were never found. With that in mind, *Fossan's Journal* ventures to suggest that the eerie singing could be some poor witless soul who escaped the fire, and who wanders the streets.

Your diligent reporter, increasingly curious, sallied forth into the streets, where tales of the past linger. Within the huddle of houses and shops and taverns, dwell people who tell how stories have always been whispered about The Thrawl – how the word itself was an old word for larder, and how, as children, they believed the place was the larder of a family of ogres, who, in the best fairy-tale tradition, liked human flesh for their tables.

It was, though, surprisingly difficult to find people prepared to talk about the strange singing heard around the ruins. An imaginative or a superstitious mind might almost think that they were frightened to talk about it.

But one doughty soul who has lived in The Thrawl's shadow for almost her entire life, did speak out. She told your reporter how she had brought up three daughters in Rogues Well Yard and one son. A small lady, she was, brown as to complexion and grey as to hair, which she wore twisted back in a wispy bun on her neck. No longer young, she declined to give her name, not wishing her children to know she had spoken to reporters – particularly not wanting her eldest daughter to know, on account of the daughter being in service to a famous lady who was on the stage.

This lady had work at a local rag-shop – Peg the Rags, it was called, and all the folk hereabouts knew it. They had a street stall, too, of a Friday and a Saturday, and there'd be nights when they'd be late packing things away, and afterwards they'd have a nip of gin at the Cock & Sparrow.

'That means I have to go home along by Fossan's Yard, and what's left of The Thrawl. That's when I heard the singing,' she explained. 'Last month it was –

November, and perishing cold. Misty, as well, so's you couldn't hardly see your hand in front of your face. I'm always a bit nervous in those streets, I don't mind saying it, for I'm old enough to remember those nights when you dursen't go out after dark for fear of . . . Well, you'll know who I mean. Him as prowled the streets hereabouts, killing women in a mad frenzy.

'Walking along that bit of road, I was, and thinking to go along a bit sharpish. That was when I heard it.'

'The singing?' I asked.

'Froze my bones, it did'

'Could you hear the words?'

'Not so's I could repeat them exactly. But I can tell you it's about listening for prowling footsteps at midnight.' She paused, then, drawing a bit closer, said, 'I recognized it, 'cause I'd heard it before. It used to get sung hereabouts – years ago, it was. But it was kind of a warning. You'd hear it and you knew to run for safety.'

'Safety from what?'

She leaned forward, one hand curling around your reporter's wrist for a moment. 'From *him*,' she said, in a whisper. 'Bad luck to even say the name, even after so long. But around here, we don't forget. You'll know who I mean.' She glanced over her shoulder as if fearful of being overheard, then wrapped the woollen shawl more tightly around her shoulders, and darted away, leaving your reporter staring after her.

It is not, of course, difficult to guess to what – and to whom – the good lady had been referring. Many stories cling to this part of London's East End, but there is one that lifts its drippingly gory head above the rest. That is the story that belongs to dark, fogbound streets and a very particular terror. A story that stretches back a good ten years and that may even stretch as far again into the future.

It is the story of how the women of Whitechapel learned and sang a strange and rather eerie song by night – a song intended to warn one another of the approach of Jack the Ripper.

TWENTY-TWO

P hin's first reaction was to wonder if the reporter might
have gone on to write gothic horror, and that if so he had
probably done quite well for himself, because he certainly
knew how to set a scene.

But his second reaction was to re-read the lines about how
some of the women of Whitechapel had 'learned and sung a
strange and rather eerie song'. A song that was 'about listening
for prowling footsteps at midnight', according to the worthy
Seth Strumble, and that the unnamed lady said had originally
been a warning of the approach of Jack the Ripper. She had
not actually mentioned the Ripper by name, but there did not
seem much doubt as to whom she had meant. The journalist
had certainly not had any doubts at all.

Phin reached for the notes he had brought with him, and
leafed through them for the lyrics found in Linklighters.

'Listen for the killer for he's here, just out of sight.
Listen for the footsteps 'cos it's very late at night.
I can hear his tread and he's prowling through the dark.
I can hear him breathing and I fear that I'm his mark.
Now I hear the midnight prowl,
Now I see the saw and knife.
Next will come the victim's howl.
So save yourself from him, and *run* . . .
. . . run hard to save your life.'

Was it possible that this was the song referred to by the
long-ago reporter – that it was a song that had been sung by
the women of Whitechapel as a warning that Jack the Ripper
was on the prowl? There had been stranger stories about the
Ripper, of course, but even so . . .

The curious thing, though, was that the song – or one that
sounded very like it – had been heard a good ten years after
the Ripper's killing spree had ended. But the *Journal*'s explanation was perfectly credible – that some poor soul shut away

in The Thrawl had known the song, and, lost in the tumult and the confusion of the fire, had roamed the streets, singing the song. It might even be one of the Ripper's near misses, in fact – that would be an experience to scar you for life, and one that would very likely print the song's words indelibly on your mind.

It was all intriguing and fairly sinister, and one day Phin might see if more details could be uncovered. But it had been Links he had been trying to find, and he had not in fact found anything at all. Links could have drawn The Thrawl at any time after it had burned, from memory or simply from imagination. Equally, he could have drawn it before it had burned, from reality – from his own acquaintance with it.

He obtained a printout of the article, handed over what he hoped was a suitable donation, promised that he would certainly use the library's excellent facilities again, and took himself back to his flat.

He had hoped that Toby might be at home and free for a drink, or even a meal; Phin would have been glad of anything that would disperse the clinging darknesses of The Thrawl, Jack the Ripper, and eerie disembodied singing in fogbound streets. It was remarkable how, having read the *Journal*'s article, the lyrics of the song framed in Linklighters conjured up the classic images of the lamplit streets through which the Ripper had prowled. How had those lyrics found their way to Linklighters, though?

However, Toby's flat was in darkness, so Phin made himself some scrambled eggs, added a wedge of bread and cheese, and ate it at his desk, the notes from the afternoon's gleanings spread out.

It was only when he had washed up the plate and had carried a cup of coffee back into the study, that he checked emails, and saw there was one from Gregory at Thumbprints.

'Sorry to have missed you, and we're about to close,' said the email, which was timed just before five p.m. 'But we can speak on Monday? Meanwhile, I've turned up an anthology with something that might possibly relate to your research. The poems in it are mostly fairly dull and turgid – they're mainly from around the end of the nineteenth century. But there's one that might connect to Linklighters. I've scanned it and it's come out a bit fuzzily, but it's readable, so I'm attaching it. I've put the anthology itself on one side in case you'd like to come in and take a look. Again, this isn't a "hard sell" – it's more that with this being such a long-owned family shop, and being next to Linklighters in its various incarnations, I've become interested in your research.

All best,

Gregory.'

Phin clicked on the attachment, hoping it would not be scornfully rejected by a too-stern virus checker, or that Gregory had not sent it via some arcane programme which Phin's own, slightly elderly, computer would refuse to recognize.

But it was all right, the attachment was opening. Probably it would not be anything of any special interest, but it was nice of Gregory to have taken the trouble, and it would be worth checking.

The attachment, once open, was, as Gregory had said, a bit fuzzy, especially at the edges, but when Phin zoomed it up a notch, it was perfectly readable.

The title was 'The Harlequin's Last Dance'.

The last dance, thought Phin. It's not so long since that would have a romantic ring to it – the last dance of the night; the final waltz and an unspoken understanding that the one you danced with was the one who would be taking you, or whom you would be taking, home. 'After the Ball', and 'Goodnight Irene', and 'Some Enchanted Evening'. It would have been gentle and polite, and, if it had not always been entirely innocent, it had certainly been light years away from today's 'Your place or mine?' culture.

But there had been an earlier time when the term, *the last dance*, had had a far more macabre meaning. It had referred to the frenetic jerkings on the gallows, after the gallows trap had been released. Dancing on air, it had sometimes been called, and it had been the description of the last moments of the slowly strangling hanged man. Or the hanged woman.

Woman. Had Scaramel been the Harlequin of this poem? Phin had the sudden feeling that he was about to take a step forward into a cold darkness, but he quelled it, and began to read.

Sunlight bleeding on the old stone court –
The place where Jack Ketch's own ghost might still
    walk.
The stage is all set and the lines are all learned,
The script is well Thumbed, and the movements
    ordained,
For Murder's the sin that can not be condoned.
And the Harlequin's dance must perforce be performed.

The great and the good do not dare intervene
So the Harlequin's last dance must darken the scenes.
A death for a death – that was ever the rule
Tho' barbaric the punishment, ugly the means.

Once people would gather to hear the death knell
And to Linklight the moment the deep Grave Trap fell.
But today are no watchers, today no stage doors,
The Harlequin's last dance will have no applause.

Phin read this twice through, then sat back, staring at it.
The verses were hardly Shakespearean sonnet or lyric poetry,
but there was a rhythm and a resonance to them, and the
images they conjured up were vivid.

The Harlequin's last dance, he thought. That doesn't have
to mean Scaramel, of course. Or might it? The references are
all there. The upper case T for 'Thumbed' in the well-thumbed
script – that could be a nod to Thumbprints. And certainly the
capital L for 'Linklight' could mean Linklighters.

Even so, this could be referring to anyone, and the date
could be anywhere from . . . Well, from the time that hangings
stopped being public events. The mention of people no longer
being able to watch or hear the death knell indicated that. The
group Phin had met in the Marble Arch pub had said something
about public hangings stopping in the mid-nineteenth century.
He got up to scour the reference books. The last public hanging
turned out to have been in 1868. That was well before
Scaramel's time; it meant that the hanging referred to in this
poem could have been in her era.

What else? Jack Ketch was the old name for a hangman,

of course, and the reference to his ghost walking in the old stone court probably meant Tyburn. As for linklighting the moment when the old Grave Trap fell – that was surely a theatrical reference. Phin pulled out a couple more reference books specifically dealing with the theatre, and, as he had thought, stage traps – the devices used for raising scenery and actors from beneath the stage – had been given names, according to their shape and size. In theatre parlance, a grave trap was quite simply a rectangle which could be lowered and raised – it was supposed to have acquired its name from early use for the graveyard scene in *Hamlet*. But by only a slight stretch of the imagination, it could also mean the trapdoor of a gallows, surely?

He sat back, frowning. Whoever this had been – whoever had danced that last dance on the gallows, whoever it had been for whom the great and the good had not dared intervene – he did not want it to have been Scaramel.

He began to search for details of hangings. It seemed that what had been known as the long drop had been introduced in the 1870s – only a few years after public executions had been stopped. So if this hanging had taken place after public hangings, it had also most likely taken place after the long drop had become practice. It could be Scaramel's era. And that line about dancing on air was most likely poetic licence, because the long drop would have been used – the carefully calculated snapping of the condemned man's neck. Or woman's.

In *commedia dell'arte*, Harlequin had been a man. Yes, but Scaramel had carved out her infamous career in a place called Harlequin Court.

But Scaramel had been the insouciant lady who cavorted saucily across nineteenth-century stages – she was the one who had danced on card tables at a gaming party at three in the morning, who had performed on a grand piano, and who reportedly had danced for the Prince of Wales wearing hardly any clothes at all. Phin did not want her to be a murderess.

And yet the rumour that she had committed murder clung to her legend. There had been that song about the ghost river beds that might refer to the old ditch beneath Linklighters.

It was now after midnight, but he doubted if he could sleep – the image of Scaramel being led to the gallows and standing on the trap was so strongly with him.

But after all, it seemed that life was not entirely made up of darknesses and ghosts, because while he was still seated at his desk, an email from Arabella came bouncing in.

'I'm missing you a huge amount,' she wrote. 'And I meant to dash back to London on Monday, but it seems that while Toby's plumbers were fitting the new bathroom, they inadvertently screwdrivered or power-hammered (is that the right expression, do you suppose?) straight into the main sewer pipe, and it's the pipe that serves the whole house, wouldn't you know it would be, so there was a flood of biblical proportions and revolting content. The first floor wasn't too badly affected, but the ground floor was awash with unmentionable effluent. All the occupants had to be temporarily rehoused (and probably won't ever speak to me again), but I shall send Toby to talk to them, because the whole thing was his idea. Fortunately, generous offers of reimbursement are forthcoming, and it sounds as if everyone's going to be compensated very adequately.

But if you happen to have a spare hour (ha!) when you could just dash out to take a look at the place, I would be really grateful. Just so I know the whole house isn't dissolving into a lake of loathsome putrescence, like that man in the Edgar Allen Poe story did.

I expect you'll say I could spend a couple of days at your flat, but nice as that would be, I'm not sure if I could relax knowing Toby is on the other side of your bedroom wall. If you see what I mean, Phin, dear. Or if you can tear yourself away from Scaramel and dash over to Paris, that would be great. The company apartment is quite small, but the bed is very substantial. And the black silk underwear is still folded up in my case, and it isn't going to be unfolded for anyone else.'

Phin read this with a mixture of amusement and affectionate exasperation, made a mental note to berate Toby for wishing such incompetent plumbers on Arabella, then replied to her email saying he would look in at her flat tomorrow. He hesitated over mentioning his latest discoveries, but they all seemed so far removed from both the Liszt project and the Scaramel/ Links search, that he decided against it. Instead, he said he would try to get to Paris next weekend, and that he was looking forward to unfolding the black silk underwear.

When finally he got into bed, it was not that sad and macabre account of what might have been Scaramel's execution that was with him, or even the flickering image beloved by film-makers of a cloaked gentleman stalking Victorian London carrying a surgeon's bag.

It was the fact that the *Fossan's Journal* reporter seemed to think the 'Listen' song had been composed as a warning about Jack the Ripper. As Phin fell asleep, he was wondering how far he could trust that opinion. And if so, who the composer had been.

TWENTY-THREE

Shortly after nine o'clock the next morning, Phin tapped on Toby's door to borrow the key to Arabella's flat. As he did so, it flickered on his mind as to whether he and Arabella might be reaching a stage where they would exchange door-keys anyway. This was a very pleasant thought.

'You're an early bird,' said Toby, opening the door. 'Good thing I was up.'

'I knew you were up,' said Phin. 'I heard you singing the rugby version of "The Girl I Left Behind Me" in the shower half an hour ago.'

'We'll have to get that wall sound-proofed sometime,' said Toby, unrepentant. 'But you won't need a key to Arabella's place. The plumbers are working today. They'll let you in.'

'They're working on a Sunday?' said Phin, incredulously.

'Yes, because the insurers are paying and they've doubled the rate or maybe tripled it. Or it might be the plumbers' professional indemnity set-up who are paying. Anyway, somebody's footing the bill for Sunday work, so they'll be at the flat all day.'

'Well, that's good anyway,' said Phin. 'I'm only whizzing over to Linklighters for another quick look through the stuff in the cellar, but I'm setting off earlier than I need so that I can check Arabella's place beforehand.'

'Ah, but is the luscious Loretta likely to check on you while you're at Linklighters?' asked Toby. 'And if so, what's it worth for me not to tell Arabella?'

'I'm not going to be checked on by Loretta or anyone else,' said Phin. 'I'll only be there for an hour or two anyway.'

'It is,' said Toby, solemnly, 'now only quarter past nine, and a good deal can be achieved on a Sunday morning before lunch.'

'You speak as one who knows. How is the physiotherapist?'

'Very well indeed, as a matter of fact.'

Arabella's flat was a hive of activity. Carpets had been discarded and furniture was stacked in a corner, shrouded in what looked like waterproof covering.

'Sort of thing that could happen to anyone,' said a rotund man in overalls, who appeared to be directing proceedings. 'But a young apprentice – what they call "traineeship work placement" – was helping chisel up a section of the floor so we could drop the new toilet in – very smart it's going to look when it's done, one of those wall-hung affairs, she's got an eye for class, hasn't she, that Miss Tallis? But the lad, well-meaning as anything, switched on the power-hammer, and it got away with him, and powered straight down into a main sewer pipe. And, of course, it was the pipe that serves the whole house – wouldn't you know it would be.'

'Wouldn't you just,' said Phin. He checked all the rooms so he could describe everything to Arabella, considered taking a couple of photographs to send her, but decided against it. Even Arabella's buoyancy might be deflated by the actual sight of the devastation.

Instead, he thanked the man, and set off for Harlequin Court. He had not needed to be at Arabella's flat as long as he had thought, and he would probably reach Linklighters a bit earlier than he had arranged with Loretta Farrant. It was a nice morning, though, and he could sit on the little bench outside Thumbprints and wait until she arrived.

'Do you think,' said Loretta, as she and Roland finished breakfast, 'that you could come with me to the restaurant this morning? Just for an hour or so?'

She sounded a bit defensive, and Roland turned to look at her. They had been avoiding one another's eyes since they got up, and they had only exchanged the most necessary comments, mostly about whether there was any more coffee, or whether Roland had finished in the bathroom because Loretta wanted to wash her hair. It was not exactly as if they were embarrassed because he had found the sketch and because Loretta had poured out the story of her ancestors; it was more as if neither of them knew whether or not they should reopen the subject. Roland would have quite liked to know more about those shadowy figures and about the tragic ancestor who had been consigned to an asylum. If nothing else, it might have meant bringing a few things into the open, and it might even have meant he could find a way of coming to terms with the almost-certain knowledge that Loretta had brought about Mother's death. But he had no idea if it would anger Loretta to ask about the sketch and the ancestor, or if it might upset her. She was hardly ever upset about anything – it was one of the strengths in her he had admired so much at the beginning. But there was, of course, also the possibility that she was regretting what she had said.

He had just been deciding that he would ask if he could look at the sketch again, when Loretta made her request about going to the restaurant. It surprised him slightly, because she hardly ever went there on a Sunday. They did not normally do very much at all on Sundays, in fact. Loretta might spend a desultory hour or two working out menus for the forthcoming week, or drafting PR ideas, and Roland usually went out to buy Sunday newspapers, which then got spread around the flat during the reading of them. This always annoyed Loretta, because she said she was the one who had to pick them up and tidy them away for recycling, and she wished Roland would remember that he no longer lived in a sprawling old house where you could shut the door on any clutter and just go into one of the other rooms. Roland usually said he could do his own tidying up, and in any case he was generally the one who took the newspapers to the recycling place.

But slightly waspish as these exchanges were, there was a degree of comfortable familiarity about them, and in a curious way Roland looked forward to them. It helped to put from his mind how they used to stay in bed until almost lunchtime on Sundays, making sleepy love, listening to the news on the radio, then sharing a shower before getting up to eat a huge brunch. It was also important not to remember the struggling, embarrassing failures on those mornings, after he had found Loretta's earring outside Mother's door.

To push these thoughts away, he said, 'Why on earth are you going to the restaurant on a Sunday?'

'I'm meeting Phineas Fox again, if you remember.'

'Oh, yes, I do remember, now you mention it. But you said I didn't need to be there.'

'It's just that the quarterly inspection of the sluice gate and the panel's due next week.'

'Is it?'

'There was a letter – I thought I told you. The Health and Safety people are going in on Wednesday, so I want to have a quick look beforehand, to make sure everything's all right. Only I hate that place – the sluice gate place – and it'd be a whole lot easier if you were with me. It's less disruption to do it while the restaurant's closed, as well. It needn't take more than half an hour, then you could go straight home, and I'd stay to see Phineas.'

'Have we got to actually raise the sluice gate?'

'Yes, but only a couple of feet, just so we can shine a torch through.'

The thought of raising the gate, of cranking up the ancient machinery and exposing the shrivelled old river was a shivery one. Roland had only seen the gate once, during the renovations, but he had thought it was the most macabre thing he had ever encountered.

But he said, temperately, 'Yes, all right, I'll come with you.'

'Good. I'll wash up the breakfast things, and throw on a jacket. If we go a bit early at least there won't be many people around.'

There were not many people around at all, and Harlequin Court, when they got to it, was deserted and silent.

'It's strange to see it like this,' said Roland, looking about him, as Loretta unlocked the door.

'Sunday morning mode.'

As they went inside, it occurred to Roland that Loretta was a bit overdressed for a casual Sunday morning meeting. He thought the jacket she had offhandedly mentioned throwing on was new, and it looked expensive. It was for this man, of course, this Phineas Fox who was quite ordinary looking, but who had remarkable eyes and a nice voice. Probably Loretta would flirt with him after Roland had gone home, and maybe even try to seduce him. Once this would have caused a deep pain, but Roland realized sadly that he no longer cared much what she did, or who she did it with, or where it was done.

'Phineas Fox won't be here until eleven,' said Loretta, locking the door and going down the stairs. 'But we'll deal with checking the gate right away, shall we?'

It was shadowy and still in the restaurant, and there was somehow a feeling that they were being watched. The figures in the framed posters and playbills had a ghostly aspect, and the eyes might almost have been alive.

As Roland followed Loretta down to the deep cellar, he had the sensation of something old and dank brushing across the air. But then Loretta switched on a light, and there was only a faint drift of lavender from the plug-in air freshener she kept down here, and the room was its usual ordinary office-self.

'Let's unlock the panel and get that out of the way,' she said, reaching in her bag and handing him the key.

Roland had forgotten the panel was kept locked, but he took the small key and reached up. There was a faint creak as the lock turned and the panel's seams were released, and then a cold dank stench really did seep into the room. Roland ignored it, and swung the panel back so that it was flat against the wall. The light from the office spilled into the yawning space, showing the old stone walls, pitted and scarred with age. As his eyes began to adjust to the dimness, the gate seemed almost to materialize out of the darkness. It was massive; easily fifteen feet high, and probably ten or twelve feet wide, and it was just as monstrous and sinister as he remembered. There was a row of iron spikes at the very top, melting into the darkness, but just visible. On the right of the gate was a huge wheel, with thick black spokes and levers. That was the mechanism that would raise the gate.

'It's darker in there than I expected,' he said, half over his shoulder to Loretta.

'Is it? Haven't you got your phone? There's a torch on it, isn't there?'

Roland always forgot about having a torch on the phone, because he was hardly ever in a situation where he needed to use it. He fumbled a bit, then finally managed to switch it on. Shining the light, he swung one leg over the low sill of the panel, and stepped through. The sour dankness came at him like a blow, but he stepped across to the gate, and put the torch on the ground, so that its small light fell directly on to the iron wheel. The wheel felt cold to his touch, almost slimy, and he was about to grasp it, when Loretta said,

'Roland, I think there's a kind of key for the wheel. I've never operated it, but I remember seeing the Health and Safety people doing it. You have to slot it in just under the actual wheel, and then turn it – I think it works on the same principle as the key on a tin of sardines. It was fitted as an extra security thing.'

'I can't see anything . . .' Roland moved the torch. 'Oh, wait, yes, this must be it – just under the wheel itself.'

It was indeed like a massive key. It was a good eighteen inches in length with a kind of ring handle, and the other end of the shaft was shaped to slot into the spokes of the wheel to give leverage. Roland saw what Loretta meant about a tin of sardines. He slotted it in place, then turned it, pulling hard. There was a shudder of movement deep within the tunnel, then from beyond the gate came a dull clanking sound, and with it the impression of immense iron cogs meshing and huge chains uncoiling. The gate creaked and shivered, then a thin rim of dull light showed at the bottom. Roland had to fight a sudden compulsion to get out of the horrible old cellar as fast as possible. But he stayed where he was, his hands on the wheel, and with agonizing slowness, the sluice gate began to rise. It was like the slow yawn of a monster. Mud and silt dripped like strings from a second row of iron spikes along the bottom rim – black iron teeth, thought Roland, repressing a shudder. The stench that gusted out was like a solid wall.

He stepped back from the wheel, but the gate continued to rise, as if the mechanism, once activated, had to finish its course. It struggled up to a three-quarters position – the spikes along the bottom edge four or five feet over Roland's head – then stopped. Beyond the opening, he could see what looked like a brick-lined tunnel, with curved sides and a roof that stretched away into a cobwebby gloom. There was a yawning blackness at the core of the tunnel, which must be where the ancient ditch had been. The ghost river. Roland had not seen it at such close quarters before, and it was much wider than he had expected. Alongside it was a brick ledge, three feet wide at the most.

Loretta had climbed through the panel, and had come to stand next to him. 'Is everything all right?'

'Yes, I think so. The gate seemed to go up all right.'

'Good. It's a strange place, that tunnel, isn't it?' she said, softly.

'Very.'

She linked her hand through his arm and leaned against him. 'You get the feeling that it's a place that might have seen – and kept – a few secrets in its time, don't you?'

'Yes.'

'What secrets might it keep about us, d'you think, Roland?' she said. 'About you and me.'

There was an odd silence, then Roland turned his head to look at her. 'I don't know that I've got any particularly dark secrets.'

Loretta smiled, but for some reason it struck Roland as an odd smile. As if somebody else's smile had been pasted on to her face. He wondered suddenly if that was how she had looked on the night she'd crept up the stairs to pull the carpet into ridges for Mother to stumble over . . .? Sly, calculating . . . No, surely it was just the strange light down here.

Loretta said, in a perfectly normal voice, 'Of course you haven't got any dark secrets. Let's close this gate, shall we?'

'Yes, as quickly as possible. Loathsome place.' Roland shivered. 'Still, I should think it'll pass the insurance inspection all right.'

'Oh, yes. Useful things, insurance inspections,' said Loretta, in an odd voice. As she turned back to the wheel, the sly, unfamiliar look seemed to fall across her face again. Roland saw her pick up the key and he was about to go to help turn the wheel back, when there was suddenly a whirl of movement, and the heavy key came at him from out of nowhere. It hit him in the centre of his chest and there was the sensation of something splintering inside him. He cried out with the pain, falling forwards towards the open gate. Two hard, firm hands pushed him straight into the yawning tunnel, and thick darkness closed around him, sick and confusing.

When the darkness receded slightly, he realized he had fallen on the narrow ledge that ran alongside the old river bed, and that he was half lying against the wall. He sat up, meaning to scramble straight back under the gate, but such agony clenched around his ribcage that he cried out again, and the darkness spun and swooped around him again. He fought against it, and through blurred vision saw Loretta framed in the partly open gate, the heavy key still in her hands. The light from his discarded phone fell partly across her, so that she was half in and half out of its beam. And there was an air of such menace about her . . . If I try to get out she'll hit me with that thing again, thought Roland, in horror.

In a gasping voice, he said, 'What are you doing?' and Loretta smiled.

'Protecting my interests. You see, yesterday, when I was cleaning out cupboards, I found my earring in your dressing-table drawer,' she said. 'And I know exactly which night I lost that earring. It was the night I set the murder-trap for your mother.'

Roland's entire chest felt as if iron spikes were being hammered into it, but at some level he was aware that this was the moment he had always known would come. He had always known that one day this would be dragged into the

open, although he had not known how it would come about
or when it would happen. But now here it was.

'There was,' Loretta was saying, 'only one place you could
have found that earring, and that was outside the door of your
mother's bedroom. And if you found it, you must have guessed
what I did that night.'

Roland said, 'I did find it. I did guess what you'd done. I
realized you'd heard what she said to me.'

'About making sure I wouldn't get any of the money if we
got married. Yes.' Loretta did not move. She seemed perfectly
prepared to stand like this, talking to him. Through the pain,
Roland thought it was as if she suddenly wanted – or even
needed – to make sure he understood everything she had done
and why she had done it.

She said, 'You'd gone upstairs to help her into bed after
supper – a stupid ritual that, I always thought. Your mother
was perfectly capable of getting herself into bed. I washed up,
and then I went halfway up the stairs to call that I'd made
some coffee, and to ask if your mother wanted a cup. And I
heard everything. My God, it was like the opening chapter of
a Victorian novel,' she said, scornfully.

'I know. I told her that.'

'Did you ever tell anyone you found my earring?' said
Loretta.

'No.' Against the swirling darkness, Roland thought: and that
was a supremely stupid thing to say! I should have told her
there was someone who knew – it would have been safer if I
had said that.

'Ah,' she said, on a pleased note. 'That's very good.'

'I wouldn't have wanted anyone to find out my wife
was—'

'A murderess?'

'Yes. And I still won't tell anyone.' He could hear the pleading
note in his voice. 'Why would I say anything after so long?'

'You might,' said Loretta. 'I can't trust you not to. I can't
take that risk.' She took a step back, and Roland tried to
calculate if he could spring forward and be through the yawning
gap of the open gate before she reached the wheel. But when
he tried to move the pain sent him into sick dizziness again.

'I don't think you'll get out,' she said, as if she were considering the matter from all angles. 'I've seen the maps of those underground rivers and the tunnels – the later ones, I mean – and everywhere is sealed off. There's no other way out, except through this gate. And the gate doesn't have a mechanism on the inside. I lay awake most of last night working it out, and I know that, as plans go, it's foolproof. You'll disappear, and of course I shan't know where you are. I'll be the distraught wife, and no one will suspect me of anything. Why would they? I've got that meeting with Phineas Fox later this morning, as well, and that's going to provide a kind of alibi. I'd hardly have killed my husband with someone due for a meeting here in . . .' She glanced at her watch, and said, 'In three-quarters of an hour.'

Three-quarters of an hour, thought Roland, and a frail hope brushed his mind. Could he keep her talking until Fox got here? He might be early. But he might be late. He tried again to move towards the gate, but the pain grabbed him again and he sank back, gasping.

'Nobody saw us come into Harlequin Court,' said Loretta. 'I was keeping an eye out for that. And when Phineas does get here, he'll find me outside in the square, apparently having just arrived. We'll come down here, and we'll talk about his research, and afterwards we'll walk to the tube together. We might even have some lunch somewhere – I shall pretend to phone you, and let you know that, I think. It's all going to seem like a perfectly innocent Sunday morning, entirely free of any murderous intentions.'

'And at some point you'll try to seduce Phineas Fox, I expect,' said Roland. 'Because you'll just have committed a second murder, and you'll be so turned on by that . . . Just as you were after you killed Mother,' he said, with a sudden angry memory.

'You didn't object at the time,' said Loretta, at once. 'It was only later that you . . . Was it after you found the earring that you went cold on me in bed?' she said, suddenly. 'Was that why?'

'Yes.'

'I see. Some men would be rampant at the thought of screwing a murderess, but not you. It was when you went out to get a taxi that I did it,' she said, suddenly. 'It was pouring with rain, and Wynne couldn't possibly have heard me. But creeping up those stairs – they were in shadow and I didn't dare switch on a light – it felt as though I'd stepped into a different world. I don't know how to explain it, but it was as if the rules had changed. As if what I was going to do wasn't in the least wrong.'

Roland saw a faint puzzlement flicker on her face, then she said, 'When I got up to that landing, I simply knelt down and pulled a bit of the carpet free – just across the doorway – just where she'd come out of her room next morning. I didn't know if it would work, but it did.' She made an impatient gesture. 'D'you know, I didn't even realize I'd lost that earring until much later – then I thought I must have dropped it in the street, or maybe in the taxi. I suppose you wouldn't notice it had gone, because I had on that twenties-style hat against the rain.'

'I found it while I was clearing out the house that last weekend,' said Roland.

'When I saw it in your dressing-table drawer yesterday, for a moment I didn't understand. I couldn't think why, if you'd found it, you simply hadn't given it back to me. That would have been the normal thing to do, wouldn't it? To say, "I found this – you must have dropped it sometime." The fact that you never did – that you hid it all these months . . . Well, I could only think of one reason for that.'

'Loretta – listen, Mother's death was put down to an accident, and it can stay that way,' said Roland, desperately. 'But what you're doing now – this is different. As soon as people know I'm missing . . .'

'But they won't know until at least tomorrow night,' said Loretta. 'I shan't report you as missing until then.'

'They'll search down here, though . . .'

'Not at once. It could be days. And even if they do find you, I've got that letter about the insurance check on the gates. I told you it was useful, that letter. Actually, that was what gave me the idea for all this.' Again there was the smile that was so eerily not Loretta's smile. 'I'll suggest that you must have come down here to make sure everything was all

right for the inspection,' she said. 'But that you must have
fumbled the mechanism. It's so old, anyway, that nobody
would have trouble believing me. And in any case, by the
time they do open the tunnel—'

'It will be too late,' said Roland, in a horrified whisper.

'Yes. I'm sorry,' said Loretta. 'I really am. I liked you,
Roland – more than liked.'

'It wasn't just the money, then?' This had to be the most
bizarre conversation anyone had ever had.

Loretta said, 'Oh, the money – yes, of course it was about
the money. But really, it was about this place. Linklighters . . .'

'Linklighters reclaimed,' said Roland, half to himself. 'For
your ancestor.'

'Yes. There it was, empty, vandalized, slowly rotting away.
It made me so angry. I used to sit on that seat near the bookshop, and stare at it. I had to have it.'

Her eyes were inward looking, and Roland tensed his
muscles to move, because if he could just catch her off guard
. . . But even the small effort sent the pain tearing through his
ribs again, making him cry out. The sound pulled Loretta out
of her strange memories. She frowned, then turned back to
the wheel, and bent over, slotting the key in place, then
wrenching the wheel around. Roland felt the shudder of movement from the gate, and panic rose up. He tried again to crawl
forwards, but this time as the pain engulfed him, nausea rose
up, and he bent over to be sick, almost screaming with the
pain that the retching caused.

When he fell back, shivering and gasping, the clanking of
the gate was echoing everywhere, monstrously magnified
within the tunnel. Slowly and ponderously, the gate began to
descend, the shark's teeth spikes coming slowly down.

Roland clawed desperately at the brick wall again, trying
to get to his feet. Then, from beyond the monstrous sounds
of the machinery, he heard a door opening, then a rush of
movement from the office beyond the open panel. A man's
voice shouted, 'Stop! For God's sake, don't shut the gate –
there's someone in there!'

From where he was lying, Roland saw a dark-haired man
scramble through the open panel – a man who could only be

Phineas Fox. Had Loretta mistimed it all? No, she was too efficient – Fox must have arrived early, and found the street door unlocked. He would have seen the light on and come down here.

Fox stopped short just inside the panel, staring at the scene, clearly not entirely understanding what had happened. Roland saw the panic flare in Loretta's face, and he saw her start forward.

But Fox had already darted towards the still half-open gate, and he was reaching out to Roland, clearly intending to grab his arm and pull him out to safety.

As he did so, Loretta almost threw herself at him, so that he fell sideways into the gaping darkness where Roland was struggling to stand up. His head smacked against the side of the tunnel, and for a breath-snatching second he was on the very edge of the gaping channel. Then Roland managed to grab his hand and pull him to safety. Pain from his damaged ribs tore through him and he cried out again, but he had pulled Fox back to safety.

Except that neither of them was safe, because the gate's mechanism, once activated, was coming down, the clanking of the old mechanism echoing through the tunnel, and the dripping iron spikes were only a foot above them.

The light was draining, and then, with a final dreadful scraping noise, the gate clanged into place.

TWENTY-FOUR

London, 1890s

Daisy often went out to Whitechapel to Ma's new rooms. They were very smart indeed; Lissy and Vi and their husbands had spruced the place up a treat. And Ma loved being part of the lively street trade, selling and buying at the stall with Peg the Rags, gossiping with local people.

There was only one thing against the new rooms as far as

Daisy was concerned, and that was that they were a bit nearer
to The Thrawl; in fact they were almost in the shadow of the
great grim wall that was the Paupers' Wing. Still, you could
not have everything in life, and Ma did not seem to mind. She
liked knowing she was still surrounded by the people she had
known all her life, she said; the people she had grown up with.
It made her feel safe. Daisy understood that, of course. And
looked at sensibly, Ma had always lived near The Thrawl; it
was part of her life, and even its horrible stories were part of
it. The stories had been part of Daisy's life as well until she
went to live with Madame, just as they had been part of the
lives of all the children growing up in that area of Whitechapel.
She knew the tales of the gaolers who were supposed to trade
with the body-snatchers, and who sold the lunatics' bodies to
them for the physicians' experiments. And when Daisy and
her sisters were small, somebody had started a rumour that
the devil lived in a deep dungeon beneath the Paupers' Ward,
and sometimes crept out at night and cut out the hearts of the
living people to add to his collection. The children had found
that terrifying, and everyone had attended church and ragged
Sunday school for weeks.

Later, Daisy heard the adults' tales. How there were poor
souls shut away who were not mad at all. Chained and forgotten
and left to rot. And a good many of them as sane as anyone
in the outside world. Daisy knew, too, the stories of how
husbands used The Thrawl – and places like it – to shut away
unwanted wives, or wives to shut away unwanted husbands.

She knew, as well, about daughters who used The Thrawl
to shut away fathers who sexually abused them, their two
sisters, and their young brother.

Daisy could still remember how she had felt when she followed
Pa along the canal towpath after she caught him with Joe. She
could remember how it had felt to run forward and push him
so hard he went straight down into the canal.

But there was another layer to that memory – the memory
of how she had crouched, shivering and shocked at what
she had done, grateful for the wall of the empty warehouse
behind her. She clung to the knowledge that what she had

done had been necessary, in order to protect Ma and girls. And Joe. Above and beyond all of that, to protect Joe.

She had been about to make a shaky way back along the canal path, and return to Maida Vale as quickly as possible. Nobody had seen what she had done. Pa's body would be discovered at some point, and it would be assumed he had fallen into the canal while he was sozzled. Daisy was just thinking she felt strong enough to stand up and set off, when something happened that sent fear coursing through her.

A few yards along from where she was standing, near to a narrow bridge that spanned the canal for the drays, the filthy water was churning violently, and, as Daisy turned to look, a figure came up out of the filthy water, and reached out to grasp the edges of the bank. Water streamed from the figure, tangled weeds trailed from its head, half covering the face, and, as it struggled on to the path, there was a moment when it was silhouetted in the faint phosphorescence coming off the canal.

'*Daisy . . .*'

It was a slurred sound, forced from a mouth choked with mud. Sodden, mud-crusted hands clawed at the ground, and Daisy backed away, one hand at her throat. But already he had managed to climb on to the path, and he was half lying there, coughing and gasping wetly.

'Bitch,' he said, spitting the words out. 'I'll tell them what you did – sly cat you are . . . They'll string you up – you'll dance at Tyburn . . .' There was another bout of coughing, and he vomited slime and mud over his boots.

Daisy shuddered, then thought: if I went forward now, I could push him back into the canal and it would finish him off this time. But she could not do it. Having once screwed up her courage to give that earlier push, she could not deal a second blow. And, ridiculously and illogically, she could not take advantage of the weakness and the helplessness. And yet if she did not, he would tell people what she had done. He would go back to Rogues Well Yard. To Ma. To Joe.

Barely a foot from where he was lying was a door opening into one of the abandoned warehouses. Even in the dull, early evening light, Daisy could see that it gave straight on to the warehouse's cavernous interior.

She had not thought she could bring herself to touch Pa again, but fear was lending her strength and courage, and she seized his arms, and dragged him across the ground into the bad-smelling blackness of the old warehouse. He swore, and tried feebly to resist her, mouthing threats again, but he was still struggling to breathe, and it was easy to shove him into the black interior. He fell to the ground, against the wall.

Daisy said, 'I'll get help.' She had no idea if he believed her, or even if he heard her, but she sped across the floor. Once outside she wrenched the sagging door shut, wincing as the hinges shrieked like souls in torment, but seeing gratefully that it finally closed.

And now it was a matter of speed – of getting to the one person in all the world Daisy trusted, and doing so as fast as possible.

She ran towards the Commercial Road, and blessedly and thankfully a hansom came rattling along within minutes. Daisy climbed breathlessly inside.

Madame listened as Daisy gabbled out what had happened, and what she had done. It sounded confused and muddled, but Daisy knew Madame had understood. She had no idea if she was about to be thrown out into the street, or if she would end up in Newgate, or . . .

Madame said, 'Daisy, listen carefully. You're not going to be punished for this – I won't let you be. But that man must be . . .' She thought for some moments, then said, 'Yes. I see a way.'

'What are we going to do?' said Daisy, as Madame whisked into her bedroom and snatched a long dark cape from the cupboard.

Madame had flung the cape around her shoulders, and thrust her feet into button boots. When she looked back at Daisy, there was a light in her eyes. 'There are times,' she said, 'when having led a somewhat disreputable life – and having known a few gentlemen of influence – comes in useful.'

*   *   *

The afternoon was darkening as their hansom cab rattled through the streets, and pulled up outside a large white house just off Eaton Square.

This was a part of London Daisy had never been to, and she found it daunting. But Madame walked briskly up the wide, white steps and rang the bell. Challenged by a uniformed servant as to her business, she said, 'My business is with your employer. Please give him my card and say I want to see him at once. I shan't take up very much of his time.'

It was the first time Daisy had seen Madame use a visiting card. Posh ladies and gentlemen had them, but she had not realized Madame had, too. The servant nodded, and as he padded away, Madame glanced at Daisy. 'Surprised to hear me being posh?' she said. 'But I can talk as posh as anyone if I have to. Don't worry, Daisy. Just agree with everything I say.'

The servant returned, took them across a large hall, and showed them into a warm, comfortably furnished room, with book-lined walls and a fire glowing in the grate. Behind a big leather-topped desk was a man with silver hair and a thin face. He came across the room and took Madame's hand.

'Scaramel,' he said, looking down at her. 'After all these years.'

'After all these years,' agreed Madame, composed as a cat. She sat down and studied him, in her turn. 'The years have been remarkably kind to you, Charles.'

'It would be in the nature of an insult to say they've been kind to you,' said the man, seating himself opposite to her. 'Because you're ageless, Scaramel. To what do I owe this pleasure?'

Madame smiled. 'Do you recall that I once helped you in a difficult situation?' she said. 'And that you said if ever you could repay that favour . . .?'

'I do remember,' he said. 'Three hundred guineas was the sum in question. A gambling debt.'

'Yes. I daresay three hundred guineas is a mere fleabite to you now, but in those days—'

'In those days it was more than I had in the world,' he said.

'So it was. You gave the other players a draft on your bank, knowing it would not be honoured.'

'I did. I was very young and very foolish – and very much in love with you, if you recall that, as well?'

'Oh yes,' she said, softly. 'I recall that.'

They both seemed to have forgotten Daisy's presence. She did not dare move.

'You gave me the money,' said Charles. 'The draft was honoured, and I got away with it.'

'Yes.'

'And now you want that – that favour to be repaid?'

Madame paused, as if deciding on her next words. Then she said, 'Yes, I do. It's asking a good deal of you, but since you're who and what you are nowadays, I think you're the one man who can help me.'

'My present position sounds better than it is,' he said, and Daisy suddenly liked him for saying this.

'Nevertheless, you're very high up in the police service, Charles. With a particular responsibility for the city's mental institutions, yes? And I hear there's a knighthood in the wings.'

'Minx. How did you know about that? It's supposed to be a closely guarded secret.'

'I still have friends,' said Madame, demurely. 'Services to the mentally sick, isn't that what the knighthood will be for?'

'Something like that.'

'Well, now, my maid here, Daisy, has a father who is going to be . . . arrested and almost certainly hanged.'

'Ah. For a capital crime? Yes, of course it must be. Murder?'

'Yes,' said Madame, without hesitating, and Daisy managed to bite down a small gasp of surprise. 'There was a fight and the other man died.'

She's spinning a story for him, thought Daisy. She's taking him into a make-believe world. Exactly as she takes her audiences into make-believe worlds. She tried to think if this was better than telling the man the truth, and did not know.

Madame said, 'The thing is that this man, Daisy's father, is – well, almost witless,' and Daisy saw that she was feeling her way along this fragile strand of fantasy.

'Has there been medical advice?' said Charles.

There was a split-second pause, then Madame said, 'No. The

family have never had the money for that. They've cared for him themselves – you know that's the way with poorer people.'

'They look after their own,' he said, half to himself.

'Yes. But now, with this charge hanging over him . . . He wouldn't stand a chance in the dock. And it would deeply damage Daisy here – also her brother. Her brother is a gifted artist, Charles – there's a promising career ahead of him.'

'Which you've helped with,' he said, smiling.

Madame gave one of her shrugs. 'Something like this could ruin several lives,' she said. 'Daisy's, her brother's. Their mother, of course. But if this man could simply be – be put out of the way for a time – to allow the matter to die down and be forgotten.' She sat back, but her eyes never left him.

'And you're thinking he could be kept safely out of the way inside a mental institution?'

'It's where he ought to be anyway.' Madame said this without any hesitation at all. 'He has no memory of the fight that killed the other man, but he's now having wild delusions – one of them is that Daisy attacked him earlier today. Quite ridiculous, of course. You only have to look at Daisy to see she's a little shrimp of a thing who certainly couldn't attack a grown man. In any case, she hasn't been away from my house for the last two days. I don't think she's even seen her father for at least a week; that's so, isn't it Daisy?'

'Yes,' said Daisy, and the man turned to look at her. Daisy tried not to flinch from the direct regard.

Then he said, 'If I refuse? What would you do? Bring up that old gambling debt matter? I wouldn't have thought you capable of blackmail, Scaramel.'

Madame put out a hand, her fingers curling around the man's. Daisy held her breath, then saw him turn his hand up so that it clasped hers.

'Of course I'm not capable of it. But don't refuse, Charles,' she said, softly. 'Please do this for me.'

'For old times' sake?'

She smiled. 'Auld Lang Syne? It was New Year's Eve, wasn't it, that first night?'

'It was. It was the night you danced on the card tables at four in the morning and sang . . . What was it called?'

'"If Only They Knew Where I Keep My Little Bit of Luck",' said Madame, promptly.

His lips twitched, but he said, gravely, 'Highly appropriate to the occasion.'

'That was the night you lost the three hundred guineas,' said Madame.

'Scaramel, I lost a great deal more that night. We both know that.' He seemed suddenly to realize he was still holding her hand, and he took his own hand back, and said, in a different voice, 'For how long would you want this to be? This stay in an institution?'

'Certainly until the hue and cry dies down, I think, don't you, Daisy?' she said.

'Yes,' said Daisy, again. She was terrified of saying the wrong thing, of shattering the fragile make-believe that Madame was creating.

'And,' said Madame, looking back at Charles, 'as you know, a hue and cry can go on for months.' A pause, then, 'I would not expect him to be on the parish, of course,' she said. 'Not kept in a Paupers' Ward – that's what you call them, isn't it?'

'It is.'

'There will be funds to avoid that.'

'You always were one for the underdog,' said Charles. This time he smiled properly, and Daisy saw why Madame might, on her own account, have lost her head a little bit over him all those years ago, and why she would have settled his gambling debt. He made a rueful gesture. 'Donations for those places are always seized on gratefully, no matter the reason for them. Most of the asylums are run on a shoestring, I'm afraid.' He frowned, then said, 'Yes. All right.'

'You'll take him into one of the institutions?'

'I will. Where exactly is he now?'

'He's hiding out in Whitechapel. Where did you tell me it was, Daisy?'

Daisy said, 'In an abandoned warehouse, along by the canal. You go across Fossan's Yard, and turn off Canal Alley on to a towpath.' Something prompted her to add, 'He's weak and confused.'

'All right. I'll send word for him to be picked up as quickly as possible. Tonight, certainly.' He hesitated, then said, 'I don't have much control over which asylum he'll go to, but if he's in Whitechapel – if that's the area where he lives – it'll almost certainly be The Thrawl.'

The Thrawl. The name lay on the warm room as if an icy finger had traced it. Daisy drew breath to say something, then stopped, because Madame was already standing up, clearly considering matters to be resolved. Charles stood up as well, and she took both his hands in hers. 'Thank you,' she said. 'You were always a gentleman, Charles.' Then, with the sudden mischievous smile, she said, 'Although we both remember those nights after that card party when you weren't entirely a gentleman.'

'I remember those nights too, Scaramel.' He took her hand and held it against his cheek for a moment. 'I've never forgotten you, my dear.'

'Nor I you, Charles.'

'If only—'

'It wasn't to be,' she said, at once. 'There were too many differences. The gulf was too wide between us.' She held his hand against her cheek for a moment longer, then, as if throwing off the memories, he said,

'God help us all, if this is ever found out.'

'It'd be farewell to that knighthood, wouldn't it?'

'It'd be farewell to a great many things,' said Charles, and walked with them to the door.

It was a wild plan, of course, but it was exactly the kind of plan Madame would have thought up. It was also, Daisy thought afterwards, exactly like Madame to produce a former lover who could help.

'Who was he, exactly?' she said, later that night.

'An admirer.' Madame smiled the smile that made her look like a mischievous cat. 'Well, admirer's a polite word. He was a bit wild in his youth, but he's a very good man. He really does care about justice and fairness. He went into the police force after that gambling business, and some years ago he started to campaign for things like better conditions in prisons and asylums. I've often seen mention of him in newspapers. He's well thought of, and he deserves that knighthood.

And – what's important here, Daisy – he's the very last person anyone would suspect of bending the law a bit.' She turned to look at Daisy. 'No regrets about this plan?'

'No, except—'

'You wish it didn't have to be The Thrawl.'

'Yes.'

'I'll make sure the funds are sent, though. So that he gets a degree of comfort.'

'Thank you. How long—'

'Will he stay in there? I suppose as long as we want,' said Madame. 'He raped his own daughters, remember. All three of you. He would have done the same to Joe,' said Madame. 'For all we know, he already had.' She made an angry gesture. 'We'd never be able to get a police case against him. If I thought there was the least chance of that, I'd do it. But they'd never listen. The law favours men anyway – always remember that, Daisy. But if he's left free, Joe isn't safe, and nor are other young girls – boys, too. As for you – you certainly aren't safe,' she said. 'He'll accuse you of trying to kill him. That's something that might well get into court.'

'Because the law favours men.'

'Yes. If you can, see this as a kind of prison sentence.'

'I will.'

Incredibly, the mad plan, conjured out of nothing on the spur of the moment, pulled almost at random from Madame's lively imagination, had worked. It was unexpectedly easy to tell people that Pa had fallen into the canal and been drowned, and that Madame had made herself responsible for the funeral. Ma had to be told the truth, of course, but no one else knew. Lissy and Vi didn't know. Joe certainly didn't know, and Daisy vowed he never would. Let them all think the evil creature could never trouble them again.

The man called Charles was awarded his knighthood later that year – Madame showed Daisy the newspaper announcement.

'Well deserved,' she said. 'I shall send a very ladylike card of congratulations. And I shall sign it simply as "S". Nicely mysterious and anonymous, but he'll know who it is, of course'

Later she said, 'Daisy, no one will ever know the truth about what we did that night. There's no way this can ever get out – and no way your father can ever get out.'

But then came the night when The Thrawl burned.

TWENTY-FIVE

London, 1890s

Daisy had told Madame she was going to visit Pa.

'Visit him?' said Madame, staring at her in disbelief. 'Daisy, you can't. You mustn't. In any case, I don't think it'd be allowed. He did get taken to The Thrawl, you know, and The Thrawl is—'

'One of the tunnel houses. I know.'

'But it must be five – no, more like seven – years now.'

'I know,' said Daisy again. 'But I've been thinking about him for a long time. I have dreams about him. Like he might be calling out to me,' she said, in an ashamed mumble. 'Like he might need help. I got to know he's all right. I know he was a vicious evil monster, but—'

'I understand.' Madame frowned, then said, 'I don't think I can ask Charles to help with arranging a visit. Or even to make any kind of check for you. I can't involve him again. But I wonder if we simply turned up at The Thrawl and asked to be admitted . . .'

'Could we?'

'We could try. Would I need to look prosperous, I wonder – Lady Bountiful; in which case I'd want the velvet cloak and the feather boa? Or would it be better to be a bit shabby and hoping to visit a relative? No, I don't like that idea. But I might be thinking of consigning a poor witless relative to the place, in which case I could have a veil and dab my eyes sadly and use that white face powder that Rhun said made me look like a corpse. Or—'

'Lady Bountiful,' said Daisy, before Madame could get too

carried away. 'That's the one to be. It'd look as if you're there to help them.'

'You're right.'

'When could we go?' said Daisy.

'Well, on Saturday afternoon the twins will be with the Thumbprints for their music session,' said Madame. 'That means we don't need to worry about leaving them for a couple of hours. Saturday afternoon it shall be. Lay out the velvet cloak, will you, Daisy – oh, and that bonnet with crimson plumes. I'll use my most refined voice, and I'll be inspecting the place to see if it's deserving of an endowment – that'll do it if anything will. Money,' said Madame, sagely, 'will open almost any door in the world. All you need is the confidence. Walk in as if you own the place, and the odds are that most people will think you do.'

Daisy had never really visualized driving up to the gates of The Thrawl in a hansom cab, grasping the twisted iron bell pull and hearing it ring dolefully inside the terrible place.

At first it seemed as if no one was going to respond, then a small, inset door was pushed open to no more than six inches, and a rheumy eye peered suspiciously out. A gravelly voice demanded to know their business.

Daisy's heart bumped with nervousness, but Madame, very haughty, said something about a tour of inspection, and the promise of a donation – making it seem, thought Daisy admiringly, as if the arrangement had already been made, and as if they were expected.

'And we realize it will be putting you to considerable trouble,' she said, grandly, 'so perhaps . . .'

There was the chink of a coin, and a hand came out to seize the proffered half-sovereign. Even through the narrow gap in the door, Daisy saw the doorkeeper perform the classic gesture of biting on the coin to make sure it was genuine. Then he nodded, pocketed it, and opened the door wider for them to enter.

Daisy hesitated, because after all this was the place of all those childhood tales – this was the ogre's castle, the giant's larder, the place built over the devil's own dungeons. But

Madame, who would probably be able to defy a dozen ogres if the situation required it, swirled her velvet cloak around her ankles with a flourish, and stepped through, so Daisy followed.

The doorkeeper clanged the door shut, observing that there was a shocking cold wind out there, and it got into folks' tubes something chronic. This was followed by the rather revolting clearing of his throat, after which he wiped the back of his hand across his mouth, then crooked a grimy finger at them, indicating that they were to follow him. In the dull light of the stone hall, Daisy saw that he was very stunted, barely coming up to her shoulder, and that one of his shoulders was higher than the other. His face made her think of old, gnarled tree-trunks.

But at least he had not questioned their right to be here, although the half-sovereign probably had a good deal to do with that. Scuttling along, he led them down a dank corridor, thick with the stench of dirt and despair. A kind of dark heaviness lay on the air, and Daisy almost felt it pressing down on her head. At intervals, gas flares sent out a dispirited light, and Daisy began to feel as if the grotesque people of those old stories might suddenly appear and gibber at them from the shadows.

The walls of the corridor were dark and scarred and running with damp, and they had to step over puddles that might have been caused by the dripping of water from above, but that might be other fluids. They reached an intersection, where three corridors converged, when from somewhere within the building, a harsh, loud bell sounded.

'That means dinner,' said their guide, at once. 'I got to go. Y'can see what you want, though. Over there – and there.' He waved vaguely in the direction of the corridors. 'Come back to the main door when you're ready. If I ain't there, someone'll be around to unlock it for you.'

'But can't you show us where—'

'I ain't missing my dinner, not for you, nor the Queen of England,' he said, at once. 'You go where you want, I ain't bothered, and nobody else will be, neither.'

He sped off, leaving them staring after him. Then Madame seemed to stand up a little straighter, as if squaring her shoulders, and said, 'Pity about that, but at least we're inside, and we've been told we can go wherever we want. Let's start with this corridor.'

'There's a door just along there,' said Daisy, in a whisper. 'It'll probably be locked, but still . . .'

But the door was not locked. It opened outwards, and as Madame pulled it, a thick stench came at them, causing Daisy to flinch and clap a hand over her mouth.

'Daisy, if you're going to be sick, go and do it in that corner as quietly as you can manage.'

'I'm all right.'

'Good.' But Madame, too, had flinched, and she closed the door quickly, and stepped back. 'No need to go in there,' she said, a bit sharply. 'Paupers' Ward. He won't be there – I made an arrangement, remember? Let's try these other corridors.'

The left-hand corridor was lit by more of the gas jets, and several doors opened off it. Each had a tiny grille.

'They'll be locked,' said Madame, but she tapped on each door. 'Daisy, call out that we're visitors. If your Pa's in any of the rooms, he'll know your voice.'

Several times the person in the room cried out in response to Daisy's voice, but the words did not make any sense. Twice there were eerie wails and screams, and Daisy shivered.

'Are they answering us? Or do they wail like that anyway?'

'I don't know. Let's just try this last one,' said Madame.

'Yes.'

As Madame reached out to tap on the surface, a voice from within the room, 'Daise? That you out there, gel? That my little murdering bitch of a daughter, is it? It is, isn't it? I'd reckernize your voice anywhere, you vicious little shrew.'

There was a movement from beyond the grille, and hands came up to curl around the thin bars. Eyes, angry and filled with hatred, glared out.

'Pa,' said Daisy, torn between relief and fear. 'Yes, it's me. We came to make sure you was all right.'

'Course I ain't fucking all right, stupid bitch. Shut up in here all this time, is it likely I'm all right? Come to gloat, have you?'

'No, we've come to make sure you're getting reasonable treatment,' said Madame. There was no trace of nervousness or fear in her voice. She said, 'Daisy was worried about you. You know, you might be shut away in here, but you're lucky not to be in Newgate.'

'Might's well be,' he said, sullenly. 'Might's well be hanging from Jack Ketch's rope. That's where she should be,' he said, jabbing a finger at Daisy. 'Bleedin' murderer, that one.'

'No, she isn't,' said Madame, as Daisy flinched. 'And we're not here to gloat – we're here to make sure you're being treated properly. You're supposed to have food and exercise and things you want within reason. Are you?'

'Might be.' There was the impression of a sullen shrug.

Daisy said, 'Do they – um – let you out of this room sometimes?' Because it was unbearable to think of him – to think of any human being – locked away like this all day and all night. She glanced along the corridor, and had the impression that a shadow moved behind one of the grilles.

'Well?' Madame was saying. 'Do they let you out?'

'They might do,' he said, grudgingly. 'Yes, all right, I come out for dinner and tea every day. Bit of a walk round the yard, too. They let me work a bit in the gardens some days. See the others then. See the women.' Incredibly, there was a leery glint from beyond the grille. 'And we all got to go to church service on Sundays. You should hear the chains of them paupers clanking then. Vicar got to shout to make hisself heard sometimes. They got to chain some of them, see, 'cos they're wild and mad.'

Again, Daisy caught the movement from the far room. Like someone whisking back out of sight, not wanting to be seen.

'I don't get chained, though,' Pa was saying, and now there was a dreadful kind of pride. 'I ain't mad, see, so they don't do that. But I shouldn't be in here at all.'

Daisy said, a bit desperately, 'It won't be for ever. It really isn't meant to be for ever.'

'I ain't been a saint,' he said. 'But I might change. Vicar, he's talked about that. He helps folk change their ways.' There was a wheedling note in his voice now.

Daisy said, 'We could see if—'

But Madame's hand came down warningly, and she stopped.

'We got to go now,' said Daisy. 'But we'll see what might be done. Talk to the vicar, maybe. No promises, though.'

'Never were none. But you see about it, gel,' he said.

'I wish I hadn't come,' said Daisy, softly, as she and Madame walked back along the dim passage. The cries of the men and women in the locked rooms still echoed around them, bouncing off the old stones.

'Later on, you'll be glad you did come,' said Madame. 'You saw for yourself that he's not being treated so very badly. He's not with the really mad ones, and he told you himself that he comes out for meals and a bit of work in the gardens. And there's some companionship.'

'I know, but . . .'

Daisy stopped, because the cries from within the rooms suddenly sounded different. She turned to look back, and saw that Madame had done the same.

'Daisy – d'you hear that?' she said. 'It's not shouting voices any longer, it's as if—'

Daisy said, in a whisper, 'It's as if someone's singing.'

'Yes.'

'It's coming from that room at the end. I thought someone was standing at the grille, trying to peer out to see us – trying to listen to us . . .'

They stood very still, and Daisy thought they were both trying to think that there was nothing so very unusual about hearing tuneless singing inside a place like The Thrawl. Most of the people who were locked away in here were poor helpless souls whose senses had become warped and distorted, or whose minds had gone astray. A good many of them might very well hum to themselves, or sing wordlessly. There might be comfort for them in such a thing.

But this was not humming, and this was not wordless singing.

This was the song written by Rhun using the long-ago composer's music. Somewhere inside The Thrawl someone was singing 'Listen for the Killer'.

It seemed to Daisy that the two of them stood frozen and unable to move or speak, while the whispering echoes of The

Thrawl's strangeness swirled and eddied around them. And lying on top of those echoes . . .

As the final lines of the song faded, Daisy drew in a shaky breath, then said, 'That was the whole thing. The entire song that Rhun wrote.'

'Yes. But it doesn't mean anything,' said Madame, a bit too firmly. 'It's not so many years since we taught people that music and those words. There's nothing to say there isn't someone in here who learned it then.'

Daisy was about to say this could be true, when the singing started again, and this time – oh, dear God, although the tune was the same, now the singer was using words that neither of them had ever heard – words that Rhun had certainly never written. And now it was not 'Listen', it was 'Harken'.

'Harken to the killer for he's here, just out of sight.
Harken to my footsteps when it's very late at night.
At pallid church and bishop's head,
With eager hands and furtive tread,
By midnight's knell you'll hear the prowl,
And then you'll hear the victim's howl.
And then you'll know the killer stalks
With needle and knife and butcher hooks –
You'll know that I still walk.'

'It is that room,' said Daisy, after a moment. 'He's in there.'

They both stared at the door – Daisy thought they were both trying to find the courage to go up to it and peer through the grille, but before either of them could move, there was a patter of footsteps, and the doorkeeper appeared.

'Seen what you wanted?' he said.

'Some things.' Madame pointed to the end door. 'The man there—'

'Oh, that one,' said the doorkeeper. 'Heard him, have you? Real mad, that one.'

'Who is he?'

'Don't think anyone knows. Don't think he knows, either. One story is he was found wandering in them old dried-out rivers underground. Ghost rivers, they call them. They say he lost his wits down there in the dark. Enough to make anyone lose their wits, ain't it, being down there in the dark?'

Cold sick horror was washing over Daisy. She thought: it
is him. It really is. Because of course he'd get out of the tunnel
– I should have known he'd get out.

'But another story says the high-ups put him in here so's
he wouldn't have to stand his trial and end up being hanged,'
said the doorkeeper. 'I reckon that happens more'n folks know.
British justice, huh.' He jabbed a thumb in the direction of
the room. 'Sings like he done just now some of the time. Other
times you hear him kind of chanting to himself.'

'Chanting what?'

'Odd, it is. Names of streets,' said the doorkeeper. 'Knows
the East End like you wouldn't believe. Whitechapel,
Spitalfields. All the streets and the little alleyways – Hanbury
Street, Dorset Street, Miller's Court – he chants them all, over
and over. Even parts of the City. Mitre Square, and the like.
It's like as if he's saying a prayer to himself. I hear some
things in this place, but that one . . . Gives you the shivering
creeps.' He turned to lope back down the passageway, turning
to make sure they were following.

'Had my dinner,' he said. 'I'll unlock the door for you, then
I'll be off to my own bit of room. I got a twist of baccy and
a nice drop o' whiskey to warm me. Last a few nights to come,
that will, thanks to your jimmy o'goblin.'

As Daisy and Madame walked across Fossan's Yard, Daisy
said, 'That song – that other verse he sang. I didn't understand
that line—'

'The one about "At pallid church and bishop's head"?'

'Yes. What did it mean?'

'I've been thinking about that. Pallid church – I should think
would be Whitechapel,' said Madame. 'And bishop's head would
be Mitre Square, most likely.' She glanced at Daisy.

Daisy said slowly, 'And those places the doorkeeper said
he chants to himself – Hanbury Street, Miller's Court. They
were all—'

'All places where the Ripper's victims were found,' said
Madame.

TWENTY-SIX

London, 1890s

The week after the visit to The Thrawl was Ma's birthday. Daisy and Joe were going to take her out to supper at the Cock & Sparrow, and Lissy and Vi and their husbands were coming as well. Lissy's Lita was making a whole batch of mutton and onion pies for the evening. Daisy was greatly looking forward to it.

'Shall I turn up and give a surprise performance for her birthday?' Madame asked.

'Oh! Could you? She'd love it,' said Daisy, delighted. 'They'd all love it.'

'I'll do it, then. The twins can go up to the Thumbprints' for the evening – they like that, and the Thumbprints like having them. Thaddeus is reading *The Adventures of Pinocchio* to them. And Rhun can go along later to get them back down here to their beds. See now, what shall I sing . . .?'

Ma was pleased to see Daisy and Joe, and thrilled to her toes when Madame came in and threw off her velvet cloak to reveal one of her saucy costumes. Bowler Bill was there, of course, delighted to be playing an accompaniment, and Old Shaky was in his corner, happily strumming his banjo. He mightn't be able to stand up for more than five minutes at a time on account of his bad legs, but he could join in and play any music you cared to sing, could Shaky.

Madame gave them the Marie Lloyd song, 'A Bit of a Ruin That Cromwell Knocked About a Bit', performing Miss Lloyd's dance, in which she pretended to be tipsy for the last line about, '*Outside the Cromwell Arms last Saturday night/I was one of the ruins that Cromwell knocked about a bit.*' Everyone applauded and roared out the lines with her. After that, she did, 'Oh, Mr Porter', which was very saucily meant, with everyone delightedly roaring the lines.

Then Bowler Bill struck up, 'For She's a Jolly Good Fellow', with Old Shaky plunking away at his banjo. Everyone got up to sing, Peg the Rags stood on a table and pretended to conduct, and people cheered. Daisy was pleased to see what good friends Ma had around her, and proud of her family. Lissy's girl was taking round the trays of mutton pies, and everyone was eating and laughing. Joe did not say very much – he never did – but Daisy could see he was enjoying it all in his quiet way, drinking in the scene; probably, when he got home, he would draw it all.

The party was still going on when Daisy and Joe, together with Madame, left, laughing when Bowler Bill shouted across the room that it was raining, and he would lend them his umbrella. Madame retorted that they would not melt from a drop of rain, but Daisy took the umbrella, and in fact they were glad of it because when they got out to the street it was raining quite heavily.

The three of them walked in silence, Daisy and Joe on each side of Madame, all sharing the umbrella. It was a companionable silence, though. Once or twice Joe slowed his steps, looking up at a building or peering down a dimly lit alley, and Daisy smiled. One day, she would see Joe having a proper display of his work in an expensive gallery. That was a very good thought.

They were nearing the Commercial Road, when they heard the shouts.

'Fire! There's a fire!'

'Get help! Fire!'

'Where?' said Madame, looking about her in bewilderment. 'I can't see any fire.'

'Nor can I . . .'

But Joe had run back to the corner of the street, and was beckoning. 'Over here,' he said. 'Across from Fossan's Yard. Flames and smoke.'

Huge clouds of smoke, shot with crimson and scarlet flames, were already billowing into the night sky. There was no need to ask where it was coming from. There was only one building hereabouts that was large enough to give forth that amount of smoke and flames.

The Thrawl was burning.

People were starting to run towards it, shouting for help to be brought, and Joe went forward with them. But there was a moment when Daisy and Madame hesitated, and looked at one another, and Daisy knew they were sharing the same thought. You did not, of course, run away from something so disastrous, something where people might be needing help, but—

But this was The Thrawl. And inside it were secrets that needed to remain secret. Then the moment passed, and they were going after Joe, becoming swept along with the rest of the people running towards the fire, because of course they must do what they could.

Black, evil-smelling smoke gusted into Daisy's face as she ran, making her cough, and half blinding her. The flames were lighting up the sky now, and people were shouting and clutching at children to keep them away from the flames.

They rounded the corner on the edge of Fossan's Yard, and there it was – The Thrawl, with its rearing walls glowing from the heat. Bricks and huge chunks of stone were falling into the street, showering down everywhere, and men who seemed to be in charge were shouting to everyone to keep back – couldn't they see it was bloody dangerous? You'd get crushed to fragments by a bit of falling wall if you didn't look out.

But already some form of order was being established. People had formed a line across the main part of the square, and buckets were being filled from a nearby pump, and passed from hand to hand, then flung on to the flames. Daisy saw Madame go over to join them, and she saw Joe helping to pump the water. She went to stand with Madame, taking her place in the line, but churning in her mind was the fact that Pa had been inside this place, and that he might have escaped in the confusion. What if he was somewhere in this throng of people, peering into their faces, searching for the daughter who had nearly killed him, and who had then got him shut inside a madhouse? He might be quite close this very minute.

And what about that other one – that one who had sung his own version of 'Listen' and who chanted the names of all the murder sites to himself in the dark quiet of his room? Daisy shivered and looked nervously about her, but everyone seemed intent on the fire.

Police constables had come running to help, their shrill whistles blowing to summon others. They were already rounding up people who were clearly the asylum's residents – ragged, bewildered-looking creatures, they were, wandering around in fearful puzzlement. Several of them had been wrapped in what somebody told Daisy were called restraining jackets, and the warders were leading them away from the square. A woman next to Daisy said the church and a mission hall had been opened up as a temporary shelter. They would all be looked after, she said comfortably, but one of the men further down the line said this was rubbish – it was a safe bet that not all the lunatics would have been found, poor sods.

'Too many of them,' he said. 'That place was stuffed to the attics with them. Ask me, not even the warders knew everyone who was in there. Mark my words, there'll be some strange ones wandering the streets for many a night to come.'

'But what happened?' said Daisy, frantically passing the heavy buckets along. 'How did it start?'

'Somebody said there was a doorkeeper took to smoking a pipe near the main doors,' he said. 'Took a drop too much whiskey one night – although God alone knows how he could afford whiskey! – and fell asleep with his pipe burning. Place'd go up like a tinderbox.'

Daisy stared at the man in horror, understanding that the doorkeeper had only afforded the whiskey because of Madame's half-sovereign, and that this fire was the result of it. No time to think about it now, though – they all had to concentrate on getting the fire under control and getting people to safety.

More and more people had joined in, and people had come running out of the Cock & Sparrow. Bowler Bill had organized a second bucket-and-pump line – Daisy saw Lissy and Vi and their husbands helping. Even Old Shaky had done his best to carry buckets, although he soon had to give up, and he told Daisy he was a useless old wreck who could not help out in trouble. Fortunately, Madame heard this, and said Shaky was not a wreck at all, in fact he could be extremely helpful to her, because here was the fare for a hansom cab for him to go

out to Maida Vale and explain to Rhun and the Thumbprints
what had happened and that she would be late home. Rhun
would be sure to give him a drop of whiskey when he got
there, she said, at which Shaky went off, feeling that he might
not be so useless after all.

By midnight the fire had been quenched almost entirely,
although it was clear that the ruins would smoulder for some
time. There were heaps of blackened rubble everywhere, and
great pieces of masonry and chunks of chimneys that had
fallen away. Most of the main walls were still standing,
although the windows had fallen out, and the rooms were open
to the sky where ceilings and great sections of the roof had
fallen in.

'I think we can safely leave it now,' said Madame, wiping
the back of her hand across her forehead. 'We should be able
to pick up a cab – there'll still be plenty around. Where's Joe
got to? Oh, there you are, Joe. We're going home now – you
going to come with us, are you? Good. We'll get you taken
to your lodgings first.'

As they walked away, they could still hear the clattering of
buckets and swooshing of water hosing on to the walls, but
after they had turned a couple of corners, the sounds faded,
and the ordinary night street noises of London started to take
over. There was the rattle of carts and the clop of hooves from
the cabs in the main thoroughfares. A cab would come past
them at any minute, and Daisy thought they would all be very
grateful to climb in and get home. They could hear people
who had not known about the fire calling goodnight to one
another, and a snatch of drunken singing from a tavern somewhere. Once a brace of cats yowled, and there was the sound
of a window being flung up, and angry shouts to the cats to
clear off. The word used was not actually 'clear'. There were
the sounds of footsteps, as well, so other people could not be
far off.

Footsteps. Daisy glanced over her shoulder, because it was
not sounding like several sets of footsteps – it was a single
set.

'Nothing wrong in a few footsteps,' said Madame, very
softly. 'There're plenty of people around.'

'Tisn't all that late anyway,' put in Joe.

But it seemed to Daisy that, as they walked on, the footsteps walked with them. It did not mean someone was following them, of course – simply that someone was walking in the same direction.

They were nearing the Commercial Road, when Joe suddenly said, 'The footsteps – they're still there. Somebody *is* following us.'

Even as he was saying this, Madame's hand was closing on Daisy's arm, and she said, 'He's right. Someone's creeping along behind us.'

Daisy listened, and although she could not hear footsteps, for a dreadful moment a snatch of singing reached her. Her heart leapt, because it felt as if the night of the fire was being replayed. Then she realized it was only a burst of song from the nearby tavern, and she relaxed and almost laughed with relief.

Madame laughed, as well. She said, 'Lot of scared-cats, ain't we? It's only the people from the bar over there. Drunken lot, they are . . .'

She stopped, because a figure had stepped out from a side alley and was coming towards them at a lurching run. The glow from the ruins of The Thrawl was behind him, and his eyes were fierce with hatred. The familiar voice came to them.

'Murdering bitch of a daughter! I got you at last! I been following you ever since you left the fire, an' now I got you cornered!' The eyes slewed round to Joe. 'I got you as well, useless thing for a son that you are! Part of the plot, weren't you!'

Daisy grabbed Joe's hand, but Joe was standing stock-still, staring with horror at the man he had thought dead, and when Daisy tried to pull him back down the street, he seemed unaware that she was even there.

Pa came straight at them, seizing Daisy with one hand, and dealing her a hard blow across her face with the other. She fell back against a shop window, hitting her head on the stone frame. The pain of the fall spun her into dizziness, blurring her vision, but she saw Joe bound forward and attack Pa, and

she understood at once that his mind had gone spinning back
to those squalid years in Rogues Well Yard.

It took Pa by surprise. He almost fell back, but then he
righted himself and fell on Joe, knocking him to the ground
with almost contemptuous ease. He crouched over him, his
thick fingers closing around Joe's throat.

'And you're next, you bitch,' he said in a dreadful snarling
voice, not loosening his grip, but looking round to where
Daisy was attempting to get up. 'Di'n't I say you wouldn't
escape me?'

'Stop it!' That was Madame, yelling fit to wake the dead.
'Let him go, you madman. They'll hang you if you kill him!'

'Don't hang madmen, darlin',' said Pa, leerily. 'They'll put
me back in one of those places, that's all they'll do.'

Joe's hands were flailing helplessly and his face was
becoming suffused with crimson. Daisy struggled frantically
to get up, but the street was spinning and tilting all around
her, and she fell back again, sobbing with frustration and with
terror for Joe. But through the sick dizziness she saw Madame
run forward – Pa had disregarded Madame as a threat, in the
way he would have disregarded any female, but Madame was
already pulling at Pa's arms, trying to loosen his grip on Joe's
throat. She would never do it – Pa was too heavy, too powerful
– but then Daisy saw that Madame was clutching the umbrella,
half jokingly given to them in the Cock & Sparrow. It was
not very heavy, but Madame was raising it over her head, and
from that height it would deal a telling blow. Even as Daisy
was thinking this, the shaft came smashing down on the back
of Pa's head. He gave a kind of half grunt of pain or fury, but
his hands did not loosen their grip. Madame, her face white,
but her eyes blazing, dealt a second blow, and then a third.
And with the third blow, there was a sickening crunch of bone
splintering, and Pa let out a cry that echoed around the deserted
square, then fell back. His body jerked a few times, then his
head lolled to one side, and his eyes fell open, wide and staring.

Joe scrambled back from the prone figure, then turned to
Daisy, his eyes frightened pits in his face. Daisy's head was
still throbbing from the blow and her mind felt as if it were
stuffed with cotton, but she grabbed Joe's hands and finally

was able to stand up. Madame was bending over Pa's prone form, and Daisy thought she was feeling for a heartbeat, which was what people did if they thought somebody was dead.

Then she sat back on her heels, and in a voice that shook, said, 'He's gone. There's no heartbeat.'

'He's dead,' whispered Joe, and before Daisy could speak, Madame was there, her arms about him.

'Yes, Joe, he's really dead now – he can't hurt anyone again.'

Daisy was still holding Joe's hands. She said, 'Did you mean to do that? To kill him?'

'No. Oh, God, no. But I'm not sorry for what I did.'

Daisy looked at her, and strongly in her mind was the knowledge of how, that long-ago night by the canal, she had not been sorry for what she had done, either.

'But,' said Madame, 'I'm not sure what we do now,' and for the first time Daisy saw that Madame really did have no idea what to do. She realized that she had no idea, either.

It was Joe who said, 'We hide him. Now. Tonight.'

'But where—?'

'In the ghost river,' said Joe.

TWENTY-SEVEN

London, 1890s

'Passed out, has he?' said the hansom cab driver, cheerfully, as they half dragged Pa's body into the cab. Joe had wound his scarf around Pa's face, almost completely hiding it.

'Fraid he has.' Daisy was only grateful that they had managed to find a cab in the Commercial Road and had not had to lug him any further.

'Got sozzled, did he?'

'In the Ten Bells,' said Daisy, choosing the largest of the nearby taverns, and one where a single drunk would not be noticed out of the others.

'Happens to us all. Hope he ain't gonna be sick in my cab. Where to?'

Daisy started to say Harlequin Court, but Madame said, firmly, 'Maida Vale. We need to pick someone up while you wait for us.'

As the cab drew up outside the house, Joe said, 'I'll stay here.' He caught Daisy's eye, and said, 'Be all right, Daise.' Then, with a glance to the cab seat, he said a bit louder, 'He won't wake up – too drunk for that, but I'll stay anyway.'

'Anyone in there'll be in bed and fast asleep at this hour,' said the cabby, cheerfully, leaning forward to look up at the house. 'No, you're all right – lights burning in one of the rooms.'

'We shouldn't be very long,' said Madame.

'Odds to me how long you are, darlin'. You're paying the fare. Bit of a rest for me and the old nag to just stand here, anyway.'

Rhun was sitting by the fire, drinking a glass of whiskey, and discussing the works of Walter Scott with Thaddeus Thumbprint. They were both startled when Daisy and Madame came in, tumbling out their story. Neither of them minded about Thaddeus being there; the Thumbprints were very nearly family, and they could be trusted with anything in the world.

After Rhun and Thaddeus had heard the story, Thaddeus said, 'Rhun, you go with them. I'll stay here with the twins. I'd be no use in a job like that, anyway. I'll just run down and put a note through my own door, letting Cedric know what's going on.'

'Daisy can stay here with you,' said Madame.

'No! I got to be there,' said Daisy, at once. 'Joe, too. He was our pa, no matter what he did. We need to stay with him.'

Madame and Rhun exchanged looks, then nodded.

'I'll get rid of this cloak,' said Madame, suddenly. 'It's covered in soot and flinders, and some great clumping person's trodden on the hem and torn it.'

'That's bloody like you to think of your clothes at such a time . . .' began Rhun, hotly, but Madame had already darted into the bedroom, and snatched up one of her velvet hooded cloaks.

'We'll burn that other one tomorrow,' she said.

'And now,' said Rhun, impatiently, 'come on down the stairs.'

Daisy thought they were all grateful that the cabby did not ask any awkward questions. He did, in fact, get them across London very quickly – probably because he was still worried about his drunken fare being sick. As they went past Regent's Park, Madame leaned forward, and flung something from the window. It fell with a clatter, and the horse reared slightly. The cabby shouted to know what had happened.

'Empty bottles he had in his pocket,' said Rhun, cheerfully. 'Getting rid of them.'

The cabby observed that empty bottles were no use to man nor beast, and he hoped they had not hit some poor sod.

'You'd have heard the yell if I had,' said Rhun, and, leaning back, he said very softly to Madame, 'The umbrella?'

'Yes.'

They got Pa out of the carriage reasonably easily, with Rhun entering into the deception by addressing remarks to Pa, such as, 'Soon get you inside, boyo,' and, 'My word, you had a skinful tonight.'

Daisy understood that this was for the cabby's benefit, in case anything were to come out afterwards. There was nothing in the least remarkable about driving a drunk across London, to be carried into his house – the cabby would very likely have forgotten about it by morning. What he would not forget was discovering he had driven a corpse from Whitechapel to Maida Vale and then out to Charing Cross Road.

As they were set down at the entrance to Harlequin Court, Rhun called to the cabby that they would get their charge along to his rooms very easily now, and thank you very much for all your help. Madame paid the fare, adding a deliberately modest tip. 'Because,' she said, as the cab clopped away, 'we don't want to draw attention to ourselves.'

Harlequin Court was not completely quiet, of course; even at this hour there were the sounds of carriages rumbling along beyond the alleyway, and people's voices calling out, or even singing. A church clock – most likely St Martin-in-the-Fields – chimed three. In another hour the barrow boys and the costers would be making for Covent Garden.

They manoeuvred Pa across the court, with Rhun on one side of him and Joe on the other. The shops were all in darkness at this hour, of course, and the only light came from the streetlamp that brooded over the little square, and flickered a grudging light across the cobbles.

Linklighters was locked and silent – 'But I've got a key,' Madame said.

As she felt for it, Joe suddenly said, very quietly, 'Daise, what if that other one's still down there? You know who I mean.'

Daisy felt as if she had received a sudden smack across her face. Joe was thinking that the body of the killer – *their* killer, Whitechapel's killer – might still be in the ghost river. That he might have died in the lonely darkness. She could not possibly say that he had almost certainly been inside The Thrawl last week.

'Hear him chanting to himself,' the doorkeeper had said. 'Names of streets – like as if he's saying a prayer . . . Knows the East End like you wouldn't believe . . .'

And Daisy had heard for herself the sly, sinister singing of the 'Listen' music coming from the locked room.

She said, as casually as she could manage, 'Don't matter if he is, Joe. Remember Rhun said people go down there every few years, and they often find bodies and have to bring them out. So if that one did die down there, he likely won't be there now.'

He appeared to accept this, and he turned to watch Madame unlocking the door and opening it.

'Inside as quickly as we can,' she said. 'Before anyone sees us.'

'No one's about,' said Daisy, but she glanced uneasily over her shoulder.

'There're shadows, though,' said Joe, staring around the court. 'If you look into them, you'd imagine people standing there, watching.'

Daisy suddenly had the impression that there was someone who had stolen along the narrow alleyway, and who was standing just out of sight, watching them. She was glad when Madame had the door unlocked. Rhun and Joe took Pa's shoulders between them, and Daisy took his feet, while Madame held the door open.

They got him down the steps. Everywhere was in shadow, but there was a faint spill of light from the open door at the top of the stairs, and Daisy darted back up to close it. Madame had not left the key in the lock, but there was no one around, and they would make sure to lock it when they went out.

'Where now?' said Rhun, when Daisy came down the stairs again.

'Through that door. It goes down to the deep cellar.'

Joe said, very softly, 'And the deep cellar goes through to the ghost river.'

'Had we better light some of the gas jets?'

'No,' said Rhun, at once. 'We don't want any lights that might show from upstairs. Joe can get a couple of the oil lamps from the back of the stage, and we'll take them down there. And a tinder, Joe.'

The lamps duly lighted, Daisy went down the steps ahead of them, carrying one of the lamps so they could all see their way.

It was even more difficult to get Pa down the narrow, steep stone steps, but in the end they pushed him part of the way, and he slithered all the way down, landing in an ungainly heap at the foot.

'Sorry about that, boyo,' said Rhun, not unkindly. 'But it won't make any difference to you what we do now.'

Madame said, 'No, but . . .' She pulled the velvet cloak from about her shoulders, and bent down to wrap it around the dead man. 'You were an evil, vicious man,' she said, softly. 'But you'll be getting what's due to you now, and I daresay Daisy and Joe will keep one or two good memories of you.' She straightened up, brushing the dust from her skirts. 'Through there, Daisy? God Almighty, is that where you and Joe went all those years ago?'

'Yes. There's a gap in the wall just here. Two bits of wall overlap – one bit behind the other, and you can squeeze between them. Only it's very narrow, so—'

'We'll never do it,' said Madame, as Daisy held up one of the lamps. 'There's barely room for one person to squeeze through, never mind two of us carrying a—'

'We can chip some of the stone away,' said Joe. 'It's old and it'll break up. And nobody'll ever know, on account of nobody ever comes down here.'

'He's right,' said Rhun, who was inspecting the wall. 'This is crumbly old stonework – dry as you could imagine. It won't take much to knock some of it away – widen the gap so we can get through.'

'There're hammers and chisels in the carpenter's room,' said Joe. 'I can get them.'

'And bring another lamp and a couple of candles,' called Daisy, as he went back up the stairs.

'And a bottle of brandy if you can find one,' shouted Rhun.

By the time Joe returned, Daisy was starting to feel as if she was being pulled into a world where nothing was real any longer. The lamplight and the candlelight burned up, washing over the cobwebbed old walls, and the smell of tallow and oil mingled with the stench of the old ditch beyond the wall. And all the while, Pa's body lay there on the ground, wrapped in Madame's velvet cloak, his face covered with Joe's scarf . . . Don't look, thought Daisy. It's not him – that's not a person any longer; it's just an overcoat that he's cast off. And I ain't going to pretend I'm sorry, because he ruined my childhood, and Vi's and Lissy's, and Joe's as well. And he nearly ruined Ma's life, too. But Madame had been right when she had said that there would be one or two good memories to keep. Daisy wiped a tear away angrily.

Clouds of brick dust billowed out into the old cellar as Rhun swung the hammer at the wall, and chunks of stone began to fall away – small pieces at first, and then larger ones.

'Said it'd be easy,' said Joe. 'Let me have a go at it now.'

'No, it's all right, boy, and it's nearly done, anyway. Daisy, hold up that lamp a bit more, will you?'

'I can make out the sluice gate,' said Daisy, putting the lamp up against the wall.

'Good God, so can I,' said Rhun, coming to look through the gap with her. 'That's a fearsome-looking thing. If ever you'd see Time's iron gates, ready to close slowly . . .'

'Never mind Time's iron gates, can we get him through now?' demanded Madame. 'And get the gate open?'

'We can. But Scaramel, my love, you and Daisy go upstairs, will you, and make sure there's no one around in the square? Just in case someone comes along – a drunk or someone looking for a night's shelter. You keep a watchful eye for that, and Joe and I can manage very well between us. Can't we, Joe?'

'Yes.'

Daisy understood that Rhun wanted to shield her from seeing Pa's body taken into the tunnel. She hesitated, then nodded, and reached for one of the candles to light the way.

She and Madame stood just inside the street door, looking out across Harlequin Court. The night air was cold, but it felt good after the dank, sour cellar, and also after the smoke-filled streets of Whitechapel. Daisy realized with a shock that it could only be three or four hours since they had fought the fire at The Thrawl.

They could hear faint sounds from below. There was a deep groaning creak, that would be the sluice gate being lifted, and then the sensation of something under their feet shuddering.

'Is that the gate being cranked up?' said Madame, half turning her head to look back through the door.

'Yes.' Memory showed Daisy the yawning tunnel, and the ledge running alongside the channel where the old ditch had been. How far along would they take Pa? Would they simply throw him into the channel and leave him? Would the rats come teeming out? She stared into the shadows.

'If you look into them, you'd imagine people standing there, watching,' Joe had said earlier. *As the killer had stood there that night, waiting for them, following them inside . . .* Where was he now, that man? Had he got out of The Thrawl as Pa had? Daisy shivered, and drew her cloak more firmly around her shoulders.

'Odd how you get the feeling someone's watching,' said Madame, looking round the court, and shivering in the same way. She had wrapped her own cloak around Pa, of course; Daisy, remembering this, dragged off her own cloak and offered it to Madame, but Madame waved it away.

'I don't need it,' she said. 'I'm not really cold. If I shivered just then, it's probably nothing more than a guilty conscience.' She looked round the court again. 'No one's watching,' she said. 'That's guilty conscience, too, making us think there might be someone. Let's go back inside. They should have finished by now.'

And so they had. The sluice gate was in its place, and Rhun and Joe were gathering up the hammers and chisels. Daisy could almost find faint amusement at the sight of Madame wielding a large broom, sweeping dust into corners.

'Found it in the carpenter's room,' she said, looking up. 'By the time we've done, no one will know what's happened tonight.'

'I shouldn't think anyone ever comes down here from one year to the next,' said Rhun.

'Nor should I,' said Madame. Then, suddenly, 'Rhun, was there anything to mark him as being from The Thrawl?'

'No.'

'Did you look?'

'Yes. Even if they found him, they wouldn't know who he was.'

'Good. Let's go home. Joe, you'd better stay at Maida Vale tonight. No point waking up the people at your lodgings.'

'I'll get another broom to help with the sweeping up,' said Daisy. 'Joe, you bring the hammers and things and we'll put them back in the workshop.'

They were just closing the workshop door, when they heard the street door overhead bang, and voices and the sounds of people coming down the main stairs, and then down the stone steps.

A man's voice cried, with considerable authority, 'Police! None of you move! Nobody down there move!'

There was the clatter of footsteps going down the stone steps – it sounded like at least three people, all with heavy boots, then the man's voice came again.

'Sergeant Blunt,' he said, clearly by way of introduction. 'And this is a very strange sight to see. Excavating the walls, were the pair of you?'

'Our presence here is perfectly innocent,' said Rhun. 'We've been working on a new routine for this lady – she performs here.'

'In the middle of the night? And in the cellar?' said the man, sarcastically. 'Tell that to a judge and twelve good men and true, and see what they think! Now then, you, my dear, are under arrest.'

Madame's voice, very cool, said, 'Am I, indeed? Well, this is a new experience for me, at any rate. What am I being arrested for?'

'Murder,' said Sergeant Blunt, and the word fell on the air like a gobbet of blood on to black water. Incredibly and dreadfully there was the chink of iron. Gyve, thought Daisy, her mind reeling, and she made an instinctive move towards the steps.

Joe's hand came out, stopping her. 'Don't let them know we're here,' he said, very softly. 'Not yet.'

'Who am I supposed to have murdered?' Madame was saying.

'An inmate of The Thrawl.'

It could not have been anything else, of course, and even though Daisy had expected it, the words still came like a blow. She and Joe crept to the head of the cellar stairs, and crouched there, listening.

Rhun was saying, angrily, 'This is nonsense. Why would you think Scaramel had killed someone?'

'We know she did,' said Sergeant Blunt. 'She was seen doing it.'

Daisy and Joe exchanged horrified looks. In a whisper, Daisy said, 'But she can't have been seen. There was no one around.'

'Don't always see folks who hide themselves,' said Joe. 'Plenty of little doorways and alleys.'

Even as he said it, Daisy was remembering how they had all felt, at different times tonight, that they were being watched.

'I take it you're Mr Rhydderch, are you, sir?' Blunt was saying.

'Yes, he is. The writer and poet,' said Madame, at once. 'A very distinguished gentleman.'

'And if you're to make free with my name, Constable, you'll do me the courtesy of pronouncing it correctly,' said Rhun, coldly, and pronounced it in ringing syllables.

'I'll make a note,' said the sergeant. 'But for the moment, we're going to take a look behind that wall that you seem to have half knocked down. My men will bring lights down, and I think they might find something very interesting.'

'There's an old sluice gate, Sergeant,' said a different, younger voice.

'Is there now? Well, we'll raise that. Get those lights. And a couple of good hammers – we'll need to knock out a bit more of this wall to work properly, I should think.'

There was the sound of people coming up the steps again, and Joe and Daisy shrank back, and saw two young policemen go up to the street.

Rhun was saying, 'What are you expecting to find, Sergeant?'

'The body, sir,' said Blunt.

'Oh, you'll probably find half a dozen,' said Rhun, carelessly. 'Vagrants, trying to find a night's shelter, and getting trapped.'

'Ah, but there's only likely to be one body that's been put there in the last half-hour. And, quite apart from that, sir, as I've already told you, this lady was actually seen committing the act. There was what we call an eyewitness.'

'A what?'

'An eyewitness,' said another voice – female this time. 'And I'm the eyewitness. Earlier tonight, I saw that hellcat smash a man's head to splinters, and then drag his body into a hansom cab.'

Daisy and Joe looked at one another, then Daisy said in a shocked whisper, 'That's Belinda Baskerville.'

'Yes. We'd better stay here,' said Joe. 'So we can listen, and see if there's a way to help.'

It felt odd for it to be Joe who was saying what they should do, but it also felt very comforting.

Belinda was saying, 'She used the shaft of an umbrella – big, sturdy old thing it was. She beat his head to a pulp with it.'

Daisy's legs suddenly would no longer hold her up, and she sank to the ground, shivering, wrapping her arms around herself as if to force warmth and strength back. Belinda really had seen it – she had described exactly what had happened. They had thrown the umbrella out of the cab, but the police might be able to find it, and it would be covered in blood and bits of bone . . .

And when they raised the sluice gate, they would find Pa's body in the ghost river, the head splintered and broken, exactly as Belinda had described.

Rhun was saying, 'Sergeant, you can't possibly trust anything that this . . . this female says. She's got a long-standing grudge against Scaramel, and she'd say anything that would injure her.'

'He's right,' said Madame, eagerly. 'You can ask anyone – she's a vicious, spiteful cat and she's been trying to get even with me for years.'

'Oh, a cat am I!' shrieked Belinda. 'You've got a bloody cheek, you hell-hag, when you've cheated and lied and whored your way through your life – and now you've committed a murder to save your miserable skin! I saw you do it, and I'm going to see you pay for it!'

'You'll be the one who'll pay for this, Madame Useless-on-a-stage, Mistress Dull-in-a-Bed Baskerville!' shouted Madame. 'Because I'll drag you through the courts for this, see if I don't! It's libel and . . . and the spoiling of a person's character . . . and—'

Rhun said, 'Be quiet for a moment. Sergeant Blunt, why would Scaramel need to kill anyone? Answer me that, if you can.'

'I can answer it,' said Belinda, and Daisy and Joe crept closer to the top of the steps, fearful of missing anything.

'Several years ago, you helped to get a man locked away in an asylum,' said Belinda, clearly addressing Madame directly. 'But he was as sane as anyone.'

Daisy thrust her fist into her mouth to stop herself from gasping. Belinda knew, she thought in horror. She knew what we did all those years ago.

But then Belinda said, 'I don't know who he was, that man, but I heard the whispers – and there were plenty of them if you knew where to listen. And it sounded as if this was someone important. Someone who ought to face justice for something, only they wouldn't – or couldn't – allow it. So they decided to shuffle him out of the way. And don't try to tell me that kind of thing don't happen, for we all know it does! Look after their own, the toffs! And you helped them,' she said.

'But how could I have been part of that?' demanded Madame. 'And why would I help?'

''Cause you knew them all, those toffs in the prison service and the . . . what do they call it? The Lunacy Board. Well, I say *know*, but you'd been in the beds of half of them.'

'Malicious lies,' said Rhun, at once. 'Jealousy.'

'It's true!' shrieked Belinda. 'The number of blokes as've dipped their wick in that one, you wouldn't believe—'

'Now then, madam, this isn't really needed—'

'Oh, fuck what's needed! This bloke she killed tonight – he was the one they hid. And she'd been the go-between. A sneaky little nark, she'd been, watching him for them, and then telling them where they could pick him up. Well paid for it, she'd have been – and that's why you did it, Scaramel. Do anything for money and a spot at Collins', wouldn't you!'

Rhun said, in a scoffing voice, 'Just where did they pick him up, this mystery man?'

'Think I don't know that?' said Belinda, scoffingly. 'Well, I do. I got my own spies. He was on an old towpath off Canal Alley, that's where. In the shadow of The Thrawl itself, it is. He was hiding out in one of the empty warehouses, and that's where they took him.'

Daisy felt so sick she thought she might throw up on the ground. Belinda knew all this – she had known it all these years.

'How could you possibly know something like that?' demanded Rhun.

'I kept my ear to the ground and I heard the gossip. Servants in posh houses. People who work in places like The Thrawl. I told you, I got spies of my own. And people will tell you things if you pay them. I even got to know those two boring old farts who live in your house. Thought I was after their bit of money, didn't you? Ha! Chicken-feed, that'd have been. No, it was so I could pick up the talk about you, Scaramel.' She drew in a breath, and went on. 'I looked round those rooms of yours while you were in Paris. Didn't find nothing, but it was worth a go. When you came back, I watched where you went and what you did and who you got friendly with. Had some posh friends, dintcha?'

'You lying bitch!' shouted Madame. 'You're making it up! And it's sheer, spiteful jealousy, because I got the bookings – and the men! – that you wanted. And it's because I stopped you defrauding poor little Cedric Thumbprint of all his savings, too. I never thought you hated me this much, Belinda,' she said, suddenly serious.

'If you knew all this, Belinda,' said Rhun, 'why in God's name didn't you speak out?'

'Because I could never prove it,' said Belinda. 'But I didn't mind how long it took. I didn't mind that it went on for years – I *enjoyed* watching and listening. Making notes – I kept a journal, too, same as the high-up ladies do about their mimsy parties and dances, only mine was a journal about you, Scaramel. Dates and places and everything.'

'How disgusting,' said Rhun.

'Whatever it is, it's all there for the police to read. Di'n't expect it to go on quite so long, though, I'll admit that,' said Belinda. 'But it was worth it, because tonight when The Thrawl burned down – that prisoner – *the* prisoner escaped. And I knew that was my chance. Soon's the street-boys started shouting what was happening. I thought – it's The Thrawl, and it's where *he* is—'

'"He"?' said Rhun.

'The bloke she helped get put in there. The one they had to keep hidden. I told you,' said Belinda, impatiently. 'So I went out there at once. I thought you'd be there, Scaramel, because I knew you'd be frit to death of *him* escaping and it all coming out. And you were – so much so that you bashed the poor sod over the head, and then you dragged his body down here to hide it.'

There was a pause, and Daisy dug her fingernails into the palms of her hands. The 'toffs' and the people within the Lunacy Board that Belinda had talked about would include Charles – the man in the Eaton Square house. He had done it because he and Madame had once loved one another. Would that all come out?

Belinda had got a twisted version of things, but Daisy, remembering the soft singing they had heard inside The Thrawl, thought Belinda had not got it so very wrong. Daisy would stake her life on that man being the killer – *her* killer, the Whitechapel murderer. Leather Apron – Jack the Ripper. Had he been put in The Thrawl to keep him from justice, as Belinda had said? But why? Was he someone so important, so high-up, that they could not put him on trial for his butchery?

But at the moment all that mattered was that Belinda had seen Madame kill a man with the fire from The Thrawl still tinting the sky blood-red all around them. It was obvious that she was prepared to stand up in a court and say so. It was also obvious that she would produce the journal she had kept, and, sick and bitter as it might be, it was the kind of thing that people in courts would take notice of.

Madame would fight all this, of course, and Rhun and the Thumbprints and everyone who knew Madame would fight for her and with her. But Daisy was already realizing that it might not be possible to persuade people that Belinda Baskerville was lying. Because she was not lying. She really had seen Madame commit murder and it had happened exactly as she had described it.

As the realization of this swept over Daisy in sick, icy waves, there was a shudder of movement from below, and then the grinding cranking of the old machinery as the policemen began to raise the sluice gate.

TWENTY-EIGHT

London, 1890s

They carried Pa's body out just as faint streaks of light were touching the sky. Three policemen carried it up to Harlequin Court, and Daisy heard one of them say something about how it was going to be a bit bloody grim to be lugging a corpse along to Charing Cross Road, where the wagons were.

'Couldn't we have wrapped him up a bit better, too? There's only that old scarf over his head. He'd got that cloak or cape or some such around him, hadn't he?'

'It slid off when we lifted him up.'

'Pity you didn't grab it, then.'

'Come to that, pity you didn't. But neither of us had a free hand, if you remember. Dead weight, wasn't he? And that ledge no wider than a couple of feet. Ask me, we did well to get him out at all. Anyway, there ain't likely to be anyone around to see him, and even if there is, his face is covered up.'

'Best it stays like that,' said another man. 'Who d'you reckon he is? Really, I mean?'

There was a brief pause, then, 'Best not ask,' said the first man. 'Let's just get this done and over with.'

Daisy and Joe had retreated to the side of the stage by this time, and they were huddled together behind a fall of velvet curtain. But they were able to see Madame being brought out by two police offices – Daisy thought she hesitated at the top of the steps and looked around. She hoped Madame would guess that Daisy and Joe were still there, and that they had not abandoned her.

Rhun was behind Madame, looking as if he would like to punch everyone in sight, and lastly came Belinda Baskerville. Her eyes were bright, and she looked so pleased with herself that Daisy wanted to run out and smack the stupid smirk from the bitch's face. She thought she had never hated anyone so much in her life.

As they all went up the main stairs to the street door, she heard Sergeant Blunt say to one of the constables, 'So far so good. We've got the body and we've got the Baskerville woman's statement. There'll be that journal she kept, too. I reckon it's as near watertight as you could wish. But later on – when it's full daylight – we'll go back into that hellhole beyond the sluice gate, and we'll see if there's any other evidence to find.'

'We've left the gate open for that, Sarge.'

'Good man. No harm in seeing what else is to be found – judges like as much detail as possible. Juries, too. So we'll fill in the charge sheets, and we'll get ourselves a bit of break-fast and a wash, then we'll be back.'

As the street door closed, Daisy and Joe emerged from their hiding place. They were stiff and cramped, but there was no thought of going back to Maida Vale. Rhun would go out there as soon as he could, and the twins would not in the least mind being with one or both of the Thumbprints. The Thumbprints would be perfectly happy to stay with them for as long as necessary.

Joe said, 'They're coming back later. Does that mean they haven't got all the – what did they call it? – all the evidence they need?'

'I don't know,' said Daisy. 'There isn't anything for them to find in the ghost river, though, except—'

'What?'

'Her cloak,' said Daisy, slowly. 'She'd wrapped it round him, but it slid off when those two policemen carried him out. Remember we heard them talking about it? That means it'll still be in the tunnel. Joe, that cloak might be the final thing that would hang her.'

'Not if we go into the tunnel and find it first,' said Joe.

They looked at one another.

'We'll have to do it now,' said Daisy, with decision, although everything in her was shuddering from going through the sluice gate. 'Before they come back. We'd better get the oil lamps again—'

'Police left a couple of their bullseye lanterns,' said Joe. 'We can use one – it's a better light.'

Once lit and the flap opened, the lantern gave a strong yellow light, and they went cautiously back down the stone steps. As soon as they were at the foot, the cold, sour breath of the dried-out ditch came at them. And there it was. The sluice gate, half open like the hungering maw of some ancient monster.

'Horrid,' said Daisy. 'But let's get this over with.'

The last time they had gone into the ghost river tunnel, it had been thickly, suffocatingly dark, and they had had to feel their way along the narrow ledge. This time they could see their way, and they could see the worn stones, shiny and dripping with damp. Twice there was a scuttling of tiny clawed feet.

'How far along did you bring Pa?'

'Not far, because the narrow ledge made it awkward. Only about to here.'

'There are footprints,' said Daisy. 'Tilt the light a bit, will you? Yes, they stop here. This must be as far as you came.'

'Can't see the cloak, though,' said Joe.

'It might have slipped off the ledge. Fallen into the channel – Joe, be careful,' said Daisy, as he leaned over the rim of the channel to look down. 'Because . . .'

She broke off, and Joe looked back at her. 'What's wrong?'

'I heard something.'

'What?'

Daisy turned her head, and looked back down the tunnel, to where a faint light came from the open gate. Then, in a voice from which most of the breath had been driven, she said, 'Joe, there's someone in the tunnel with us.'

She felt him flinch, but then he said, 'It'll be the police come back. Bit sooner than we thought.'

'They'd have made more noise – boots and calling to one another.'

'I can't hear anything,' said Joe. 'There's no one here.'

But as he said this, a sly, soft voice reached them.

'Oh, but, my dears, there *is* someone here with you.' The throaty whisper echoed horridly in the enclosed space. 'Did you really think I'd let you get away from me?' said the voice. 'The two people in the world who could identify me . . . Who still could identify me and get me hanged. The two who saw what I did on one of those nights.'

He was coming towards them now – in the light from the lantern his shadow was already on the far wall and the tunnel roof, monstrous and distorted. The hands were already reaching out, and Daisy had to beat down the impulse to run, because even with the lantern's light it would be so easy to stumble and fall into the channel. But Joe had grabbed her hand, and was already pulling her away from the menacing shadow.

And if they could find their way to the grating with the iron
ladder – the ladder *he* had climbed down before . . .

'You won't escape,' said the voice. 'I can't let you live, of
course – you know what I look like. You'll give the police
that last piece of evidence they need to hang me. They never
had that, you know – or did you know? They weren't able to
prove anything against me – that's why they put me in that
place: The Thrawl. They couldn't put me on trial, but they
didn't dare let me go free. They knew what I'd do if they did.'

'You'd go on murdering,' whispered Daisy. We're hearing
his confession, she thought, her mind tumbling. He's telling
us what happened, what he did, why he was locked away in
The Thrawl. And once he's finished telling us that . . .

He was much nearer to them now, even though they were
moving as fast as they dared. But the shadows were shivering,
because Joe was shaking with terror, making the lantern shake
as well. The shadows on the tunnel walls and the roof were
becoming fantastical, unreal outlines.

The massive black shadow suddenly swooped forward, and
Daisy cried out. In the lantern's beam, the remembered face
came out of the gloom, and with it was the glint of something
sharp and pointed – something that would tear and maim and
torture . . . Something he must have stolen – a knife, a razor
. . . It did not matter; all that mattered was escaping him.

Then Joe's arm came up, and a spear of light seemed to fly
like a burning arrow through the darkness. Daisy gasped, then
realized that Joe had flung the oil lamp straight into the face of
the murderer. It struck him full on, and he let out a screech
of pain and terror, flinging up his hands in defence. But already
a small flame had shot up from the lamp where the oil had
spilled out on to the candle and the wick, and fire blazed up.
The flames licked across the wet stone walls, but although it
found no hold there, it continued to rage upwards. As the hot
smell of burning oil gusted out, Daisy and Joe recoiled,
throwing up their own hands to shield their faces and their
eyes from the flames, backing away.

And then the screaming began.

It filled up the tunnel, splintering the brooding silence of
the ghost river. Against the flames, sharply limned, was the

struggling black figure, the arms flung up as if for help. But there was nothing Daisy or Joe could do to save him – they could only save themselves; they could only try to get away from the burning shape and out of the sound of the screams that must be tearing his throat to bloodied tatters . . .

They half ran, sobbing and gasping, along the tunnel, until finally and blessedly they saw faint spears of daylight filtering in from overhead – light that showed them the iron rungs of the ladder that would take them up to the street.

As they went towards it, behind them, the man London had known as Jack the Ripper screamed as he burned alive in the ghost river.

St Martin-in-the-Fields was chiming six as they made their exhausted way through the streets, and people were around, and there was a strange air of normality everywhere, because for a great many people another ordinary day had begun.

'Maida Vale first,' said Daisy. 'I think I've got enough to pay a cab, and if I haven't, Rhun or the Thumbprints will pay when we get there.'

'Do we tell people about . . . about what's just happened?'

'I don't know. We'll tell Rhun and see.'

'What's going to happen to Madame?' said Joe.

Daisy looked at him in the grey dawn of the London street.

'I don't know,' she said.

TWENTY-NINE

Phin came up out of a confused nightmare, in which pain had been clenching around his head in throbbing waves. Deep within the nightmare was something about a huge gate clanking down.

He fought against the pain, and forced himself to think what had led to this. He could remember setting off for Linklighters to meet Loretta Farrant – that had only been this morning,

hadn't it? He remembered, as well, that he had been a bit
early, but that the restaurant door had been unlocked, so he
had gone inside, and then down to the deep cellar. He frowned,
feeling the confusion clear slightly. The panel leading to the
old Cock & Pye ditch had been open and, incredibly, what
had to be a sluice gate was being cranked down. Phin had
barely had time to take this in, when he'd realized there was
someone beyond the gate – someone inside the dark tunnel,
who looked injured. Phin had instinctively gone towards the
huddled-up figure, and that had been when a pair of small,
strong hands had pushed him, so hard that he had tumbled
through the narrowing gap between the edge of the gate and
the ground. He thought he had banged his head against
something hard and cold, but as he spun down into uncon-
sciousness, he knew he had heard the sound of the gate clanging
down into place.

His head was still banging with maddeningly rhythmic
waves of pain, but the pain was starting to recede slightly, and
Phin tried to see about him. The darkness was thick, but it
was not absolutely complete – or perhaps his eyes were
adjusting. There was the impression of someone sitting quite
near to him. He had just acknowledged this, and he was just
realizing it must be whoever he had seen earlier, when a voice
said, a bit breathlessly, 'You've come round? Thank God for
that, at any rate. Are you all right?'

'I think so. Who—'

'Roland Farrant,' said the voice. 'You must be Phineas Fox.'

'Yes.' Phin managed to add, 'As introductions go, this has
to be the weirdest ever. What happened?'

There was a considerable pause, as if Roland Farrant was
working out what to say. Probably, though, he was in pain.
He had certainly sounded as if he was.

'I'm not entirely sure. We were testing the sluice gate –
there's an insurance inspection due. The mechanism jammed
and I think Loretta panicked.'

'Ah,' said Phin. 'I thought she pushed me through.'

'I don't think so. No, she wouldn't do that. She was trying
to reach up to unjam the gate,' said Roland, then broke off on
a gasp.

'Are you injured?' Phin thought they could both be fairly sure that Loretta had pushed him, and he thought it was likely she had done the same to Roland, although he could not imagine why. But that was not the immediate concern. He managed to half sit up, which made his head spin again, but made him feel a bit more in control of the situation.

'I think I've got a broken rib,' said Roland. 'I crunched it against the edge of the wall. It's as painful as hell, but I don't think there's any more damage. Have you got a phone? Mine's on the other side of that hellish gate.'

'Yes, hold on . . . Damn,' said Phin, after a moment. 'No signal. I suppose we're too far underground. Wait a minute, I'll put the torch on – at least we'll have a bit of light. Can we open the gate from this side?'

'I don't think so,' said Roland. 'I think this whole place was sealed up years ago.'

'We'd better try, though. Until,' said Phin, carefully, 'help comes.'

He made a cautious way to the gate. The ledge was perilously narrow – it would be easy to make a misstep and fall into the yawning channel where the old ditch had been. He got to the gate, although when he shone the phone's torchlight all around it, he saw it was flush with the wall, and metal plates overlaid the entire frame. There was no switch, no lever, nothing to operate it. Phin, wishing his head was not aching so violently, examined the entire wall again, then returned to where Roland half lay.

'Nothing doing, I'm afraid.'

Roland, clearly still struggling against pain, said, 'I didn't think there would be. The tunnel was closed off – oh, years and years ago. Loretta found out about it, because there were all kinds of Health and Safety regulations she had to comply with. She had to make sure that the place could be accessed and that's why that panel was built in.'

Phin felt despair close over him. He thought it seemed unlikely that Loretta would get them out; as for shouting, they could shout until they were voiceless, but they would never be heard down here. Toby certainly knew Phin had the meeting with Loretta, but there was no reason for him to wonder where Phin was. But there would be a way to get out – Phin would concentrate on how to do it, and he would not think that he had been lured down here by Loretta Farrant. In any case, he had not been lured at all; he had instigated today's meeting himself.

Lured. The word scratched against his mind. He frowned, then memory clicked into place. The old verse from the Marble Arch pub had been about London's old rivers – hadn't it even mentioned this one? It had certainly talked about luring, though; Phin forced his mind to yield up the exact words. There had been something about only sleeping in beds where you were safe, and about never letting yourself be lured to a ghost river bed, because you could end up dead. The verse slid into his mind.

'Never be lured to the ghost river beds,

Only sleep in a bed where you're safe.

In a ghost river bed, you could end up quite dead . . .'

Then had come the quirky mentions of the old, lost London rivers. Tyburn and the Earl's Sluice. And this one, of course. The Cock and Pye.

'And there's really no use

To try raising the sluice.

Street grids and street grilles will not help your ills,

For you can't reach the grilles when you're dead.'

Grilles, thought Phin, sitting up, and wincing from the jab of pain against his temples. Street grids and street grilles. That verse was saying there would be street grids or grilles along those old rivers.

Would there still be grilles from this river that opened on to the streets? For drainage? For maintenance? Phin thought there would have to be, and he had a sudden vivid memory of walking across Harlequin Court with Arabella, and of Arabella getting the heel of her boot stuck in a grille. Was that grille directly over the Cock & Pye? But it did not have to be that one – any grille would do. Because if they could find one, and even if they could not climb through, they could use it to attract attention. They would probably be able to get a phone signal, too.

Phin got to his feet again.

'Roland – can you walk?'

'Just about. If I have to.'

'This might not work out, but we've got to go along this tunnel until we see light coming in from overhead.'

'Loretta said the ditch came out somewhere in St Martin's Lane,' said Roland. 'But it's anybody's guess if it still does. And she said the whole tunnel had been sealed. Wouldn't that mean any grids would have been covered over?'

'Let's hope not,' said Phin.

It was eerie and it was perilous in the extreme to make their way along the narrow ledge. Phin was still fighting the dizziness from having hit his head against the tunnel wall, and Roland was clearly in a good deal of pain from his cracked – or broken – rib. But it had to be done. If they crawled on their hands and feet, they had to find a way of reaching the streets above.

Phin shone the torchlight carefully, praying the charge would last. Several layers below those thoughts, he tried not to think that there would almost certainly be rats down here.

Their footsteps echoed in the enclosed space, and once, when Roland stumbled and sent a shower of small stones skittering into the yawning channel, the sound was magnified a dozen times over. The tunnel curved slightly round to the left after a time, and Phin was just starting to think that a thread of light might be showing from somewhere, and wondering if he dared hope they were approaching a street grid, when Roland said, 'What's that?'

'What? Where?'

'There's something lying on the ground up ahead.'

'What kind of something?' Phin moved the torch, trying to quell apprehension, because anything might be down here.

'I don't know. It's a sort of huddled shape.'

'We'll have to step over it a bit carefully,' said Phin, shining the torch. 'Because . . . Oh. Oh God.'

They both stood very still, staring down at the huddled shape. It lay on the ground, half against the wall, and in the torchlight it was unmistakable. A human head. A human body. The bones black—

'Black with age,' said Roland, half to himself, and even as he said it, Phin thought: no, it's black because it's been burned. It's *charred*.

The nightmare possibilities reared up at once, and he pushed them away, and finally managed to say, 'It must have been down here for years. Decades.'

'Yes. Trapped down here,' said Roland, horror rising in his voice.

A dreadful silence seemed to close down. Phin thought – he knows we're trapped, because he knows Loretta deliberately pushed him through that gate. She pushed me after him, because I saw what happened.

But I can't die down here like this, he thought. I won't. He said, 'Let's go on. I still think there could be a grid or something – or that we'll reach somewhere where there's a phone signal.'

They stepped over the hunched-up bones with difficulty, Phin going first, then shining his torch back for Roland to follow. Roland was pressing both hands against his chest, and his face was drenched in sweat, and Phin hoped the injury was as straightforward as a broken rib, and that the rib itself had not caused any internal injury.

But now there was no doubt about the tunnel becoming lighter. From somewhere daylight was trickling in, and even if there was not a grille through which they could climb, there would almost certainly be a phone signal. Phin switched off the torch, and tried dialling.

He had never been so grateful in his life to see the stored numbers come up, and to hear, when he tapped out Toby's number, the ringing tone at the other end.

London, 1890s

Daisy sat on the edge of the circle of people, her eyes fixed on the thin face of the man behind the desk. There had been something called an Appeal following Madame's trial. Daisy was not entirely clear about the details, but it might mean that a different judge would say Madame's trial had been wrong – that Madame was not guilty after all, and she could go free.

They were here in the Eaton Square house to be told what had happened.

Rhun sat next to her, with Thaddeus Thumbprint on his other side. Cedric had remained at Maida Vale with Joe and the twins.

It was strange to see these two men – Rhun and the distinguished gentleman called Charles – facing one another. It was probably impossible to say which of them had loved her more or which one she had loved more.

'The Appeal was turned down,' said Charles, and Daisy felt as if a massive black weight had fallen around her shoulders. 'I couldn't save her. I'm truly sorry.' He spread his hands in a gesture of apology that was so humble Daisy wanted to cry. 'They ruled that the evidence was clear and couldn't be overturned.'

'Baskerville's statement clinched it, of course,' said Rhun, bitterly. 'And the irony is that what she said was perfectly true.'

'Yes. Scaramel did kill Daisy's father. Belinda saw her do it. Scaramel was defending Daisy's brother, of course, but even so . . . They produced her journal again,' said Charles. 'Even allowing for her jealousy, it was as damning as it had been at the trial. She knew about the visit here when we dealt with your father, Daisy. That counted for a lot, I'm afraid.'

'Are you likely to be drawn in, sir?' asked Daisy, nervously. 'Because of how you helped that night?'

'So far I've fought my way clear,' he said, smiling at her.

'What Belinda said about there being a cover-up was perfectly true, of course,' put in Rhun. 'There was a cover-up.'

'Yes, but Miss Baskerville only got pieces of the story, and it got twisted. It was very believable, though,' said Thaddeus. He and Cedric had gone to court each day, and had made careful notes in case there was anything that could be picked up and used for Madame's defence.

'I'm afraid a good many of the lawyers – and the judges and the police chiefs – knew about the real cover-up,' said Charles. 'That was what tipped the balance, I think. They knew the Ripper had been shut away in The Thrawl – they knew there must have been informants who helped with putting him there, even though they could never pin down the final piece of evidence they needed to charge him.'

'Identification,' said Daisy, with a shiver.

'Yes. So it all made it very easy for them to believe that Scaramel really did kill the Ripper that night. May the evil creature continue to burn in hell.'

'And because of it, Scaramel will hang,' said Rhun, bleakly.

'Yes. Murder's the crime that can't be condoned – that's what the Appeal Court said in the summing-up.'

'We're very grateful for all you've done,' said Thaddeus.

'I haven't done enough to save her life, though. I suppose the only other thing I could do . . .'

'Yes?' said Rhun, as Charles hesitated.

Charles said, slowly, 'You hadn't better take this too seriously and I would probably have to deny I ever even said it – but the only other thing I could do is to see whether the door of a certain cell – and I mean *the* cell – inside Newgate Gaol could be left unlocked before eight o'clock tomorrow morning.' He looked at them. 'It's the maddest thought in the world, though.'

'Completely mad,' said Rhun, staring at him. And then, 'Or is it?'

Rhun, with Daisy and the Thumbprints, sat in the familiar room in Maida Vale the following day, looking across the dark gardens.

Rhun said, 'The maddest thought in the world.'

'D'you think he'll do it? Get someone to leave the cell door unlocked?'

'D'you think he can?' said Cedric.

'I think he was telling us he'll try,' said Rhun.

'And warning us to be ready,' nodded Thaddeus. 'Well, we can be. We can be there – outside the gaol. Rhun, where would you take her? If it were to succeed?'

'Paris,' said Rhun, at once. 'I'm taking the twins back there anyway – they can't stay in London to hear all the talk.'

'We'd all come under suspicion.'

'Oh, yes. But I think it will seem perfectly acceptable for me to take the twins away from London,' said Rhun. 'Daisy will come with us to look after them. That, too, would be normal and believable.'

'What about Joe?'

'Joe could come with us, too,' said Rhun. 'There are one or two artists over there I got to know – people who might help him to get into one of the art schools. It's what he'd like, I think.'

'Wouldn't it look like a kind of mass exodus?' said Thaddeus. 'Attract more attention?'

But Cedric came in eagerly at that. 'Not if there seemed to be a different reason for Joe vanishing,' he said. 'We could say he'd disappeared – that we didn't know where he was. We could even advertise him as missing.'

'Even put out a news-sheet asking for information about him,' said Thaddeus. 'Something about information being sought regarding the whereabouts of the young artist known as Links. That would make him seem unconnected to Daisy and the rest of you,' he said.

They looked at one another. Then Rhun said, 'We'll do it. All of it. I'll make the arrangements right away. Tomorrow night – or the next night – we'll all be in Paris.' He paused. 'But I don't know whether we'll have Scaramel with us,' he said.

THIRTY

'St Martin's Lane?' said Arabella, regarding Phin across a table in a Paris restaurant a week later. 'You came out of the ghost river tunnel in St Martin's Lane?'

'Well, near enough. But Toby had to call out the police and they had to call out a water board – no idea which one. And I think the fire service might have been involved at one stage. They got us out through the street grid – they thought it was safer than the sluice gate, because we'd have had to go all the way back through the tunnel, and Roland was in a good deal of pain. But,' said Phin, ruefully, 'it was all very dramatic and public.'

'I wouldn't care if it had been screened on national television and across the entire world if it meant you were safe.' Arabella reached for Phin's hand across the table, and held it for a moment.

'Actually, by that time, I was beyond caring,' said Phin. 'The paramedics insisted on carting us off to the nearest A&E. I was pronounced as a bit concussed, but they let me out next day. They kept Roland in for a couple more days.' He paused, as the waiter placed before them plates of wild salmon.

Arabella said, 'Did Loretta really trap you both in there?'

Phin hesitated, then said, 'It seemed like it at the time, but it all happened so fast and I wouldn't swear to it now. Roland's sticking to his story that they were testing the gate for an insurance check, and I got the impression that he won't be bringing any charges against her. I think it'd probably be difficult to prove she did anything criminal, in fact, and she's a tough lady – she'd fight her corner strenuously. But I have the feeling that there'll be a quick divorce, and I bet Roland will try to keep her from getting her hands on a share in Linklighters.'

'Will he keep it on himself? Maybe put in a good manager?'

'I don't know.' Phin ate a mouthful of the salmon, which was very good, and said, 'Farrant's a bit of a wimp on several levels, but I suspect that when it comes to the sordid matter of coinage, he's no fool.'

'Or knows people who aren't. Yes, I see. Phin, you haven't said anything about this restaurant.'

'I like it – you made a good choice. Or is there something special about it?' said Phin. 'Because I thought you simply wanted to gaze at me across a candlelit dinner table, and anticipate the moment when I'd sweep you into a cab and we'd go back to the apartment, and—'

'Well, that is partly the reason,' said Arabella. 'But didn't you see the name over the door when we came in?'

'I had eyes only for you,' said Phin, solemnly. 'Well, and for avoiding the puddles, because it was raining like fury. Why? Where are we?'

'This,' said Arabella, with gleeful triumph, 'is the famous Maison dans le Parc. It's where Scaramel and her merry band held that supper party for Rhun Rhydderch. Reported in *La Vie Parisienne.*'

'Are you sure they haven't just used the name?' said Phin, sitting back and looking about him with more attention.

'I am. Because,' said Arabella, standing up and pushing back her chair, 'when I came in yesterday to book the table, I found this.'

She led him to the far side of the restaurant, where several small alcoves, clearly meant for semi-private dinner parties, opened off the main restaurant area.

In the second of these was a series of framed sketches – some of them lightly tinted. Arabella slipped her hand into Phin's. 'Look,' she said.

Over the sketches was framed lettering. It said, '*La série macabre,* Darkness, *par l'artiste Anglais, Links – b. 1878 (est), d. 1946.*'

Phin said, softly, 'The macabre *Darkness* series by the English artist, Links.'

'Born around 1878, and died in 1946,' said Arabella. 'That would make him about sixty-eight.'

'And it means he was found,' said Phin. 'Or he wasn't missing in the first place.'

'Or even that somebody made a mistake.'

'Whatever it was, I'm glad.'

'I was, too, when I found this.'

The first sketch showed a narrow street with crammed-together buildings and low arches across the road. Shadows lay across the cobblestones, and there was the impression of a single figure standing menacingly within the darkness, and the silver line of a knife. The title was, *The Darkness Begins.*

The next showed a crowded room, clearly a tavern, with drinkers at the tables, and a brightly dressed figure wearing scarlet and magenta at the centre. She was holding out what were obviously sheets of music. The expressions in all the faces were very vivid; there was absorption in them, and in some there was fear. The title was, *Driving Back the Darkness.*

'It's the music we found in Linklighters,' said Phin, leaning over to inspect it more closely. 'Can you see the lyrics on some of the music she's holding? Tiny, but readable. Links often seems to have done that – reproduce every last detail. It's "Listen for the Killer".'

'You're right.'

'I found an article in *Fossan's Journal*, which I think referred to it,' he said. 'There was something about local people hearing it sung after a fire at an old asylum in Whitechapel – and how the older ones recognized it from music once used as a sort of warning against . . . well, against Jack the Ripper. I do know how gothic and melodramatic that sounds.' He studied the tavern sketch more closely. 'It's making a bit of a leap,' he said, 'but I wonder if that's Scaramel at the centre.'

'It's not much of a leap,' said Arabella. 'If you look really closely, you can see she's wearing a tiny necklace made up of harlequin diamond-shapes.'

'You're right. The motif again. Then it could well be Scaramel.'

The third sketch showed an underground tunnel with a curved roof. Two figures – one male, one female, were walking along it, and there was the impression that they were walking along the edges of a river that was not quite there – a river that was partly hidden by smoky mist and drifting shadows. But what was definitely there was a dark figure engulfed by fire – flames blazed up around it like scarlet licking tongues, and its arms were flung out as if imploring for help. Eyes, just discernible, stared out with agonized terror. The title was, *The Darkness Dies.*

'Could it,' said Arabella, 'possibly be the tunnel under Linklighters? With the ghost river?'

'It looks like it. Although I should think most of those old tunnels look the same. But . . .'

Arabella said, 'But you and Roland Farrant found those bones down there.'

'And they were charred,' said Phin. 'As if whoever it was had—'

'Had burned. And this is called, *The Darkness Dies*,' said Arabella. 'Phin, was the "Darkness" Jack the Ripper?'

'I wonder if it was,' said Phin, thoughtfully.

Arabella shivered, then said, 'Look at the fourth sketch. In some ways it's the strangest of them all.'

The fourth sketch was called, *The Darkness Cheated.* It

depicted a vast grim-looking building, with a courtyard packed with people.

'It's Newgate Gaol,' said Arabella, indicating a tiny oblong with the words on it on one side of a grilled gate. 'You said Links put in all the details.'

The sketch was tinted in shades of dark greys and near-blacks, and the famous old gaol, long since demolished, but its legend woven into the warp of London's history, crouched beneath a lowering sky that might have been a sullen dawn or a thundery twilight. But there was a single piece of colour in the sketch. It came from a figure falling headlong from a high roof ledge – a figure dressed in scarlet and purple, with dark hair streaming wildly in the wind, and a cloak billowing out like wings. But here and there, the underside of the cloak had been touched with tiny harlequin diamond-shapes.

'If that "Listen for the Killer" song really was written as a warning about the Ripper,' said Arabella, 'then the second sketch in a pub – *Driving Back the Darkness* – definitely links Scaramel to him. Because she's fairly obviously distributing the song to the locals, isn't she? And then there was a body in the ghost river, and then there's the rumour that Scaramel committed a murder that nobody ever talked about . . . Am I getting carried away?'

They looked at one another, then Phin said, 'You're saying Scaramel killed the Ripper.'

'And was going to be hanged, only she staged a dramatic escape. Or somebody tried to stage it for her,' said Arabella.

'Yes, that's credible. You can imagine they'd want to try setting the killer of Jack free.'

'Only it went wrong.'

'I wonder if that's the truth,' said Phin, looking back at the last sketch. 'You know, somehow, it's like her to have failed to escape so spectacularly. I'm glad, though, that she never had to perform that last dance on air.'

Arabella shivered again, and he put his arm round her. 'Let's go back to our table. Is that our pudding being brought over?'

'It looks like it,' said Arabella. 'Crêpes Suzette, flambéed with curaçao.' She regarded him as they sat down, then said,

'After we've eaten it, I thought maybe we could go back to the apartment.'

'For coffee?'

'Well,' said Arabella, demurely, 'we can certainly have some coffee. But I was thinking more that you could finally help me to unpack that black silk underwear.'

Roland had spent two days in the hospital ward, and once they had strapped up his broken rib and administered pain relief, it had not been so uncomfortable. It had even been possible to think – about what had happened, and to decide whether he had handled it all correctly, and then to decide what he would do about the future.

On the whole, he thought he had done right to let Phineas Fox believe that being in the ghost river tunnel had been a pure accident. The hospital staff had wanted to know if there were any charges to be brought – any suspicious circumstances – but Roland had said, as firmly as he could, that there was most certainly no question of that. They had been checking the sluice gate prior to an insurance inspection, and his wife had muddled the operation of control wheel. She had gone off to get help, but it had taken some time, because it was difficult to know exactly who to call for in that situation, and people could not always be easily reached. Meanwhile, he and Phineas Fox had managed to find their way out by themselves.

He had definitely decided not to officially or openly accuse Loretta of anything. He had no proof that she had brought about Mother's death, or that she had attempted to kill Roland himself, and he was certainly not going to have Mother's name dragged into the spotlight and splattered across newspapers. On consideration, he thought the best way to deal with Loretta was to arrange a quiet divorce, and – here was the real crunch – to ensure she didn't get her hands on any of the money. She would try to insist on her legal share, of course, but Roland would simply tell her that if she did that he would make a very damning statement to the police about her. Two murder attempts, he could remind her, and one of them successful. Nothing could actually be proved, of course, but it could all be very unpleasant, and it would certainly damage Loretta's reputation and her future prospects. Roland knew, really, that he would never carry out such a threat, but Loretta would not know that. Yes, it was a good plan. Probably he would end up having to allow her something, but what he would not do was let her have any share in Linklighters. That would be a real punishment for her. He wondered whether he should sell Linklighters or whether he could put in a reliable manager. The present staff were all very good, and they were keen to make a go of the place, so there might be some kind of incentive that could be arranged – a small profit-share, perhaps. He would ask about that at the office.

There was a nurse on the ward – a pretty little thing – who spent quite a lot of time with him. When she asked about his wife – would she be coming in to take him home? – Roland told her that she would not. The marriage had been an unhappy one, he said. A tragic mistake. There would be a divorce fairly soon. It was all very sad, but you had to move forward and see what might be ahead next.

The nurse was sympathetic. She was very interested to hear about Linklighters, to know that Mr Farrant – well, all right, Roland – actually owned a restaurant in a central part of London. Would he be keeping that?

'Oh, yes,' said Roland, suddenly realizing that the decision had already been made in his mind. 'My wife cheated me and deceived me so severely that I'm determined she won't get her hands on the restaurant – nor on very much of the money I got from the sale of my family's house if I can help it.'

The nurse thought this was all very brave indeed. She admired a man who could stick to his principles, and she was very sorry that Roland had had such a bad time. He must definitely look to the future – to the making of new friends. You never knew who you might meet. And what was the name of the restaurant? Oh, Linklighters. That sounded very interesting. She would love to see it sometime and hear about its history.

Roland said, 'You must come and have dinner with me there as soon as I'm able to get about.'

'Don't expect to find too much,' said Phin, as he and Arabella sat at the corner desk in Tower Hamlets library. 'In fact, don't expect to find anything. The odds of turning up a piece of news about an escape attempt from Newgate Gaol over a hundred years ago are just about zero.'

'But we've got the exact year,' said Arabella, eagerly. 'It was on the sketch. And it must have been a very vivid attempt at escape – always supposing Links's sketch can be believed. It's got to be recorded somewhere.'

'I bet it won't be.'

'I bet it will.'

Incredibly, it was. Phin was rather pleased that it was again in *Fossan's Journal*. It was quite a short piece and there were no names, but it was too much of a coincidence to be referring to anyone other than Scaramel.

REMARKABLE SCENE AT NEWGATE GAOL

Newgate Gaol has its share of dramas and vivid tales, but last week's event must rank highly among them.

An execution was to take place at the traditional hour of eight in the morning – the hanging of a lady recently convicted of murdering a man whose identity, intriguingly, was never disclosed, even at the trial, which your diligent reporter attended.

For legal reasons, we are not permitted to print the lady's name, but can tell our readers that she has been very well known in the lively world of the music hall – both in London and in Paris – and is said to have caught the eye of several influential gentlemen.

The rumour is that shortly after seven o'clock on the morning of the execution, the condemned lady's devoted maid was permitted to pay her a last visit, to take her a set of clothes, since, so it is said, the lady had declared she would not go to the gallows in drab prison garb.

The maid discharged her errand, was seen to leave, in considerable distress, and the turnkey locked the cell door.

However, at half-past seven, with crowds gathering in the square outside (as crowds always do for a hanging of even the smallest interest), a disturbance broke out on a roof ledge on the older part of the gaol. The prisoner was seen not only to be free, but to be running across the parapet. She wore scarlet and black, and she had a long cloak that swirled about her. Perhaps if she could have been ten – even five – minutes sooner, her attempt might have been successful. As it was, two of the turn-keys, who were coming on duty, caught sight of her, and raised the alarm, sprinting up to the roof to give chase.

The lady broke away from them, but in her headlong flight she missed her footing and tumbled straight over the parapet's edge, plummeting to her death in the yard below, her cloak billowing out as she fell, like the wings and the plumage of an exotic scarlet and black bird of paradise.

Murder can not, of course, ever be condoned, but the process of hanging – even in these humane times – is an ugly business, and we confess to a rather guilty feeling of gladness that this warm and vivid lady did not endure it, and that she met her death in the spectacular and dramatic way she would probably have wished.

As they walked back along the Mile End Road, Phin said, 'So she really did escape the hangman.'

'I'm glad she did. That reporter was glad, too.'

Phin said, suddenly, 'I'd like to have heard that "Listen" song. I know we've got what were probably the words, or some of them, but I'd like to know what it would have sounded like.'

'So would I.'

'I'd like to know who composed it, too,' said Phin. He looked at her. 'I refuse to make a connection to Liszt,' he said.

'Do you? I'd make it.'

'All right, just between us, I will make it, but I shouldn't think it could ever be proved. And promise you'll never tell Liripine or Purslove about it.'

'I won't. Where are we going?'

'Well, I thought,' said Phin, 'that we might go across to Linklighters for some lunch.'

'And raise a glass to Scaramel?'

'Yes.'

'I think she'd like that,' said Arabella, slipping her hand through his arm.

AUTHOR'S NOTE

It's possibly fair to say that no mass-murderer has left quite such a wealth of dark legends as the man that nineteenth-century England came to know as Jack the Ripper.

Even today, the truth about Jack's identity and his eventual fate remain the subject of discussion and speculation. Films have been made about him, books have been written about him, and the theories posed as to his motives and his identity range from the sensible and near credible to the outright bizarre and the wildly fantastical.

He has, severally, been credited with being a person of some prominence – a leading doctor or surgeon, a member of the police force, or the government, or a famous painter. Some theories connect him to royalty – even to having been royal himself.

The suggestions as to why his killing spree stopped are almost as thick on the ground. But one of those suggestions is that it stopped because he was incarcerated in one of the grim lunacy asylums of his day – either because he had not been recognized for who and what he was, or because he had been recognized, but was too well-known a figure to stand trial.

When I set out to write this book, I had not intended Jack to be an especially major player. Phineas Fox, happily pursuing scholarly research into the life of Franz Lizst, was to unexpectedly come upon a fragment of music – a song – that the women of Whitechapel had used as an alarm signal at the height of the Ripper's reign.

But very gradually – almost without my realizing it – Jack got into the story in a far stronger and much more insistent way than I had bargained for. He was present in every plot twist, he influenced characters' motives and directed their actions – it was as if he peered out of every dark shadow surrounding the nineteenth-century players, and reached out to the present day through them.

Jack the Ripper – the Whitechapel Murderer, Leather Apron – seized the public's horrified imagination more than a century ago and never seems to have let go.

His dark legacy has reached into the present, and it was that dark legacy that brought about *Music Macabre*.